AT FAULT

AT FAULT
Kate Chopin

A SCHOLARLY EDITION WITH
BACKGROUND READINGS

Edited by
Suzanne Disheroon Green
David J. Caudle

THE UNIVERSITY OF TENNESSEE PRESS
KNOXVILLE

Editorial Assistant: Susie Scifres Kuilan.

Selection from *A Visit to Uncle Tom's Cabin* by D. B. Corley. Chicago: Baird & Lee, 1892. Bound vol. 80. Reprinted by permission of Northwestern State University of Louisiana, Watson Memorial Library, Cammie G. Henry Research Center, Melrose Collection.

Selection from "Property Offenses, Social Tension and Racial Antagonism in Post–Civil War Rural Louisiana" by Gilles Vandal. Copyright © 1997 by *Journal of Social History*. Reprinted by permission of *Journal of Social History*.

Selection from "'Bloody Caddo': White Violence Against Blacks in a Louisiana Parish, 1865–1876" by Gilles Vandal. Copyright © 1991 by *Journal of Social History*. Reprinted by permission of *Journal of Social History*.

Selection from *Louisiana and the Fair: An Exposition of the World, Its People and Their Achievements* by J. W. Buel, ed. St. Louis: World's Progress Pub. Co., 1905. Reprinted by permission of Watson Memorial Library, Cammie G. Henry Research Center, Rare Book Collection, F351B93, vol. 10.

Selection from *"Indescribably Grand" Diaries and Letters from the 1904 World's Fair.* "Recollections of the Fair" by Sam P. Hyde. Ed. Martha R. Clevenger. Copyright © 1996 by Missouri Historical Society. Reprinted by permission of Missouri Historical Society.

Selection from *Apologetics & Catholic Doctrine, Part III: Catholic Morality* by Rev. Bernard J. Kelly. Copyright © 1951 by Holy Ghost Congregation. Reprinted by permission of Holy Ghost Congregation.

Selection from "Early New Orleans Society: A Reappraisal" by Joseph G. Tregle Jr. Copyright © 1952 by the Southern Historical Association. Reprinted by permission of the Managing Editor.

Selection from "On That Word 'Creole' Again: A Note" by Joseph G. Tregle Jr. Copyright © 1982 by *Louisiana History*. Reprinted by permission of the Louisiana Historical Association.

Selection from *The Forgotten People: Cane River's Creoles of Color* by Gary B. Mills. Copyright © 1977 by Louisiana State University Press. Reprinted by permission of Louisiana State University Press.

Selection from "The Plantation Mistress: Her Working Life." *Southern Exposure* 11.1 (1983): 58–63. Copyright © 1983 by Catherine Clinton. Reprinted by permission of Catherine Clinton.

Selection from *St. Louis Spectator.* Copyright © 1890. Reprinted by permission of The State Historical Society of Missouri, Columbia.

Selection from *St. Louis Post-Dispatch.* Copyright © 1890. Reprinted by permission of The State Historical Society of Missouri, Columbia.

LIBRARY OF CONGRESS CATALOGING-IN-PUBLICATION DATA

Chopin, Kate, 1851–1904.
At fault / Kate Chopin ; a scholarly edition with background readings edited by Suzanne Disheroon Green and David J. Caudle.—1st ed.
   p. cm.
Includes bibliographical references and index.
ISBN 1-57233-120-8 (cl.: alk. paper)—ISBN 1-57233-121-6 (pbk.: alk.paper)
1. Women plantation owners—Fiction. 2. Chopin, Kate, 1851–1904. At fault. 3. Plantation life—Fiction. 4. Young women—Fiction. 5. Louisiana—Fiction. 6. Creoles—Fiction. 7. Widows—Fiction. I. Green, Suzanne Disheroon, 1963– II. Caudle, David J., 1956–   III. Title.
PS1294.C63 A63 2001
813'.4—dc21   00-011384

This volume is dedicated to our
families and friends who helped
make this project a reality

Contents

At Fault

The Text

Part 1

Part 2

Backgrounds and Contexts

Contemporary Reviews

Literary Sources

Legal, Historic, and Economic Influences

Illustrations

Following Page 150

Figures

Maps

Preface

Despite its relative obscurity, Kate Chopin's first novel, *At Fault,* has received increased attention from literary critics in recent years. Although perhaps lacking some of the artistic qualities of her later masterpiece, *The Awakening,* and at times a bit didactic for the taste of modern readers, *At Fault* is an important piece of the Chopin canon. Surprisingly, given the significance of this novel in terms of evaluating and understanding Chopin's complete body of work, *At Fault* has not been widely available, except as part of Per Seyersted's *The Complete Works of Kate Chopin,* since shortly after its initial publication in 1890.

This volume originally was intended simply to make the text of *At Fault* available in a more affordable and accessible form for scholars of American, southern, and women's literature; the general reading public; and students in college classrooms. However, as we began to develop this project, it became clear that the cultural milieu that surrounds this novel is quite different from that of either *The Awakening* or most of Chopin's short fiction. Certainly, Chopin draws upon many of the same elements that characterize her later work: recurring characters; a fictional community based upon the Cane River region of Natchitoches Parish in Northwestern Louisiana; Creole dialects; and Louisiana landscapes, to name just a few. However, she develops themes that remain relevant today, despite the fact that at the time *At Fault* was written, Chopin clearly was not the polished writer she would become later.

The narrative of *At Fault* revolves around a young Creole widow who runs a plantation on her own, despite her neighbors' expectations that she would soon remarry and assume a more traditional role. Her story illustrates both the development of railroad systems in the rural South and its effect upon the agrarian provincialism of small town life in Louisiana. *At Fault* also documents the threat felt by those who had lived in these rural regions their entire lives upon encountering such profound and unstoppable changes. Chopin also documents—none too subtly—her opinions of the urban *nouveau riche,* the Temperance Movement, and several renowned contemporary writers.

At Fault is quite an ambitious undertaking for a first novel, and we realized that to make this novel truly accessible, especially to readers who are unfamiliar with the gumbo that is Louisiana culture, it would be necessary to examine the context within which Chopin placed her novel. Accordingly, this volume consists of two parts: the text of *At Fault,* with explanatory notes; and a collection of supplementary materials—many of which were available and familiar to Chopin herself—assembled to provide context for the novel. These materials allow a fuller reading of *At Fault.*

ACKNOWLEDGMENTS

As with any volume of this scope, the list of people and organizations to whom we owe a debt of gratitude is extensive. Without the help of these, and doubtless others whom we have inadvertently neglected to mention, this volume would not have been possible.

We owe particular thanks to our families, who provided not only moral support and encouragement, but in many cases economic support as well. Their generosity made possible several extended research trips. Jay Caudle, Jolene Caudle, Fred Disheroon, Diane Donley, Charles L. Green, Elaine Green, and Richard Green have been instrumental in the completion of this volume. Special thanks also go to Kathryn Amanda Green and J. Alexander Green for their patience with a mom who too often said that she had to work instead of going outside to throw baseballs or paint flower pots. J. Alexander Green also helped proofread some of the manuscript materials, and Kathryn Amanda Green took on extra chores, especially cooking, to help.

Without the help of our tireless, unflagging, and uncomplaining editorial assistant, Susie Scifres Kuilan, we undoubtedly would have pulled each other's hair out and possibly our own as well. She was invaluable in helping to get the manuscript together, spending countless hours—even on her days off—typing, correcting, and organizing our material. She deserves a substantial measure of credit for the successful completion of this volume. We also thank the Department of Language and Communication at Northwestern State University of Louisiana for providing institutional support for Kuilan's services. The students in English 3150 (Spring 2000) provided feedback on material that we needed to annotate in the text of the novel.

Our dear friend and colleague, Lisa Abney of the Louisiana Folklife Center, Natchitoches, Louisiana, not only contributed an original essay to the volume, but also went out of her way to secure photos of maps from Special

Collections, Louisiana Collection, Tulane University Library. We still owe her and her new husband dinner at Antoine's for her efforts. Michelle Pichon contributed an insightful and thought-provoking essay created especially for this volume. The members of the weekly research and "save our mental health" group—Lisa Abney, Helaine Razovsky, Helen Sugarman, and Shelisa Theus—were kind enough to review the introduction to the volume and make excellent suggestions for revision. After we returned to Louisiana to finish writing the book, Jerry Alexandratos made several trips to acquire materials that were available only at the Library of Congress; he also assisted in clarifying several copyright issues. He too, will be the recipient of a Creole dinner and a bottle of Merlot.

Marie François Conin-Jones translated the French and Creole passages in *At Fault* with the same pleasing professionalism she demonstrated in working with us on our previous Chopin volume. We owe her a special *merci* for her patience with our lateness in getting materials to her. Shelley Svidal aided us in locating the Cicero quotation cited in the endnotes.

At the Cammie G. Henry Research Center, Watson Library, Northwestern State University of Louisiana, Archivist Mary Linn Wernet and Assistant Archivist Catherine Jannik helped us locate information about Chopin, her husband, and their family landholdings. Sonny Newton Carter made photographic copies of several maps in the Research Center collections on very short notice, and we are grateful. Bill Meneray at the Special Collections, Tulane University, was a great help in securing both maps of Louisiana and permission to reproduce them in this volume.

Charles L. Green and Anitra Kinder photographed many of the historical sites pictured in this volume and were instrumental in getting them developed and enlarged. Finally, Gary Hardamon, supervisor of photography at Northwestern State University of Louisiana, developed and enlarged several prints for us; he was extremely kind and efficient in doing so on short notice.

We owe thanks to the research librarians at the following institutions: the Library of Congress; the McKeldin Library, University of Maryland; Tulane University; Missouri Historical Society; and the University of North Texas Libraries. The staff at the St. Louis Cemetery aided us in locating the Chopin family plot.

Finally, the editors at the University of Tennessee Press—especially Joyce Harrison, acquisitions editor, who initially approached us about doing this volume; and Stan Ivester, managing editor—were extremely helpful throughout the editing and production process. They patiently answered our multitudinous questions and helped the publication process run smoothly.

Editorial Practices

This edition of *At Fault* conforms as closely as possible to the first edition, which was published privately in 1890 by Nixon-Jones Publishing. No substantial reprint has been undertaken until this time. A short-run reprinting of the first edition was issued by Green Street Press in 1986, but this edition has been out of print for some time. The only other version presently available is included in Per Seyersted's *The Complete Works of Kate Chopin* (1969), but the expense of this excellent volume makes its acquisition prohibitive for most readers.

No manuscript of the novel or author's notes related to the text are known to exist, and thus a true critical edition of this text is not possible. Chopin was notorious for destroying her notes and drafts, a reputation that is confirmed by the recently published *Kate Chopin's Private Papers*. This collection demonstrates that Chopin kept exacting financial accounts of both the disposition of her manuscripts and the fate of those manuscript pages after publication. Given Chopin's well-documented writing habits, new evidence is unlikely. Because of the lack of archival evidence, we have little alternative but to rely exclusively on the first edition, with a few minor deviations which are outlined below.

Editorial Changes from the First Edition

Perhaps because it was privately—and therefore inexpensively—published, the first edition of *At Fault* contains a number of irregularities in spelling, punctuation, and other usage. We have regularized spelling when such changes are not at variance with nineteenth-century conventions, and have verified these spellings using Funk and Wagnall's *A Standard Dictionary of the English Language* (1899). Chopin's spelling inconsistencies—such as her use of *aint* and *ain't* interchangeably—have been modernized throughout the text.

We have made minimal changes in punctuation, because many changes of this nature could affect the reading of the text, and we have attempted to avoid such forced readings. Where punctuation *clearly* is a typographical error (e.g., a missing period at the end of a sentence), we have corrected it, and we have annotated any such changes in the endnotes to the text.

EDITORIAL CHANGES IN BACKGROUND PIECES

Because of copyright considerations, we have not corrected the few typographical errors in the secondary material included in this volume. However, we have noted such items where they occur. Many of these secondary sources were written contemporaneously with *At Fault*; hence many of the same types of irregularities in usage, spelling, and especially punctuation, occur. Several of these pieces, and most notably the excerpts from Thorstein Veblen's *The Theory of the Leisure Class,* employ spellings common to British English.

Most of the pieces in the "Backgrounds and Contexts" section are drawn from primary source material. However, in a few cases, we have taken excerpts from scholarly sources, each of which has its own documentation. In the interest of clarity, we have renumbered the relevant notes or tables so that they appear consecutively in the excerpt. Such changes in the numbering scheme of the original versions are indicated by brackets. Because of copyright restrictions, we have made no other changes to these essays.

EDITORIAL PRACTICES IN TEXTUAL NOTES

Unless otherwise noted, definitions of English words are paraphrased from the *Oxford English Dictionary* (New York: Oxford University Press, 1989). French translations are the work of Marie François Conin-Jones of the University of North Texas, Denton, Texas. Explanatory notes, except where otherwise noted, are the work of the editors.

Introduction

A New Generation
Reads *At Fault*

t Fault, one of Kate Chopin's first efforts as a professional writer, was published in 1890 in a private printing of only one thousand copies. While on the surface *At Fault* appears to be a prototypical example of the nineteenth-century domestic novel or a light piece of local color fiction, Chopin's early effort transcends the limitations inherent in these genres. Indeed, *At Fault* addresses many of the same issues that would come to be identified as the hallmarks of Chopin's best fiction. In her first novel, she deals with the ideological questions arising from the redefinition of gender, race, and class roles that foreshadow the more explicit treatment of these themes in much of her short fiction and in *The Awakening.* In addition, she explores many of the issues that came to dominate America's Gilded Age: urbanization and industrialization, along with the resulting economic dislocation. Although these issues are not often considered from the perspective of vanquished southerners prior to the rise of the Vanderbilt Agrarians over thirty years later, in many ways these changes had an even more profound impact on the South than on other parts of the country. Chopin's novel depicts a traditional agrarian society in the throes of recovery from defeat in war and its adaptation to unprecedented subsequent changes in its economic structure. *At Fault* demonstrates that, even at the very beginning of her literary career, Chopin was already an astute observer of human nature, social relations, and historically and economically significant events.

At Fault introduces the reader to the Cane River region and its people—a community that provides the setting and characters for many of Chopin's later works. By the late nineteenth century, this isolated region, the earliest to be settled by Europeans in what was to become the Louisiana Purchase, was home to a unique Creole culture infused with French, Spanish, Anglo-American, Native American, African, and Caribbean influences. These influences resulted in the development of a system of ethnic and social relations which was, because of its complexity, utterly foreign to that found throughout the rest of the American South. Chopin's realistic and detailed depiction of this unique society, whose heritage remains influential to this day, would of itself make *At Fault* an important contribution to American literature.

In addition to its importance as a work of cultural and historical documentary, *At Fault* provides a baseline for the study of Chopin's development as one of America's most renowned fiction writers. Many of her recurrent themes—including her somewhat cynical view of religion, shameless social climbers, and especially, her attention to the struggles of women to expand their social and economic opportunities—are further developed in Chopin's later work. Thus *At Fault* provides the reader with a greater understanding and appreciation of Creole culture, of American social and economic history, and of Chopin's development as a writer.

THE LIFE OF KATE CHOPIN

Kate O'Flaherty Chopin was born in St. Louis, Missouri, on February 8, 1850. She was the eldest daughter of Thomas O'Flaherty and his second wife, Eliza Faris. O'Flaherty was a well-to-do merchant and railroad executive in what was then a burgeoning city on the edge of the western frontier. Because of his Irish heritage in an era in which Irish immigrants were not held in high esteem by most Americans, he needed entrée if he was going to be accepted at the highest levels of St. Louis society. Faris, with her aristocratic French roots, provided this calling card.

O'Flaherty's position with the Missouri-Pacific Railroad led to his early death. To celebrate the completion of the first railroad bridge in St. Louis, the railroad executives boarded a train for a ceremonial trip across the structure. The bridge collapsed, plunging into the Gasconade River, taking with it three of the train cars and their passengers. The accident left Faris a twenty-six-year-old widow with two young children.

Kate Chopin's maternal ancestors numbered among the founders of St. Louis, and several came from Old World Huguenot stock. Chopin was immersed in the French-Creole culture that informs much of her fiction from the time she was a small child, spending a good deal of time with her great-grandmother who spoke only French. Chopin herself spoke fluent French from childhood, and her dialect was influenced by her great-grandmother's "soft Creole patois, [which was] less sharp than the French of Paris."[1] Chopin received her education at the Sacred Heart Academy, whose reputation for high academic standards, as well as for producing "better Catholic wives and mothers,"[2] was well known, and Chopin proved herself to be an able student who received numerous honors during her years at the academy.

Kate married Creole businessman Oscar Chopin in 1870 and moved with him to Louisiana, where he became a cotton factor in New Orleans.[3] Oscar had already left the family plantation because of his distaste for his father's harshness and rough handling of his slaves. The couple resided in New Orleans until Oscar lost his business, at which time they moved to Cloutierville, where he managed the town's general store. Kate bore six children in nine years, and the family lived in relative comfort until Oscar contracted "swamp fever," probably malaria, in 1882 and died, leaving Kate with a substantial debt and a house full of small children. She then worked diligently to pay all of Oscar's debts, while conducting a semi-public affair with local planter Albert Sampite. She ultimately left Cloutierville to return with her children to St. Louis, where she lived, wrote, and published for the remainder of her life. She died of a brain hemorrhage in August 1904, less than five years after the appearance of her masterpiece, *The Awakening.*

CULTURAL CONTEXTS

At Fault reflects the many literary and cultural influences to which Chopin was exposed during her life and travels. In addition to being a talented writer of fiction, she was an astute literary critic, publishing a number of reviews and critical essays. She was an avid reader who also translated French literature, demonstrating a particular affinity for the work of Guy de Maupassant. Her frequent literary and philosophical allusions, many of which are annotated in this edition of *At Fault,* also attest to Chopin's extensive knowledge of the literature, philosophy, and popular culture of her time. Numerous critics have remarked on Chopin's familiarity with philosophical works, especially the German Romanticism of Friedrich Schopenhauer and Friedrich Nietzsche. Also, she would certainly have been familiar with the work of Nathaniel Hawthorne and quite likely with his well-documented hostility toward women writers. Her satirical references to "The Custom House" in *At Fault* reveal a disdain for Hawthorne that would be consistent with a knowledge of this hostility. Ralph Waldo Emerson, one of nineteenth-century America's preeminent philosophers and public speakers, appears to fare even worse in Chopin's novels, although Chopin quotes from his work in her response to a reviewer of *At Fault,* included in this volume, whom she believed to be in error. In *The*

Awakening, Edna Pontellier quickly falls asleep while reading from a collection of Emerson's essays, and in *At Fault,* another Emerson volume is not only ridiculed by Belle Worthington, it is reduced to the status of a paperweight, serving as an anchor for dry goods airing on the roof of a St. Louis apartment building. The same unfortunate fate befalls a copy of John Ruskin's *Miscellanies,* one of the most popular critical works of the late nineteenth century. Clearly, prevailing literary and philosophical currents influenced the type of fiction that Chopin produced.

At Fault also demonstrates Chopin's knowledge of the local legends popular among the residents of the Cane River region, as illustrated by her references in *At Fault* to the graves of the alleged inspirations for Simon Legree and Uncle Tom from Harriet Beecher Stowe's *Uncle Tom's Cabin.* Emily Toth, in her first biography of Chopin, notes that Chopin's father-in-law purchased his plantation from Robert McAlpin, the real-life alter-ego of Old McFarlane in the novel, whose family retained some of the adjoining property. Toth also notes that the elder Chopin was sometimes mistaken for McAlpin as the model for Legree in local gossip because of his harsh treatment of his own family and slaves. This site, located in Chopin, Louisiana, is about five miles from Oscar Chopin's residence in Cloutierville and is still visited by residents of Natchitoches Parish.

In addition to this knowledge of local folklore, Chopin was also steeped in the Creole culture of Louisiana and was familiar with the economy of the region by virtue of her husband's business ventures outside of the family plantation and her own experiences settling his affairs after his death. Settling the estate required her to regain the legal custody of her children. Closing succession after the father's death when the custody of minor children was involved was a complicated economic and legal task because of the influence of the Napoleonic Code on Louisiana state laws. Upon Oscar's death, the legal guardianship of the six Chopin children automatically devolved to his closest male relative, his brother, Lamy Chopin. Kate Chopin was forced to petition the court, in a complicated and time-consuming ordeal, to gain full custody of her children, despite her brother-in-law's lack of opposition. When she was finally granted custody, Lamy Chopin was named "Under Tutor," which implied that her competence in the eyes of the law was still questionable.[4]

As *At Fault* shows, Chopin put her knowledge of business and legal issues, knowledge rare for a woman of her era, to good use in her writing career, as *At Fault* faithfully portrays the economic milieu of late nineteenth-century Louisiana. In the aftermath of the Civil War and Reconstruction, the economic order of the Old South was in shambles due to the collapse of slavery and damage from the war. The region was home to many displaced persons, both African American and white, who had no prospects and who benefited from no social support system. As a result, crime in northwestern Louisiana, ranging from petty theft to murder, reached its historic peak in the last quarter of the nineteenth century.

Thérèse Lafirme, the protagonist of *At Fault,* expresses well-founded trepidation about the coming of the railroad to northwestern Louisiana. Her concern is not born of simple nostalgia for a way of life whose time was soon to end, although she realizes that the railroad will quickly alter the economy, the social structure, and the landscape of the region. Chopin's depiction of the rapidly changing economy is realistic, as demonstrated by Thérèse's mixed emotions regarding the arrival of the lumber mill and David Hosmer. Though pleased by the financial windfall from the sale of timber rights on her property, she does not look forward to the changes to the land and the culture of her community that will inevitably follow. Joçint is even less pleased by the advent of the lumber mill and the regimentation of his formerly carefree lifestyle because of the demands of industrial labor. He longs for the time when his days were filled with hunting and fishing, and he resents the infringement of the production line into his way of life. His resentment leads him first to petty sabotage of Hosmer's mill and, ultimately, to arson. Hosmer himself represents the changing of the economic guard as well. *At Fault* illustrates that wealth and social prominence were no longer tied to land ownership and the patronage of a large number of agricultural laborers. Thérèse manages to maintain the status quo of the antebellum economy because of the income from her timber leases; however, such relief could only be temporary. In the future, the new money and the ability to acquire it quickly would come from the industrial exploitation of raw materials, not from agriculture. Thérèse's marriage to Hosmer becomes not only a love match but a symbolic representation of the shotgun wedding between agriculture and industry that was occurring all over the post-Reconstruction South.

The disruption of the established social order of late nineteenth-century Louisiana brought by industrialization was compounded by the fact that respect for the government had evaporated and legal authority was largely nonexistent. The few active law enforcement officials were held in disdain by most of the community, and for safety's sake, they seldom ventured far from the courthouse. Such a turn of events is not surprising, given that Louisiana had been under four different national governments and had survived a bloody Civil War, all within a single century. Furthermore, northwestern Louisiana did not suffer from the same vanquished mentality as the rest of the South following the Civil War. The northwestern portion of the state was never overrun by the dreaded Yankees, nor did it suffer the same massive physical destruction inflicted on much of the rest of the South. The result of this escape from total subjugation was an attitude which approached invincibility on the part of the white male population. Not surprisingly, both property crimes, born of economic necessity, and crimes of violence, born of social disorder, were rampant. Court records indicate that, in the years immediately following Reconstruction in many Louisiana parishes, including those of the Cane River region, as much as one-third of the adult male population was either the victim or the perpetrator of a serious assault or murder. Local vigilance committees meted out most of the justice to be had, most often in the form of intimidation or lynchings. In addition, citizens were not only well armed, they knew how to use their weapons, and they were encouraged by the authorities to do so freely in the event of trouble. In light of this situation, the response, or lack thereof, to the murders of Joçint and Grégoire indicate the widespread social disorder which Chopin herself had experienced first-hand.

At Fault also illustrates the influence of the Temperance Movement on American society in the late nineteenth century. Begun in the early 1800s, this social movement grew in influence, ultimately resulting in the passage of the Volstead Act in 1919, the controversial Eighteenth Amendment to the Constitution that banned the production and sale of alcoholic beverages in the United States. The leadership of the abolitionist, temperance, and women's suffrage movements overlapped to a large extent, and their efforts were often coordinated; at one point, the leaders of these movements decided to defer the suffrage issue until abolition was accomplished. Following the Civil War, efforts directed toward women's suffrage and temperance increasingly gained momentum. The temperance cause was viewed by many, including many of its leaders, as an essentially female issue, since women's economic dependence on men, and their lack of protection under the law should a man victimize them, made women especially vulnerable to the consequences of excessive drinking.[5] The physical abuse and financial irresponsibility that resulted from the excessive consumption of alcohol, more often than not, affected women and young children most dramatically. Chopin was also personally acquainted with these issues because of her relationship with Albert Sampite, a prominent Natchitoches Parish planter. In her recent biography of Chopin, Toth notes that Sampite, a charming man when sober, sometimes abused his wife when he had been drinking.[6] *At Fault* accurately portrays contemporary attitudes with regard to the subject of temperance, and the fact that alcoholism leads to Fanny's divorce, and ultimately to her death, emphasizes this point. Grégoire's death is also associated with excessive drinking, as his alcohol-induced aggression leads to the confrontation during which he is shot, as well as to several lesser altercations leading up to it.

Another aspect of late nineteenth-century culture reflected in *At Fault* is the popularity of exhibitions and fairs. Chopin herself was a fan of such expositions, as evidenced in part by her suffering a fatal cerebral hemorrhage after spending a day at the 1904 St. Louis World's Fair. These expositions began in Europe as a showcase for the technological advances of burgeoning industrial powers. Such events soon became popular in the United States as well, and St. Louis hosted numerous such expositions leading up to the year-long extravaganza in 1904. The excerpts from *Indescribably Grand*[7] and *Louisiana and the Fair,*[8] though describing the 1904 World's Fair, are representative of the scene that Hosmer would have witnessed on the Pike, or midway, following his remarriage to Fanny. The physical setting would have been similar as well, since in St. Louis expositions and fairs of all types were held in the same locale, Forest Park, and differed from each other primarily in their scale.

Chopin's novel is also deeply influenced by the rapid changes in social roles that accompanied industrialization and the transformation of the economy that led to the Gilded Age. By the end of the nineteenth century, St. Louis had become a major urban center, transforming in less than a century from a rustic frontier outpost into the fourth largest city in the United States, behind only New York, Chicago, and Philadelphia. St. Louis was expanding rapidly in both wealth and population, and accordingly, offered amenities such as large, modern apartment buildings, telephones, electricity, paved roads, and public transportation. The middle class was on the rise, as corporate growth provided new career opportunities to those with skills and ambition. The contrast with the rural agrarianism of northwest Louisiana could not be more pronounced, as the social and economic changes transforming St. Louis were the barest of suggestions in Natchitoches Parish.

The plantation economy of which Thérèse is matriarch is a vestige of the Old South. As the novel opens, the static economic system of the plantation community—its social hierarchy little changed from antebellum days—is experiencing the first effects of industrialization. Thérèse occupies the unusual position of a woman who is both economically independent and upon whom many other people depend for financial support. With the exception of Hosmer's lumber mill, Place-du-Bois and the surrounding regions are an entirely agrarian society. The economic and social differences between St. Louis and rural Louisiana are best illustrated in the contrast between Fanny's lifestyle and Thérèse's. Chopin characterizes the "professional time wasters" of St. Louis as anti-intellectual, vulgar, and immoral, contrasting them unfavorably with the gentility, hospitality, and cultivated manners of the Louisiana natives. This dichotomy is most clearly seen when Fanny's friends from St. Louis come to visit her in Louisiana on their way to Mardi Gras. Belle Worthington is portrayed as loud and pushy, demanding a pack of cards so that she can school the uneducated rural folk in the ways of six-handed euchre, while Fanny is in turn either irritable, sulky, or rude. Thérèse and her guests are reserved and a bit taken aback by the St. Louis set. In fact, the ostentatious appearance and behavior of Belle Worthington leads Mr. Duplan to wonder in a manner that is only half-joking if she is in fact Hosmer's mistress, rather than the supposedly respectable matron that she presents herself to be. Thérèse, on the other hand, epitomizes the best of the myths of southern honor and womanhood, ideals held in high esteem, even if, as Bertram Wyatt-Brown notes in *Southern Honor: Ethics and Behavior in the Old South,*[9] it was the rare individual who lived up to the myths. Despite rapidly accumulating wealth, the industrial classes could never hope to approach the cultivated gentility of the southern aristocracy, and at best were viewed as little more than an urban variety of "plain white trash."

The selections from Thorstein Veblen's *The Theory of the Leisure Class,* along with the excerpts from contemporary etiquette manuals in this volume, shed light on the social expectations and strict social codes of the time. For example, the formal mourning restrictions placed on those who lost a loved one illustrate the often extreme demands placed on nineteenth-century women. Women were expected not only to mourn the passing of their own relatives but to withdraw from public view to grieve the passing of their husband's relatives with equal fervor. This expectation at times even extended to the family of a husband's earlier wives. Mourning traditions also depict the implicit social hierarchy that kept everyone in a well-defined place. This hierarchy especially concerned domestic servants, who were far more common during the time in which *At Fault* is set than they are today. The roles and behavior of both worker and employer were carefully defined, even if these unwritten codes were not always enforced. Despite the low pay and often difficult working conditions, many people were forced to seek employment as domestic servants, and for women this was often the only type of work available. The excerpts from *The Young Lady's Friend,* which advocates kind and fair treatment of domestic servants, implies that such treatment was not necessarily the norm.

Given the Catholic background of both Thérèse and of Chopin herself, we might expect religion to play an important role in *At Fault*. Chopin was raised as a Catholic, but by the time her mother died, shortly after her return to St. Louis, she had fallen away from practicing the religion of her youth.

Similarly, Thérèse self-identifies as a Catholic but does not appear to be overly devout. Nevertheless, Hosmer's divorce makes it impossible for her to marry him without committing a mortal sin. She also arranges for a requiem mass to be said for Grégoire, but this is the only occasion in the novel when Thérèse actively takes part in any sort of religious ceremony. She is also interested in the temperance cause, perhaps in part because of the Catholic teachings regarding moderation, but more likely because she is a moralist at heart. However, Catholicism is not the only religion that is given voice in *At Fault.* Melicent speaks of several Unitarian beliefs, including the absence of an everlasting hell. She also rejects Grégoire after he kills Joçint, in part because her religious convictions cause her to find his crime reprehensible and unforgivable. In addition, Hosmer and Fanny are married by a Unitarian minister, although neither appears to be particularly concerned with religious issues. Chopin's novel addresses these and many other thorny issues in *At Fault* that are further explored in her later and better-known works.

Contemporary Reviews

Contemporary reviews of *At Fault* were largely positive, and most focused on its local color. The novel was praised for its depiction of the Cane River region, even by those most familiar with the area, and critics also appreciated it because the "plot of the novel is full of interest," according to the *Natchitoches Enterprise.* This reviewer went on to express her satisfaction with the novel: "The perusal of the work afforded us much pleasure and we hope that Mrs. Kate Chopin will again favor us with another. Upon the whole 'tis our humble opinion that while we cannot accord genius to the fair authoress we are willing to admit that she is a lady who possesses talents of no common order." Despite Chopin herself having composed a response to this review because she believed that the writer had misrepresented the roles of Fanny and Thérèse in the novel, she also expressed appreciation for his kind reception of her work. Her view of Chopin's talent was shared by a reviewer for *St. Louis Life,* who remarked that *At Fault* "is a pleasing story, exceptionally well-told, and proves that Mrs. Chopin possesses a talent that should prove a source of pleasure to the public and profit to herself."

The novel received similar positive reviews in other publications. The *St. Louis Republic* remarked that "some of the secondary characters are particularly well drawn, and the local color is excellent," while the *New Orleans Daily Picayune* called *At Fault* "charming." *At Fault's* local color elements, specifically Chopin's depiction of local dialects, was praised by *The Nation,* which commented that Chopin had "an aptitude for seizing dialects of whites and blacks alike, and no little skill in perceiving and defining character." Despite its inexpensive production, abundant typographical and mechanical errors, and the small press run which limited its availability, *At Fault* was a promising start to Chopin's literary career.

Despite the positive, if understandably limited, response of contemporary critics to *At Fault,* the nine years that intervened between the appearance of Chopin's two published novels—a period that saw the production of almost her entire corpus[10]—influenced the reaction of later critics. *At Fault* is clearly the work of a novice writer who had demonstrable, if undeveloped, talent. The experience that Chopin gained writing short fiction helped her to become a far more polished artist by the time she wrote *The Awakening.* Both novels were restored to the attention of critics and general readers simultaneously with the publication of *The Complete Works of Kate Chopin* in 1969, and Chopin's first novel was understandably overshadowed by what most readers consider to be her masterpiece.

CRITICAL RECEPTION

Although some literary critics have argued that *At Fault* suffers in comparison to Chopin's masterpiece, *The Awakening,* such a comparison is misleading on several grounds. Because it was self-published, *At Fault* was produced without the benefit of either professional editing or proofreading. Because of these restrictions, numerous typographical and spelling errors occurred throughout the production process. Unfortunately, this poorly produced edition too often reflects on the quality of the writing itself, causing some readers to, perhaps subconsciously, mistakenly question the quality of the narrative as well. Since no subsequent edition of *At Fault* was published for almost eighty years, serious critical study of this novel was not only delayed, upon its return to critical attention it was at once overshadowed by the tremendous response to *The Awakening.*

At Fault introduces many of the elements that would later be recognized as the basis for Chopin's later success: a strong emphasis on the unusual regional aspects of northwestern Louisiana, where many of her narratives are set; a substantial and enduring community of interrelated families on all levels of the social hierarchy, along with their servants and former slaves; and an interest in questions that transcend the merely regional in favor of the universal: the changing roles of women in society, the influence that religion should hold over an individual's life, and the effects of trying to rebuild a society that has been leveled by war, economic upheaval, and racial oppression. Chopin's first novel is also considered a part of the local color tradition that characterized southern writing during this era, even though Chopin herself did not care for this label because she found it limiting. Further, despite its superficial conformity to the trappings of domestic fiction, the thematic focus of *At Fault* deals with subject matter that was not nearly so traditional. For example, its treatment of divorce is realistic, and ultimately non-judgmental, given Thérèse's change of heart after she has the opportunity to observe Fanny's behavior and Hosmer's unhappiness. Chopin's portrayal of Fanny's struggle with alcohol and her efforts to hide her abuse of it are equally frank and unusual for the time.

Chopin also places two of *At Fault*'s female characters in non-traditional roles, an unusual occurrence in nineteenth-century domestic fiction. Thérèse successfully runs a large plantation without the benefit of a husband, despite the expectations that she would either make a major mistake or succumb to the pressures of the day-to-day operations of the plantation and remarry to relieve herself of the burden. Even after her marriage to Hosmer at the end of the novel, Chopin makes it clear that Thérèse will continue to manage the plantation. Hosmer tells Thérèse that he does not wish to interfere in its operation because he is, quite simply, unqualified to do so.

By the end of the novel, Melicent, the capricious, materialistic, and vain Anglo-American woman, has found a female mentor—a scholar—and is making plans to travel west to study with her. She also takes to wearing eyeglasses so that she will appear to be more serious, remarkable in an era when most women eschewed spectacles as the marker of a bluestocking, regardless of the quality of their eyesight. In short, Chopin does not rely solely on the conventional marriage plot, an important element in many lesser pieces of women's fiction of this era.

Chopin also develops characters, such as David Hosmer, Joçint, and Grégoire, who possess an unusual, at least for the time, awareness of the dark side of industrial expansion and a sensitivity to the environmental degradation that often accompanied it. Thus, in some respects, *At Fault* was as far ahead of its time as Chopin's better known and far more controversial final novel.

Although *At Fault* received less scholarly attention than *The Awakening* and the short fiction in the years immediately following the recovery of Chopin's work in the late 1960s and early 1970s, it has received an increasing amount of critical attention in recent years. Much of the critical attention to *At Fault* has focused on comparisons with *The Awakening,* on efforts to place *At Fault* in the tradition of local color or regionalism, on examinations of racial and gender issues, or on studies of the influence of French culture on the novel. For example, Larzer Ziff, in *The American 1890s: Life and Times of a Lost Generation,* argues that Chopin's novel was overly ambitious for a writer who was just beginning her career, and that this fact largely accounts for its flaws. He also notes that while *At Fault* revolves around a very conventional version of the traditional marriage plot, Chopin's characterization of Grégoire takes "open delight in the difference between the sexes [that] was not a mentionable feeling until [Chopin] brought to American literature a setting in which it could be demonstrated with open geniality."[11]

Robert D. Arner, in "Landscape Symbolism in Kate Chopin's *At Fault*,"[12] warns of the danger of reading this early novel exclusively in terms of her later work, particularly *The Awakening*. He argues that, in so doing, readers risk narrowing their critical vision and thereby distorting the novel's emphasis. He examines the landscape symbolism of Chopin's first novel, noting that it is perhaps the most traditionally southern of her works, and he argues that it is better read as a foreshadowing of William Faulkner's work than in the context of *The Awakening*. William Warkin's "Fire, Light, and Darkness in Kate Chopin's *At Fault*" also studies the novel's symbolism and imagery. He especially notes the light-dark contrast portrayed through the novel's African American characters, arguing that they bridge this symbolic contrast in a way that many of the white characters do not. He also states that in *At Fault* Chopin attempts to "shed the limits of Romanticism and stride into Realism."[13] Lewis Leary, in "Kate Chopin's Other Novel,"[14] argues that, although *At Fault* is seldom read, it illustrates Chopin's potential as a writer and introduces themes and stylistic elements that will appear in her later, more polished work. He notes that this is particularly the case with her characterizations and her ear for dialogue, which are already well developed in *At Fault*.

In contrast, Thomas Bonner Jr., in "Kate Chopin's *At Fault*" and "*The Awakening*: A Study in Structure," argues that, in comparison to Chopin's masterpiece, her first novel is episodic, subconscious, and awkward."[15] Jo Ridgley, in *Nineteenth Century Southern Literature*,[16] criticizes *At Fault* as "weak," again in comparison to *The Awakening*. However, she also notes that in both novels Chopin envisions a "newer" South in which women would not be bound by the stereotype of the southern lady.[17] Donald A. Ringe, in "Cane River World: Kate Chopin's *At Fault* and Related Stories," takes a nineteenth-century social and historical perspective, noting that this novel, along with the short fiction set in the Cane River region, presents a coherent representation of the region and its people and society."[18] Bert Bender, in "The Teeth of Desire: *The Awakening* and *The Descent of Man*,"[19] notes that *At Fault* stands apart from *The Awakening* and Chopin's short fiction in terms of its courtship plots, while devoting most of his attention to the latter novel.

At Fault fares better with critics when they avoid superficial or stylistic comparisons with *The Awakening* and Chopin's more polished short fiction.

For example, in "Christianity and Catholicism in the Fiction of Kate Chopin"[20] Bonner again examines *At Fault,* arguing that it reflects the same themes and influences as her better known and more highly regarded works. Jane Hotchkiss's "Confusing the Issue: Who's *At Fault?*"[21] notes Barbara Ewell's observation in her book length study, *Kate Chopin,*[22] that although many of the novel's themes are derived from late nineteenth-century sentimental and domestic fiction, it critiques, as it realistically portrays, the intellectual and social conventions and traditional gender roles of the time. Ewell concludes that, despite the superficial form of *At Fault* as a traditional sentimental novel, it proves to be a multi-layered text hiding a critique of judgmental moralism and argues that it suggests a new order of moral thinking. Dorys Crow Grover, in "Kate Chopin and the Bayou Country,"[23] states that, while *At Fault* did not transcend its regionalist roots, it raises issues that extend beyond the usual domain of regional fiction. In "Fissure as Art in Kate Chopin's *At Fault,*"[24] Pamela Glenn Menke argues that this novel contains two disjointed texts that reflect the tension between Chopin's personal and artistic lives. She concludes that a close reading of *At Fault* reveals a subversive subtext shared by much of the sentimental fiction of the nineteenth century. In a second essay, "The Catalyst of Color and Women's Regional Writing: *At Fault, Pembroke,* and *The Awakening,*"[25] Menke argues that critics have too hastily dismissed much nineteenth-century women's fiction as mere local color. She states that these conventions are often the guise adopted by serious women writers of the time and that a careful examination of the underlying themes of works such as *At Fault* is needed to invigorate the criticism of nineteenth-century women's fiction.

Critics who have explored beyond the limits of local color conventions and comparisons of *At Fault* to Chopin's better known work have found their efforts rewarded. Philip Tarpley in "Kate Chopin's Sawmill: Technology and Change in *At Fault*"[26] presents a historical analysis of this novel and its depiction of the birth of the Louisiana timber industry. He notes that it is the earliest work of fiction set in the Cane River region and that its portrayal of the social changes brought by technological innovation is both detailed and accurate. Violet Harrington Bryan, in *The Myth of New Orleans in Literature,*[27] observes that *At Fault,* along with some of Chopin's short fiction, serves as a valuable counterweight to the work of some of her male contemporaries in its treatment of issues related to race and gender. In "Kate Chopin: Tradition and the Moment,"[28] Thomas Bonner Jr. argues that Chopin, unlike many late nineteenth-century southern writers, was not an apologist for the romanticized Old South. He further notes that Chopin's bold yet ambiguous treatment of controversial issues such as race, caste, and gender set her apart from most of her contemporaries.

In "Kate Chopin's Local Color Fiction and the Politics of White Supremacy,"[29] Sandra Gunning argues that Chopin's body of work is as much a response to racial stereotypes as it is a reaction to patriarchal domination, and that it provides a hitherto neglected site from which to consider the racialization of gender within turn-of-the-century women's fiction.

Critics have also expressed a good deal of interest in the French influence on *At Fault* since Chopin's interest in French literature, exemplified by her translation of the works of Guy de Maupassant, is well documented. For example, Jean Bardot, in "French Creole Portraits: The Chopin Family from Natchitoches Parish,"[30] draws on biographical sources in both Louisiana and France, concluding that characters reminiscent of Chopin's in-laws appear in both *At Fault* and in her short fiction set in the Cane River region. In "Kate Chopin's *At Fault:* The Usefulness of Louisiana French for the Imagination,"[31] Winfried Fluck argues that, like *The Awakening,* Chopin's first novel combines elements of the domestic novel, local color fiction, and "New Woman" fiction with French influences. Christopher Benfey, in *Degas in New Orleans: Encounters in the Creole World of Kate Chopin and George Washington Cable,*[32] examines the interconnected lives, friendships, and family ties of these three artists. He discusses some of the cultural features, particularly the French, that influenced Chopin's two published novels and much of her short fiction.

Given its cultural, historical, and literary merits, *At Fault* is a novel deserving of renewed attention from literary critics, other students of literature, and general readers alike. Critics are studying this novel with increased interest and frequency, and despite its shortcomings when compared to the best of Chopin's work, it nevertheless demonstrates significant literary merit. *At Fault* provides an accurate and fascinating glimpse into a time in American history which is too often forgotten over a century later. Many of the social and economic issues addressed by Chopin in *At Fault* remain unresolved, yet her insight into human nature and her understanding of social relations remains timeless. Chopin's career spanned a time which, although it seems remote, had much in common with our own turn-of-the-century society. An observer at either end of the twentieth century is dazzled by this era's rapid technological advances, troubled by the accompanying economic dislocations, and forced to deal, consciously or not, with long-standing issues of gender, ethnicity, and class that defy simple solutions, even as they invite conflict. If past is indeed prologue, the time has come for a new generation to read *At Fault,* and for this novel to assume its proper place as an important part of Chopin's literary legacy.

AT FAULT

Part One

I

THE MISTRESS OF PLACE-DU-BOIS

W hen Jérôme Lafirme died, his neighbors awaited the results of his sudden taking off with indolent watchfulness. It was a matter of unusual interest to them that a plantation of four thousand acres had been left unincumbered to the disposal of a handsome, inconsolable, childless Creole widow of thirty. A *bêtise*[1] of some sort might safely be looked for. But time passing, the anticipated folly failed to reveal itself; and the only wonder was that Thérèse Lafirme so successfully followed the methods of her departed husband.

Of course Thérèse had wanted to die with her Jérôme, feeling that life without him held nothing that could reconcile her to its further endurance. For days she lived alone with her grief; shutting out the appeals that came to her from the demoralized "hands," and unmindful of the disorder that gathered about her. Till Uncle Hiram[2] came one day with a respectful tender of sympathy, offered in the guise of a reckless misquoting of Scripture—and with a grievance.

"Mistuss," he said, "I 'lowed 'twar best to come to de house an' tell you; fur Massa he alluz did say 'Hi'urm, I counts on you to keep a eye open endurin' my appersunce;' you ricollic, marm?" addressing an expanse of black bordered cambric[3] that vailed the features of his mistress.[4] "Things is a goin' wrong; dat dey is. I don't wants to name no names doubt I'se 'bleeged to; but dey done start a kiarrin' de cotton seed off de place,[5] and dats how."

If Hiram's information had confined itself to the bare statement of things "goin' wrong," such intimation, of its nature vague and susceptible of uncertain

3

interpretation, might have failed to rouse Thérèse from her lethargy of grief. But that wrong doing presented as a tangible abuse and defiance of authority, served to move her to action. She felt at once the weight and sacredness of a trust, whose acceptance brought consolation and awakened unsuspected powers of doing.

In spite of Uncle Hiram's parting prediction "de cotton 'll be a goin' naxt" no more seed was hauled under cover of darkness from Place-Du-Bois.[6]

The short length of this Louisiana plantation stretched along Cane River, meeting the water when that stream was at its highest, with a thick growth of cotton-wood trees; save where a narrow convenient opening had been cut into their midst, and where further down the pine hills started in abrupt prominence from the water and the dead level of land on either side of them. These hills extended in a long line of gradual descent far back to the wooded borders of Lac du Bois;[7] and within the circuit which they formed on the one side, and the irregular half circle of a sluggish bayou[8] on the other, lay the cultivated open ground of the plantation—rich in its exhaustless powers of reproduction.

Among changes which the railroad brought soon after Jérôme Lafirme's death, and which were viewed by many as of questionable benefit, was one which drove Thérèse to seek another domicile. The old homestead that nestled to the hill side and close to the water's edge, had been abandoned to the inroads of progressive civilization; and Mrs. Lafirme had rebuilt many rods[9] away from the river and beyond sight of the mutilated dwelling, converted now into a section house.[10] In building, she avoided the temptations offered by modern architectural innovations,[11] and clung to the simplicity of large rooms and broad verandas: a style whose merits had stood the test of easy-going and comfort-loving generations.

The negro quarters were scattered at wide intervals over the land, breaking with picturesque irregularity into the systematic division of field from field; and in the early spring-time gleaming in their new coat of whitewash against the tender green of the sprouting cotton and corn.

Thérèse loved to walk the length of the wide verandas, armed with her field-glass, and to view her surrounding possessions with comfortable satisfaction. Then her gaze swept from cabin to cabin; from patch to patch; up to the pine-capped hills, and down to the station which squatted a brown and ugly intruder within her fair domain.

She had made pouting resistance to this change at first, opposing it step by step with a conservatism that yielded only to the resistless. She pictured a visionary troop of evils coming in the wake of the railroad, which, in her eyes no conceivable benefits could mitigate. The occasional tramp, she foresaw as an army; and the travelers whom chance deposited at the store that adjoined the station, she dreaded as an endless procession of intruders forcing themselves upon her privacy.

Grégoire, the young nephew of Mrs. Lafirme, whose duty on the plantation was comprehended in doing as he was bid, qualified by a propensity for doing as he liked, rode up from the store one day in the reckless fashion peculiar to Southern youth, breathless with the information that a stranger was there wishing audience with her.

Thérèse at once bristled with objections. Here was a confirmation of her worst dread. But encouraged by Grégoire's reiteration "he 'pear to me like a nice sort o' person," she yielded a grudging assent to the interview.

She sat within the wide hall-way beyond the glare and heat that were beating mercilessly down upon the world out of doors, engaged in a light work not so exacting as to keep her thoughts and glance from wandering. Looking through the wide open back doors, the picture which she saw was a section of the perfect lawn that encircled the house for an acre around, and from which Hiram was slowly raking the leaves cast from a clump of tall magnolias. Beneath the spreading shade of an umbrella-China tree, lay the burly Hector, but half awake to the possible nearness of tramps; and Betsy, a piece of youthful ebony in blue cottonade,[12] was crossing leisurely on her way to the poultry yard; unheeding the scorching sun-rays that she thought were sufficiently parried by the pan of chick feed that she balanced adroitly on her bushy black head.

At the front, the view at certain seasons would have been clear and unbroken: to the station, the store, and out-lying hills. But now she could see beyond the lawn only a quivering curtain of rich green which the growing corn spread before the level landscape, and above whose swaying heads appeared occasionally the top of an advancing white sun-shade.

Thérèse was of a roundness of figure suggesting a future of excessive fullness if not judiciously guarded; and she was fair, with a warm whiteness that a passing thought could deepen into color. The waving blonde hair, gathered in an abundant coil on top of her head, grew away with a pretty sweep from the temples, the low forehead and nape of the white neck that showed above a frill of soft lace. Her eyes were blue, as certain gems are; that deep blue that lights, and glows, and tells things of the soul. When David Hosmer presented himself, they were intense only with expectancy and the color was in her cheek like the blush in a shell.

He was a tall individual of perhaps forty; thin and sallow. His black hair was streaked abundantly with grey, and his face marked with premature lines;

left there by care, no doubt, and, by a too close attention to what men are pleased to call the main chances of life.

"A serious one," was Thérèse's first thought in looking at him. "A man who has never learned to laugh or who has forgotten how." Though plainly feeling the effects of the heat, he did not seem to appreciate the relief offered by the grateful change into this shadowy, sweet smelling, cool retreat; used as he was to ignore the comforting things of life when presented to him as irrelevant to that dominant main chance. He accepted under protest a glass of ice water from the wide-eyed Betsy, and suffered a fan to be thrust into his hand, seemingly to save his time or his timidity by its possibly unheeded rejection.

"Lor'-zee folks," exclaimed the observant Betsy on re-entering the kitchen, "dey'se a man in yonda, look like he gwine eat somebody up. I was fur gittin' 'way quick me."

It can be readily imagined that Hosmer lost little time in preliminary small talk. He introduced himself vaguely as from the West; then perceiving the need of being more specific as from Saint Louis. She had guessed he was no Southerner. He had come to Mrs. Lafirme on the part of himself and others with a moneyed offer for the privilege of cutting timber from her land for a given number of years. The amount named was alluring, but here was proposed another change and she felt plainly called on for resistance.

The company which he represented had in view the erection of a saw-mill some two miles back in the woods, close beside the bayou and at a convenient distance from the lake. He was not wordy, nor was he eager in urging his plans; only in a quiet way insistent in showing points to be considered in her own favor which she would be likely herself to overlook.

Mrs. Lafirme, a clever enough business woman, was moved by no undue haste to give her answer. She begged for time to think the matter over, which Hosmer readily agreed to; expressing a hope that a favorable answer be sent to him at Natchitoches, where he would await her convenience. Then resisting rather than declining all further hospitality, he again took his way through the scorching fields.

Thérèse wanted but time to become familiar with this further change. Alone she went out to her beloved woods, and at the hush of mid-day, bade a tearful farewell to the silence.

II

AT THE MILL

David Hosmer sat alone in his little office of roughly fashioned pine board. So small a place, that with his desk and his clerk's desk, a narrow bed in one corner, and two chairs, there was scant room for a man to more than turn himself comfortably about. He had just dispatched his clerk with the daily bundle of letters to the post-office, two miles away in the Lafirme store, and he now turned with the air of a man who had well earned his moment of leisure, to the questionable relaxation of adding columns and columns of figures.

The mill's unceasing buzz made pleasant music to his ears and stirred reflections of a most agreeable nature. A year had gone by since Mrs. Lafirme had consented to Hosmer's proposal; and already the business more than gave promise of justifying the venture. Orders came in from the North and West more rapidly than they could be filled. That *"Cypresse Funerall"*[1] which stands in grim majesty through the dense forests of Louisiana had already won its just recognition; and Hosmer's appreciation of a successful business venture was showing itself in a little more pronounced stoop of shoulder, a deepening of pre-occupation and a few additional lines about mouth and forehead.

Hardly had the clerk gone with his letters than a light footstep sounded on the narrow porch; the quick tap of a parasol was heard on the door-sill; a pleasant voice asking, "Any admission except on business?" And Thérèse crossed the small room and seated herself beside Hosmer's desk before giving him time to arise.

She laid her hand and arm,—bare to the elbow—across his work, and said, looking at him reproachfully:—

7

"Is this the way you keep a promise?"

"A promise?" he questioned, smiling awkwardly and looking furtively at the white arm, then very earnestly at the ink-stand beyond.

"Yes. Didn't you promise to do no work after five o'clock?"

"But this is merely pastime," he said, touching the paper, yet leaving it undisturbed beneath the fair weight that was pressing it down. "My work is finished: you must have met Henry with the letters."

"No, I suppose he went through the woods; we came on the hand-car. Oh, dear! It's an ungrateful task, this one of reform," and she leaned back, fanning leisurely, whilst he proceeded to throw the contents of his desk into hopeless disorder by pretended efforts at arrangement.

"My husband used sometimes to say, and no doubt with reason," she continued, "that in my eagerness for the rest of mankind to do right, I was often in danger of losing sight of such necessity for myself."

"Oh, there could be no fear of that," said Hosmer with a short laugh. There was no further pretext for continued occupation with his pens and pencils and rulers, so he turned towards Thérèse, rested an arm on the desk, pulled absently at his black moustache, and crossing his knee, gazed with deep concern at the toe of his boot, and set of his trouser about the ankle.

"You are not what my friend Homeyer would call an individualist," he ventured, "since you don't grant a man the right to follow the promptings of his character."

"No, I'm no individualist, if to be one is to permit men to fall into hurtful habits without offering protest against it. I'm losing faith in that friend Homeyer, who I strongly suspect is a mythical apology for your own short-comings."

"Indeed he's no myth; but a friend who is fond of going into such things and allows me the benefit of his deeper perceptions."

"You having no time, well understood. But if his influence has had the merit of drawing your thoughts from business once in a while we won't quarrel with it."

"Mrs. Lafirme," said Hosmer, seeming moved to pursue the subject, and addressing the spray of white blossoms that adorned Thérèse's black hat, "you admit, I suppose, that in urging your views upon me, you have in mind the advancement of my happiness?"

"Well understood."

"Then why wish to substitute some other form of enjoyment for the one which I find in following my inclinations?"

"Because there is an unsuspected selfishness in your inclinations that works harm to yourself and to those around you. I want you to know," she continued warmly, "the good things of life that cheer and warm, that are always at hand."

"Do you think the happiness of Melicent or—or others could be materially lessened by my fondness for money getting?" he asked dryly, with a faint elevation of eyebrow.

"Yes, in proportion as it deprives them of a charm which any man's society loses, when pursuing one object in life, he grows insensible to every other. But I'll not scold any more. I've made myself troublesome enough for one day. You haven't asked about Melicent. It's true," she laughed, "I haven't given you much chance. She's out on the lake with Grégoire."

"Ah?"

"Yes, in the *pirogue*.³ A dangerous little craft, I'm afraid; but she tells me she can swim. I suppose it's all right."

"Oh, Melicent will look after herself."

Hosmer had great faith in his sister Melicent's ability to look after herself; and it must be granted that the young lady fully justified his belief in her.

"She enjoys her visit more than I thought she would," he said.

"Melicent's a dear girl," replied Thérèse cordially, "and a wise one too in guarding herself against a somber influence that I know," with a meaningful glance at Hosmer, who was preparing to close his desk.

She suddenly perceived the picture of a handsome boy, far back in one of the pigeon-holes, and with the familiarity born of country intercourse, she looked intently at it, remarking upon the boy's beauty.

"A child whom I loved very much," said Hosmer. "He's dead," and he closed the desk, turning the key in the lock with a sharp click which seemed to add—"and buried."

Thérèse then approached the open door, leaned her back against its casing, and turned her pretty profile towards Hosmer, who, it need not be supposed, was averse to looking at it—only to being caught in the act.

"I want to look in at the mill before work closes," she said; and not waiting for an answer she went on to ask—moved by some association of ideas:—

"How is Joçint doing?"

"Always unruly, the foreman tells me. I don't believe we shall be able to keep him."

Hosmer then spoke a few words through the telephone which connected with the agent's desk at the station, put on his great slouch hat, and thrusting keys and hands into his pocket, joined Thérèse in the door-way.

Quitting the office and making a sharp turn to the left, they came in direct sight of the great mill. She quickly made her way past the huge piles of sawed timber, not waiting for her companion, who loitered at each step of the way, with observant watchfulness. Then mounting the steep stairs that led to the upper portions of the mill, she went at once to her favorite spot, quite on the edge of the open platform that overhung the dam. Here she watched with fascinated delight the great logs hauled dripping from the water, following each till it had changed to the clean symmetry of sawed planks. The unending work made her giddy. For no one was there a moment of rest, and she could well understand the open revolt of the surly Joçint; for he rode the day long on that narrow car, back and forth, back and forth, with his heart in the pine hills and knowing that his little Creole pony was roaming the woods in vicious idleness and his rifle gathering an unsightly rust on the cabin wall at home.

The boy gave but ugly acknowledgment to Thérèse's amiable nod; for he thought she was one upon whom partly rested the fault of this intrusive Industry which had come to fire the souls of indolent fathers with a greedy ambition for gain, at the sore expense of revolting youth.[4]

III

In the Pirogue

ou got to set mighty still in this pirogue," said Grégoire, as with a long oar-stroke he pulled out into mid stream.

"Yes, I know," answered Melicent complacently, arranging herself opposite him in the long narrow boat, all sense of danger which the situation might arouse being dulled by the attractiveness of a new experience.

Her resemblance to Hosmer ended with height and slenderness of figure, olive tinted skin, and eyes and hair which were of that dark brown often miscalled black; but unlike his, her face was awake with an eagerness to know and test the novelty and depth of unaccustomed sensation. She had thus far lived an unstable existence, free from the weight of responsibilities, with a notion lying somewhere deep in her consciousness that the world must one day be taken seriously; but that contingency was yet too far away to disturb the harmony of her days.

She had eagerly responded to her brother's suggestion of spending a summer with him in Louisiana. Hitherto, having passed her summers North, West, or East as alternating caprice prompted, she was ready at a word to fit her humor to the novelty of a season at the South. She enjoyed in advance the startling effect which her announced intention produced upon her intimate circle at home; thinking that her whim deserved the distinction of eccentricity with which they chose to invest it. But Melicent was chiefly moved by the prospect of an uninterrupted sojourn with her brother, whom she loved blindly, and to whom she attributed qualities of mind and heart which she thought the world had discovered to use against him.

"You got to set mighty still in this pirogue."

"Yes, I know; you told me so before," and she laughed.

"W'at are you laughin' at?" asked Grégoire with amused but uncertain expectancy.

"Laughing at you, Grégoire; how can I help it?" laughing again.

"Betta wait tell I do somethin' funny, I reckon. Ain't this a putty sight?" he added, referring to the dense canopy of an overarching tree, beneath which they were gliding, and whose extreme branches dipped quite into the slow moving water.

The scene had not attracted Melicent. For she had been engaged in observing her companion rather closely; his personality holding her with a certain imaginative interest.

The young man whom she so closely scrutinized was slightly undersized, but of close and brawny build. His hands were not so refinedly white as those of certain office bred young men of her acquaintance, yet they were not coarsened by undue toil: it being somewhat an axiom with him to do nothing that an available "nigger"[1] might do for him.

Close fitting, high-heeled boots of fine quality encased his feet, in whose shapeliness he felt a pardonable pride; for a young man's excellence was often measured in the circle which he had frequented, by the possession of such a foot. A peculiar grace in the dance and a talent for bold repartée were further characteristics which had made Grégoire's departure keenly felt among certain belles of upper Red River.[2] His features were handsome, of sharp and refined cut; and his eyes black and brilliant as eyes of an alert and intelligent animal sometimes are. Melicent could not reconcile his voice to her liking; it was too softly low and feminine, and carried a note of pleading or *pathos,* unless he argued with his horse, his dog, or a "nigger," at which times, though not unduly raised, it acquired a biting quality that served the purpose of relieving him from further form of insistence.

He pulled rapidly and in silence down the bayou, that was now so entirely sheltered from the open light of the sky by the meeting branches above, as to seem a dim leafy tunnel fashioned by man's ingenuity. There were no perceptible banks, for the water spread out on either side of them, further than they could follow its flashings through the rank underbrush. The dull splash of some object falling into the water, or the wild call of a lonely bird were the only sounds that broke upon the stillness, beside the monotonous dipping of the oars and the occasional low undertones of their own voices. When Grégoire called the girl's attention to an object nearby, she fancied it was the protruding stump of a decaying tree; but reaching for his revolver and taking quiet aim, he drove a ball into the black up-turned nozzle that sent it below the surface with an angry splash.

"Will he follow us?" she asked, mildly agitated.

"Oh no; he's glad 'nough to git out 'o the way. You betta put down yo' vail,[3]" he added a moment later.

Before she could ask a reason—for it was not her fashion to obey at word of command—the air was filled with the doleful hum of a gray[4] swarm of mosquitoes, which attacked them fiercely.

"You didn't tell me the bayou was the refuge of such savage creatures," she said, fastening her vail closely about face and neck, but not before she had felt the sharpness of their angry sting.

"I reckoned you'd 'a knowed all about it: seems like you know everything." After a short interval he added, "you betta take yo' vail off."

She was amused at Grégoire's authoritative tone and she said to him laughing, yet obeying his suggestion, which carried a note of command: "you shall tell me always, why I should do things."

"All right," he replied; "because they ain't any mo' mosquitoes; because I want you to see somethin' worth seein' afta while; and because I like to look at you," which he was doing, with the innocent boldness of a forward child. "Ain't that 'nough reasons?"

"More than enough," she replied shortly.

The rank and clustering vegetation had become denser as they went on, forming an impenetrable tangle on either side, and pressing so closely above that they often needed to lower their heads to avoid the blow of some drooping branch. Then a sudden and unlooked for turn in the bayou carried them out upon the far-spreading waters of the lake, with the broad canopy of the open sky above them.

"Oh," cried Melicent, in surprise. Her exclamation was like a sigh of relief which comes at the removal of some pressure from body or brain.

The wildness of the scene caught upon her erratic fancy, speeding it for a quick moment into the realms of romance. She was an Indian maiden of the far past, fleeing and seeking with her dusky lover some wild and solitary retreat on the borders of this lake, which offered them no seeming foot-hold save such as they would hew themselves with axe or tomahawk. Here and there, a grim cypress lifted its head above the water, and spread wide its moss-covered arms inviting refuge to the great black-winged buzzards that circled over and about it in mid-air. Nameless voices—weird sounds that awake in a Southern forest at twilight's approach,—were crying a sinister welcome to the settling gloom.

"This is a place thet can make a man sad, I tell you," said Grégoire, resting his oars, and wiping the moisture from his forehead. "I wouldn't want to be yere alone, not fur any money."

"It is an awful place," replied Melicent with a little appreciative shudder; adding "do you consider me a bodily protection?" and feebly smiling into his face.

"Oh; I ain't 'fraid o' any thing I can see an on'erstan'. I can han'le mos' any thing thet's got a body. But they do tell some mighty queer tales 'bout this lake an' the pine hills yonda."

"Queer—how?"

"W'y, ole McFarlane's buried up there on the hill; an' they's folks 'round yere says he walks about o' nights; can't res' in his grave fur the niggas he's killed."

"Gracious! and who was old McFarlane?"

"The meanest w'ite man thet ever lived, seems like. Used to own this place long befo' the Lafirmes got it. They say he's the person that Mrs. W'at's her name wrote about in *Uncle Tom's Cabin*."[5]

"Legree? I wonder if it could be true?" Melicent asked with interest.

"Thet's w'at they all say: ask any body."

"You'll take me to his grave, won't you Grégoire," she entreated.

"Well, not this evenin'—I reckon not. It'll have to be broad day, an' the sun shinin' mighty bright w'en I take you to old McFarlane's grave."

They had retraced their course and again entered the bayou, from which the light had now nearly vanished, making it needful that they watch carefully to escape the hewn logs that floated in numbers upon the water.

"I didn't suppose you were ever sad Grégoire," Melicent said gently.

"Oh my! yes;" with frank acknowledgment. "You ain't ever seen me w'en I was real lonesome. 'Tain't so bad sence you come. But times w'en I git to thinkin' 'bout home, I'm boun' to cry—seems like I can't he'p it."

"Why did you ever leave home?" she asked sympathetically.

"You see w'en father died, fo' year ago, mother she went back to France, t'her folks there; she never could stan' this country—an' lef' us boys to manage the place. Hec, he took charge the firs' year an' run it in debt. Placide an' me did'n' have no betta luck the naxt year. Then the creditors come up from New Orleans an' took holt. That's the time I packed my duds an' lef'."

"And you came here?"

"No, not at firs'. You see the Santien[6] boys had a putty hard name in the country. Aunt Thérèse, she'd fallen out with father years ago 'bout the way, she said, he was bringin' us up. Father, he wasn't the man to take nothin' from nobody. Never 'lowed any of us to come down yere. I was in Texas, goin' to the devil I reckon, w'en she sent for me, an' yere I am."

"And here you ought to stay, Grégoire."

"Oh, they ain't no betta woman in the worl' then Aunt Thérèse, w'en you do like she wants. See 'em yonda waitin' fur us? Reckon they thought we was drowned."

IV

A Small Interruption

When Melicent came to visit her brother, Mrs. Lafirme persuaded him to abandon his uncomfortable quarters at the mill and take up his residence in the cottage, which stood just beyond the lawn of the big house. This cottage had been furnished *de pied en cap*[1] many years before, in readiness against an excess of visitors, which in days gone by was not of infrequent occurrence at Place-du-Bois. It was Melicent's delighted intention to keep house here. And she foresaw no obstacle in the way of procuring the needed domestic aid in a place which was clearly swarming with idle women and children.

·   "Got a cook yet, Mel?" was Hosmer's daily enquiry[2] on returning home, to which Melicent was as often forced to admit that she had no cook, but was not without abundant hope of procuring one.

Betsy's Aunt Cynthy had promised with a sincerity which admitted not of doubt, that "de Lord willin'" she would "be on han' Monday, time to make de mornin' coffee." Which assurance had afforded Melicent a Sunday free of disturbing doubts concerning the future of her undertaking. But who may know what the morrow will bring forth? Cynthy had been "tuck sick in de night." So ran the statement of the wee pickaninny who appeared at Melicent's gate many hours later than morning coffee time: delivering his message in a high voice of complaint, and disappearing like a vision without further word.

Uncle Hiram, then called to the breach, had staked his patriarchal honor on the appearance of his niece Suze on Tuesday. Melicent and Thérèse meeting Suze some days later in a field path, asked the cause of her bad faith. The girl showed them all the white teeth which nature had lavished on her, saying with the best natured laugh in the world: "I don' know how come I didn' git dere Chewsday like I promise."

If the ladies were not disposed to consider that an all-sufficient reason, so much the worse, for Suze had no other to offer.

From Mose's wife, Minervy, better things might have been expected. But after a solemn engagement to take charge of Melicent's kitchen on Wednesday, the dusky matron suddenly awoke to the need of "holpin' Mose hoe out dat co'n in the stiff lan."

Thérèse, seeing that the girl was really eager to play in the brief rôle of housekeeper had used her powers, persuasive and authoritative, to procure servants for her, but without avail. She herself was not without an abundance of them, from the white-haired Hiram, whose position on the place had long been a sinecure,[3] down to the little brown legged tot Mandy, much given to falling asleep in the sun, when not chasing venturesome poultry off forbidden ground, or stirring gentle breezes with an enormous palm leaf fan about her mistress during that lady's after dinner nap.

When pressed to give a reason for this apparent disinclination of the negroes to work for the Hosmers, Nathan, who was at the moment being interviewed on the front veranda by Thérèse and Melicent, spoke out.

"Dey 'low 'roun' yere, dat you's mean to de black folks, ma'am: dat what dey says—I don' know me."

"Mean," cried Melicent, amazed, "in what way, pray?"

"Oh, all sort o' ways," he admitted, with a certain shy brazenness; determined to go through with the ordeal.

"Dey 'low you wants to cut de little gals' plaits off, an' sich—I don' know me."

"Do you suppose, Nathan," said Thérèse attempting but poorly to hide her amusement at Melicent's look of dismay, "that Miss Hosmer would bother herself with darkies' plaits?"

"Dat's w'at I tink m'sef. Anyways, I'll sen' Ar'minty 'roun' to-morrow, sho."

Melicent was not without the guilty remembrance of having one day playfully seized one of the small Mandy's bristling plaits, daintily between finger and thumb, threatening to cut them all away with the scissors which she carried. Yet she could not but believe that there was some deeper motive underlying this systematic reluctance of the negroes to give their work in exchange for the very good pay which she offered. Thérèse soon enlightened her with the information that the negroes were very averse to working for Northern people whose speech, manners, and attitude towards themselves were unfamiliar. She was given the consoling assurance of not being the only victim of this boycott, as Thérèse recalled many examples of strangers whom she knew to have met with a like cavalier treatment at the darkies' hands.

Needless to say, Araminty never appeared.

Hosmer and Melicent were induced to accept Mrs. Lafirme's generous hospitality; and one of that lady's many supernumeraries was detailed each morning to "do up" Miss Melicent's rooms, but not without the previous understanding that the work formed part of Miss T'rèse's[4] system.

Nothing which had happened during the year of his residence at Place-du-Bois had furnished Hosmer such amusement as these misadventures of his sister Melicent, he having had no like experience with his mill hands.

It is not unlikely that his good humor was partly due to the acceptable arrangement which assured him the daily society of Thérèse, whose presence was growing into a need with him.

V

In the Pine Woods

hen Grégoire said to Melicent that there was no better woman in the world than his Aunt Thérèse, "W'en you do like she wants," the statement was so incomplete as to leave one in uncomfortable doubt of the expediency of venturing within the influence of so exacting a nature. True, Thérèse required certain conduct from others, but she was willing to further its accomplishment by personal efforts, even sacrifices—that could leave no doubt of the pure unselfishness of her motive. There was hardly a soul at Place-du-Bois who had not felt the force of her will and yielded to its gentle influence.

The picture of Joçint as she had last seen him, stayed with her, till it gave form to a troubled desire moving her to see him again and speak with him. He had always been an unruly subject, inclined to a surreptitious defiance of authority. Repeatedly had he been given work on the plantation and as many times dismissed for various causes. Thérèse would have long since removed him had it not been for his old father Morico, whose long life spent on the place had established a claim upon her tolerance.

In the late afternoon, when the shadows of the magnolias were stretching in grotesque lengths across the lawn, Thérèse stood waiting for Uncle Hiram to bring her sleek bay Beauregard around to the front. The dark close fitting habit which she wore lent brilliancy to her soft blonde coloring; and there was no mark of years about her face or figure, save the settling of a thoughtful shadow upon the eyes, which joys and sorrows that were past and gone had left there.

As she rode by the cottage, Melicent came out on the porch to wave a laughing good-bye. The girl was engaged in effacing the simplicity of her rooms with certain bizarre decorations that seemed the promptings of a disordered imagination. Yards of fantastic calico had been brought up from the store, which Grégoire with hammer and tacks was amiably forming into impossible designs at the prompting of the girl. The little darkies had been enlisted to bring their contributions of palm branches, pine cones, ferns, and bright hued bird wings—and a row of those small recruits stood on the porch, gaping in wide-mouthed admiration at a sight that stirred within their breasts such remnant of savage instinct as past generations had left there in dormant survival.

One of the small audience permitted her attention to be drawn for a moment from the gorgeous in-door spectacle, to follow the movements of her mistress.

"Jis' look Miss T'rèse how she go a lopin' down de lane. Dere she go—dere she go—now she gone," and she again became contemplative.

Thérèse, after crossing the railroad, for a space kept to the brow of the hill where stretched a well defined road, which by almost imperceptible degrees led deeper and always higher into the woods. Presently, leaving this road and turning into a bridle path where an unpracticed eye would have discovered no sign of travel, she rode on until reaching a small clearing among the pines, in the center of which stood a very old and weather beaten cabin.

Here she dismounted, before Morico knew of her presence, for he sat with his back partly turned to the open door. As she entered and greeted him, he arose from his chair, all trembling with excitement at her visit; the long white locks, straggling and unkept, falling about his brown visage that had grown old and weather beaten with his cabin. Sinking down into his seat—the hide covered chair that had been worn smooth by years of usefulness—he gazed well pleased at Thérèse, who seated herself beside him.

"Ah, this is quite the handsomest you have made yet, Morico," she said addressing him in French, and taking up the fan that he was curiously fashioning of turkey feathers.

"I am taking extra pains with it," he answered, looking complacently at his handiwork and smoothing down the glossy feathers with the ends of his withered old fingers. "I thought the American lady[1] down at the house might want to buy it."

Thérèse could safely assure him of Melicent's willingness to seize on the trophy.

Then she asked why Joçint had not been to the house with news of him. "I have had chickens and eggs for you, and no way of sending them."

At mention of his son's name, the old man's face clouded with displeasure and his hand trembled so that he was at some pains to place the feather which he was at the moment adding to the widening fan.

"Joçint is a bad son, madame, when even you have been able to do nothing with him. The trouble that boy has given me no one knows; but let him not think I am too old to give him a sound drubbing."

Joçint meanwhile had returned from the mill and seeing Thérèse's horse fastened before his door, was at first inclined to skulk back into the woods; but an impulse of defiance moved him to enter, and gave to his ugly countenance a look that was far from agreeable as he mumbled a greeting to Thérèse. His father he did not address. The old man looked from son to visitor with feeble expectancy of some good to come from her presence there.

Joçint's straight and coarse black hair hung in a heavy mop over his low retreating forehead, almost meeting the ill-defined line of eyebrow that straggled above small dusky black eyes, that with the rest of his physique was an inheritance from his Indian mother.

Approaching the safe or *garde manger,*[2] which was the most prominent piece of furniture in the room, he cut a wedge from the round loaf of heavy soggy corn bread that he found there, added a layer of fat pork, and proceeded to devour the unpalatable morsel with hungry relish.

"That is but poor fare for your old father, Joçint," said Thérèse, looking steadily at the youth.

"Well, I got no chance[3] me, fu' go fine nuttin in de 'ood" (woods), he answered purposely in English, to annoy his father who did not understand the language.

"But you are earning enough to buy him something better; and you know there is always plenty at the house that I am willing to spare him."

"I got no chance me fu' go to de 'ouse neider," he replied deliberately, after washing down the scant repast with a long draught from the tin bucket which he had replenished at the cistern before entering. He swallowed the water regardless of the "wiggles"[4] whose presence was plainly visible.

"What does he say?" asked Morico scanning Thérèse's face appealingly.

"He only says that work at the mill keeps him a good deal occupied," she said with attempted carelessness.

As she finished speaking, Joçint put on his battered felt hat, and strode out the back door; his gun on his shoulder and a yellow cur following close at his heels.

Thérèse remained a while longer with the old man, hearing sympathetically the long drawn story of his troubles, and cheering him as no one else in the world was able to do, then she went away.

Joçint was not the only one who had seen Beauregard fastened at Morico's door. Hosmer was making a tour of inspection that afternoon through the woods, and when he came suddenly upon Thérèse some moments after she had quitted the cabin, the meeting was not so wholly accidental as that lady fancied it was.

If there could be a situation in which Hosmer felt more than in another at ease in Thérèse's company, it was the one in which he found himself. There was no need to seek occupation for his hands, those members being sufficiently engaged with the management of his horse. His eyes found legitimate direction in following the various details which a rider is presumed to observe; and his manner freed from the necessity of self direction took upon itself an ease which was occasional enough to mark it as noteworthy.

She told him of her visit. At mention of Joçint's name he reddened: then followed the acknowledgment that the youth in question had caused him to lose his temper and forget his dignity during the afternoon.

"In what way?" asked Thérèse. "It would be better to dismiss him than to rail at him. He takes reproof badly and is extremely treacherous."

"Mill hands are not plentiful, or I should send him off at once. Oh, he is an unbearable fellow. The men told me of a habit he has of letting the logs roll off the carriage, causing a good deal of annoyance and delay in replacing them. I was willing enough to believe it might be accidental, until I caught him to-day in the very act. I am thankful not to have knocked him down."

Hosmer felt exhilarated. The excitement of his encounter with Joçint had not yet died away; this softly delicious atmosphere; the subtle aroma of the pines; his unlooked for meeting with Thérèse—all combined to stir him with unusual emotions.

"What a splendid creature Beauregard is," he said, smoothing the animal's glossy mane with the end of his riding whip. The horses were walking slowly in step, and close together.

"Of course he is," said Thérèse proudly, patting the arched neck of her favorite. "Beauregard is a blooded animal, remember. He quite throws poor Nelson in the shade," looking pityingly at Hosmer's heavily built iron-grey.

"Don't cast any slurs on Nelson, Mrs. Lafirme. He's done me service that's worthy of praise—worthy of better treatment than he gets."

"I know. He deserves the best, poor fellow. When you go away you should turn him out to pasture, and forbid any one to use him."

"It would be a good idea; but—I'm not so certain about going away."

"Oh I beg your pardon. I fancied your movements were directed by some unchangeable laws."

"Like the planets in their orbits? No, there is no absolute need of my going; the business which would have called me away can be done as readily by letter. If I heed my inclination it certainly holds me here."

"I don't understand that. It's natural enough that I should be fond of the country; but you—I don't believe you've been away for three months, have you? and city life certainly has its attractions."

"It's beastly," he answered decidedly. "I greatly prefer the country—this country; though I can imagine a condition under which it would be less agreeable; insupportable, in fact."

He was looking fixedly at Thérèse, who let her eyes rest for an instant in the unaccustomed light of his, while she asked, "and the condition?"

"If you were to go away. Oh! it would take the soul out of my life."

It was now her turn to look in all directions save the one in which his glance invited her. At a slight and imperceptible motion of the bridle, well understood by Beauregard, the horse sprang forward into a quick canter, leaving Nelson and his rider to follow as they could.

Hosmer overtook her when she stopped to let her horse drink at the side of the hill where the sparkling spring water came trickling from the moist rocks, and emptied into the long out-scooped trunk of a cypress, that served as a trough. The two horses plunged their heads deep in the clear water; the proud Beauregard quivering with satisfaction, as arching his neck and shaking off the clinging moisture, he waited for his more deliberate companion.

"Doesn't it give one a sympathetic pleasure," said Thérèse, "to see the relish with which they drink?"

"I never thought of it," replied Hosmer, cynically. His face was unusually flushed, and diffidence was plainly seizing him again.

Thérèse was now completely mistress of herself, and during the remainder of the ride she talked incessantly, giving him no chance for more than the briefest answers.

VI

Melicent Talks

"David Hosmer, you are the most supremely unsatisfactory man existing."

Hosmer had come in from his ride, and seating himself in the large wicker chair that stood in the center of the room, became at once absorbed in reflections. Being addressed, he looked up at his sister, who sat sidewards on the edge of a table slightly removed, swaying a dainty slippered foot to and fro in evident impatience.

"What crime have I committed now, Melicent, against your code?" he asked, not fully aroused from his reverie.

"You've committed nothing; your sin is one of omission. I absolutely believe you go through the world with your eyes, to all practical purposes, closed. Don't you notice anything; any change?"

"To be sure I do," said Hosmer, relying on a knowledge lent him by previous similar experiences, and taking in the clinging artistic drapery that enfolded her tall spare figure, "you've a new gown on. I didn't think to mention it, but I noticed it all the same."

This admission of a discernment that he had failed to make evident, aroused Melicent's uncontrolled mirth.

"A new gown!" and she laughed heartily. "A threadbare remnant! A thing that holds by shreds and tatters."

She went behind her brother's chair, taking his face between her hands, and turning it upward, kissed him on the forehead. With his head in such a position, he could not fail to observe the brilliant folds of muslin that were arranged across the ceiling to simulate the canopy of a tent. Still holding his face, she moved it sidewards, so that his eyes, knowing now what office was expected of them, followed the line of decorations about the room.

"It's immense, Mel; perfectly immense. When did you do it all?"

"This afternoon, with Grégoire's help," she answered, looking proudly at her work. "And my poor hands are in such condition! But really, Dave," she continued, seating herself on the side of his chair, with an arm about his neck, and he leaning his head back on the improvised cushion, "I wonder that you ever got on in business, observing things as little as you do."

"Oh, that's different."

"Well, I don't believe you see half that you ought to," adding naively, "How did you and Mrs. Lafirme happen to come home together this evening?"

The bright lamp-light made the flush quite evident that arose to his face under her near gaze.

"We met in the woods; she was coming from Morico's."

"David, do you know that woman is an angel. She's simply the most perfect creature I ever knew."

Melicent's emphasis of speech was a thing so recurrent, so singularly her own, as to startle an unaccustomed hearer.

"That opinion might carry some weight, Mel, if I hadn't heard it scores of times from you, and of as many different women."

"Indeed you have not. Mrs. Lafirme is exceptional. Really, when she stands at the end of the veranda, giving orders to those darkies, her face a little flushed, she's positively a queen."

"As far as queenliness may be compatible with the angelic state," replied Hosmer, but not ill pleased with Melicent's exaggerated praise of Thérèse.

Neither had heard a noiseless step approaching, and they only became aware of an added human presence, when Mandy's small voice was heard to issue from Mandy's small body which stood in the mingled light and shadow of the door-way.

"Aunt B'lindy 'low supper on de table gittin' cole."

"Come here, Mandy," cried Melicent, springing after the child. But Mandy was flying back through the darkness. She was afraid of Melicent.

Laughing heartily, the girl disappeared into her bedroom, to make some needed additions to her toilet;[1] and Hosmer, waiting for her, returned to his interrupted reflections. The words which he had spoken during a moment of emotion to Thérèse, out in the piny[2] woods, had served a double purpose with him. They had shown him more plainly than he had quite been certain of, the depth of his feeling for her; and also had they settled his determination. He was not versed in the reading of a woman's nature, and he found himself at a loss to interpret Thérèse's actions. He recalled how she had looked away from him when he had spoken the few tender words that were yet whirling in his memory; how she had impetuously ridden ahead,—leaving him to follow alone; and her incessant speech that had forced him into silence. All of which might or might not be symptoms in his favor. He remembered her kind solicitude for his comfort and happiness during the past year; but he as readily recalled that he had not been the only recipient of such favors. His reflections led to no certainty, except that he loved her and meant to tell her so.

Thérèse's door being closed, and moreover locked, Aunt Belindy, the stout negress who had superintended the laying of supper, felt free to give low speech to her wrath as she went back and forth between dining-room and kitchen.

"Suppa gittin' dat cole 'tain' gwine be fittin' fu' de dogs te' tech. Believe half de time w'ite folks ain't got no feelin's, no how. If dey speck I'se gwine stan' up heah on my two feet all night, dey's foolin' dey sef. I ain't gwine do it. Git out dat doo' you Mandy! you want me dash dis heah coffee pot at you—blockin' up de doo's' dat away? W'ar dat good fu' nuttin' Betsy? Look yonda, how she done flung dem dere knife an' forks on de table. Jis let Miss T'rèse kotch'er. Good God A'mighty, Miss T'rèse mus' done gone asleep. G'long dar an' see."

There was no one on the plantation who would have felt at liberty to enter Thérèse's bedroom without permission, the door being closed; yet she had taken the needless precaution of bringing lock and bolt to the double security of her moment of solitude. The first announcement of supper had found her still in her riding habit, with head thrown back upon the cushion of her lounging chair, and her mind steeped in a semi-stupor that it would be injustice to her brighter moments to call reflection.

Thérèse was a warm-hearted woman, and a woman of clear mental vision; a combination not found so often together as to make it ordinary. Being a woman of warm heart, she had loved her husband with the devotion which good husbands deserve; but being a clear-headed woman, she was not disposed to rebel against the changes which Time brings, when so disposed, to the human sensibilities. She was not steeped in that agony of remorse which many might consider becoming in a widow of five years' standing at the discovery that her heart which had fitted well the holding of a treasure, was not narrowed to the holding of a memory,—the treasure being gone.

Mandy's feeble knock at the door was answered by her mistress in person who had now banished all traces of her ride and its resultant cogitations.

The two women, with Hosmer and Grégoire, sat out on the veranda after supper as their custom was during these warm summer evenings. There was no attempt at sustained conversation; they talked by snatches to and at one another, of the day's small events; Melicent and Grégoire having by far the most to say. The girl was half reclining in the hammock which she kept in a slow, unceasing motion by the impetus of her slender foot; he sitting some distance removed on the steps. Hosmer was noticeably silent; even Joçint as a theme failing to rouse him to more than a few words of dismissal. His will and tenacity were controlling him to one bent. He had made up his mind that he had something to say to Mrs. Lafirme, and he was impatient at any enforced delay in the telling.

Grégoire slept now in the office of the mill, as a measure of precaution. To-night, Hosmer had received certain late telegrams that necessitated a return to the mill, and his iron-grey was standing outside in the lane with Grégoire's horse, awaiting the pleasure of his rider. When Grégoire quitted the group to go and throw the saddles across the patient animals, Melicent, who contemplated an additional hour's chat with Thérèse, crossed over to the cottage to procure a light wrap for her sensitive shoulders against the chill night air. Hosmer, who had started to the assistance of Grégoire, seeing that Thérèse had remained alone, standing at the top of the stairs, approached her. Remaining a few steps below her, and looking up into her face, he held out his hand to say good-night, which was an unusual proceeding, for they had not shaken hands since his return to Place-du-Bois three months before. She gave him her soft hand to hold and as the warm, moist palm met his, it acted like a charged electric battery turning its subtle force upon his sensitive nerves.

"Will you let me talk to you to-morrow?" he asked.

"Yes, perhaps; if I have time."

"Oh, you will make the time. I can't let the day go by without telling you many things that you ought to have known long ago." The battery was still doing its work. "And I can't let the night go by without telling you that I love you."

Grégoire called out that the horses were ready. Melicent was approaching in her diaphanous envelope, and Hosmer reluctantly let drop Thérèse's hand and left her.

As the men rode away, the two women stood silently following their diminishing outlines into the darkness and listening to the creaking of the saddles and the dull regular thud of the horses' feet upon the soft earth, until the sounds grew inaudible, when they turned to the inner shelter of the veranda. Melicent once more possessed herself of the hammock in which she now reclined fully, and Thérèse sat near enough beside her to intertwine her fingers between the tense cords.

"What a great difference in age there must be between you and your brother," she said, breaking the silence.

"Yes—though he is younger and I older than you perhaps think. He was fifteen and the only child when I was born. I am twenty-four, so he of course is thirty-nine."

"I certainly thought him older."

"Just imagine, Mrs. Lafirme, I was only ten when both my parents died. We had no kindred living in the West, and I positively rebelled against being separated from David; so you see he's had the care of me for a good many years."

"He appears very fond of you."

"Oh, not only that, but you've no idea how splendidly he's done for me in every way. Looked after my interest and all that, so that I'm perfectly independent. Poor Dave," she continued, heaving a profound sigh, "he's had more than his share of trouble, if ever a man had. I wonder when his day of compensation will come."

"Don't you think," ventured Thérèse, "that we make too much of our individual trials. We are all so prone to believe our own burden heavier than our neighbor's."

"Perhaps—but there can be no question about the weight of David's. I'm not a bit selfish about him, though; poor fellow, I only wish he'd marry again."

Melicent's last words stung Thérèse like an insult. Her native pride rebelled against the reticence of this man who had shared her confidence while keeping her in ignorance of so important a feature of his own life. But her dignity would not permit a show of disturbance; she only asked:—

"How long has his wife been dead?"

"Oh," cried Melicent, in dismay. "I thought you knew, of course; why—she isn't dead at all—they were divorced two years ago."

The girl felt intuitively that she had yielded to an indiscretion of speech. She could not know David's will in the matter, but since he had all along left Mrs. Lafirme in ignorance of his domestic trials, she concluded it was not for her to enlighten that lady further. Her next remark was to call Thérèse's attention to the unusual number of glow-worms that were flashing through the darkness, and to ask the sign of it, adding "everything seems to be the sign of something down here."

"Aunt Belindy might tell you," replied Thérèse, "I only know that I feel the signs of being very sleepy after that ride through the woods to-day. Don't mind if I say good night?"

"Certainly not. Good night, dear Mrs. Lafirme. Let me stay here till David comes back; I should die of fright, to go to the cottage alone."

VII

Painful Disclosures

Thérèse possessed an independence of thought exceptional enough when considered in relation to her life and its surrounding conditions. But as a woman who lived in close contact with her fellow-beings she was little given to the consideration of abstract ideas, except in so far as they touched the individual man. If ever asked to give her opinion of divorce, she might have replied that the question being one which did not immediately concern her, its remoteness had removed it from the range of her inquiry. She felt vaguely that in many cases it might be a blessing; conceding that it must not infrequently be a necessity, to be appealed to however only in an extremity beyond which endurance could scarcely hold. With the prejudices of her Catholic[1] education coloring her sentiment, she instinctively shrank when the theme confronted her as one having even a remote reference to her own clean existence. There was no question with her of dwelling upon the matter; it was simply a thing to be summarily dismissed and as far as possible effaced from her remembrance.

Thérèse had not reached the age of thirty-five without learning that life presents many insurmountable obstacles which must be accepted, whether with the callousness of philosophy, the revolt of weakness or the dignity of self-respect. The following morning, the only sign which she gave of her mental disturbance, was an appearance that might have succeeded a night of unrefreshing sleep.

Hosmer had decided that his interview with Mrs. Lafirme should not be left further to the caprice of accident. An hour or more before noon he rode up from the mill knowing it to be a time when he would likely find her alone. Not seeing her, he proceeded to make inquiry of the servants; first appealing to Betsy.

"I don' know whar Miss T'rèse," with a rising inflection on the "whar." "I yaint seed her sence mornin', time she sont Unc' Hi'um yonda to old Morico wid de light bread an' truck,"[2] replied the verbose Betsy. "Aunt B'lindy, you know whar Miss T'rèse?"

"How you want me know? standin' up everlastin' in de kitchen a bakin' light-bread fu' lazy trash det betta be in de fiel' wurkin' a crap like people, stid o' 'pendin' on yeda folks."

Mandy, who had been a silent listener, divining that she had perhaps better make known certain information that was exclusively her own, piped out:—

"Miss T'rèse shet up in de parla; 'low she want we all lef'er 'lone."

Having, as it were, forced an entrance into the stronghold where Thérèse had supposed herself secure from intrusion, Hosmer at once seated himself beside her.

This was a room kept for the most part closed during the summer days, when the family lived chiefly on the verandas or in the wide open hall. There lingered about it the foreign scent of cool clean matting, mingled with a faint odor of rose which came from a curious Japanese jar that stood on the ample hearth. Through the green half-closed shutters the air came in gentle ripples, sweeping the filmy curtains back and forth in irregular undulations. A few tasteful pictures hung upon the walls, alternating with family portraits, for the most part stiff and unhandsome, except in the case of such as were of so remote date that age gave them a claim upon the interest and admiration of a far removed generation.

It was not entirely clear to the darkies whether this room were not a sort of holy sanctuary, where one should scarce be permitted to breathe, except under compulsion of a driving necessity.

"Mrs. Lafirme," began Hosmer, "Melicent tells me that she made you acquainted last night with the matter which I wished to talk to you about to-day."

"Yes," Thérèse replied, closing the book which she had made a pretense of reading, and laying it down upon the window-sill near which she sat; adding very simply, "Why did you not tell me long ago, Mr. Hosmer?"

"God knows," he replied; the sharp conviction breaking upon him, that this disclosure had some how changed the aspect of life for him. "Natural reluctance to speak of a thing so painful—native reticence—I don't know what. I hope you forgive me; that you will let it make no difference in whatever regard you may have for me."

"I had better tell you at once that there must be no repetition of—of what you told me last night."

Hosmer had feared it. He made no protest in words; his revolt was inward and showed itself only in an added pallor and increased rigidity of face lines. He arose and went to a near window, peering for a while aimlessly out between the partly open slats.

"I hadn't thought of your being a Catholic," he said, finally turning towards her with folded arms.

"Because you have never seen any outward signs of it. But I can't leave you under a false impression: religion doesn't influence my reason in this."

"Do you think then that a man who has had such misfortune, should be debarred the happiness which a second marriage could give him?"

"No, nor a woman either, if it suit her moral principle, which I hold to be something peculiarly one's own."

"That seems to me to be a prejudice," he replied. "Prejudices may be set aside by an effort of the will," catching at a glimmer of hope.

"There are some prejudices which a woman can't afford to part with, Mr. Hosmer," she said a little haughtily, "even at the price of happiness. Please say no more about it, think no more of it."

He seated himself again, facing her; and looking at him all her sympathetic nature was moved at sight of his evident trouble.

"Tell me about it. I would like to know every thing in your life," she said, feelingly.

"It's very good of you," he said, holding a hand for a moment over his closed eyes. Then looking up abruptly, "It was a painful enough experience, but I never dreamed that it could have had this last blow in reserve for me."

"When did you marry?" she asked, wishing him to start with the story which she fancied he would feel better for the telling.

"Ten years ago. I am a poor hand to analyze character: my own or another's. My reasons for doing certain things have never been quite clear to me; or I have never schooled myself to inquiry into my own motives for action. I have been always thoroughly the business man. I don't make a boast of it, but I have no reason to be ashamed of the admission. Socially, I have mingled little with my fellow-beings, especially with women, whose society has had little attraction for me; perhaps, because I have never been thrown much into it, and I was nearly thirty when I first met my wife."

"Was it in St. Louis?" Thérèse asked.

"Yes. I had been inveigled[3] into going on a river excursion," he said, plunging into the story, "Heaven knows how. Perhaps I was feeling unwell—I really can't remember. But at all events I met a friend who introduced me early in the day to a young girl—Fanny Larimore. She was a pretty little thing, not more than twenty, all pink and white and merry blue eyes and stylish clothes. Whatever it was, there was something about her that kept me at her side all day. Every word and movement of hers had an exaggerated importance for me. I fancied such things had never been said or done quite in the same way before."

"You were in love," sighed Thérèse. Why the sigh she could not have told.

"I presume so. Well, after that, I found myself thinking of her at the most inopportune moments. I went to see her again and again—my first impression deepened, and in two weeks I had asked her to marry me. I can safely say, we knew nothing of each other's character. After marriage, matters went well enough for a while." Hosmer here arose, and walked the length of the room.

"Mrs. Lafirme," he said, "can't you understand that it must be a painful thing for a man to disparage one woman to another: the woman who has been his wife to the woman he loves? Spare me the rest."

"Please have no reservations with me; I shall not misjudge you in any case," an inexplicable something was moving her to know what remained to be told.

"It wasn't long before she attempted to draw me into what she called society," Hosmer continued. "I am little versed in defining shades of distinction between classes, but I had seen from the beginning that Fanny's associates were not of the best social rank by any means. I had vaguely expected her to turn from them, I suppose, when she married. Naturally, I resisted anything so distasteful as being dragged through rounds of amusement that had no sort of attraction whatever for me. Besides, my business connections were extending, and they claimed the greater part of my time and thoughts.

"A year after our marriage our boy was born." Here Hosmer ceased speaking for a while, seemingly under pressure of a crowding of painful memories.

"The child whose picture you have at the office?" asked Thérèse.

"Yes," and he resumed with plain effort. "It seemed for a while that the baby would give its mother what distraction she sought so persistently away from home; but its influence did not last and she soon grew as restless as before. Finally there was nothing that united us except the child. I can't really say that we were united through him, but our love for the boy was the one feeling that we had in common. When he was three years old, he died. Melicent had come to live with us after leaving school. She was a high-spirited girl full of conceits as she is now, and in her exaggerated way became filled with horror of what she called the *mésalliance*[4] I had made. After a month she went away to live with friends. I didn't oppose her. I saw little of my wife, being often away from home; but as feebly observant as I was, I had now and again marked a peculiarity of manner about her that vaguely troubled me. She seemed to avoid me and we grew more and more divided.

One day I returned home rather early. Melicent was with me. We found Fanny in the dining-room lying on the sofa. As we entered, she looked at us wildly and in striving to get up grasped aimlessly at the back of a chair. I felt on a sudden as if there were some awful calamity threatening my existence. I suppose, I looked helplessly at Melicent, managing to ask her what was the matter with my wife. Melicent's black eyes were flashing indignation. 'Can't you see she's been drinking. God help you,' she said. Mrs. Lafirme, you know now the reason which drove me away from home and kept me away. I never permitted my wife to want for the comforts of life during my absence; but she sued for divorce some years ago and it was granted, with alimony which I doubled. You know the miserable story now. Pardon me for dragging it to such a length. I don't see why I should have told it after all."

Thérèse had remained perfectly silent; rigid at times, listening to Hosmer often with closed eyes.

He waited for her to speak, but she said nothing for a while till finally: "Your—your wife is still quite young—do her parents live with her?"

"Oh no, she has none. I suppose she lives alone."

"And those habits; you don't know if she continues them?"

"I dare say she does. I know nothing of her, except that she receipts for the amount paid her each month."

The look of painful thought deepened on Thérèse's face but her questions having been answered, she again became silent.

Hosmer's eyes were imploring her for a look, but she would not answer them.

"Haven't you a word to say to me?" he entreated.

"No, I have nothing to say, except what would give you pain."

"I can bear anything from you," he replied, at a loss to guess her meaning.

"The kindest thing I can say, Mr. Hosmer, is that I hope you have acted blindly. I hate to believe that the man I care for, would deliberately act the part of a cruel egotist."

"I don't understand you."

"I have learned one thing through your story, which appears very plain to me," she replied. "You married a woman of weak character. You furnished her with every means to increase that weakness, and shut her out absolutely from your life and yourself from hers. You left her then as practically without moral support as you have certainly done now, in deserting her. It was the act of a coward." Thérèse spoke the last words with intensity.

"Do you think that a man owes nothing to himself?" Hosmer asked, in resistance to her accusation.

"Yes. A man owes to his manhood, to face the consequences of his own actions."

Hosmer had remained seated. He did not even with glance follow Thérèse who had arisen and was moving restlessly about the room. He had so long seen himself as a martyr; his mind had become so habituated to the picture, that he could not on a sudden look at a different one, believing that it could be the true one. Nor was he eager to accept a view of the situation that would place him in his own eyes in a contemptible light. He tried to think that Thérèse must be wrong; but even admitting a doubt of her being right, her words carried an element of truth that he was not able to shut out from his conscience. He felt her to be a woman with moral perceptions keener than his own and his love, which in the past twenty-four hours had grown to overwhelm him, moved him now to a blind submission.

"What would you have me do, Mrs. Lafirme?"

"I would have you do what is right," she said eagerly, approaching him.

"O, don't present me any questions of right and wrong; can't you see that I'm blind?" he said, self accusingly. "What ever I do, must be because you want it; because I love you."

She was standing beside him and he took her hand.

"To do a thing out of love for you would be the only comfort and strength left me."

"Don't say that," she entreated. "Love isn't everything in life; there is something higher."

"God in heaven, there shouldn't be!" he exclaimed, passionately pressing her hand to his forehead, his cheek, his lips.

"Oh, don't make it harder for me," Thérèse said softly, attempting to withdraw her hand.

It was her first sign of weakness, and he seized on it for his advantage. He arose quickly—unhesitatingly—and took her in his arms.

For a moment that was very brief, there was danger that the task of renunciation would not only be made harder, but impossible, for both; for it was in utter blindness to everything but love for each other, that their lips met.

The great plantation bell was clanging out the hour of noon; the hour for sweet and restful enjoyment; but to Hosmer, the sound was like the voice of a derisive demon, mocking his anguish of spirit, as he mounted his horse, and rode back to the mill.

VIII

TREATS OF MELICENT

elicent knew that there were exchanges of confidence going on between her brother and Mrs. Lafirme, from which she was excluded. She had noted certain lengthy conferences held in remote corners of the verandas. The two had deliberately withdrawn one moonlight evening to pace to and fro the length of gravel walk that stretched from door front to lane; and Melicent had fancied that they rather lingered when under the deep shadow of the two great live-oaks that overarched the gate. But that of course was fancy; a young girl's weakness to think the world must go as she would want it to.

She was quite sure of having heard Mrs. Lafirme say, "I will help you." Could it be that David had fallen into financial straights and wanted assistance from Thérèse? No, that was improbable and furthermore, distasteful, so Melicent would not burden herself with the suspicion. It was far more agreeable to believe that affairs were shaping themselves according to her wishes regarding her brother and her friend. Yet her mystification was in no wise made clearer, when David left them to go to St. Louis.

Melicent was not ready or willing to leave with him. She had not had her "visit out" as she informed him, when he proposed it to her. To remain in the cottage during his absence was out of the question, so she removed herself and all her pretty belongings over to the house, taking possession of one of the many spare rooms. The act of removal furnished her much entertainment of a mild sort, into which, however, she successfully infused something of her own intensity by making the occasion one to bring a large detachment of the plantation force into her capricious service.

Melicent was going out, and she stood before her mirror to make sure that she looked properly.[1] She was black from head to foot. From the great ostrich plume that nodded over her wide-brimmed hat, to the pointed toe of the patent leather boot that peeped from under her gown—a filmy gauzy thing setting loosely to her slender shapely figure. She laughed at the somberness of her reflection, which she at once set about relieving with a great bunch of geraniums—big and scarlet and long-stemmed, that she thrust slantwise through her belt.

Melicent, always charming, was very pretty when she laughed. She thought so herself and laughed a second time into the depths of her dark handsome eyes. One corner of the large mouth turned saucily upward, and the lips holding their own crimson and all that the cheeks were lacking, parted only a little over the gleaming whiteness of her teeth. As she looked at herself critically, she thought that a few more pounds of flesh would have well become her. It had been only the other day that her slimness was altogether to her liking; but at present, she was in love with plumpness as typified in Mrs. Lafirme. However, on the whole, she was not ill pleased with her appearance, and gathering up her gloves and parasol, she quitted the room.

It was "broad day," one of the requirements which Grégoire had named as essential for taking Melicent to visit old McFarlane's grave. But the sun was not "shining mighty bright," the second condition, and whose absence they were willing enough to overlook, seeing that the month was September.

They had climbed quite to the top of the hill, and stood on the very brink of the deep toilsome railroad cut all fringed with matted grass and young pines, that had but lately sprung there. Up and down the track, as far as they could see on either side the steel rails glittered on into gradual dimness. There were patches of the field before them, white with bursting cotton which scores of negroes, men, women and children were dexterously picking and thrusting into great bags that hung from their shoulders and dragged beside them on the ground; no machine having yet been found to surpass the sufficiency of five human fingers for wrenching the cotton from its tenacious hold. Elsewhere, there were squads "pulling fodder" from the dry corn stalks; hot and distasteful work enough. In the nearest field, where the cotton was young and green, with no show of ripening, the overseer rode slowly between the rows, sprinkling plentifully the dry powder of paris green[2] from two muslin bags attached to the ends of a short pole that lay before him across the saddle.

Grégoire's presence would be needed later in the day, when the cotton was hauled to gin to be weighed; when the mules were brought to stable, to see them properly fed and cared for, and the gearing all put in place. In the meanwhile he was deliciously idle with Melicent.

They retreated into the woods, soon losing sight of everything but the trees that surrounded them and the underbrush that was scant and scattered over the turf which the height of the trees permitted to grow green and luxuriant.

There, on the far slope of the hill they found McFarlane's grave, which they knew to be such only by the battered and weather-worn cross of wood that lurched disreputably to one side—there being no hand in all the world that cared enough to make it straight—and from which all lettering had long since been washed away. This cross was all that marked the abiding place of that mist-like form, so often seen at dark to stalk down the hill with threatening stride, or of moonlight nights to cross the lake in a *pirogue,* whose substance though visible was nought; with sound of dipping oars that made no ripple on the lake's smooth surface. On stormy nights, some more gifted with spiritual insight than their neighbors, and with hearing better sharpened to delicate intonations of the super-natural, had not only seen the mist figure mounted and flying across the hills, but had heard the panting of the blood-hounds, as the invisible pack swept by in hot pursuit of the slave so long ago at rest.

But it was "broad day," and here was nothing sinister to cause Melicent the least little thrill of awe. No owl, no bat, no ill-omened creature hovering near; only a mocking bird high up in the branches of a tall pine tree, gushing forth his shrill staccatoes as blithely as though he sang paeans[3] to a translated soul in paradise.

"Poor old McFarlane," said Melicent, "I'll pay a little tribute to his memory; I dare say his spirit has listened to nothing but abuse of himself there in the other world, since it left his body here on the hill;" and she took one of the long-stemmed blood-red flowers and laid it beside the toppling cross.

"I reckon he's in a place w'ere flowers don't git much waterin', if they got any there."

"Shame to talk so cruelly; I don't believe in such places."

"You don't believe in hell?" he asked in blank surprise.

"Certainly not. I'm a Unitarian."[4]

"Well, that's new to me," was his only comment.

"Do you believe in spirits, Grégoire? I don't—in day time."

"Neva mine 'bout spirits," he answered, taking her arm and leading her off, "let's git away f'om yere."

They soon found a smooth and gentle slope where Melicent sat herself comfortably down, her back against the broad support of a tree trunk, and Grégoire lay prone upon the ground with—his head in Melicent's lap.

When Melicent first met Grégoire, his peculiarities of speech, so unfamiliar to her, seemed to remove him at once from the possibility of her consideration. She was not then awake to certain fine psychological differences distinguishing man from man; precluding the possibility of naming and classifying him in the moral as one might in the animal kingdom. But shortcomings of language, which finally seemed not to detract from a definite inheritance of good breeding, touched his personality as a physical deformation might, adding to it certainly no charm, yet from its pathological aspect not without a species of fascination, for a certain order of misregulated mind.

She bore with him, and then she liked him. Finally, whilst indulging in a little introspection; making a diagnosis of various symptoms, indicative by no means of a deep-seated malady, she decided that she was in love with Grégoire. But the admission embraced the understanding with herself that nothing could come of it. She accepted it as a phase of that relentless fate which in pessimistic moments she was inclined to believe pursued her.

It could not be thought of, that she should marry a man whose eccentricity of speech would certainly not adapt itself to the requirements of polite society.

He had kissed her one day. Whatever there was about the kiss—possibly an over exuberance—it was not to her liking, and she forbade that he ever repeat it, under pain of losing her affection. Indeed, on the few occasions when Melicent had been engaged, kissing had been excluded as superfluous to the relationship, except in the case of the young lieutenant out at Fort Leavenworth who read Tennyson to her, as an angel might be supposed to read, and who in moments of rapturous self-forgetfulness, was permitted to kiss her under the ear: a proceeding not positively distasteful to Melicent, except in so much as it tickled her.

Grégoire's hair was soft, not so dark as her own, and possessed an inclination to curl about her slender fingers.

"Grégoire," she said, "you told me once that the Santien boys were a hard lot; what did you mean by that?"

"Oh no," he answered, laughing good-humoredly up into her eyes, "You didn' yere me right. W'at I said was that we had a hard name in the country. I don' see w'y eitha, excep' we all'ays done putty much like we wanted. But my! a man can live like a saint yere at Place-des-Bois, they ain't no temptations o' no kine."

"There's little merit in your right doing, if you have no temptations to withstand," delivering the time worn aphorism with the air and tone of a pretty sage, giving utterance to an inspired truth.

Melicent felt that she did not fully know Grégoire; that he had always been more or less under restraint with her, and she was troubled by something other than curiosity to get at the truth concerning him. One day when she was arranging a vase of flowers at a table on the back porch, Aunt Belindy, who was scouring knives at the same table, had followed Grégoire with her glance, when he walked away after exchanging a few words with Melicent.

"God! but dats a diffunt man sence you come heah."

"Different?" questioned the girl eagerly, and casting a quick sideward look at Aunt Belindy.

"Lord yas honey, 'f you warn't heah dat same Mista Grégor 'd be in Centaville ev'y Sunday, a raisin' Cain. Humph—I knows 'im."

Melicent would not permit herself to ask more, but picked up her vase of flowers and walked with it into the house; her comprehension of Grégoire no wise advanced by the newly acquired knowledge that he was liable to "raise Cain" during her absence—a proceeding which she could not too hastily condemn, considering her imperfect apprehension of what it might imply.

Meanwhile she would not allow her doubts to interfere with the kindness which she lavished on him, seeing that he loved her to desperation. Was he not at this very moment looking up into her eyes, and talking of his misery and her cruelty? turning his face downward in her lap—as she knew to cry—for had she not already seen him lie on the ground in an agony of tears, when she had told him he should never kiss her again?

And so they lingered in the woods, these two curious lovers, till the shadows grew so deep about old McFarlane's grave that they passed it by with hurried step and averted glance.

IX

FACE TO FACE

fter a day of close and intense September heat, it had rained during the night. And now the morning had followed chill and crisp, yet with possibilities of a genial sunshine breaking through the mist that had risen at dawn from the great sluggish river and spread itself through the mazes of the city.

The change was one to send invigorating thrills through the blood, and to quicken the step; to make one like the push and jostle of the multitude that thronged the streets; to make one in love with intoxicating life, and impatient with the grudging dispensation that had given to mankind no wings wherewith to fly.

But with no reacting warmth in his heart, the change had only made Hosmer shiver and draw his coat closer about his chest, as he pushed his way through the hurrying crowd.

The St. Louis Exposition[1] was in progress with all its many allurements that had been heralded for months through the journals of the State.

Hence, the unusual press of people on the streets this bright September morning. Home people, whose air of ownership to the surroundings classified them at once, moving unobservantly about their affairs. Women and children from the near and rich country towns, in for the Exposition and their fall shopping; wearing gowns of ultra fashionable tendencies; leaving in their toilets nothing to expediency; taking no chances of so much as a ribbon or loop set in disaccordance with the book.

There were whole families from across the bridge, hurrying towards the Exposition. Fathers and mothers, babies and grandmothers, with baskets of lunch and bundles of provisional necessities, in for the day.

Nothing would escape their observation nor elude their criticism, from the creations in color lining the walls of the art gallery, to the most intricate mechanism of inventive genius in the basement. All would pass inspection, with drawing of comparison between the present, the past year, and the "year before," likely in a nasal drawl with the R's brought sharply out, leaving no doubt as to their utterance.

The newly married couple walking serenely through the crowd, young, smiling, up-country, hand-in-hand; well pleased with themselves, with their new attire and newer jewelry, would likely have answered Hosmer's "beg pardon" with amiability if he had knocked them down. But he had only thrust them rather violently to one side in his eagerness to board the cable car that was dashing by, with no seeming willingness to stay its mad flight. He still possessed the agility in his unpracticed limbs to swing himself on the grip, where he took a front seat, well buttoned up as to top-coat, and glad of the bodily rest that his half hour's ride would bring him.

The locality in which he descended presented some noticeable changes since he had last been there. Formerly, it had been rather a quiet street, with a leisurely horse car depositing its passengers two blocks away to the north from it; awaking somewhat of afternoons when hordes of children held possession. But now the cable had come to disturb its long repose, adding in the office, nothing to its attractiveness.

There was the drug store still at the corner, with the same proprietor, tilted back in his chair as of old, and as of old reading his newspaper with only the change which a newly acquired pair of spectacles gave to his appearance. The "drug store boy" had unfolded into manhood, plainly indicated by the mustache that in adding adornment and dignity to his person, had lifted him above the menial office of window washing. A task relegated to a mustacheless urchin with a leaning towards the surreptitious abstraction of caramels and chewing gum in the intervals of such manual engagements as did not require the co-operation of a strategic mind.

Where formerly had been the vacant lot "across the street," the Sunday afternoon elysium of the youthful base ball field from Biddle Street, now stood a row of brand new pressed-brick "flats."[2] Marvelous must have been the architectural ingenuity which had contrived to unite so many dwellings into so small a space. Before each spread a length of closely clipped grass plot, and every miniature front door wore its fantastic window furnishing; each set of decorations having seemingly fired the next with efforts of surpassing elaboration.

The house at which Hosmer rang—a plain two-storied red brick, standing close to the street—was very old-fashioned in face of its modern opposite neighbors, and the recently metamorphosed dwelling next door, that with added porches and appendages to tax man's faculty of conjecture, was no longer recognizable for what it had been. Even the bell which he pulled was old-fashioned and its tingle might be heard throughout the house long after the servant had opened the door, if she were only reasonably alert to the summons. Its reverberations were but dying away when Hosmer asked if Mrs. Larimore were in. Mrs. Larimore was in; an admission which seemed to hold in reserve a defiant "And what if she is, sir."

Hosmer was relieved to find the little parlor into which he was ushered, with its adjoining dining-room, much changed. The carpets which he and Fanny had gone out together to buy during the early days of their house-keeping, were replaced by rugs that lay upon the bare, well polished floors. The wall paper was different; so were the hangings. The furniture had been newly re-covered. Only the small household gods were as of old: things—trifles—that had never much occupied or impressed him, and that now, amid their altered surroundings stirred no sentiment in him of either pleased or sad remembrance.

It had not been his wish to take his wife unawares, and he had previously written her of his intended coming, yet without giving her a clue for the reason of it.

There was an element of the bull-dog in Hosmer. Having made up his mind, he indulged in no regrets, in no nursing of if's and and's, but stood like a brave soldier to his post, not a post of danger true—but one well supplied with discomfiting possibilities. And what had Homeyer said of it? He had railed of course as usual, at the submission of a human destiny to the exacting and ignorant rule of what he termed moral conventionalities. He had startled and angered Hosmer with his denunciation of Thérèse's sophistical guidance. Rather—he proposed—let Hosmer and Thérèse marry, and if Fanny were to be redeemed—though he pooh-poohed the notion as untenable with certain views of what he called the rights to existence: the existence of wrongs—sorrows—diseases—death—let them all go to make up the conglomerate whole—and let the individual man hold on to his personality. But if she must be redeemed—granting this point to their littleness, let the redemption come by different ways than those of sacrifice: let it be an outcome from the capability of their united happiness.

Hosmer did not listen to his friend Homeyer. Love was his god now, and Thérèse was Love's prophet.

So he was sitting in this little parlor waiting for Fanny to come.

She came after an interval that had been given over to the indulgence of a little feminine nervousness. Through the open doors Hosmer could hear her coming down the back stairs; could hear that she halted mid-way. Then she passed through the dining-room, and he arose and went to meet her, holding out his hand, which she was not at once ready to accept, being flustered and unprepared for his manner in whichever way it might direct itself.

They sat opposite each other and remained for a while silent: he with astonishment at sight of the "merry blue eyes" faded and sunken into deep, dark round sockets; at the net-work of little lines all traced about the mouth and eyes, and spreading over the once rounded cheeks that were now hollow and evidently pale or sallow, beneath a layer of rouge that had been laid on with an unsparing hand. Yet was she still pretty, or pleasing, especially to a strong nature that would find an appeal in the pathetic weakness of her face. There was no guessing at what her figure might be, it was disguised under a very fashionable dress, and a worsted shawl covered her shoulders, which occasionally quivered as with an inward chill. She spoke first, twisting the end of this shawl.

"What did you come for, David? why did you come now?" with peevish resistance to the disturbance of his coming.

"I know I have come without warrant," he said, answering her implication. "I have been led to see—no matter how—that I made mistakes in the past, and what I want to do now is to right them, if you will let me."

This was very unexpected to her, and it startled her, but neither with pleasure nor pain; only with an uneasiness which showed itself in her face.

"Have you been ill?" he asked suddenly as the details of change in her appearance commenced to unfold themselves to him.

"Oh no, not since last winter, when I had pneumonia so bad. They thought I was going to die. Dr. Franklin said I would 'a died if Belle Worthington hadn't 'a took such good care of me. But I don't see what you mean coming now. It'll be the same thing over again: I don't see what's the use, David."

"We won't talk about the use Fanny. I want to take care of you for the rest of your life—or mine—as I promised to do ten years ago; and I want you to let me do it."

"It would be the same thing over again," she reiterated, helplessly.

"It will not be the same," he answered positively. "I will not be the same, and that will make all the difference needful."

"I don't see what you want to do it for, David. Why we'd haf to get married over again and all that, wouldn't we?"

"Certainly," he answered with a faint smile. "I'm living in the South now, in Louisiana, managing a sawmill down there."

"Oh, I don't like the South. I went down to Memphis, let's see, it was last spring, with Belle and Lou Dawson, after I'd been sick; and I don't see how a person can live down there."

"You would like the place where I'm living. It's a fine large plantation, and the lady who owns it would be the best of friends to you. She knew why I was coming, and told me to say she would help to make your life a happy one if she could."

"It's her told you to come," she replied in quick resentment. "I don't see what business it is of hers."

Fanny Larimore's strength of determination was not one to hold against Hosmer's will set to a purpose, during the hour or more that they talked, he proposing, she finally acquiescing. And when he left her, it was with a gathering peace in her heart to feel that his nearness was something that would belong to her again; but differently as he assured her. And she believed him, knowing that he would stand to his promise.

Her life was sometimes very blank in the intervals of street perambulations and matinées and reading of morbid literature. That elation which she had felt over her marriage with Hosmer ten years before, had soon died away, together with her weak love for him, when she began to dread him and defy him. But now that he said he was ready to take care of her and be good to her, she felt great comfort in her knowledge of his honesty.

X

Fanny's Friends

It was on the day following Hosmer's visit, that Mrs. Lorenzo Worthington, familiarly known to her friends as Belle Worthington, was occupied in constructing a careful and extremely elaborate street toilet before her dressing bureau which stood near the front window of one of the "flats" opposite Mrs. Larimore's. The Nottingham curtain[1] screened her effectually from the view of passers-by without hindering her frequent observance of what transpired in the street.

The lower portion of this lady's figure was draped, or better, seemingly supported, by an abundance of stiffly starched white petticoats that rustled audibly at her slightest movement. Her neck was bare, as were the well shaped arms that for the past five minutes had been poised in mid-air, in the arrangement of a front of exquisitely soft blonde curls, which she had taken from her "top drawer" and was adjusting, with the aid of a multitude of tiny invisible hair-pins, to her own very smoothly brushed hair. Yellow hair it was, with a suspicious darkness about the roots, and a streakiness about the back, that to an observant eye would have more than hinted that art had assisted nature in coloring Mrs. Worthington's locks.

Dressed, and evidently waiting with forced patience for the termination of these overhead maneuvers of her friend, sat Lou,—Mrs. Jack Dawson,—a woman whom most people called handsome. If she were handsome, no one could have told why, for her beauty was a thing which could not be defined. She was tall and thin, with hair, eyes, and complexion of a brownish neutral tint, and bore in face and figure, a stamp of defiance which probably accounted for a certain eccentricity in eschewing hair dyes and cosmetics. Her face was full of little irregularities; a hardly perceptible cast in one eye; the nose drawn a bit to one side, and the mouth twitched decidedly to the other when she talked or laughed. It was this misproportion which gave a piquancy to her expression and which in charming people, no doubt made them believe her handsome.

Mrs. Worthington's coiffure being completed, she regaled herself with a deliberate and comprehensive glance into the street, and the outcome of her observation was the sudden exclamation.

"Well I'll be switched! come here quick, Lou. If there ain't[2] Fanny Larimore getting on the car with Dave Hosmer!"

Mrs. Dawson approached the window, but without haste; and in no wise sharing her friend's excitement, gave utterance to her calm opinion.

"They've made it up, I'll bet you what you want."

Surprise seemed for the moment to have deprived Mrs. Worthington of further ability to proceed with her toilet, for she had fallen into a chair as limply as her starched condition would permit, her face full of speculation.

"See here, Belle Worthington, if we've got to be at the 'Lympic at two o'clock, you'd better be getting a move on yourself."

"Yes, I know; but I declare, you might knock me down with a feather."

A highly overwrought figure of speech on the part of Mrs. Worthington, seeing that the feather which would have prostrated her must have met a resistance of some one hundred and seventy-five pounds of solid *avoir-dupois*.[3]

"After all she said about him, too!" seeking to draw her friend into some participation in her own dumbfoundedness.

"Well, you ought to know Fanny Larimore's a fool, don't you?"

"Well, but I just can't get over it; that's all there is about it." And Mrs. Worthington went about completing the adornment of her person in a state of voiceless stupefaction.

In full garb, she presented the figure of a splendid woman; trim and tight in a black silk gown of expensive quality, heavy with jets which hung and shown, and jangled from every available point of her person. Not a thread of her yellow hair was misplaced. She shone with cleanliness, and her broad expressionless face and meaningless blue eyes were set to a good-humored readiness for laughter, which would be wholesome if not musical. She exhaled a fragrance of patchouly or jockey-club,[4] or something odorous and "strong" that clung to every article of her apparel, even to the yellow kid gloves which she would now be forced to put on during her ride in the car. Mrs. Dawson, attired with equal richness and style, showed more of individuality in her toilet.

As they quitted the house she observed to her friend:

"I wish you'd let up on that smell; it's enough to sicken a body."

"I know you don't like it, Lou," was Mrs. Worthington's apologetic and half disconcerted reply, "and I was careful as could be. Give you my word, I didn't think you could notice it."

"Notice it? Gee!" responded Mrs. Dawson.

These were two ladies of elegant leisure, the conditions of whose lives, and the amiability of whose husbands, had enabled them to develop into finished and professional time-killers.

Their intimacy with each other, as also their close acquaintance with Fanny Larimore, dated from a couple of years after that lady's marriage, when they had met as occupants of the same big up-town boarding house. The intercourse had never since been permitted to die out. Once, when the two former ladies were on a visit to Mrs. Larimore, seeing the flats in course of construction, they were at once assailed with the desire to abandon their hitherto nomadic life, and settle to the responsibilities of housekeeping; a scheme which they carried into effect as soon as the houses became habitable.

There was a Mr. Lorenzo Worthington; a gentleman employed for many years past in the custom house. Whether he had been overlooked, which his small, unobtrusive, narrow-chested person made possible—or whether his many-sided usefulness had rendered him in a manner indispensable to his employers, does not appear; but he had remained at his post during the various changes of administration that had gone by since his first appointment.

During intervals of his work—intervals often occurring of afternoon hours, when he had been given night work—he was fond of sitting at the sunny kitchen window, with his long thin nose, and short-sighted eyes plunged between the pages of one of his precious books: a small hoard of which he had collected at some cost and more self-denial.

One of the grievances of his life was the necessity under which he found himself of protecting his treasure from the Philistine abuse and contempt of his wife. When they moved into the flat, Mrs. Worthington, during her husband's absence, had ranged them all, systematically enough, on the top shelf of the kitchen closet to "get them out of the way." But at this he had protested, and taken a positive stand, to which his wife had so far yielded as to permit that they be placed on the top shelf of the bedroom closet; averring that to have them laying around was a thing that she would not do, for they spoilt the looks of any room.[5]

He had not foreseen the possibility of their usefulness being a temptation to his wife in so handy a receptacle.

Seeking once a volume of Ruskin's *Miscellanies,* he discovered that it had been employed to support the dismantled leg of a dressing bureau. On another occasion, a volume of Schopenhauer, which he had been at much difficulty and expense to procure, Emerson's *Essays,*[6] and two other volumes much prized, he found had served that lady as weights to hold down a piece of dry goods which she had sponged and spread to dry on an available section of roof top.

He was glad enough to transport them all back to the safer refuge of the kitchen closet, and pay the hired girl a secret stipend to guard them.

Mr. Worthington regarded women as being of peculiar and unsuitable conformation to the various conditions of life amid which they are placed; with strong moral proclivities, for the most part subservient to a weak and inadequate mentality.

It was not his office to remodel them; his rôle was simply to endure with patience the vagaries of an order of human beings, who after all, offered an interesting study to a man of speculative habit, apart from their usefulness as propagators of the species.

As regards this last qualification, Mrs. Worthington had done less than her fair share, having but one child, a daughter of twelve, whose training and education had been assumed by an aunt of her father's, a nun of some standing in the Sacred Heart Convent.[7]

Quite a different type of man was Jack Dawson, Lou's husband. Short, round, young, blonde, good looking and bald—as what St. Louis man past thirty is not? he rejoiced in the agreeable calling of a traveling salesman.

On the occasions when he was at home; once in two weeks—sometimes seldomer—never oftener—the small flat was turned inside out and upside down. He filled it with noise and merriment. If a theater party were not on hand, it was a spin out to Forest park[8] behind a fast team, closing with a wine supper at a road-side restaurant. Or a card party would be hastily gathered to which such neighbors as were congenial were bid in hot haste; deficiencies being supplied from his large circle of acquaintances who happened not to be on the road, and who at the eleventh hour were rung up by telephone. On such occasions Jack's voice would be heard loud in anecdote, introduced in some such wise as "When I was in Houston, Texas, the other day," or "Tell you what it is, sir, those fellers over in Albuquerque are up to a thing or two."

One of his standing witticisms was to inquire in a stage whisper of Belle or Lou—whether the little gal over the way had taken the pledge yet.[9]

This gentleman and his wife were on the most amiable of terms together, barring the small grievance that he sometimes lost money at poker. But as losing was exceptional with him, and as he did not make it a matter of conscience to keep her at all times posted as to the fluctuations of his luck, this grievance had small occasion to show itself.

What he thought of his wife might best be told in his own language: that Lou was up to the mark and game every time; feminine characteristics which he apparently held in high esteem.

The two ladies in question had almost reached the terminus of their ride, when Mrs. Worthington remarked incidentally to her friend, "It was nothing in the God's world but pure sass brought those two fellers to see you last night, Lou."

Mrs. Dawson bit her lip and the cast in her eye became more accentuated, as it was apt to do when she was ruffled.

"I notice you didn't treat 'em any too cool yourself," she retorted.

"Oh, they weren't my company, or I'd a give 'em a piece of my mind pretty quick. You know they're married, and they know you're married, and they hadn't a bit o' business there."

"They're perfect gentlemen, and I don't see what business 'tis of yours, anyway."

"Oh, that's a horse of another color," replied Mrs. Worthington, bridling and relapsing into injured silence for the period of ten seconds, when she resumed, "I hope they ain't going to poke[10] themselves at the matinée."

"Likely they will 's long as they gave us the tickets."

One of the gentlemen was at the matinée: Mr. Bert Rodney, but he certainly had not "poked" himself there. He never did any thing vulgar or in bad taste. He had only "dropped in!" Exquisite in dress and manner, a swell of the upper circles, versed as was no one better in the code of gentlemanly etiquette—he was for the moment awaiting disconsolately the return of his wife and daughter from Narragansett.

He took a vacant seat behind the two ladies, and bending forward began to talk to them in his low and fascinating drawl.

Mrs. Worthington, who often failed to accomplish her fierce designs, was as gracious towards him as if she had harbored no desire to give him a piece of her mind; but she was resolute in her refusal to make one of a proposed supper party.

A quite sideward look from Mrs. Dawson, told Mr. Rodney as plainly as words, that in the event of his *partie-carrée*[11] failing him, he might count upon her for a *tête-à-tête*.[12]

XI

The Self-Assumed Burden

he wedding was over. Hosmer and Fanny had been married in the small library of their Unitarian minister whom they had found intent upon the shaping of his Sunday sermon.

Out of deference, he had been briefly told the outward circumstances of the case, which he knew already; for these two had been formerly members of his congregation, and gossip had not been reluctant in telling their story. Hosmer, of course, had drifted away from his knowledge, and in late years, he had seen little of Fanny, who when moved to attend church at all usually went to the Redemptorist's Rock Church with her friend Belle Worthington. This lady was a good Catholic to the necessary extent of hearing a mass on Sundays, abstaining from meat on Fridays and Ember days, and making her "Easters." Which concessions were not without their attendant discomforts, counterbalanced, however, by the soothing assurance which they gave her of keeping on the safe side.

The minister had been much impressed with the significance of this re-marriage which he was called upon to perform, and had offered some few and well chosen expressions of salutary advice as to its future guidance. The sexton and housekeeper had been called in as witnesses. Then Hosmer had taken Fanny back home in a cab as she requested, because of her eyes that were red and swollen.

Inside the little hall-way he took her in his arms and kissed her, calling her "my child." He could not have told why, except that it expressed the responsibility he accepted of bearing all things that a father must bear from the child to whom he has given life.

"I should like to go out for an hour, Fanny; but if you would rather not, I shall stay."

"No, David, I want to be alone," she said, turning into the little parlor, with eyes big and heavy from weariness and inward clashing emotions.

Along the length of Lindell avenue from Grand avenue west to Forest park,[1] reaches for two miles on either side of the wide and well kept gravel drive a smooth stone walk, bordered its full extent with a double row of trees which were young and still uncertain, when Hosmer walked between them.

Had it been Sunday, he would have found himself making one of a fashionable throng of promenaders; it being at that time a fad with society people to walk to Forest park and back of a Sunday afternoon. Driving was then considered a respectable diversion only on the six work days of the week.[2]

But it was not Sunday and this inviting promenade was almost deserted. An occasional laborer would walk clumsily by; apathetic; swinging his tin bucket and bearing some implement of toil with the yellow clay yet clinging to it. Or it might be a brace of strong-minded girls walking with long and springing stride,[3] which was then fashionable; looking not to the right nor left; indulging in no exchange of friendly and girlish chatter, but grimly intent upon the purpose of their walk.

A steady line of vehicles was pushing on towards the park at the moderate speed which the law required. On both sides of the wide boulevard tasteful dwellings, many completed, but most of them in the course of construction, were in constant view. Hosmer noted every thing, but absently; and yet he was not pre-occupied with thought. He felt himself to be hurrying away from something that was fast overtaking him, and his faculties for the moment were centered in the mere act of motion. It is said that motion is pleasurable to man. No doubt, in connection with a healthy body and free mind, movement brings to the normal human being a certain degree of enjoyment. But where the healthful conditions are only physical, rapid motion changes from a source of pleasure to one of mere expediency.

So long as Hosmer could walk he kept a certain pressing consciousness at bay. He would have liked to run if he had dared. Since he had entered the park there were constant trains of cars speeding somewhere overhead; he could hear them at near intervals clashing over the stone bridge. And there was not a train which passed that he did not long to be at the front of it to measure and let out its speed. What a mad flight he would have given it, to make men hold their breath with terror! How he would have driven it till its end was death and chaos!—so much the better.

There suddenly formed in Hosmer's mind a sentence—sharp and distinct. We are all conscious of such quick mental visions whether of words or pictures, coming sometimes from a hidden and untraceable source, making us quiver with awe at this mysterious power of mind manifesting itself with the vividness of visible matter.

"It was the act of a coward."

Those were the words which checked him, and forbade him to go farther: which compelled him to turn about and face the reality of his convictions.

It is no unusual sight, that of a man lying full length in the soft tender grass of some retired spot of Forest park—with his face hidden in his folded arms. To the few who may see him, if they speculate at all about him he sleeps or he rests his body after a day's fatigue. "Am I never to be the brave man?" thought Hosmer, "always the coward, flying even from my own thoughts?"

How hard to him was this unaccustomed task of dealing with moral difficulties, which all through his life before, however lightly they had come, he had shirked and avoided! He realized now, that there was to be no more of that. If he did not wish his life to end in disgraceful shipwreck, he must take command and direction of it upon himself.

He had felt himself capable of stolid endurance since love had declared itself his guide and helper. But now—only to-day—something beside had crept into his heart. Not something to be endured, but a thing to be strangled and thrust away. It was the demon of hate; so new, so awful, so loathsome, he doubted that he could look it in the face and live.

Here was the problem of his new existence.

The woman who had formerly made his life colorless and empty he had quietly turned his back upon, carrying with him a pity that was not untender. But the woman who had unwittingly robbed him of all possibility of earthly happiness—he hated her. The woman who for the remainder of a life-time was to be in all the world the nearest thing to him, he hated her. He hated this woman of whom he must be careful, to whom he must be tender, and loyal and generous. And to give no sign or word but of kindness; to do no action that was not considerate, was the task which destiny had thrust upon his honor.

He did not ask himself it if were possible of accomplishment. He had flung hesitancy away, to make room for the all-powerful "Must be."[4]

He walked slowly back to his home. There was no need to run now; nothing pursued him. Should he quicken his pace or drag himself ever so slowly, it could henceforth make no difference. The burden from which he had fled was now banded upon him and not to be loosed, unless he fling himself with it into forgetfulness.

XII

SEVERING OLD TIES

Returning from the matinée, Belle and her friend Lou Dawson, before entering their house, crossed over to Fanny's. Mrs. Worthington tried the door and finding it fastened, rang the bell, then commenced to beat a tattoo upon the pane with her knuckles; an ingenuous manner which she had of announcing her identity. Fanny opened to them herself, and the three walked into the parlor.

"I haven't seen you for a coon's age, Fanny," commenced Belle, "where on earth have you been keeping yourself?"

"You saw me yesterday breakfast time, when you came to borrow the wrapper pattern,"[1] returned Fanny, in serious resentment to her friend's exaggeration.

"And much good the old wrapper pattern did me: a mile too small every way, no matter how much I let out the seams. But see here—"

"Belle's the biggest idiot about her size: there's no convincing her she's not a sylph."[2]

"*Thank* you, Mrs. Dawson."

"Well, it's a fact. Didn't you think Furgeson's scales were all wrong the other day because you weighed a hundred and eighty pounds?"

"O that's the day I had that heavy rep[3] on."

"Heavy nothing. We were coming over last night, Fanny, but we had company," continued Mrs. Dawson.

"Who d'you have?" asked Fanny mechanically and glad of the respite.

"Bert Rodney and Mr. Grant. They're so anxious to meet you. I'd 'a sent over here for you, but Belle—"

"See here, Fanny, what the mischief was Dave Hosmer doing here to-day, and going down town with you and all that sort 'o thing?"

Fanny flushed uneasily. "Have you seen the evening paper?" she asked.

"How d'you want us to see the paper? we just come from the matinée."

"David came yesterday," Fanny said working nervously at the window shade. "He'd wrote me a note the postman brought right after you left with the pattern. When you saw us getting on the car, we were going down to Dr. Martin's, and we've got married again."

Mrs. Dawson uttered a long, low whistle by way of comment. Mrs. Worthington gave vent to her usual "Well I'll be switched," which she was capable of making expressive of every shade of astonishment, from the lightest to the most pronounced; at the same time unfastening the bridle of her bonnet which plainly hindered her free respiration after such a shock.

"Say that Fanny isn't sly, after that, Belle."

"Sly? My God, she's a fool! If ever a woman had a snap! and to go to work and let a man get around her like that."

Mrs. Worthington seemed powerless to express herself in anything but disconnected exclamations.

"What are you going to do, Fanny?" asked Lou, who having aired all the astonishment which she cared to show, in her whistle, was collected enough to want her natural curiosity satisfied.

"David's living down South. I guess we'll go down there pretty soon. Soon's he can get things fixed up here."

"Where—down South?"

"O, I don't know. Somewheres in Louisiana."

"It's to be hoped in New Orleans," spoke Belle didactically, "that's the only decent place in Louisiana where a person could live."

"No, 'taint in New Orleans. He's got a saw-mill somewhere down there."

"Heavens and earth! a saw mill?" shrieked Belle. Lou was looking calmly resigned to the startling news.

"Oh, I ain't going to live in a saw mill. I wisht you'd all let me alone, any way," she returned pettishly. "There's a lady keeps a plantation, and that's where he lives."

"Well of all the rigamaroles! a lady, and a saw mill and a plantation. It's my opinion that man could make you believe black's white, Fanny Larimore."

As Hosmer approached his house, he felt mechanically in his pocket for his latch key; so small a trick having come back to him with the old habit of misery. Of course he found no key. His ring startled Fanny, who at once sprang from her seat to open the door for him; but having taken a few steps, she hesitated and irresolutely re-seated herself. It was only his second ring that the servant unamiably condescended to answer.

"So you're going to take Fanny away from us, Mr. Hosmer," said Belle, when he had greeted them and seated himself beside Mrs. Dawson on the small sofa that stood between the door and window. Fanny sat at the adjoining window, and Mrs. Worthington in the center of the room; which was indeed so small a room that any one of them might have reached out and almost touched the hand of the others.

"Yes, Fanny has agreed to go South with me," he answered briefly. "You're looking well, Mrs. Worthington."

"Oh, Law yes, I'm never sick. As I tell Mr. Worthington, he'll never get rid of me, unless he hires somebody to murder me. But I tell you what, you came pretty near not having any Fanny to take away with you. She was the sickest woman! Did you tell him about it, Fanny? Come to think of it, I guess the climate down there'll be the very thing to bring her round."

Mrs. Dawson without offering apology interrupted her friend to inquire of Hosmer if his life in the South were not of the most interesting, and begging that he detail them something of it; with a look to indicate that she felt the deepest concern in anything that touched him.

A masculine presence had always the effect of rousing Mrs. Dawson into an animation which was like the glow of a slumbering ember, when a strong pressure of air is brought to bear upon it.

Hosmer had always considered her an amiable woman, with rather delicate perceptions; frivolous, but without the vulgarisms of Mrs. Worthington, and consequently a less objectionable friend for Fanny. He answered, looking down into her eyes, which were full of attentiveness.

"My life in the South is not one that you would think interesting. I live in the country where there are no distractions such as you ladies call amusements— and I work pretty hard. But it's the sort of life that one grows attached to and finds himself longing for again if he have occasion to change it."

"Yes, it must be very satisfying," she answered; for the moment perfectly sincere.

"Oh very!" exclaimed Mrs. Worthington, with a loud and aggressive laugh. "It would just suit you to a T, Lou, but how it's going to satisfy Fanny! Well, I've got nothing to say about it, thanks be; it don't concern me."

"If Fanny finds that she doesn't like it after a fair trial, she has the privilege of saying so, and we shall come back again," he said looking at his wife whose elevation of eyebrow, and droop of mouth gave her the expression of martyred resignation, which St. Lawrence[4] might have worn, when invited to make himself comfortable on the gridiron—so had Mrs. Worthington's words impressed her with the force of their prophetic meaning.

Mrs. Dawson politely hoped that Hosmer would not leave before Jack came home; it would distress Jack beyond everything to return and find that he had missed an old friend whom he thought so much of.

Hosmer could not say precisely when they would leave. He was in present negotiation with a person who wanted to rent the house, furnished; and just as soon as he could arrange a few business details, and Fanny could gather such belongings as she wished to take with her, they would go.

"You seem mighty struck on Dave Hosmer, all of a sudden," remarked Mrs. Worthington to her friend, as the two crossed over the street. "A feller without any more feelings than a stick; it's what I always said about him."

"Oh, I always did like Hosmer," replied Mrs. Dawson. "But I thought he had more sense than to tie himself to that little gump again, after he'd had the luck to get rid of her."

A few days later Jack came home. His return was made palpable to the entire neighborhood; for no cab ever announced itself with quite the dash and clatter and bang of door that Jack's cabs did.

The driver had staggered behind him under the weight of the huge yellow valise, and had been liberally paid for the service.

Immediately the windows were thrown wide open, and the lace curtains drawn aside until no smallest vestige of them remained visible from the street. A condition of things which Mrs. Worthington upstairs bitterly resented, and naturally, spoiling as it necessarily did, the general *coup d'œil*[5] of the flat to passers-by. But Mrs. Dawson had won her husband's esteem by just such acts as this one of amiable permission to ventilate the house according to methods of his own and essentially masculine; regardless of dust that might be flying, or sun that might be shining with disastrous results to the parlor carpet.

Clouds of tobacco smoke were seen to issue from the open windows. Those neighbors whose openings commanded a view of the Dawson's alley-gate might have noted the hired girl starting for the grocery with unusual animation of step, and returning with her basket well stocked with beer and soda bottles—a provision made against a need for "dutch-cocktails,"[6] likely to assail Jack during his hours of domesticity.

In the evening the same hired girl, breathless from the multiplicity of errands which she had accomplished during the day, appeared at the Hosmers with a message that Mrs. Dawson wanted them to "come over."

They were preparing to leave on the morrow, but concluded that they could spare a few moments in which to bid adieu to their friends.

Jack met them at the very threshold, with warm and hearty hand-shaking, and loud protest when he learned that they had not come to spend the evening and that they were going away next day.

"Great Scott! you're not leaving to-morrow? And I ain't going to have a chance to get even with Mrs. Hosmer on that last deal? By Jove, she knows how to do it," he said, addressing Hosmer and holding Fanny familiarly by the elbow. "Drew to the middle, sir, and hang me, if she didn't fill. Takes a woman to do that sort o' thing; and me a laying for her with three aces.[7] Hello there, girls! here's Hosmer and Fanny," in response to which summons his wife and Mrs. Worthington issued from the depths of the dining-room, where they had been engaged in preparing certain refreshments for the expected guests.

"See here, Lou, we'll have to fix it up some way to go and see them off to-morrow. If you'd manage to lay over till Thursday I could join you as far as Little Rock. But no, that's a fact," he added reflectively, "I've got to be in Cincinnati on Thursday."

They had all entered the parlor, and Mrs. Worthington suggested that Hosmer go up and make a visit to her husband, whom he would find up there "poking over those everlasting books."

"I don't know what's got into Mr. Worthington lately," she said, "he's getting that religious. If it ain't the Bible he's poring over, well it's something or other just as bad."

The brightly burning light guided Hosmer to the kitchen, where he found Lorenzo Worthington seated beside his student-lamp at the table, which was covered with a neat red cloth. On the gas-stove was spread a similar cloth and the floor was covered with a shining oil-cloth.

Mr. Worthington was startled, having already forgotten that his wife had told him of Hosmer's return to St. Louis.

"Why, Mr. Hosmer, is this you? come, come into the parlor, this is no place," shaking Hosmer's hand and motioning towards the parlor.

"No, it's very nice and cozy here, and I have only a moment to stay," said Hosmer, seating himself beside the table on which the other had laid his book, with his spectacles between the pages to mark his place. Mr. Worthington then did a little hemming and hawing preparatory to saying something fitting the occasion; not wishing to be hasty in offering the old established form of congratulation, in a case whose peculiarity afforded him no precedential guide. Hosmer came to his relief by observing quite naturally that he and his wife had come over to say good-bye, before leaving for the South, adding "no doubt Mrs. Worthington has told you."

"Yes, yes, and I'm sure we're very sorry to lose you; that is, Mrs. Larimore—I should say Mrs. Hosmer. Isabella will certainly regret her departure, I see them always together, you know."

"You cling to your old habit, I see, Mr. Worthington," said Hosmer, indicating his meaning by a motion of the hand towards the book on the table.

"Yes, to a certain extent. Always within the forced limits, you understand. At this moment I am much interested in tracing the history of various religions which are known to us; those which have died out, as well as existing religions. It is curious, indeed, to note the circumstances of their birth, their progress and inevitable death; seeming to follow the course of nations in such respect. And the similitude which stamps them all, is also a feature worthy of study. You would perhaps be surprised, sir, to discover the points of resemblance which indicate in them a common origin. To observe the slight differences, indeed technical differences, distinguishing the Islam from the Hebrew, or both from the Christian religion. The creeds are obviously ramifications from the one deep-rooted trunk which we call religion. Have you ever thought of this, Mr. Hosmer?"

"No, I admit that I've not gone into it. Homeyer would have me think that all religions are but mythological creations invented to satisfy a species of sentimentality—a morbid craving in man for the unknown and undemonstrable."

"That is where he is wrong; where I must be permitted to differ from him. As you would find, my dear sir, by following carefully the history of mankind, that the religious sentiment is implanted, a true and legitimate attribute of the human soul—with peremptory right to its existence. Whatever may be faulty in the creeds—that makes no difference, the foundation is there and not to be dislodged. Homeyer, as I understand him from your former not infrequent references, is an Iconoclast, who would tear down and leave devastation behind him; building up nothing. He would deprive a clinging humanity of the supports about which she twines herself, and leave her helpless and sprawling upon the earth."

"No, no, he believes in a natural adjustment," interrupted Hosmer. "In an innate reserve force of accommodation. What we commonly call laws in nature, he styles accidents—in society, only arbitrary methods of expediency, which, when they outlive their usefulness to an advancing and exacting civilization, should be set aside. He is a little impatient to always wait for the inevitable natural adjustment."

"Ah, my dear Mr. Hosmer, the world is certainly to-day not prepared to stand the lopping off and wrenching away of old traditions. She must take her stand against such enemies of the conventional. Take religion away from the life of man—"

"Well, I knew it—I was just as sure as preaching," burst out Mrs. Worthington, as she threw open the door and confronted the two men—resplendent in "baby blue" and much steel ornamentation. "As I tell Mr. Worthington, he ought to turn Christian Brother or something and be done with it."

"No, no, my dear; Mr. Hosmer and I have merely been interchanging a few disjointed ideas."

"I'll be bound they were disjointed. I guess Fanny wants you, Mr. Hosmer. If you listen to Mr. Worthington he'll keep you here till daylight with his ideas."

Hosmer followed Mrs. Worthington down-stairs and into Mrs. Dawson's. As he entered the parlor he heard Fanny laughing gaily, and saw that she stood near the sideboard in the dining-room, just clicking her glass of punch to Jack Dawson's, who was making a gay speech on the occasion of her new marriage.

They did not leave when they had intended. Need the misery of that one day be told?

But on the evening of the following day, Fanny peered with pale, haggard face from the closed window of the Pullman car as it moved slowly out of Union depôt, to see Lou and Jack Dawson smiling and waving good-bye, Belle wiping her eyes and Mr. Worthington looking blankly along the line of windows, unable to see them without his spectacles, which he had left between the pages of his Schopenhauer on the kitchen table at home.

Part Two

I

Fanny's First Night
at Place-Du-Bois

The journey South had not been without attractions for Fanny. She had that consciousness so pleasing to the feminine mind of being well dressed; for her husband had been exceedingly liberal in furnishing her the means to satisfy her fancy in that regard. Moreover the change holding out a promise of novelty, irritated her to a feeble expectancy. The air, that came to her in puffs through the car window, was deliciously soft and mild; steeped with the rich languor of the Indian summer, that had already touched the tree tops, the sloping hill-side, and the very air, with russet and gold.

Hosmer sat beside her, curiously inattentive to his newspaper; observant of her small needs, and anticipating her timid half expressed wishes. Was there some mysterious power that had so soon taught the man such methods to a woman's heart, or was he not rather on guard and schooling himself for the rôle which was to be acted out to the end? But as the day was approaching its close, Fanny became tired and languid; a certain mistrust was creeping into her heart with the nearing darkness. It had grown sultry and close, and the view from the car window was no longer cheerful, as they whirled through forests, gloomy with trailing moss, or sped over an unfamiliar country whose features were strange and held no promise of a welcome for her.

They were nearing Place-du-Bois, and Hosmer's spirits had risen almost to the point of gaiety as he began to recognize the faces of those who loitered about the stations at which they stopped. At the Centerville station, five miles before reaching their own, he had even gone out on the platform to shake hands with the rather mystified agent who had not known of his absence. And he had waved a salute to the little French priest of Centerville who stood out in the open beside his horse, booted, spurred and all equipped for bad weather, waiting for certain consignments which were to come with the train, and who answered Hosmer's greeting with a sober and uncompromising sweep of the hand. When the whistle sounded for Place-du-Bois, it was nearly dark. Hosmer hurried Fanny on to the platform, where stood Henry, his clerk. There were a great many negroes loitering about, some of whom offered him a cordial "how'dy Mr. Hosma," and pushing through was Grégoire, meeting them with the ease of a courtier, and acknowledging Hosmer's introduction of his wife, with a friendly hand shake.

"Aunt Thérèse sent the buggy down fur you," he said, "we had rain this mornin' and the road's putty heavy. Come this way. Mine out fur that ba'el, Mrs. Hosma, it's got molasses in. Hirum bring that buggy ova yere."

"What's the news, Grégoire?" asked Hosmer, as they waited for Hiram to turn the horses about.

"Jus' about the same's ev'a. Miss Melicent wasn't ver' well a few days back; but she's some betta. I reckon you're all plum wore out," he added, taking in Fanny's listless attitude, and thinking her very pretty as far as he could discover in the dim light.

They drove directly to the cottage, and on the porch Thérèse was waiting for them. She took Fanny's two hands and pressed them warmly between her own; then led her into the house with an arm passed about her waist. She shook hands with Hosmer, and stood for a while in cheerful conversation, before leaving them.

The cottage was fully equipped for their reception, with Minervy in possession of the kitchen and the formerly reluctant Suze as housemaid: though Thérèse had been silent as to the methods which she had employed to prevail with these unwilling damsels.

Hosmer then went out to look after their baggage, and when he returned, Fanny sat with her head pillowed on the sofa, sobbing bitterly. He knelt beside her, putting his arm around her, and asked the cause of her distress.

"Oh it's so lonesome, and dreadful, I don't believe I can stand it," she answered haltingly through her tears.

And here was he thinking it was so home-like and comforting, and tasting the first joy that he had known since he had gone away.

"It's all strange and new to you, Fanny; try to bear up for a day or two. Come now, don't be a baby—take courage. It will all seem quite different by and by, when the sun shines."

A knock at the door was followed by the entrance of a young colored boy carrying an armful of wood.

"Miss T'rèse sont me kin'le fiar fu' Miss Hosma; 'low he tu'nin' cole," he said depositing his load on the hearth; and Fanny, drying her eyes, turned to watch him at his work.

He went very deliberately about it, tearing off thin slathers from the fat pine, and arranging them into a light frame-work, beneath a topping of kindling and logs that he placed on the massive brass andirons.[1] He crawled about on hands and knees, picking up the stray bits of chips and moss that had fallen from his arms when he came in. Then sitting back on his heels he looked meditatively into the blaze which he had kindled and scratched his nose with a splinter of pine wood. When Hosmer presently left the room, he rolled his big black eyes towards Fanny, without turning his head, and remarked in a tone plainly inviting conversation "yo' all come f'om way yonda?"

He was intensely black, and if Fanny had been a woman with the slightest sense of humor, she could not but have been amused at the picture which he presented in the revealing fire-light with his elfish and ape like body much too small to fill out the tattered and ill-fitting garments that hung about it. But she only wondered at him and his rags, and at his motive for addressing her.

"We're come from St. Louis," she replied, taking him with a seriousness which in no wise daunted him.

"Yo' all brung de rain," he went on sociably, leaving off the scratching of his nose, to pass his black yellow-palmed hand slowly through the now raging fire, a feat which filled her with consternation. After prevailing upon him to desist from this salamander like exhibition, she was moved to ask if he were not very poor to be thus shabbily clad.

"No 'um," he laughed, "I got some sto' close yonda home. Dis yere coat w'at Mista Grégor gi'me," looking critically down at its length, which swept the floor as he remained on his knees. "He done all to'e tu pieces time he gi' him tu me, whar he scuffle wid Joçint yonda tu de mill. Mammy 'low she gwine mek him de same like new w'en she kin kotch de time."

The entrance of Minervy bearing a tray temptingly arranged with a dainty supper served to silence the boy, who at seeing her, threw himself upon all fours and appeared to be busy with the fire. The woman, a big raw-boned field hand, set her burden awkwardly down on a table, and after staring comprehensively around, addressed the boy in a low rich voice, "Dar ain't no mo' call to bodda wid dat fiar, you Sampson; how come Miss T'rèse sont you lazy piece in yere tu buil' fiar?"

"Don' know how come," he replied, vanishing with an air of the utmost self-depreciation.

Hosmer and Fanny took tea together before the cheerful fire and he told her something of methods on the plantation, and made her further acquainted with the various people whom she thus far encountered. She listened apathetically; taking little interest in what he said, and asking few questions. She did express a little bewilderment at the servant problem. Mrs. Lafirme, during their short conversation, had deplored her inability to procure more than two servants for her; and Fanny could not understand why it should require so many to do the work which at home was accomplished by one. But she was tired—very tired, and early sought her bed, and Hosmer went in quest of his sister whom he had not yet seen.

Melicent had been told of his marriage some days previously, and had been thrown into such a state of nerves by the intelligence, as to seriously alarm those who surrounded her and whose experience with hysterical girls had been inadequate.

Poor Grégoire had betaken himself with the speed of the wind to the store to procure bromide, valerian,[2] and whatever else should be thought available in prevailing with a malady of this distressing nature. But she was "some betta," as he told Hosmer, who found her walking in the darkness of one of the long verandas, all enveloped in filmy white wool. He was a little prepared for a cool reception from her, and ten minutes before she might have received him with a studied indifference. But her mood had veered about and touched the point which moved her to fall upon his neck, and in a manner, condole with him; seasoning her sympathy with a few tears.

"Whatever possessed you, David? I have been thinking, and thinking, and I can see no reason which should have driven you to do this thing. Of course I can't meet her; you surely don't expect it?"

He took her arm and joined her in her slow walk.

"Yes, I do expect it, Melicent, and if you have the least regard for me, I expect more. I want you to be good to her, and patient, and show yourself her friend. No one can do such things more amiably than you, when you try."

"But David, I had hoped for something so different."

"You couldn't have expected me to marry Mrs. Lafirme, a Catholic," he said, making no pretense of misunderstanding her.

"I think that woman would have given up religion—anything for you."

"Then you don't know her, little sister."

It must have been far in the night when Fanny awoke suddenly. She could not have told whether she had been awakened by the long, wailing cry of a traveler across the narrow river, vainly trying to rouse the ferryman; or the creaking of a heavy wagon that labored slowly by in the road and moved Hector to noisy enquiry. Was it not rather the pattering rain that the wind was driving against the window panes? The lamp burned dimly upon the high old-fashioned mantel-piece and her husband had thoughtfully placed an improvised screen before it, to protect her against its disturbance. He himself was not beside her, nor was he in the room. She slid from her bed and moved softly on her bare feet over to the open sitting-room door.

The fire had all burned away. Only the embers lay in a glowing heap, and while she looked, the last stick that lay across the andirons, broke through its tapering center and fell amongst them, stirring a fitful light by which she discovered her husband seated and bowed like a man who has been stricken. Uncomprehending, she stood a moment speechless, then crept back noiselessly to bed.

II

"Neva To See You!"

hérèse judged it best to leave Fanny a good deal to herself during her first days on the plantation, without relinquishing a certain watchful supervision of her comfort, and looking in on her for a few moments each day. The rain which had come with them continued fitfully and Fanny remained in doors, clad in a warm handsome gown, her small slippered feet cushioned before the fire, and reading the latest novel of one of those prolific female writers who turn out their unwholesome intellectual sweets so tirelessly, to be devoured by the girls and women of the age.

Melicent, who always did the unexpected, crossed over early on the morning after Fanny's arrival; penetrated to her sleeping room and embraced her effusively, even as she lay in bed, calling her "poor dear Fanny" and cautioning her against getting up on such a morning.

The tears which had come to Fanny on arriving, and which had dried on her cheek when she turned to gaze into the cheer of the great wood fire, did not return. Everybody seemed to be making much of her, which was a new experience in her life; she having always felt herself as of little consequence, and in a manner, overlooked. The negroes were overawed at the splendor of her toilettes[1] and showed a respect for her in proportion to the money value which these toilettes reflected. Each morning Grégoire left at her door his compliments with a huge bouquet of brilliant and many colored crysanthemums, and enquiry if he could serve her in any way. And Hosmer's time, that was not given to work, was passed at her side; not in brooding or pre-occupied silence, but in talk that invited her to friendly response.

With Thérèse, she was at first shy and diffident, and over watchful of herself. She did not forget that Hosmer had told her "The lady knows why I have come" and she resented that knowledge which Thérèse possessed of her past intimate married life.

Melicent's attentions did not last in their ultra-effusiveness, but she found Fanny less objectionable since removed from her St. Louis surroundings; and the evident consideration with which she had been accepted at Place-du-Bois seemed to throw about her a halo of sufficient distinction to impel the girl to view her from a new and different stand-point.

But the charm of plantation life was letting go its hold upon Melicent. Grégoire's adoration alone, and her feeble response to it, were all that kept her.

"I neva felt anything like this befo'," he said, as they stood together and their hands touched in reaching for a splendid rose that hung invitingly from its tall latticed support out in mid lawn. The sun had come again and dried the last drop of lingering moisture on grass and shrubbery.

"W'en I'm away f'om you, even fur five minutes, 't seems like I mus' hurry quick, quick, to git back again; an' w'en I'm with you, everything 'pears all right, even if you don't talk to me or look at me. Th' otha day, down at the gin," he continued, "I was figurin' on some weights an' wasn't thinkin' about you at all, an' all at once I remember'd the one time I'd kissed you. Goodness! I couldn't see the figures any mo', my head swum and the pencil mos' fell out o' my han'. I neva felt anything like it: hones', Miss Melicent, I thought I was goin' to faint fur a minute."

"That's very unwise, Grégoire," she said, taking the roses that he handed her to add to the already large bunch. "You must learn to think of me calmly: our love must be something like a sacred memory—a sweet recollection to help us through life when we are apart."

"I don't know how I'm goin' to stan' it. Neva to see you! neva—my God!" he gasped, paling and crushing between his nervous fingers the flower she would have taken from him.

"There is nothing in this world that one cannot grow accustomed to, dear," spoke the pretty philosopher, picking up her skirts daintily with one hand and passing the other through his arm—the hand which held the flowers, whose peculiar perfume ever afterwards made Grégoire shiver through a moment of pain that touched very close upon rapture.

He was more occupied than he liked during those busy days of harvesting and ginning, that left him only brief and snatched intervals of Melicent's society. If he could have rested in the comfort of being sure of her, such moments of separation would have had their compensation in reflective anticipation. But with his undisciplined desires and hot-blooded eagerness, her half-hearted acknowledgments and inadequate concessions, closed her about with a chilling barrier that staggered him with its problematic nature. Feeling himself her equal in the aristocracy of blood, and her master in the knowledge and strength of loving, he resented those half understood reasons which removed him from the possibility of being anything to her. And more, he was angry with himself for acquiescing in that self understood agreement. But it was only in her absence that these thoughts disturbed him. When he was with her, his whole being rejoiced in her existence and there was no room for doubt or dread.

He felt himself regenerated through love, and as having no part in that other Grégoire whom he only thought of to dismiss with unrecognition.

The time came when he could ill conceal his passion from others. Thérèse became conscious of it, through an unguarded glance. The unhappiness of the situation was plain to her; but to what degree she could not guess. It was certainly so deplorable that it would have been worth while to have averted it. Yet, she felt great faith in the power of time and absence to heal such wounds even to the extent of leaving no tell-tale scar.

"Grégoire, my boy," she said to him, speaking in French, and laying her hand on his, when they were alone together. "I hope that your heart is not too deep in this folly."

He reddened and asked, "What do you mean, aunt?"

"I mean, that unfortunately, you are in love with Melicent. I do not know how much longer she will remain here, but taking any possibility for granted, let me advise you to leave the place for a while; go back to your home, or take a little trip to the city."

"No, I could not."

"Force yourself to it."

"And lose days, perhaps weeks, of being near her? No, no, I could not do that, aunt. There will be plenty time for that in the rest of my life," he said, trying to speak calmly and forcing his voice to a harshness which the nearness of tears made needful.

"Does she know? Have you told her?"

"Oh yes, she knows how much I love her."

"And she does not love you," said Thérèse, seeming rather to assert than to question.

"No, she does not. No matter what she says—she does not. I can feel that here," he answered, striking his breast. "Oh aunt, it is terrible to think of

her going away; forever, perhaps; of never seeing her. I could not stand it."
And he stood the strain no longer, but sobbed and wept with his aunt's consoling arms around him.

Thérèse, knowing that Melicent would not tarry much longer with
them, thought it not needful to approach her on the subject. Had it been otherwise, she would not have hesitated to beg the girl to desist from this unprofit-
able amusement of tormenting a human heart.

III

A Talk Under
the Cedar Tree

Day by day, Fanny threw off somewhat of the homesickness which had weighted her at coming. Not by any determined effort of the will, nor by any resolve to make the best of things. Outside influences meeting half-way the workings of unconscious inward forces, were the agents that by degrees were gently ridding her of the acute pressure of dissatisfaction, which up to the present, she had stolidly borne without any personal effort to cast it off.

Thérèse affected her forcibly. This woman so wholesome, so fair and strong; so un-American as to be not ashamed to show tenderness and sympathy with eye and lip, moved Fanny like a new and pleasing experience. When Thérèse touched her caressingly, or gently stroked her limp hand, she started guiltily, and looked furtively around to make sure that none had witnessed an exhibition of tenderness that made her flush, and the first time found her unresponsive. A second time, she awkwardly returned the hand pressure, and later, these mildly sensuous exchanges prefaced the outpouring of all Fanny's woes, great and small.

"I don't say that I always done what was right, Mrs. Laferm, but I guess David's told you just what suited him about me. You got to remember there's always two sides to a story."

She had been to the poultry yard with Thérèse, who had introduced her to its feathery tenants, making her acquainted with stately Brahmas and sleek Plymouth-Rocks and hardy little "Creole chickens"[1]—not much to look at, but very palatable when converted into *fricassée*.[2]

Returning, they seated themselves on the bench that encircled a massive cedar—spreading and conical. Hector, who had trotted attendance upon them during their visit of inspection, cast himself heavily down at his mistress' feet and after glancing knowingly up into her face, looked placidly forth at Sampson, gathering garden greens on the other side of a low dividing fence.

"You see if David'd always been like he is now, I don't know but things 'd been different. Do you suppose he ever went any wheres with me, or even so much as talked to me when he came home? There was always that everlasting newspaper in his pocket, and he'd haul it out the first thing. Then I used to read the paper too sometimes, and when I'd to go talk to him about what I read, he'd never even looked at the same things. Goodness knows what he read in the paper, I never could find out; but here'd be the edges all covered over with figuring. I believe it's the only thing he ever thought or dreamt about; that eternal figuring on every bit of paper he could lay hold of, till I was tired picking them up all over the house. Belle Worthington used to say it'd of took an angel to stand him. I mean his throwing papers around that way. For as far as his never talking went, she couldn't find any fault with that; Mr. Worthington was just as bad, if he wasn't worse. But Belle's not like me; I don't believe she'd let poor Mr. Worthington talk in the house if he wanted to."

She gradually drifted away from her starting point, and like most people who have usually little to say, became very voluable, when once she passed into the humor of talking. Thérèse let her talk unchecked. It seemed to do her good to chatter about Belle and Lou, and Jack Dawson, and about her home life, of which she unknowingly made such a pitiable picture to her listener.

"I guess David never let on to you about himself," she said moodily, having come back to the sore that rankled: the dread that Thérèse had laid all the blame of the rupture on her shoulders.

"You're mistaken, Mrs. Hosmer. It was a knowledge of his own short-comings that prompted your husband to go back and ask your forgiveness. You must grant, there's nothing in his conduct now that you could reproach him with. And," she added, laying her hand gently on Fanny's arm, "I know you'll be strong, and do your share in this reconciliation—do what you can to please him."

Fanny flushed uneasily under Thérèse's appealing glance.

"I'm willing to do anything that David wants," she replied, "I made up my mind to that from the start. He's a mighty good husband now, Mrs. Laferm. Don't mind what I said about him. I was afraid you thought that—"

"Never mind," returned Thérèse kindly, "I know all about it. Don't worry any farther over what I may think. I believe in you and in him, and I know you'll both be brave and do what's right."

"There isn't anything so very hard for David to do," she said, depressed with a sense of her inadequate strength to do the task which she had set herself. "He's got no faults to give up. David never did have any faults. He's a true, honest man; and I was a coward to say those things about him."

Melicent and Grégoire were coming across the lawn to join the two, and Fanny, seeing them approach, suddenly chilled and wrapt[3] herself about in her mantle of reserve.

"I guess I better go," she said, offering to rise, but Thérèse held out a detaining hand.

"You don't want to go and sit alone in the cottage; stay here with me till Mr. Hosmer comes back from the mill."

Grégoire's face was a study. Melicent, who did what she wanted with him, had chosen this afternoon, for some inscrutable reason, to make him happy. He carried her shawl and parasol; she herself bearing a veritable armful of flowers, leaves, red berried sprigs, a tangle of richest color. They had been in the woods and she had bedecked him with garlands and festoons of autumn leaves, till he looked a very Satyr;[4] a character which his flushed, swarthy cheeks, and glittering animal eyes did not belie.

They were laughing immoderately, and their whole bearing still reflected their exuberant gaiety as they joined Thérèse and Fanny.

"What a '*Mater Dolorosa*'[5] Fanny looks!" exclaimed Melicent, throwing herself into a picturesque attitude on the bench beside Thérèse, and resting her feet on Hector's broad back.

Fanny offered no reply, but to look helplessly resigned; an expression which Melicent knew of old, and which had always the effect of irritating her. Not now, however, for the curve of the bench around the great cedar tree removed her from the possibility of contemplating Fanny's doleful visage, unless she made an effort to that end, which she was certainly not inclined to do.

"No, Grégoire," she said, flinging a rose into his face when he would have seated himself beside her, "go sit by Fanny and do something to make her laugh; only don't tickle her; David mightn't like it. And here's Mrs. Lafirme looking almost as glum. Now, if David would only join us with that 'pale cast of thought'[6] that he bears about usually, what a merry go round we'd have."

"When Melicent looks at the world laughing, she wants it to laugh back at her," said Thérèse, reflecting something of the girl's gaiety.

"As in a looking-glass, well isn't that square?" she returned, falling into slang, in her recklessness of spirit.

Endeavoring to guard her treasure of flowers from Thérèse, who was without ceremony making a critical selection among them of what pleased her, Melicent slid around the bench, bringing herself close to Grégoire and begging his protection against the Vandalism of his aunt. She looked into his eyes for an instant as though asking him for love instead of so slight a favor and he grasped her arm, pressing it till she cried out from the pain: which act, on his side, served to drive her again around to Thérèse.

"Guess what we are going to do to-morrow: you and I and all of us; Grégoire and David and Fanny and everybody?"

"Going to Bedlam[7] along with you?" Thérèse asked.

"Mrs. Lafirme is in need of a rebuke, which I shall proceed to administer," thrusting a crumpled handful of rose leaves down the neck of Thérèse's dress, and laughing joyously in her scuffle to accomplish the punishment.

"No, madam; I don't go to Bedlam; I drive others there. Ask Grégoire what we're going to do. Tell them, Grégoire."

"They ain't much to tell. We'a goin' hoss back ridin'."

"Not me; I can't ride," wailed Fanny.

"You can get up Torpedo for Mrs. Hosmer, can't you, Grégoire?" asked Thérèse.

"Certainly. W'y you could ride ole Torpedo, Mrs. Hosma, if you neva saw a hoss in yo' life. A li'l chile could manage him."

Fanny turned to Thérèse for further assurance and found all that she looked for.

"We'll go up on the hill and see that dear old Morico, and I shall take along a comb, and comb out that exquisite white hair of his and then I shall focus[8] him, seated in his low chair and making one of those cute turkey fans."

"Ole Morico ain't goin' to let you try no monkeyshines on him; I tell you that befo' han'," said Grégoire, rising and coming to Melicent to rid him of his sylvan ornamentations, for it was time for him to leave them. When he turned away, Melicent rose and flung all her flowery wealth into Thérèse's lap, and following took his arm.

"Where are you going?" asked Thérèse.

"Going to help Grégoire feed the mules," she called back looking over her shoulder; the sinking sun lighting her handsome mischievous face.

Thérèse proceeded to arrange the flowers with some regard to graceful symmetry; and Fanny did not regain her talkative spirit that Melicent's coming had put to flight, but sat looking silent and listlessly into the distance.

As Thérèse glanced casually up into her face, she saw it warmed by a sudden faint glow—an unusual animation, and following her gaze, she saw that Hosmer had returned and was entering the cottage.

"I guess I better be going," said Fanny rising, and this time Thérèse no longer detained her.

IV

Thérèse Crosses the River

To shirk any serious duties of life would have been entirely foreign to Thérèse's methods or even instincts. But there did come to her moments of rebellion—or repulsion, against the small demands that presented themselves with an unfailing recurrence; and from such, she at times indulged herself with the privilege of running away. When Fanny left her alone—a pathetic little droop took possession of the corners of her mouth that might not have come there if she had not been alone. She laid the flowers, only half arranged, on the bench beside her, as a child would put aside a toy that no longer interested it. She looked towards the house and could see the servants going back and forth. She knew if she entered, she would be met by appeals from one and the other. The overseer would soon be along, with his crib[1] keys, and stable keys; his account of the day's doings and consultations for to-morrow's work, and for the moment, she would have none of it.

"Come, Hector—come, old boy," she said rising abruptly; and crossing the lawn she soon gained the gravel path that led to the outer road. This road brought her by a mild descent to the river bank. The water, seldom stationary for any long period, was at present running low and sluggishly between its red banks.

Tied to the landing was a huge flat-boat that was managed by the aid of a stout cable reaching quite across the river; and beside it nestled a small light skiff. In this Thérèse seated herself, and proceeded to row across the stream, Hector plunging into the water and swimming in advance of her.

The banks on the opposite shore were almost perpendicular; and their summit to be reached only by the artificial road that had been cut into them:

broad and of easy ascent. This river front was a standing worry to Thérèse, for when the water was high and rapid, the banks caved constantly, carrying away great sections from the land. Almost every year, the fences in places had to be moved back, not only for security, but to allow a margin for the road that on this side followed the course of the small river.

High up and perilously near the edge stood a small cabin. It had once been far removed from the river, which had now, however, eaten its way close up to it—leaving no space for the road-way. The house was somewhat more pretentious than others of its class, being fashioned of planed painted boards, and having a brick chimney that stood fully exposed at one end. A great rose tree climbed and spread generously over one side, and the big red roses grew by hundreds amid the dark green setting of their leaves.

At the gate of this cabin Thérèse stopped, calling out, "*Grosse tante!—oh, Grosse tante!*"[2]

The sound of her voice brought to the door a negress—coal black and so enormously fat that she moved about with evident difficulty. She was dressed in a loosely hanging purple calico garment of the mother Hubbard type—known as a *volante*[3] amongst Louisiana Creoles; and on her head was knotted and fantastically twisted a bright *tignon*.[4] Her glistening good-natured countenance illumined at the sight of Thérèse.

"*Quo faire to pas voulez rentrer, Tite maîtresse?*"[5] and Thérèse answered in the same Creole dialect: "Not now, *Grosse tante*—I shall be back in half an hour to drink a cup of coffee with you." No English words can convey the soft music of that speech, seemingly made for tenderness and endearment.

As Thérèse turned away from the gate, the black woman re-entered the house, and as briskly as her cumbersome size would permit, began preparations for her mistress' visit. Milk and butter were taken from the safe; eggs, from the India rush basket that hung against the wall; and flour, from the half barrel that stood in convenient readiness in the corner: for *Tite Maîtresse* was to be treated to a dish of *croquignoles*.[6] Coffee was always an accomplished fact at hand in the chimney corner.

Grosse tante, or more properly, Marie Louise, was a Creole—Thérèse's nurse and attendant from infancy, and the only one of the family servants who had come with her mistress from New Orleans to Place-du-Bois at that lady's marriage with Jérôme Lafirme. But her ever increasing weight had long since removed her from the possibility of usefulness, otherwise than in supervising her small farm yard. She had little use for "*ces néges Américains,*"[7] as she called the plantation hands—a restless lot forever shifting about and changing quarters.

It was seldom now that she crossed the river; only two occasions being considered of sufficient importance to induce her to such effort. One was in the event of her mistress' illness, when she would install herself at her bedside as a fixture, not to be dislodged by any less inducement than Thérèse's full recovery. The other was when a dinner of importance was to be given: then Marie Louise consented to act as *chef de cuisine*,[8] for there was no more famous cook than she in the State; her instructor having been no less a personage than old Lucien Santien[9]—a *gourmet* famed for his ultra Parisian tastes.

Seated at the base of a great China-berry on whose gnarled protruding roots she rested an arm languidly, Thérèse looked out over the river and gave herself up to doubts and misgivings. She first took exception with herself for that constant interference in the concerns of other people. Might not this propensity be carried too far at times? Did the good accruing counterbalance the personal discomfort into which she was often driven by her own agency? What reason had she to know that a policy of non-interference in the affairs of others might not after all be the judicious one? As much as she tried to vaguely generalize, she found her reasoning applying itself to her relation with Hosmer.

The look which she had surprised in Fanny's face had been a painful revelation to her. Yet could she have expected other, and should she have hoped for less, than that Fanny should love her husband and he in turn should come to love his wife?

Had she married Hosmer herself! Here she smiled to think of the storm of indignation that such a marriage would have roused in the parish. Yet, even facing the impossibility of such contingency, it pleased her to indulge in a short dream of what might have been.

If it were her right instead of another's to watch for his coming and rejoice at it! Hers to call him husband and lavish on him the love that awoke so strongly when she permitted herself, as she was doing now, to invoke it! She felt what capability lay within her of rousing the man to new interests in life. She pictured the dawn of an unsuspected happiness coming to him: broadening; illuminating; growing in him to answer to her own big-heartedness.

Were Fanny, and her own prejudices, worth the sacrifice which she and Hosmer had made? This was the doubt that bade fair to unsettle her; that called for a sharp, strong out-putting of the will before she could bring herself to face the situation without its accessions of personalities. Such communing with herself could not be condemned as a weakness with Thérèse, for the effect which it left upon her strong nature was one of added courage and determination.

When she reached Marie Louise's cabin again, twilight, which is so brief in the South, was giving place to the night.

Within the cabin, the lamp had already been lighted, and Marie Louise was growing restless at Thérèse's long delay.

"Ah *Grosse tante*, I'm so tired," she said, falling into a chair near the door; not relishing the warmth of the room after her quick walk, and wishing to delay as long as possible the necessity of sitting at table. At another time she might have found the dish of golden brown *croquignoles* very tempting with its accessory of fragrant coffee; but not to-day.

"Why do you run about so much, *Tite Maîtresse?* You are always going this way and that way; on horseback, on foot—through the house. Make those lazy niggers work more. You spoil them. I tell you if it was old mistress that had to deal with them, they would see something different."

She had taken all the pins from Thérèse's hair which fell in a gleaming, heavy mass; and with her big soft hands she was stroking her head as gently as if those hands had been of the whitest and most delicate.

"I know that look in your eyes, it means headache. It's time for me to make you some more *eau sédative*[10]—I am sure you haven't any more; you've given it away as you give away every thing."

"*Grosse tante,*" said Thérèse seated at table and sipping her coffee; *Grosse tante* also drinking her cup—but seated apart, "I am going to insist on having your cabin moved back; it is silly to be so stubborn about such a small matter. Some day you will find yourself out in the middle of the river—and what am I going to do then?—no one to nurse me when I am sick—no one to scold me—nobody to love me."

"Don't say that, *Tite maîtresse,* all the world loves you—it isn't only Marie Louise. But no. You must remember the last time poor Monsieur Jérôme moved me, and said with a laugh that I can never forget, 'well, *Grosse tante,* I know we have got you far enough this time out of danger,' away back in Dumont's field you recollect? I said then, Marie Louise will move no more; she's too old. If the good God does not want to take care of me, then it's time for me to go."

"Ah, but *Grosse tante,* remember—God does not want all the trouble on his own shoulders," Thérèse answered humoring the woman, in her conception of the Diety. "He wants us to do our share, too."

"Well, I have done my share. Nothing is going to harm Marie Louise. I thought about all that, do not fret. So the last time Père Antoine[11] passed in the road—going down to see that poor Pierre Pardou at the Mouth—I called him in, and he blessed the whole house inside and out, with holy water—notice how the roses have bloomed since then—and gave me medals of the holy Virgin to hang about. Look over the door, *Tite maîtresse,* how it shines, like a silver star."

"If you will not have your cabin removed, *Grosse tante*, then come live with me. Old Hatton has wanted work at Place-du-Bois, the longest time. We will have him build you a room wherever you choose, a pretty little house like those in the city."

"*Non—non, Tite maîtresse, Marie Louise 'prè créver icite avé tous son butin, si faut*" (no, no, *Tite maîtresse*, Marie Louise will die here with all her belongings if it must be).

The servants were instructed that when their mistress was not at home at a given hour, her absence should cause no delay in the household arrangements. She did not choose that her humor or her movements be hampered by a necessity of regularity which she owed to no one. When she reached home supper had long been over.

Nearing the house she heard the scraping of Nathan's violin, the noise of shuffling feet and unconstrained laughter. These festive sounds came from the back veranda. She entered the dining-room, and from its obscurity looked out on a curious scene. The veranda was lighted by a lamp suspended from one of its pillars. In a corner sat Nathan; serious; dignified, scraping out a monotonous but rhythmic minor strain to which two young negroes from the lower quarters—famous dancers—were keeping time in marvelous shuffling and pigeon-wings; twisting their supple joints into astonishing contortions and the sweat rolling from their black visages. A crowd of darkies stood at a respectful distance, an appreciative and encouraging audience. And seated on the broad rail of the veranda were Melicent and Grégoire, patting Juba and singing a loud accompaniment to the breakdown.[12]

Was this the Grégoire who had only yesterday wept such bitter tears on his aunt's bosom?

Thérèse turning away from the scene, the doubt assailed her whether it were after all worth while to strive against the sorrows of life that can be so readily put aside.

V

One Afternoon

Whatever may have been Torpedo's characteristics in days gone by, at this advanced period in his history he possessed none so striking as a stoical inaptitude for being moved. Another of his distinguishing traits was a propensity for grazing which he was prone to indulge at inopportune moments. Such points taken in conjunction with a gait closely resembling that of the camel in the desert, might give much cause to wonder at Thérèse's motive in recommending him as a suitable mount for the unfortunate Fanny, were it not for his wide-spread reputation of angelic inoffensiveness.

The ride which Melicent had arranged and in which she held out such promises of a "lark" proved after all but a desultory affair. For with Fanny making but a sorry equestrian debut and Hosmer creeping along at her side; Thérèse unable to hold Beauregard within conventional limits, and Melicent and Grégoire vanishing utterly from the scene, sociability was a feature entirely lacking to the excursion.

"David, I can't go another step: I just can't, so that settles it."

The look of unhappiness in Fanny's face and attitude would have moved the proverbial stone.

"I think if you change horses with me, Fanny, you'll find it more comfortable, and we'll turn about and go home."

"I wouldn't get on that horse's back, David Hosmer, if I had to die right here in the woods, I wouldn't."

"Do you think you could manage to walk back that distance then? I can lead the horses," he suggested as a *pis aller.*[1]

"I guess I'll haf to; but goodness knows if I'll ever get there alive."

They were far up on the hill, which spot they had reached by painfully slow and labored stages, each refraining from mention of a discomfort that might interfere with the supposed enjoyment of the other, till Fanny's note of protest.

Hosmer cast about him for some expedient that might lighten the unpleasantness of the situation, when a happy thought occurred to him.

"If you'll try to bear up, a few yards further, you can dismount at old Morico's cabin and I'll hurry back and get the buggy. It can be driven this far anyway: and it's only a short walk from here through the woods."

So Hosmer set her down before Morico's door: her long riding skirt, borrowed for the occasion, twisting awkwardly around her legs, and every joint in her body aching.

Partly by pantomimic signs interwoven with a few French words which he had picked up within the last year, Hosmer succeeded in making himself understood to the old man, and rode away leaving Fanny in his care.

Morico fussily preceded her into the house and placed a great clumsy home-made rocker at her disposal, into which she cast herself with every appearance of bodily distress. He then busied himself in tidying up the room out of deference to his guest; gathering up the scissors, waxen thread and turkey feathers which had fallen from his lap in his disturbance, and laying them on the table. He knocked the ashes from his corn-cob pipe which he now rested on a projection of the brick chimney that extended into the room and that served as mantel-piece. All the while he cast snatched glances at Fanny, who sat pale and tired. Her appearance seemed to move him to make an effort towards relieving it. He took a key from his pocket and unlocking a side of the *garde manger,* drew forth a small flask of whisky. Fanny had closed her eyes and was not aware of his action, till she heard him at her elbow saying in his feeble quavering voice:—

"*Tenez madame; goutez un peu; ça va vous faire du bien,*"[2] and opening her eyes she saw that he held a glass half filled with strong "toddy" for her acceptance.

She thrust out her hand to ward it away as though it had been a reptile that menaced her with its sting.

Morico looked nonplussed and a little abashed: but he had much faith in the healing qualities of his remedy and urged it on her anew. She trembled a little, and looked away with rather excited eyes.

"*Je vous assure madame, ça ne peut pas vous faire du mal.*"[3]

Fanny took the glass from his hand, and rising went and placed it on the table, then walked to the open door and looked eagerly out, as though hoping for the impossibility of her husband's return.

She did not seat herself again, but walked restlessly about the room, intently examining its meager details. The circuit of inspection bringing her again to the table, she picked up Morico's turkey fan, looking at it long and critically. When she laid it down, it was to seize the glass of "toddy" which she unhesitatingly put to her lips and drained at a draught. All uneasiness and fatigue seemed to leave her on the instant as though by magic. She went back to her chair and reseated herself composedly. Her eyes now rested on her old host with a certain quizzical curiosity strange to them.

He was plainly demoralized by her presence, and still made pretense of occupying himself with the arrangement of the room.

Presently she said to him: "Your remedy did me more good than I'd expected," but not understanding her, he only smiled and looked at her blankly.

She laughed good-humoredly back at him, then went to the table and poured from the flask which he had left standing there, liquor to the depth of two fingers, this time drinking it more deliberately. After that she tried to talk to Morico and thought it very amusing that he could not understand her.

Presently Joçint came home and accepted her presence there very indifferently. He went to the *garde manger* to stay his hunger, much as he had done on the occasion of Thérèse's visit; talked in grim abrupt utterances to his father, and disappeared into the adjoining room where Fanny could hear him and occasionally see him polishing and oiling his cherished rifle.

Morico, more accustomed to foreign sounds in the woods than she, was the first to detect the approach of Grégoire, whom he went out hurriedly to meet, glad of the relief from the supposed necessity of entertaining his puzzling visitor. When he was fairly out of the room, she arose quickly, approached the table and reaching for the flask of liquor, thrust it hastily into her pocket, then went to join him. At the moment that Grégoire came up, Joçint issued from a side door and stood looking at the group.

"Well, Mrs. Hosma, yere I am. I reckon you was tired waitin'. The buggy's yonda in the road."

He shook hands cordially with Morico saying something to him in French which made the old man laugh heartily.

"Why didn't David come? I thought he said he was coming; that's the way he does," said Fanny complainingly.

"That's a po' compliment to me, Mrs. Hosma. Can't you stan' my company for that li'le distance?" returned Grégoire gallantly. "Mr. Hosma had a good deal to do w'en he got back, that's w'y he sent me. An' we betta hurry up if we expec' to git any suppa' to-night. Like as not you'll fine your kitchen cleaned out."

Fanny looked her inquiry for his meaning.

"Why, don't you know this is 'Tous-saint' eve[4]—w'en the dead git out o' their graves an' walk about? You wouldn't ketch a nigga out o' his cabin to-night afta dark to save his soul. They all gittin' ready now to hustle back to the quartas."

"That's nonsense," said Fanny, drawing on her gloves, "you ought to have more sense than to repeat such things."

Grégoire laughed, looking surprised at her unusual energy of speech and manner. Then he turned to Joçint, whose presence he had thus far ignored, and asked in a peremptory tone:

"W'at did Woodson say 'bout watchin' at the mill to-night? Did you ask him like I tole you?"

"Yaas, me ax um: ee' low ee an' goin'. Say how Sylveste d'wan' watch lak alluz. Say ee an' goin'. Me don' blem 'im neida, don' ketch me out de 'ouse night lak dat fu no man."

"*Sacré imbécile,*"[5] muttered Grégoire, between his teeth, and vouchsafed him no other answer, but nodded to Morico and turned away. Fanny followed with a freedom of movement quite unlike that of her coming.

Morico went into the house and coming back hastily to the door called to Joçint:

"Bring back that flask of whisky that you took off the table."

"You're a liar: you know I have no use for whisky. That's one of your damned tricks to make me buy you more." And he seated himself on an over-turned tub and with his small black eyes half closed, looked moodily out into the solemn darkening woods. The old man showed no resentment at the harshness and disrespect of his son's speech, being evidently used to such. He passed his hand slowly over his white long hair and turned bewildered into the house.

"Is it just this same old thing year in and year out, Grégoire? Don't any one ever get up a dance, or a card party or anything?"

"Jus' as you say; the same old thing f'om one yea's' en' to the othea. I used to think it was putty lonesome myse'f w'en I firs' come yere. Then you see they's no neighbo's right roun' yere. In Natchitoches now; that's the place to have a right down good time. But see yere; I didn' know you was fon' o' dancin' an' such things."

"Why, of course, I just dearly love to dance. But it's as much as my life's worth to say that before David; he's such a stick; but I guess you know that by this time," with a laugh, as he had never heard from her before—so unconstrained; at the same time drawing nearer to him and looking merrily into his face.

"The little lady's been having a 'toddy' at Morico's, that makes her lively," thought Grégoire. But the knowledge did not abash him in the least. He accommodated himself at once to the situation with that adaptability common to the American youth, whether of the South, North, East or West.

"Where abouts did you leave David when you come away?" she asked with a studied indifference.

"Hol' on there, Buckskin—w'er you takin' us? W'y, I lef' him at the sto' mailin' lettas."

"Had the others all got back? Mrs. Laferm? Melicent? did they all stop at the store, too?"

"Who? Aunt Thérèse? no, she was up at the house w'en I lef'—I reckon Miss Melicent was there too. Talkin' 'bout fun,—it's to git into one o' them big spring wagons on a moonlight night, like they do in Centaville sometimes; jus' packed down with young folks—and start out fur a dance up the coast. They ain't nothin' to beat it as fah as fun goes."

"It must be just jolly. I guess you're a pretty good dancer, Grégoire?"

"Well—'taint fur me to say. But they ain't many can out dance me: not in Natchitoches pa'ish, anyway. I can say that much."

If such a thing could have been, Fanny would have startled Grégoire more than once during the drive home. Before its close she had obtained a promise from him to take her up to Natchitoches for the very next entertainment—averring that she didn't care what David said. If he wanted to bury himself that was his own look out. And if Mrs. Laferm took people to be angels that they could live in a place like that, and give up everything and not have any kind of enjoyment out of life, why, she was mistaken and that's all there was to it. To all of which freely expressed views Grégoire emphatically assented.

Hosmer had very soon disembarrassed himself of Torpedo, knowing that the animal would unerringly find his way to the corn crib by supper time. He continued his own way now untrammelled, and at an agreeable speed which soon brought him to the spring at the road side. Here he found Thérèse, half seated against a projection of rock, in her hand a bunch of ferns which she had evidently dismounted to gather, and holding Beauregard's bridle while he munched at the cool wet tufts of grass that grew everywhere.

As Hosmer rode up at a rapid pace, he swung himself from his horse almost before the animal came to a full stop. He removed his hat, mopped his forehead, stamped about a little to relax his limbs and turned to answer the enquiry with which Thérèse met him.

"Left her at Morico's. I'll have to send the buggy back for her."

"I can't forgive myself for such a blunder," said Thérèse regretfully, "indeed I had no idea of that miserable beast's character. I never was on him you know—only the little darkies, and they never complained: they'd as well ride cows as not."

"Oh, it's mainly from her being unaccustomed to riding, I believe."

This was the first time that Hosmer and Thérèse had met alone since his return from St. Louis. They looked at each other with full consciousness of what lay in the other's mind. Thérèse felt that however adroitly another woman might have managed the situation, for herself, it would have been a piece of affectation to completely ignore it at this moment.

"Mr. Hosmer, perhaps I ought to have said something before this, to you—about what you've done."

"Oh, yes, congratulated me—complimented me," he replied with a pretense at a laugh.

"Well, the latter, perhaps. I think we all like to have our good and right actions recognized for their worth."

He flushed, looked at her with a smile, then laughed out-right—this time it was no pretense.

"So I've been a good boy; have done as my mistress bade me and now I'm to receive a condescending little pat on the head—and of course must say thank you. Do you know, Mrs. Lafirme—and I don't see why a woman like you oughtn't to know it—it's one of those things to drive a man mad, the sweet complaisance with which women accept situations, or inflict situations that it takes the utmost of a man's strength to endure."

"Well, Mr. Hosmer," said Thérèse plainly discomposed, "you must concede you decided it was the right thing to do."

"I didn't do it because I thought it was right, but because you thought it was right. But that makes no difference."

"Then remember your wife is going to do the right thing herself—she admitted as much to me."

"Don't fool yourself, as Melicent says, about what Mrs. Hosmer means to do. I take no account of it. But you take it so easily; so as a matter of course. That's what exasperates me. That you, you, you, shouldn't have a suspicion of the torture of it; the loathsomeness of it. But how could you—how could any woman understand it? Oh forgive me, Thérèse—I wouldn't want you to. There's no brute so brutal as a man," he cried, seeing the pain in her face and knowing he had caused it. "But you know you promised to help me—oh I'm talking like an idiot."

"And I do," returned Thérèse, "that is, I want to, I mean to."

"Then don't tell me again that I have done right. Only look at me sometimes a little differently than you do at Hiram or the gate post. Let me once in
a while see a look in your face that tells me that you understand—if it's only a
little bit."

Thérèse thought it best to interrupt the situation; so, pale and silently she
prepared to mount her horse. He came to her assistance of course, and when
she was seated she drew off her loose riding glove and held out her hand to
him. He pressed it gratefully, then touched it with his lips; then turned it and
kissed the half open palm.

She did not leave him this time, but rode at his side in silence with a
frown and a little line of thought between her blue eyes.

As they were nearing the store she said diffidently: "Mr. Hosmer, I wonder if it wouldn't be best for you to put the mill in some one else's charge—and
go away from Place-du-Bois."

"I believe you always speak with a purpose, Mrs. Lafirme: you have
somebody's ultimate good in view, when you say that. Is it your own, or mine,
or whose is it?"

"Oh! not mine."

"I will leave Place-du-Bois, certainly, if you wish it."

As she looked at him she was forced to admit that she had never seen
him look as he did now. His face, usually serious, had a whole unwritten tragedy in it. And she felt altogether sore and puzzled and exasperated over man's
problematic nature.

"I don't think it should be left entirely to me to say. Doesn't your own
reason suggest a proper course in the matter?"

"My reason is utterly unable to determine anything in which you are
concerned, Mrs. Lafirme," he said, checking his horse and laying a restraining
hand on her bridle, "let me speak to you one moment. I know you are a woman
to whom one may speak the truth. Of course, you remember that you prevailed upon me to go back to my wife. To you it seemed the right thing—to
me it certainly seemed hard—but no more nor less than taking up the old
unhappy routine of life, where I had left it when I quitted her. I reasoned
much like a stupid child who thinks the colors in his kaleidoscope may fall
twice into the same design. In place of the old, I found an entirely new situation—horrid, sickening, requiring such a strain upon my energies to live
through it, that I believe it's an absurdity to waste so much moral force for so
poor an aim—there would be more dignity in putting an end to my life. It
doesn't make it any the more bearable to feel that the cause of this unlooked
for change lies within myself—my altered feelings. But it seems to me that I

have the right to ask you not to take yourself out of my life; your moral support; your bodily atmosphere. I hope not to give way to the weakness of speaking of these things again: but before you leave me, tell me, do you understand
a little better why I need you?"

"Yes, I understand now; and I thank you for talking so openly to me.
Don't go away from Place-du-Bois; it would make me very wretched."

She said no more and he was glad of it, for her last words held almost the
force of action for him; as though she had let him feel for an instant her heart
beat against his own with an echoing pain.

Their ways now diverged. She went in the direction of the house and he
to the store where he found Grégoire, whom he sent for his wife.

VI

One Night

"Grégoire was right: do you know those nasty creatures have gone and left every speck of the supper
dishes unwashed? I've got half a mind to give them
both warning to-morrow morning."

Fanny had come in from the kitchen to the sitting room,
and the above homily was addressed to her husband who stood
lighting his cigar. He had lately taken to smoking.

"You'd better do nothing of the kind; you wouldn't
find it easy to replace them. Put up a little with their vagaries: this sort of thing only happens once a year."

"How do you know it won't be something else just as
ridiculous to-morrow? And that idiot of a Minervy; what
do you suppose she told me when I insisted on her staying to wash up things?
She says, last whatever you call it, her husband wanted to act hard-headed and
staid[1] out after dark, and when he was crossing the bayou, the spirits jerked
him off his horse and dragged him up and down in the water, till he was nearly
drowned. I don't see what you're laughing at; I guess you'd like to make out
that they're in the right."

Hosmer was perfectly aware that Fanny had had a drink, and he rightly
guessed that Morico had given it to her. But he was at a loss to account for the
increasing symptoms of intoxication that she showed. He tried to persuade
her to go to bed; but his efforts to that end remained unheeded, till she had
eased her mind of an accumulation of grievances, mostly fancied. He had much
difficulty in preventing her from going over to give Melicent a piece of her
mind about her lofty airs and arrogance in thinking herself better than other
people. And she was very eager to tell Thérèse that she meant to do as she
liked, and would stand no poking of noses in her business. It was a good while

before she fell into a heavy sleep, after shedding a few maudlin tears over the conviction that he intended to leave her again, and clinging to his neck with beseeching enquiry whether he loved her.

He went out on the veranda feeling much as if he had been wrestling with a strong adversary who had mastered him, and whom he was glad to be freed of, even at the cost of coming inglorious from the conflict. The night was so dark, so hushed, that if ever the dead had wished to step from their graves and take a stroll above ground, they could not have found a more fitting hour. Hosmer walked very long in the soothing quiet. He would have liked to walk the night through. The last three hours had been like an acute physical pain, that was over for the moment, and that being over, left his mind free to return to the delicious consciousness, that he had needed to be reminded of, that Thérèse loved him after all. When his measured tread upon the veranda finally ceased to mark the passing hours, a quiet that was almost pulseless fell upon the plantation. Place-du-Bois slept. Perhaps the only night in the year that some or other of the negroes did not lurk in fence corners, or make exchange of nocturnal visits.

But out in the hills there was no such unearthly stillness reigning. Those restless wood-dwellers, that never sleep, were sending startling gruesome calls to each other. Bats were flapping and whirling and darting hither and thither; the gliding serpent making quick rustle amid the dry, crisp leaves, and over all sounded the murmur of the great pine trees, telling their mystic secrets to the night.

A human creature was there too, feeling a close fellowship with these spirits of night and darkness; with no more fear in his heart than the unheeded serpent crossing his path. Every inch of the ground he knew. He wanted no daylight to guide him. Had his eyes been blinded he would no doubt have bent his body close to earth and scented his way along like the human hound that he was. Over his shoulder hung the polished rifle that sent dull and sudden gleamings into the dark. A large tin pail swung from his hand. He was very careful of this pail—or its contents, for he feared to lose a drop. And when he accidentally struck an intervening tree and spilled some upon the ground, he muttered a curse against his own awkwardness.

Twice since leaving his cabin up in the clearing, he had turned to drive back his yellow skulking dog that followed him. Each time the brute had fled in abject terror, only to come creeping again into his master's footsteps, when he thought himself forgotten. Here was a companion whom neither Joçint nor his mission required. Exasperated, he seated himself on a fallen tree and whistled softly. The dog, who had been holding back, dashed to his side, trembling with eagerness, and striving to twist his head around to lick the hand that patted him. Joçint's other hand glided quickly into his pocket, from which he drew forth a coil of thin rope that he flung deftly over the animal's head, drawing it close and tight about the homely, shaggy throat. So quickly was the action done, that no sound was uttered, and Joçint continued his way untroubled by his old and faithful friend, whom he left hanging to the limb of a tree.

He was following the same path that he traversed daily to and from the mill, and which soon brought him out into the level with its soft tufted grass and clumps of squat thorn trees. There was no longer the protecting wood to screen him; but of such there was no need, for the darkness hung about him like the magic mantle of story. Nearing the mill he grew cautious, creeping along with the tread of a stealthy beast, and halting at intervals to listen for sounds that he wished not to hear. He knew there was no one on guard to-night. A movement in the bushes near by, made him fall quick and sprawling to earth. It was only Grégoire's horse munching the soft grass. Joçint drew near and laid his hand on the horse's back. It was hot and reeking^2 with sweat. Here was a fact to make him more wary. Horses were not found in such condition from quietly grazing of a cool autumn night. He seated himself upon the ground, with his hands clasped about his knees, all doubled up in a little heap, and waited there with the patience of the savage, letting an hour go by, whilst he made no movement.

The hour past, he stole towards the mill, and began his work of sprinkling the contents of his pail here and there along the dry timbers at well calculated distances, with care that no drop should be lost. Then, he drew together a great heap of crisp shavings and slathers, plentifully besprinkling it with what remained in the can. When he had struck a match against his rough trousers and placed it carefully in the midst of this small pyramid, he found that he had done his work but too surely. The quick flame sprang into life, seizing at once all it could reach. Leaping over intervals; effacing the darkness that had shrouded him; seeming to mock him as a fool and point him out as a target for heaven and earth to hurl destruction at if they would. Where should he hide himself? He only thought now of how he might have done the deed differently, and with safety to himself. He stood with great beams and loose planks surrounding him; quaking with a premonition of evil. He wanted to fly in one direction; then thought it best to follow the opposite; but a force outside of himself seemed to hold him fast to one spot. When turning suddenly about, he knew it was too late, he felt that all was lost, for there was Grégoire, not twenty paces away—covering him with the muzzle of a pistol and—cursed luck—his own rifle along with the empty pail in the raging fire.

Thérèse was passing a restless night. She had lain long awake, dwelling on the insistent thoughts that the day's happenings had given rise to. The sleep which finally came to her was troubled by dreams—demoniac[3]—grotesque. Hosmer was in a danger from which she was striving with physical effort to rescue him, and when she dragged him painfully from the peril that menaced him, she turned to see that it was Fanny whom she had saved—laughing at her derisively, and Hosmer had been left to perish. The dream was agonizing; like an appalling nightmare. She awoke in a fever of distress, and raised herself in bed to shake off the unnatural impression which such a dream can leave. The curtains were drawn aside from the window that faced her bed, and looking out she saw a long tongue of flame, reaching far up into the sky—away over the tree tops and the whole Southern horizon a glow. She knew at once that the mill was burning, and it was the affair of a moment with her to spring from her bed and don slippers and wrapper. She knocked on Melicent's door to acquaint her with the startling news; then hurried out into the back yard and rang the plantation bell.

Next she was at the cottage rousing Hosmer. But the alarm of the bell had already awakened him, and he was dressed and out on the porch almost as soon as Thérèse had called. Melicent joined them, highly agitated, and prepared to contribute her share towards any scene that might be going forward. But she found little encouragement for heroics with Hosmer. In saddling his horse rather hastily he was as unmoved as though preparing for an uneventful morning canter. He stood at the foot of the stairs preparing to mount when Grégoire rode up as if pursued by furies;[4] checking his horse with a quick, violent wrench that set it quivering in its taut limbs.

"Well," said Hosmer, "I guess it's done for. How did it happen? who did it?"

"Joçint's work," answered Grégoire bitingly.

"The damned scoundrel," muttered Hosmer, "where is he?"

"Don' botha 'bout Joçint; he ain't goin' to set no mo' mill afire," saying which, he turned his horse and the two rode furiously away.

Melicent grasped Thérèse's arm convulsively.

"What does he mean?" she asked in a frightened whisper.

"I—I don't know," Thérèse faltered. She had clasped her hands spasmodically together, at Grégoire's words, trembling with horror of what must be their meaning.

"Maybe he arrested him," suggested the girl.

"I hope so. Come; let's go to bed: there's no use staying out here in the cold and dark."

Hosmer had left the sitting-room door open, and Thérèse entered. She approached Fanny's door and knocked twice: not brusquely, but sufficiently loud to be heard from within, by any one who was awake. No answer came, and she went away, knowing that Fanny slept.

The unusual sound of the bell, ringing two hours past midnight—that very deadest hour of the night—had roused the whole plantation. On all sides squads of men and a few venturesome women were hurrying towards the fire; the dread of supernatural encounters overcome for the moment by such strong reality and by the confidence lent them in each other's company.

There were many already gathered around the mill, when Grégoire and Hosmer reached it. All effort to save anything had been abandoned as useless. The books and valuables had been removed from the office. The few householders—mill-hands—whose homes were close by, had carried their scant belongings to places of safety, but everything else was given over to the devouring flames.

The heat from this big raging fire was intense, and had driven most of the gaping spectators gradually back—almost into the woods. But there, to one side, where the fire was rapidly gaining, and making itself already uncomfortably felt, stood a small awe-stricken group talking in whispers; their ignorance and superstition making them irresolute to lay a hand upon the dead Joçint. His body lay amongst the heavy timbers, across a huge beam, with arms outstretched and head hanging down upon the ground. The glazed eyes were staring up into the red sky, and on his swarthy visage was yet the horror which had come there, when he looked in the face of death.

"In God's name, what are you doing?" cried Hosmer. "Can't some of you carry that boy's body to a place of safety?"

Grégoire had followed, and was looking down indifferently at the dead. "Come, len' a han' there; this is gittin' too durn hot," he said, stooping to raise the lifeless form. Hosmer was preparing to help him. But there was some one staggering through the crowd; pushing men to right and left. With now a hand upon the breast of both Hosmer and Grégoire, and thrusting them with such force and violence, as to lay them prone amongst the timbers. It was the father. It was old Morico. He had awakened in the night and missed his boy. He had seen the fire; indeed close enough that he could hear its roaring; and he knew everything. The whole story was plain to him as if it had been told by a revealing angel. The strength of his youth had come back to speed him over the ground.

"Murderers!" he cried looking about him with hate in his face. He did not know who had done it; no one knew yet, and he saw in every man he looked upon the possible slayer of his child.

So here he stood over the prostrate figure; his old gray jeans hanging loosely about him; wild eyed—with bare head clasped between his claw-like hands, which the white disheveled hair swept over. Hosmer approached again, offering gently to help him carry his son away.

"Stand back," he hurled at him. But he had understood the offer. His boy must not be left to burn like a log of wood. He bent down and strove to lift the heavy body, but the effort was beyond his strength. Seeing this he stooped again and this time grasped it beneath the arms; then slowly, draggingly, with halting step, began to move backward.

The fire claimed no more attention. All eyes were fastened upon this weird picture; a sight which moved the most callous to offer again and again assistance, that was each time spurned with an added defiance.

Hosmer stood looking on, with folded arms; moved by the grandeur and majesty of the scene. The devouring element, loosed in its awful recklessness there in the heart of this lonely forest. The motley group of black and white standing out in the great red light, powerless to do more than wait and watch. But more was he stirred to the depths of his being, by the sight of this human tragedy enacted before his eyes.

Once, the old man stops in his backward journey. Will he give over? has his strength deserted him? is the thought that seizes every on-looker. But no— with renewed effort he begins again his slow retreat, till at last a sigh of relief comes from the whole watching multitude. Morico with his burden has reached a spot of safety. What will he do next? They watch in breathless suspense. But Morico does nothing. He only stands immovable as a carved image. Suddenly there is a cry that reaches far above the roar of fire and crash of falling timbers: "*Mon fils! mon garçon!*"[5] and the old man totters and falls backward to earth, still clinging to the lifeless body of his son. All hasten towards him. Hosmer reaches him first. And when he gently lifts the dead Joçint, the father this time makes no hindrance, for he too has gone beyond the knowledge of all earthly happenings.

VII

MELICENT LEAVES
PLACE-DU-BOIS

here had been no witness to the killing of Joçint; but there were few who did not recognize Grégoire's hand in the affair. When met with the accusation, he denied it, or acknowledged it, or evaded the charge with a jest, as he felt for the moment inclined. It was a deed characteristic of any one of the Santien boys, and if not altogether laudable—Joçint having been at the time of the shooting unarmed—yet was it thought in a measure justified by the heinousness of his offense, and beyond dispute, a benefit to the community.

Hosmer reserved the expression of his opinion. The occurrence once over, with the emotions which it had awakened, he was inclined to look at it from one of those philosophic stand-points of his friend Homeyer. Heredity and pathology had to be considered in relation with the slayer's character. He saw in it one of those interesting problems of human existence that are ever turning up for man's contemplation, but hardly for the exercise of man's individual judgment. He was conscious of an inward repulsion which this action of Grégoire's awakened in him,—much the same as a feeling of disgust for an animal whose instinct drives it to the doing of violent deeds,—yet he made no difference in his manner towards him.

Thérèse was deeply distressed over this double tragedy: feeling keenly the unhappy ending of old Morico. But her chief sorrow came from the callousness of Grégoire, whom she could not move even to an avowal of regret. He could not understand that he should receive any thing but praise for

95

having rid the community of so offensive and dangerous a personage as Joçint; and seemed utterly blind to the moral aspect of his deed.

An event at once so exciting and dramatic as this conflagration, with the attendant deaths of Morico and his son, was much discussed amongst the negroes. They were a good deal of one opinion in regard to Joçint having been only properly served in getting "w'at he done ben lookin' fu' dis long time." Grégoire was rather looked upon as a clever instrument in the Lord's service; and the occurrence pointed a moral which they were not likely to forget.

The burning of the mill entailed much work upon Hosmer, to which he turned with a zest—an absorption that for the time excluded everything else.

Melicent had shunned Grégoire since the shooting. She had avoided speaking with him—even looking at him. During the turmoil which closely followed upon the tragic event, this change in the girl had escaped his notice. On the next day he suspected it only. But the third day brought him the terrible conviction. He did not know that she was making preparations to leave for St. Louis, and quite accidentally overheard Hosmer giving an order to one of the unemployed mill hands to call for her baggage on the following morning before train time.

As much as he had expected her departure, and looked painfully forward to it, this certainty—that she was leaving on the morrow and without a word to him—bewildered him. He abandoned at once the work that was occupying him.

"I didn' know Miss Melicent was goin' away to-morrow," he said in a strange pleading voice to Hosmer.

"Why, yes," Hosmer answered, "I thought you knew. She's been talking about it for a couple of days."

"No, I didn' know nothin' 'tall 'bout it," he said, turning away and reaching for his hat, but with such nerveless hand that he almost dropped it before placing it on his head.

"If you're going to the house," Hosmer called after him, "tell Melicent that Woodson won't go for her trunks before morning. She thought she'd need to have them ready to-night."

"Yes, if I go to the house. I don' know if I'm goin' to the house or not," he replied, walking listlessly away.

Hosmer looked after the young man, and thought of him for a moment: of his soft voice and gentle manner—perplexed that he should be the same who had expressed in confidence the single regret that he had not been able to kill Joçint more than once.

Grégoire went directly to the house, and approached that end of the veranda on which Melicent's room opened. A trunk had already been packed and fastened and stood outside, just beneath the low-silled window that was open. Within the room, and also beneath the window, was another trunk, before which Melicent kneeled, filling it more or less systematically from an abundance of woman's toggery that lay in a cumbrous heap on the floor beside her. Grégoire stopped at the window to tell her, with a sad attempt at indifference:

"Yo' brotha says don't hurry packin'; Woodson ain't goin' to come fur your trunks tell mornin'."

"All right, thank you," glancing towards him for an instant carelessly and going on with her work.

"I didn' know you was goin' away."

"That's absurd: you knew all along I was going away," she returned, with countenance as expressionless as feminine subtlety could make it.

"W'y don't you let somebody else do that? Can't you come out yere a w'ile?"

"No, I prefer doing it myself; and I don't care to go out."

What could he do? what could he say? There were no convenient depths in his mind from which he might draw at will, apt and telling speeches to taunt her with. His heart was swelling and choking him, at sight of the eyes that looked anywhere, but in his own; at sight of the lips that he had one time kissed, pressed into an icy silence. She went on with her task of packing, unmoved. He stood a while longer, silently watching her, his hat in his hands that were clasped behind him, and a stupor of grief holding him vise-like. Then he walked away. He felt somewhat as he remembered to have felt oftentimes as a boy, when ill and suffering, his mother would put him to bed and send him a cup of bouillon perhaps, and a little negro to sit beside him. It seemed very cruel to him now that some one should not do something for him—that he should be left to suffer this way. He walked across the lawn over to the cottage, where he saw Fanny pacing slowly up and down the porch.

She saw him approach and stood in a patch of sunlight to wait for him. He really had nothing to say to her as he stood grasping two of the balustrades and looking up at her. He wanted somebody to talk to him about Melicent.

"Did you know Miss Melicent was goin' away?"

Had it been Hosmer or Thérèse asking her the question she would have replied simply "yes," but to Grégoire she said "yes; thank Goodness," as frankly as though she had been speaking to Belle Worthington. "I don't see what's kept her down here all this time, anyway."

"You don't like her?" he asked, stupefied at the strange possibility of any one not loving Melicent to distraction.

"No. You wouldn't either, if you knew her as well as I do. If she likes a person she goes on like a lunatic over them as long as it lasts; then good-bye John! she'll throw them aside as she would an old dress."

"Oh, I believe she thinks a heap of Aunt Thérèse."

"All right; you'll see how much she thinks of Aunt Thérèse. And the people she's been engaged to! There ain't a worse flirt in the city of St. Louis; and always some excuse or other to break it off at the last minute. I haven't got any use for her, Lord knows. There ain't much love lost between us."

"Well, I reckon she knows they ain't anybody born, good enough fur her?" he said, thinking of those engagements that she had shattered.

"What was David doing?" Fanny asked abruptly.

"Writin' lettas at the sto'."

"Did he say when he was coming?"

"No."

"Do you guess he'll come pretty soon?"

"No, I reckon not fur a good w'ile."

"Is Melicent with Mrs Laferm?"

"No; she's packin' her things."

"I guess I'll go sit with Mrs. Laferm, d'you think she'll mind?"

"No, she'll be glad to have you."

Fanny crossed over to go join Thérèse. She liked to be with her when there was no danger of interruption from Melicent, and Grégoire went wandering aimlessly about the plantation.

He staked great hopes on what the night might bring for him. She would melt, perhaps, to the extent of a smile or one of her old glances. He was almost cheerful when he seated himself at table; only he and his aunt and Melicent. He had never seen her look so handsome as now, in a woolen gown that she had not worn before, of warm rich tint, that brought out a certain regal splendor that he had not suspected in her. A something that she seemed to have held in reserve till this final moment. But she had nothing for him—nothing. All her conversation was addressed to Thérèse; and she hurried away from table at the close of the meal, under pretext of completing her arrangements for departure.

"Doesn't she mean to speak to me?" he asked fiercely of Thérèse.

"Oh, Grégoire, I see so much trouble around me; so many sad mistakes, and I feel so powerless to right them; as if my hands were tied. I can't help you in this: not now. But let me help you in other ways. Will you listen to me?"

"If you want to help me, Aunt," he said stabbing his fork into a piece of bread before him, "go and ask her if she doesn't mean to talk to me: if she won't come out on the gallery a minute."

"Grégoire wants to know if you won't go out and speak to him a moment, Melicent," said Thérèse entering the girl's room. "Do as you wish, of course. But remember you are going away to-morrow; you'll likely never see him again. A friendly word from you now may do more good than you imagine. I believe he's as unhappy at this moment as a creature can be!"

Melicent looked at her horrified. "I don't understand you at all, Mrs. Lafirme. Think what he's done; murdered a defenseless man! How can you have him near you—seated at your table? I don't know what nerves you have in your bodies, you and David. There's David, hobnobbing with him. Even that Fanny talking to him as if he were blameless. Never! If he were dying I wouldn't go near him."

"Haven't you a spark of humanity in you?" asked Thérèse, flushing violently.

"Oh, this is something physical," she replied, shivering, "let me alone."

Thérèse went out to Grégoire, who stood waiting on the veranda. She only took his hand and pressed it telling him good-night, and he knew that it was a dismissal.

There may be lovers, who, under the circumstances, would have felt sufficient pride to refrain from going to the depôt on the following morning, but Grégoire was not one of them. He was there. He who only a week before had thought that nothing but her constant presence could reconcile him with life, had narrowed down the conditions of his life's happiness now to a glance or a kind word. He stood close to the steps of the Pullman car that she was about to enter, and as she passed him he held out his hand, saying "Good-bye." But he held his hand to no purpose. She was much occupied in taking her valise from the conductor who had hoisted her up, and who was now shouting in stentorian tones, "All aboard," though there was not a soul with the slightest intention of boarding the train but herself.

She leaned forward to wave good-bye to Hosmer, and Fanny, and Thérèse, who were on the platform; then she was gone.

Grégoire stood looking stupidly at the vanishing train.

"Are you going back with us?" Hosmer asked him. Fanny and Thérèse had walked ahead.

"No," he replied, looking at Hosmer with ashen face, "I got to go fine my hoss."

VIII

With Loose Rein

"De Lord be praised fu' de blessin's dat he showers down 'pon us," was Uncle Hiram's graceful conclusion of his supper, after which he pushed his empty plate aside regretfully, and addressed Aunt Belindy. "'Pears to me, Belindy, as you reached a pint wid dem bacon an' greens to-night, dat you never tetched befo'. De pint o' de flavorin' is w'at I alludes to."

"All de same, dat ain't gwine to fetch no mo'," was the rather uncivil reply to this neat compliment to her culinary powers.

"Dah!" cried the youthful Betsy, who formed one of the trio gathered together in the kitchen at Place-du-Bois. "Jis listen (to) Unc' Hiurm! Aunt B'lindy neva tetched a han' to dem bacon an' greens. She tole me out o' her own mouf to put 'em on de fiar; she warn't gwine pesta wid 'em."

"Warn't gwine pesta wid 'em?" administering a cuff on the ear of the too communicative Betsy, that sent her sprawling across the table. "T'inks I'se gwine pesta wid you—does you? Messin' roun' heah in de kitchin' an' ain't tu'ned down a bed or drawed a bah, or done a lick o' yo' night wurk yit."

"I is done my night wurk, too," returned Betsy whimpering but defiantly, as she retreated beyond reach of further blows from Aunt Belindy's powerful right hand.

"Dat harshness o' yourn, Belindy, is wat's a sourin' yo' tempa, an' a turnin' of it intur gall an' wormwood. Does you know wat de Scripture tells us of de wrathful woman?"

"Whar I got time to go a foolin' wid Scripture? W'at I wants to know; whar dat Pierson boy, he don't come. He ben gone time 'nough to walk to Natch'toches an' back."

"Ain't dat him I years yonda tu de crib?" suggested Betsy, coming to join Aunt Belindy in the open doorway.

"You heahs mos' too much fu' yo' own good, you does, gal."

But Betsy was right. For soon a tall, slim negro, young and coal black, mounted the stairs and came into the kitchen, where he deposited a meal bag filled with various necessities that he had brought from Centreville. He was one of the dancers who had displayed their skill before Melicent and Grégoire. Uncle Hiram at once accosted him.

"Well, Pierson, we jest a ben a wonderin' consarnin' you. W'at was de 'casion o' dat long delay?"

"De 'casion? W'y man alive, I couldn't git a dog gone soul in de town to wait on me."

"Dat boy kin lie, yas," said Aunt Belindy, "God A'mighty knows ever time I ben to Centaville dem sto' keepas ain't done a blessed t'ing but settin' down."

"Settin' down—Lord! dey warn't settin' down to-day; you heah me."

"W'at dey doin' ef day ain't settin' down, Unc' Pierson?" asked Betsy with amiable curiosity.

"You jis drap dat 'uncle,' you," turning wrathfully upon the girl, "sence w'en you start dat new trick?"

"Lef de chile 'lone, Pierson, lef 'er alone. Come heah, Betsy, an' set by yo' Uncle Hiurm."

From the encouraging nearness of Uncle Hiram, she ventured to ask "w'at you 'low dey doin' ef dey ain't settin' down?" this time without adding the offensive title.

"Dey flyin' 'roun', Lord! dey hidin' dey sef! dey gittin' out o' de way, I tell you. Grégor jis ben a raisin' ole Cain in Centaville."

"I know'd it; could a' tole you dat mese'f. My Lan'! but dats a piece, dat Grégor," Aunt Belindy enunciated between paroxysms of laughter, seating herself with her fat arms resting on her knees, and her whole bearing announcing pleased anticipation.

"Dat boy neva did have no car' fur de salvation o' his soul," groaned Uncle Hiram.

"W'at he ben a doin' yonda?" demanded Aunt Belindy impatiently.

"Well," said Pierson, assuming a declamatory air and position in the middle of the large kitchen, "he lef' heah—what time he lef heah, Aunt B'lindy?"

"He done lef' fo' dinna, 'caze I seed 'im a lopin' to'ads de riva, time I flung dat Sampson boy out o' de doo', bringin' dem greens in heah 'dou't washin' of 'em."

"Dat's so; it war good dinna time w'en he come a lopin' in town. Dat hoss look like he ben swimmin' in Cane Riva, he done ride him so hard. He fling he se'f down front o' Grammont's sto' an' he come a stompin' in, look like gwine hu't somebody. Ole Grammont tell him, 'How you come on, Grégor? Come ova tu de house an' eat dinna wid us: de ladies be pleas tu see you.'"

"Humph," muttered Aunt Belindy, "dem Grammont gals be glad to see any t'ing dat got breeches on; lef 'lone good lookin' piece like dat Grégor."

"Grégor, he neva sey, 'Tank you dog,' jis fling he big dolla down on de counta an' 'low 'don't want no dinna: gimme some w'iskey.'"

"Yas, yas, Lord," from Aunt Belindy.

"Ole Grammont, he push de bottle to'ads 'im, an' I 'clar to Goodness ef he didn' mos fill dat tumbla to de brim, an' drink it down, neva blink a eye. Den he tu'n an treat ev'y las' w'ite man stan'in' roun'; dat ole kiarpenta man; de blacksmif; Marse Verdon. He keep on a treatin'; Grammont, he keep a handin' out de w'iskey; Grégor he keep on a drinkin' an a treatin'—Grammont, he keep a handin' out; don't make no odds tu him s'long uz dat bring de money in de draw. I ben a stan'in' out on de gallery, me, a peekin' in. An' Grégor, he cuss and swar an' he kiarry on, and 'low he want play game poka. Den dey all goes a trompin' in de back room an' sets down roun' de table, and I comes a creepin' in, me, whar I kin look frough de doo', and dar dey sets an' plays and Grégor, he drinks w'iskey an' he wins de money. An' arta w'ile Marse Verdon, he little eyes blinkin', he 'low, 'y'all had a shootin' down tu Place-du-Bois, *hein* Grégor?' Grégor, he neva say nuttin': he jis' draw he pistol slow out o' he pocket an' lay it down on de table; an' he look squar in Marse Verdon eyes. Man! ef you eva seed some pussun tu'n' w'ite!"

"Reckon dat heifa 'Milky' look black side li'le Verdon dat time," chuckled Aunt Belindy.

"Jis' uz wi'te uz Unc' Hiurm's shurt an' a trimblin', an' neva say no mo' 'bout shootin'. Den old Grammont, he keine o' hang back an' say, 'You git de jestice de peace, 'hine you, kiarrin' conceal' weepons dat a-way, Grégor.'"

"Dat ole Grammont, he got to git he gab in ef he gwine die fu' it," interrupted Aunt Belindy.

"Grégor say—'I don't 'lows to kiarr no conceal' weepons,' an he draw nudda pistol slow out o' he udda pocket an' lay et on de table. By dat time he gittin' all de money, he crammin' de money in he pocket; an' dem fellas dey gits up one arta d'udda kine o' shy-like, an' sneaks out. Den Grégor, he git up an come out o' de room, he coat 'crost he arm, an' de pistols a stickin' out an him lookin' sassy till ev'y body make way, same ef he ben Jay Goul'.[1] Ef he look one o' 'em in de eye dey outs wid, 'Howdy, Grégor—how you come on, Grégor?' jis' uz pelite uz a peacock, an' him neva take no trouble to yansa 'em. He jis' holla out fu' somebody bring dat hoss tu de steps, an' him stan'in' 's big uz life, waitin'. I gits tu de hoss fus', me, an' leads 'im up, an' he gits top dat hoss stidy like he ain't tetch a drap, an' he fling me big dolla."

"Whar de dolla, Mista Pierson?" enquired Betsy.

"De dolla in my pocket, an' et gwine stay dah. Didn't ax you fu' no, 'Mista Pierson.' Whar yu' all tink he went on dat hoss?"

"How you reckon we knows whar he wint; we wasn't dah," replied Aunt Belindy.

"He jis' went a lopin' twenty yards down to Chartrand's sto'. I goes on 'hine 'im see w'at he gwine do. Dah he git down f'um de hoss an' go a stompin' in de sto'—eve'ybody stan'in' back jis' same like fu' Jay Goul', an' he fling bill down on de counta an' 'low, "Fill me up a bottle, Chartrand, I'se gwine travelin'.' Den he 'lows, 'You treats eve'y las' man roun' heah at my 'spence, black an' w'ite—nuttin' fu' me,' an' he fole he arms an' lean back on de counta, jis' so. Chartrand, he look skeerd, he say 'François gwine wait on you.' But Grégor, he 'low he don't wants no rusty skileton a waitin' on him w'en he treat, 'Wait on de gemmen yo'se'f—step up gemmen.' Chartrand 'low, 'Damn ef nigga gwine drink wid w'ite man in dat sto',' all same he kein git 'hine box tu say dat."

"Lord, Lord, de ways o' de transgressor!" groaned Uncle Hiram.

"You want to see dem niggas sneaking 'way," resumed Pierson, "dey knows Grégor gwine fo'ce 'em drink; dey knows Chartrand gwine make it hot fu' 'em art'ards ef dey does. Grégor he spie me jis' I'se tryin' glide frough de doo' an he call out, 'Yonda a gemmen f'um Place-du-Bois; Pierson, come heah; you'se good 'nough tu drink wid any w'ite man, 'cept me; you come heah, take drink wid Mr. Louis Chartrand.'

"I 'lows don't wants no drink, much 'bleege, Marse Grégor'. 'Yis, you wants drink,' an' 'id dat he draws he pistol. 'Mista Chartrand want drink, too. I done owe Mista Chartrand somethin' dis long time; I'se gwine pay 'im wid a treat,' he say. Chartrand look like he on fiar, he so red, he so mad, he swell up same like ole bull frog."

"Dat make no odd," chuckled Aunt Belindy, "he gwine drink wid nigga ef Grégor say so."

"Yes, he drink, Lord, only he cuss me slow, an' 'low he gwine break my skull."

"Lordy! I knows you was jis' a trimblin', Mista Pierson."

"Warn't trimblin' no mo' 'en I'se trimblin' dis minute, an' you drap dat 'Mista.' Den w'at you reckon? Yonda come Père Antoine; he come an' stan' in de doo' an' he hole up he han'; look like he ain't 'feard no body an' he 'low: 'Grégor Sanchun, how is you dar' come in dis heah peaceful town frowin' of it into disorda an' confusion? Ef you isn't 'feard o' man; hasn't you got no fear o' God A'mighty wat punishes?'"

"Grégor, he look at 'im an' he say cool like, 'Howdy, Père Antoine; how you come on?' He got he pistol w'at he draw fu' make Chartrand drink wid dis heah nigga,—he foolin' wid it an' rubbin' it up and down he pants, an' he 'low 'Dis a gemmen w'at fit to drink wid a Sanchun—w'at'll you have?' But Père Antoine, he go on makin' a su'mon same like he make in chu'ch, an' Grégor, he lean he two arm back on de counta—kine o' smilin' like, an' he say, 'Chartrand, whar dat bottle I orda you put up?' Chartrand bring de bottle; Grégor, he put de bottle in he coat pocket wat hang on he arm—car'ful.

"Père Antoine, he go on preachin', he say, 'I tell you dis young man, you 'se on de big road w'at leads tu hell.'

"Den Grégor straight he se'f up an' walk close to Père Antoine an' he say, 'Hell an' damnation dar ain't no sich a place. I reckon she know; w'at you know side o' her. She say dar ain't no hell, an' ef you an' de Archbishop an' de Angel Gabriel come along an' 'low dey a hell, you all liars,' an' he say, 'Make way dah, I'se a gittin' out o' heah; dis ain't no town fittin' to hol' a Sanchun. Make way ef you don't wants to go to Kingdom come fo' yo' time.'

"Well, I 'lows dey did make way. Only Père Antoine, he look mighty sorry an' down cas'.

"Grégor go out dat sto' taking plenty room, an' walkin' car'ful like, an' he swing he se'f on de hoss; den he lean down mos' flat an' stick he spurs in dat hoss an' he go tar'in' like de win' down street, out o' de town, a firin' he pistol up in de ar."

Uncle Hiram had listened to the foregoing recital with troubled countenance, and with many a protesting groan. He now shook his old white head, and heaved a deep sigh. "All dat gwine come hard an' heavy on de madam. She don't desarve it—God knows, she don't desarve it."

"How you, ole like you is, kin look fu' somethin' diffunt, Unc' Hiurm?" observed Aunt Belindy philosophically. "Don't you know Grégor gwine be Grégor tell he die? Dat's all dar is 'bout it."

Betsy arose with the sudden recollection that she had let the time pass for bringing in Miss Thérèse's hot water, and Pierson went to the stove to see what Aunt Belindy had reserved for him in the shape of supper.

IX

The Reason Why

Sampson, the young colored boy who had lighted Fanny's fire on the first day of her arrival at Place-du-Bois, and who had made such insinuating advances of friendliness towards her, had continued to attract her notice and good will. He it was who lighted her fires on such mornings as they were needed. For there had been no winter. In mid-January, the grass was fresh and green; trees and plants were putting forth tender shoots, as if in welcome to spring; roses were blossoming, and it was a veritable atmosphere of Havana rather than of central Louisiana that the dwellers at Place-du-Bois were enjoying. But finally winter made tardy assertion of its rights. One morning broke raw and black with an icy rain falling, and young Sampson arriving in the early bleakness to attend to his duties at the cottage, presented a picture of human distress to move the most hardened to pity. Though dressed comfortably in the clothing with which Fanny had appareled him—he was ashen. Save for the chattering of his teeth, his body seemed possessed of a paralytic inability to move. He knelt before the empty fire-place as he had done on that first day, and with deep sighs and groans went about his work. Then he remained long before the warmth that he had kindled; even lying full length upon the soft rug, to bask in the generous heat that permeated and seemed to thaw his stiffened limbs.

Next, he went quietly into the bedroom to attend to the fire there. Hosmer and Fanny were still sleeping. He approached a decorated basket that hung against the wall; a receptacle for old newspapers and odds and ends. He drew something from his rather capacious coat pocket, and, satisfying himself that Hosmer slept, thrust it in the bottom of the basket, well covered by the nondescript accumulation that was there.

The house was very warm and cheerful when they arose, and after breakfasting Hosmer felt unusually reluctant to quit his fire-side and face the inclement day; for an unaccustomed fatigue hung upon his limbs and his body was sore, as from the effect of bruises. But he went, nevertheless, well incased in protective rubber; and as he turned away from the house, Fanny hastened to the hanging basket, and fumbling nervously in its depths, found what the complaisant[1] Sampson had left for her.

The cold rain had gradually changed into a fine mist, that in descending, spread an icy coat upon every object that it touched. When Hosmer returned at noon, he did not leave the house again.

During the afternoon Thérèse knocked at Fanny's door. She was enveloped in a long hooded cloak, her face glowing from contact with the sharp moist air, and myriad crystal drops clinging to her fluffy blonde hair that looked very golden under the dark hood that covered it. She wanted to learn how Fanny accepted this unpleasant change of atmospheric conditions, intending to bear her company for the remainder of the day if she found her depressed, as was often the case.

"Why, I didn't know you were home," she said, a little startled, to Hosmer who opened the door to her. "I came over to show Mrs. Hosmer something pretty that I don't suppose she ever saw before." It was a branch from a rose-tree, bearing two open blossoms and a multitude of buds, creamy pink, all encased in an icy transparency that gleamed like diamonds. "Isn't it exquisite?" she said, holding the spray up for Fanny's admiration. But she saw at a glance that the spirit of Disorder had descended and settled upon the Hosmer household.

The usually neat room was in a sad state of confusion. Some of the pictures had been taken from the walls, and were leaning here and there against chairs and tables. The mantel[2] ornaments had been removed and deposited at random and in groups about the room. On the hearth was a pail of water in which swam a huge sponge; and Fanny sat beside the center-table that was piled with her husband's wearing apparel, holding in her lap a coat which she had evidently been passing under inspection. Her hair had escaped from its fastenings; her collar was hooked away; her face was flushed and her whole bearing indicated her condition.

Hosmer took the frozen spray from Thérèse's hand, and spoke a little about the beauty of the trees, especially the young cedars that he had passed out in the hills on his way home.

"It's all well and good to talk about flowers and things, Mrs. Laferm—sit down please—but when a person's got the job that I've got on my hands, she's something else to think about. And David here smoking one cigar after another. He knows all I've got to do, and goes and sends those darkies home right after dinner."

Thérèse was so shocked that for a while she could say nothing; till for Hosmer's sake she made a quick effort to appear at ease.

"What have you do to, Mrs. Hosmer? Let me help you, I can give you the whole afternoon," she said with an appearance of being ready for any thing that was at hand to be done.

Fanny turned the coat over in her lap, and looked down helplessly at a stain on the collar, that she had been endeavoring to remove; at the same time pushing aside with patient repetition the wisp of hair that kept falling over her cheek.

"Belle Worthington'll be here before we know it; her and her husband and that Lucilla of hers. David knows how Belle Worthington is, just as well as I do; there's no use saying he don't. If she was to see a speck of dirt in this house or on David's clothes, or anything, why we'd never hear the last of it. I got a letter from her," she continued, letting the coat fall to the floor, whilst she endeavored to find her pocket.

"Is she coming to visit you?" asked Thérèse who had taken up a feather brush, and was dusting and replacing the various ornaments that were scattered through the room.

"She's going down to Muddy Graw (Mardi-Gras) her and her husband and Lucilla and she's going to stop here a while. I had that letter—I guess I must of left it in the other room."

"Never mind," Thérèse hastened to say, seeing that her whole energies were centered on finding the letter.

"Let me look," said Hosmer, making a movement towards the bedroom door, but Fanny had arisen and holding out a hand to detain him she went into the room herself, saying she knew where she'd left it.

"Is this the reason you've kept yourself shut up here in the house so often?" Thérèse asked of Hosmer, drawing near him. "Never telling me a word of it," she went on, "It wasn't right; it wasn't kind."

"Why should I have put any extra burden on you?" he answered, looking down at her, and feeling a joy in her presence there, that seemed like a guilty indulgence in face of his domestic shame.

"Don't stay," Thérèse said. "Leave me here. Go to your office or over to the house—leave me alone with her."

Fanny returned, having found the letter, and spoke with increased vehemence of the necessity of having the house in perfect trim against the arrival of

Belle Worthington, from whom they would never hear the last, and so forth.

"Well, your husband is going out, and that will give us a chance to get things righted," said Thérèse encouragingly. "You know men are always in the way at such times."

"It's what he ought to done before; and left Suze and Minervy here," she replied with grudging acquiescence.

After repeated visits to the bedroom, under various pretexts, Fanny grew utterly incapable to do more than sit and gaze stupidly at Thérèse, who busied herself in bringing the confusion of the sitting-room into some order.

She continued to talk disjointedly of Belle Worthington and her well known tyrannical characteristics in regard to cleanliness; finishing by weeping mildly at the prospect of her own inability to ever reach the high standard required by her exacting friend.

It was far in the afternoon—verging upon night, when Thérèse succeeded in persuading her that she was ill and should go to bed. She gladly seized upon the suggestion of illness; assuring Thérèse that she alone had guessed her affliction: that whatever was thought singular in her behavior must be explained by that sickness which was past being guessed at—then she went to bed.

It was late when Hosmer left his office; a rough temporary shanty, put together near the ruined mill.

He started out slowly on his long cold ride. His physical malaise of the morning had augmented as the day went on, and he was beginning to admit to himself that he was "in for it."

But the cheerless ride was lightened by a picture that had been with him through the afternoon, and that moved him in his whole being, as the moment approached when it might be changed to reality. He knew Fanny's habits; knew that she would be sleeping now. Thérèse would not leave her there alone in the house—of that he was sure. And he pictured Thérèse at this moment seated at his fire-side. He would find her there when he entered. His heart beat tumultuously at the thought. It was a very weak moment with him, possibly, one in which his unnerved condition stood for some account. But he felt that when he saw here there, waiting for him, he would cast himself at her feet and kiss them. He would crush her white hands against his bosom. He would bury his face in her silken hair. She should know how strong his love was, and he would hold her in his arms till she yield back tenderness to his own. But— Thérèse met him on the steps. As he was mounting them, she was descending; wrapped in her long cloak, her pretty head covered by the dark hood.

"Oh, are you going?" he asked.

She heard the note of entreaty in his voice.

"Yes," she answered, "I shouldn't have left her before you came; but I knew you were here; I heard your horse's tread a moment ago. She's asleep. Good night. Take courage and have a brave heart," she said, pressing his hand a moment in both hers, and was gone.

The room was as he had pictured it: order restored and the fire blazing brightly. On the table was a pot of hot tea and a tempting little supper laid. But he pushed it all aside and buried his face down upon the table into his folded arms, groaning aloud. Physical suffering; thwarted love, and at the same time a feeling of self-condemnation, made him wish that life were ended for him.

Fanny awoke close upon morning, not knowing what had aroused her. She was for a little while all bewildered and unable to collect herself. She soon learned the cause of her disturbance. Hosmer was tossing about and his outstretched arm lay across her face, where it had evidently been flung with some violence. She took his hand to move it away, and it burned her like a coal of fire. As she touched him he started and began to talk incoherently. He evidently fancied himself dictating a letter to some insurance company, in no pleased terms—of which Fanny caught but snatches. Then:

"That's too much, Mrs. Lafirme; too much—too much—Don't let Grégoire burn—take him from the fire, some one. Thirty day's credit—shipment made on tenth," he rambled on at intervals in his troubled sleep.

Fanny trembled with apprehension as she heard him. Surely he has brain fever[3] she thought, and she laid her hand gently on his burning forehead. He covered it with his own, muttering "Thérèse, Thérèse—so good—let me love you."

X

Perplexing Things

"Lucilla!"

The pale, drooping girl started guiltily at her mother's sharp exclamation, and made an effort to throw back her shoulders. Then she bit her nails nervously, but soon desisted, remembering that that also, as well as yielding to a relaxed tendency of the spinal column, was a forbidden indulgence.

"Put on your hat and go on out and get a breath of fresh air; you're as white as milk-man's cream."[1]

Lucilla rose and obeyed her mother's order with the precision of a soldier, following the directions of his commander.

"How submissive and gentle your daughter is," remarked Thérèse.

"Well, she's got to be, and she knows it. Why, I haven't got to do more than look at that girl most times for her to understand what I want. You didn't notice, did you, how she straightened up when I called 'Lucilla' to her? She knows by the tone of my voice what she's got to do."

"Most mothers can't boast of having such power over their daughters."

"Well, I'm not the woman to stand any shenanigans from a child of mine. I could name you dead loads of women that are just completely walked over by their children. It's a blessing that boy of Fanny's died, between you and I; its what I've always said. Why, Mrs. Laferm, she couldn't any more look after a youngster than she could after a baby elephant. By the by, what do you guess is the matter with her, any way?"

"How, the matter?" Thérèse asked; the too ready blood flushing her face and neck as she laid down her work and looked up at Mrs. Worthington.

"Why, she's acting mighty queer, that's all I can say for her."

110

"I haven't been able to see her for some time," Thérèse returned, going back to her sewing, "but I suppose she got a little upset and nervous over her husband; he had a few days of very serious illness before you came."

"Oh, I've seen her in all sorts of states and conditions, and I've never seen her like that before. Why, she does nothing in the God's world but whine and sniffle, and wish she was dead; it's enough to give a person the horrors. She can't make out she's sick; I never saw her look better in my life. She must of gained ten pounds since she come down here."

"Yes," said Thérèse, "She was looking so well, and—and I thought everything was going well with her too, but—" and she hesitated to go on.

"Oh, I know what you want to say. You can't help that. No use bothering your brains about that—now you just take my advice," exclaimed Mrs. Worthington brusquely.

Then she laughed so loud and suddenly that Thérèse, being already nervous, pricked her finger with her needle till the blood came; a mishap which decided her to lay aside her work.

"If you never saw a fish out of water, Mrs. Laferm, do take a peep at Mr. Worthington astride that horse; it's enough to make a cat expire!"

Mrs. Worthington was on the whole rather inclined to take her husband seriously. As often as he might excite her disapproval, it was seldom that he aroused her mirth. So it may be gathered that his appearance in this unfamiliar rôle of horseman was of the most mirth-provoking.

He and Hosmer were dismounting at the cottage, which decided Mrs. Worthington to go and look after them; Fanny for the time being—in her opinion—not having "the gumption to look after a sick kitten."

"This is what I call solid comfort," she said looking around the well appointed sitting-room, before quitting it.

"You ought to be a mighty happy woman, Mrs. Laferm; only I'd think you'd die of lonesomeness, sometimes."

Thérèse laughed, and told her not to forget that she expected them all over in the evening.

"You can depend on me; and I'll do my best to drag Fanny over; so-long."

When left alone, Thérèse at once relapsed into the gloomy train of reflections that had occupied her since the day she had seen with her bodily eyes something of the wretched life that she had brought upon the man she loved. And yet that wretchedness in its refinement of cruelty and immorality she could not guess and was never to know. Still, she had seen enough to cause her to ask herself with a shudder "was I right—was I right?"

She had always thought this lesson of right and wrong a very plain one. So easy of interpretation that the simplest minded might solve it if they would. And here had come for the first time in her life a staggering doubt as to its nature. She did not suspect that she was submitting one of those knotty problems to her unpracticed judgment that philosophers and theologians delight in disagreeing upon, and her inability to unravel it staggered her. She tried to convince herself that a very insistent sting of remorse which she felt came from selfishness—from the pain that her own heart suffered in the knowledge of Hosmer's unhappiness. She was not callous enough to quiet her soul with the balm of having intended the best. She continued to ask herself only "was I right?" and it was by the answer to that question that she would abide, whether in the stony content of accomplished righteousness, or in an enduring remorse that pointed to a goal in whose labyrinthine possibilities her soul lost itself and fainted away.

Lucilla went out to get a breath of fresh air as her mother had commanded, but she did not go far to seek it. Not further than the end of the back veranda, where she stood for some time motionless, before beginning to occupy herself in a way which Aunt Belindy, who was watching her from the kitchen window, considered highly problematical. The negress was wiping a dish and giving it a fine polish in her absence of mind. When her curiosity could no longer contain itself she called out:

"W'ats dat you'se doin' dah, you li'le gal? Come heah an' le' me see."

Lucilla turned with the startled look which seemed to be usual with her when addressed.

"Le' me see," repeated Aunt Belindy pleasantly.

Lucilla approached the window and handed the woman a small square of stiff writing paper which was stuck with myriad tiny pin-holes; some of which she had been making when interrupted by Aunt Belindy.

"W'at in God A'Mighty's name you call dat 'ar?" the darkey asked examining the paper critically, as though expecting the riddle would solve itself before her eyes.

"Those are my acts I've been counting," the girl replied a little gingerly.

"Yo' ax? I don' see nuttin' 'cep' a piece o' papah plum fill up wid holse. W'at you call ax?"

"Acts—acts. Don't you know what acts are?"

"How you want me know? I neva ben to no school whar you larn all dat."

"Why, an act is something you do that you don't want to do—or something you don't want to do, that you do—I mean that you don't do. Or if you want to eat something and don't. Or an aspiration; that's an act, too."

"Go long! W'ats dat—asp'ration?"

"Why, to say any kind of little prayer; or if you invoke our Lord, or our Blessed Lady, or one of the saints, that's an aspiration. You can make them just as quick as you can think—you can make hundreds and hundreds in a day."

"My Lan'! Dat's w'at you'se studyin' 'bout w'en you'se steppin' 'roun' heah like a droopy pullet? An' I t'ought you was studyin' 'bout dat beau you lef' yonda to Sent Lous."

"You mustn't say such things to me; I'm going to be a religious."

"How dat gwine henda you have a beau ef you'se religious?"

"The religious never get married," turning very red, "and don't live in the world like others."

"Look heah, chile, you t'inks I'se fool? Religion—no religion, whar you gwine live ef you don' live in de worl'? Gwine live up in de moon?"

"You're a very ignorant person," replied Lucilla, highly offended. "A religious devotes her life to God, and lives in the convent."

"Den w'y you neva said 'convent'? I knows all 'bout convent. W'at you gwine do wid dem ax w'en de papah done all fill up?" handing the singular tablet back to her.

"Oh," replied Lucilla, "when I have thousands and thousands I gain twenty-five years' indulgence."

"Is dat so?"

"Yes," said the girl; and divining that Aunt Belindy had not understood, "twenty-five years that I don't have to go to purgatory. You see most people have to spend years and years in purgatory, before they can get to Heaven."

"How you know dat?"

If Aunt Belindy had asked Lucilla how she knew that the sun shone, she could not have answered with more assurance "because I know" as she turned and walked rather scornfully away.

"W'at dat kine o' fool talk dey larns gals up yonda tu Sent Lous? An' huh ma a putty woman; yas, bless me; all dress up fittin' to kill. Don' 'pear like she studyin' 'bout ax."

XI

A Social Evening

r. and Mrs. Joseph Duplan with their little daughter Ninette, who had been invited to Place-du-Bois for supper, as well as for the evening, were seated with Thérèse in the parlor, awaiting the arrival of the cottage guests. They had left their rather distant plantation, Les Chênières, early in the afternoon, wishing as usual to make the most of these visits, which, though infrequent, were always so much enjoyed.

The room was somewhat altered since that summer day when Thérèse had sat in its cool shadows, hearing the story of David Hosmer's life. Only with such difference, however, as the change of season called for; imparting to it a rich warmth that invited to sociability and friendly confidences. In the depths of the great chimney glowed with a steady and dignified heat, the huge back-log, whose disposal Uncle Hiram had superintended in person; and the leaping flames from the dry hickories that surrounded it, lent a very genial light to the grim-visaged Lafirmes who looked down from their elevation on the interesting group gathered about the hearth.

Conversation had never once flagged with these good friends; for, aside from much neighborhood gossip to be told and listened to, there was the always fertile topic of "crops" to be discussed in all its bearings, that touched, in its local and restricted sense, the labor question, cultivation, freight rates, and the city merchant.

With Mrs. Duplan there was a good deal to be said about the unusual mortality among "Plymouth-Rocks"[1] owing to an alarming prevalence of "pip,"[2] which malady, however, that lady found to be gradually yielding to a heroic treatment introduced into her *basse-cour*[3] by one Coulon, a piney wood sage of some repute as a mystic healer.

This was a delicate refined little woman, somewhat old-fashioned and stranded in her incapability to keep pace with the modern conduct of life; but giving her views with a pretty self-confidence, that showed her a ruler in her peculiar realm.

The young Ninette had extended herself in an easy chair, in an attitude of graceful abandonment, the earnest brown eyes looking eagerly out from under a tangle of auburn hair, and resting with absorbed admiration upon her father, whose words and movements she followed with unflagging attentiveness. The fastidious little miss was clad in a dainty gown that reached scarcely below the knees; revealing the shapely limbs that were crossed and extended to let the well shod feet rest upon the polished brass fender.

Thérèse had given what information lay within her range concerning the company which was expected. But her confidences had plainly been insufficient to prepare Mrs. Duplan for the startling effect produced by Mrs. Worthington on that little woman in her black silk of a by-gone fashion; so splendid was Mrs. Worthington's erect and imposing figure, so blonde her blonde hair, so bright her striking color and so comprehensive the sweep of her blue and scintillating gown. Yet was Mrs. Worthington not at ease, as might be noticed in the unnatural quaver of her high-pitched voice and the restless motion of her hands, as she seated herself with an arm studiedly resting upon the table near by.

Hosmer had met the Duplans before; on the occasion of a former visit to Place-du-Bois and again at Les Chênières when he had gone to see the planter on business connected with the lumber trade.

Fanny was a stranger to them and promised to remain such; for she acknowledged her presentation with a silent bow and retreated as far from the group as decent concession to sociability would permit.

Thérèse with her pretty Creole tact was not long in bringing these seemingly incongruent elements into some degree of harmony. Mr. Duplan in his courteous and rather lordly way was presently imparting to Mrs. Worthington certain reminiscences of a visit to St. Louis twenty-five years before, when he and Mrs. Duplan had rather hastily traversed that interesting town during their wedding journey. Mr. Duplan's manner had a singular effect upon Mrs. Worthington, who became dignified, subdued, and altogether unnatural in her endeavor to adjust herself to it.

Mr. Worthington seated himself beside Mrs. Duplan and was soon trying to glean information, in his eager short-sighted way, of psychological interest concerning the negro race; such effort rather bewildering that good lady, who could not bring herself to view the negro as an interesting or suitable theme to be introduced into polite conversation.

Hosmer sat and talked good-naturedly to the little girls, endeavoring to dispel the shyness with which they seemed inclined to view each other—and Thérèse crossed the room to join Fanny.

"I hope you're feeling better," she ventured, "you should have let me help you while Mr. Hosmer was ill."

Fanny looked away, biting her lip, the sudden tears coming to her eyes. She answered with unsteady voice, "Oh, I was able to look after my husband myself, Mrs. Laferm."

Thérèse reddened at finding herself so misunderstood. "I meant in your housekeeping, Mrs. Hosmer; I could have relieved you of some of that worry, whilst you were occupied with your husband."

Fanny continued to look unhappy; her features taking on that peculiar downward droop which Thérèse had come to know and mistrust.

"Are you going to New Orleans with Mrs. Worthington?" she asked, "she told me she meant to try and persuade you."

"No; I'm not going. Why?" looking suspiciously in Thérèse's face.

"Well," laughed Thérèse, "only for the sake of asking, I suppose. I thought you'd enjoy Mardi-Gras, never having seen it."

"I'm not going anywheres unless David goes along," she said, with an impertinent ring in her voice, and with a conviction that she was administering a stab and a rebuke. She had come prepared to watch her husband and Mrs. Lafirme, her heart swelling with jealous suspicion as she looked constantly from one to the other, endeavoring to detect signs of an understanding between them. Failing to discover such, and loth[4] to be robbed of her morbid feast of misery, she set her failure down to their pre-determined subtlety. Thérèse was conscious of a change in Fanny's attitude, and felt herself unable to account for it otherwise than by whim, which she knew played a not unimportant rôle in directing the manner of a large majority of women. Moreover, it was not a moment to lose herself in speculation concerning this woman's capricious behavior. Her guests held the first claim upon her attentions. Indeed, here was Mrs. Worthington even now loudly demanding a pack of cards. "Here's a gentleman never heard of six-handed euchre.[5] If you've got a pack of cards, Mrs. Laferm, I guess I can show him quick enough that it can be done."

"Oh, I don't doubt Mrs. Worthington's ability to make any startling and pleasing revelations," rejoined the planter good humoredly, and gallantly following Mrs. Worthington who had risen with the view of putting into immediate effect her scheme of initiating these slow people into the unsuspected possibilities of euchre; a game which, however adaptable in other ways, could certainly not be indulged in by seven persons. After each one proffering, as is usual on such occasions, his readiness to assume the character of on-looker, Mr. Worthington's claim to entire indifference, if not inability—confirmed by his wife—was accepted as the most sincere, and that gentleman was excluded and excused.

He watched them as they seated themselves at table, even lending assistance, in his own awkward way, to range the chairs in place. Then he followed the game for a while, standing behind Fanny to note the outcome of her reckless offer of "five on hearts,"[6] with only three trumps in hand, and every indication of little assistance from her partners, Mr. Duplan and Belle Worthington.

At one end of the room was a long, low, well-filled book-case. Here had been the direction of Mr. Worthington's secret and stolen glances the entire evening. And now towards this point he finally transported himself by gradual movements which he believed appeared unstudied and indifferent. He was confronted by a good deal of French—to him an unfamiliar language. Here a long row of Balzac; then, the Waverley Novels in faded red cloth of very old date. Racine, Molière, Bulwer following in more modern garb; Shakespeare in a compass that promised very small type. His quick trained glance sweeping along the shelves, contracted into a little frown of resentment while he sent his hand impetuously through his scant locks, standing them quite on end.

On the very lowest shelf were five imposing volumes in dignified black and gold, bearing the simple inscription "Lives of the Saints—Rev. A. Butler."[7] Upon one of them, Mr. Worthington seized, opening it at hazard. He had fallen upon the history of St. Monica, mother of the great St. Austin[8]—a woman whose habits it appears had been so closely guarded in her childhood by a pious nurse, that even the quenching of her natural thirst was permitted only within certain well defined bounds. This mentor used to say "you are now for drinking water, but when you come to be mistress of the cellar, water will be despised, but the habit of drinking will stick by you." Highly interesting, Mr. Worthington thought, as he brushed his hair all down again the right way and seated himself the better to learn the fortunes of the good St. Monica, who, curiously enough, notwithstanding those early incentives to temperance, "insensibly contracted an inclination to wine," drinking "whole cups of it with pleasure as it came in her way." A "dangerous intemperance" which it finally pleased Heaven to cure through the instrumentality of a maid servant taunting her mistress with being a "wine bibber."

Mr. Worthington did not stop with the story of Saint Monica. He lost himself in those details of asceticism, martyrdom, superhuman possibilities which man is capable of attaining under peculiar conditions of life—something he had not yet "gone into."

The voices at the card table would certainly have disturbed a man with less power of mind concentration. For Mrs. Worthington in this familiar employment was herself again—*con fuoco*.[9] Here was Mr. Duplan in high spirits; his wife putting forth little gushes of bird-like exaltation as the fascinations of the game revealed themselves to her. Even Hosmer and Thérèse were drawn for the moment from their usual preoccupation. Fanny alone was the ghost of the feast. Her features never relaxed from their settled gloom. She played at hap-hazard, listlessly throwing down the cards or letting them fall from her hands, vaguely asking what were trumps at inopportune moments; showing that inattentiveness so exasperating to an eager player and which oftener than once drew a sharp rebuke from Belle Worthington.

"Don't you wish we could play," said Ninette to her companion from her comfortable perch beside the fire, and looking longingly towards the card table.

"Oh, no," replied Lucilla briefly, gazing into the fire, with hands folded in her lap. Thin hands, showing up very white against the dull colored "convent uniform" that hung in plain, severe folds about her and reached to her very ankles.

"Oh, don't you? I play often at home when company comes. And I play cribbage and *vingt-et-un*[10] with papa and win lots of money from him."

"That's wrong."

"No, it isn't; papa wouldn't do it if it was wrong," she answered decidedly. "Do you go to the convent?" she asked, looking critically at Lucilla and drawing a little nearer, so as to be confidential. "Tell me about it," she continued, when the other had replied affirmatively. "Is it very dreadful? you know they're going to send me soon."

"Oh, it's the best place in the world," corrected Lucilla as eagerly as she could.

"Well, mamma says she was just as happy as could be there, but you see that's so awfully long ago. It must have changed since then."

"The convent never changes: it's always the same. You first go to chapel to mass early in the morning."

"Ugh!" shuddered Ninette.

"Then you have studies," continued Lucilla. "Then breakfast, then recreation, then classes, and there's meditation."

"Oh, well," interrupted Ninette, "I believe anything most would suit you, and momma when she was little; but if I don't like it—see here, if I tell you something will you promise never, never, to tell?"

"Is it any thing wrong?"

"Oh, no, not very; it isn't a real mortal sin. Will you promise?"

"Yes," agreed Lucilla; curiosity getting something the better of her pious scruples.

"Cross your heart?"

Lucilla crossed her heart carefully, though a little reluctantly.

"Hope you may die?"

"Oh!" exclaimed the little convent girl aghast.

"Oh, pshaw," laughed Ninette, "never mind. But that's what Polly always says when she wants me to believe her: 'hope I may die, Miss Ninette.' Well, this is it: I've been saving up money for the longest time, oh ever so long. I've got eighteen dollars and sixty cents, and when they send me to the convent, if I don't like it, I'm going to run away." This last and startling revelation was told in a tragic whisper in Lucilla's ear, for Betsy was standing before them with a tray of chocolate and coffee that she was passing around.

"I yeard you," proclaimed Betsy with mischievous inscrutable countenance.

"You didn't," said Ninette defiantly, and taking a cup of coffee.

"Yas, I did, I yeard you," walking away.

"See here, Betsy;" cried Ninette recalling the girl, "you're not going to tell, are you?"

"Dun know ef I isn't gwine tell. Dun know ef I isn't gwine tell Miss Duplan dis yere ver' minute."

"Oh Betsy," entreated Ninette, "I'll give you this dress if you don't. I don't want it any more."

Betsy's eyes glowed, but she looked down unconcernedly at the pretty gown.

"Don't spec it fit me. An' you know Miss T'rèse ain't gwine let me go flyin' roun' wid my laigs stickin' out dat away."

"I'll let the ruffle down, Betsy," eagerly proposed Ninette.

"Betsy!" called Thérèse a little impatiently.

"Yas, 'um—I ben waitin' fu' de cups."

Lucilla had made many an aspiration—many an "act" the while. This whole evening of revelry, and now this last act of wicked conspiracy seemed to have tainted her soul with a breath of sin which she would not feel wholly freed from, till she had cleansed her spirit in the waters of absolution.

The party broke up at a late hour, though the Duplans had a long distance to go, and, moreover, had to cross the high and turbid river to reach their carriage which had been left on the opposite bank, owing to the difficulty of the crossing.

Mr. Duplan took occasion of a moment aside to whisper to Hosmer with the air of a connoisseur, "fine woman that Mrs. Worthington of yours."

Hosmer laughed at the jesting implication, whilst disclaiming it, and Fanny looked moodily at them both, jealously wondering at the cause of their good humor.

Mrs. Duplan, under the influence of a charming evening passed in such agreeable and distinguished company, was full of amiable bustle in leaving and had many pleasant parting words to say to each, in her pretty broken English.

"Oh, yes, ma'am," said Mrs. Worthington to that lady, who had taken admiring notice of the beautiful silver "Holy Angels" medal that hung from Lucilla's neck and rested against the dark gown. "Lucilla takes after Mr. Worthington as far as religion goes—kind of different though, for I must say it ain't often he darkens the doors of a church."

Mrs. Worthington always spoke of her husband present as of a husband absent. A peculiarity which he patiently endured, having no talent for repartée, that he had at one time thought of cultivating. But that time was long past.

The Duplans were the first to leave. Then Thérèse stood for a while on the veranda in the chill night air watching the others disappear across the lawn. Mr. and Mrs. Worthington and Lucilla had all shaken hands with her in saying good night. Fanny followed suit limply and grudgingly. Hosmer buttoned his coat impatiently and only lifted his hat to Thérèse as he helped his wife down the stairs.

Poor Fanny! she had already taken exception at that hand pressure which was to come and for which she watched, and now her whole small being was in a jealous turmoil—because there had been none.

XII

TIDINGS THAT STING

hérèse felt that the room was growing oppressive. She had been sitting all morning alone before the fire, passing in review a great heap of household linen that lay piled beside her on the floor, alternating this occupation with occasional careful and tender offices bestowed upon a wee lamb that had been brought to her some hours before, and that now lay wounded and half lifeless upon a pile of coffee sacks before the blaze.

A fire was hardly needed, except to dispel the dampness that had even made its insistent way in-doors, covering walls and furniture with a clammy film. Outside, the moisture was dripping from the glistening magnolia leaves and from the pointed polished leaves of the live-oaks, and the sun that had come out with intense suddenness was drawing it steaming from the shingled roof-tops.

When Thérèse, finally aware of the closeness of the room, opened the door and went out on the veranda, she saw a man, a stranger, riding towards the house and she stood to await his approach. He belonged to what is rather indiscriminately known in that section of the State as the "piney-woods" genus. A raw-boned fellow, lank and long of leg; as ungroomed with his scraggy yellow hair and beard as the scrubby little Texas pony which he rode. His big soft felt hat had done unreasonable service as a head-piece; and the "store clothes" that hung upon his lean person could never in their remotest freshness have masqueraded under the character of "all wool." He was in transit, as the bulging saddle-bags that hung across his horse indicated, as well as the rough brown blanket strapped behind him to the animal's back. He rode up close to the rail of the veranda near which Thérèse stood, and nodded to her without offering to raise or touch his hat. She was prepared for the drawl with which he addressed her, and even guessed what the first words would be.

"You're Mrs. Laferm I 'low?"

Thérèse acknowledged her identity with a bow.

"My name's Jimson; Rufe Jimson," he went on, settling himself on the pony and folding his long knotty hands over the hickory switch that he carried in guise of a whip.

"Do you wish to speak to me? won't you dismount?" Thérèse asked.

"I hed my dinner down to the store," he said, taking her proposal as an invitation to dine, and turning to expectorate a mouth full of tobacco juice before continuing. "Capital sardines them air," passing his hand over his mouth and beard in unctuous remembrance of the oily dainties.

"I'm just from Cornstalk, Texas, on mu way to Grant. An' them roads as I've traversed isn't what I'd call the best in a fair and square talk."

His manner bore not the slightest mark of deference. He spoke to Thérèse as he might have spoken to one of her black servants, or as he would have addressed a princess of royal blood if fate had ever brought him into such unlikely contact, so clearly was the sense of human equality native to him.

Thérèse knew her animal, and waited patiently for his business to unfold itself.

"I reckon thar hain't no ford hereabouts?" he asked, looking at her with a certain challenge.

"Oh, no; it's even difficult crossing in the flat," she answered.

"Wall, I hed calc'lated continooing on this near side. Reckon I could make it?" challenging her again to an answer.

"There's no road on this side," she said turning away to fasten more securely the escaped branches of a rose-bush that twined about a column near which she stood.

Whether there were a road on this side or on the other side, or no road at all, appeared to be a matter of equal indifference to Mr. Jimson, so far as his manner showed. He continued imperturbably, "I 'lowed to stop here on a little matter o' business. 'Tis some out o' mu way; more'n I'd calc'lated. You couldn't tell the ixact distance from here to Colfax,[1] could you?"

Thérèse rather impatiently gave him the desired information, and begged that he would disclose his business with her.

"Wall," he said, "onpleasant news 'll keep most times tell you're ready fur it. That's my way o' lookin' at it."

"Unpleasant news for me?" she inquired, startled from her indifference and listlessness.

"Rather onpleasant ez I take it. I hain't a makin' no misstatement to persume thet Grégor Sanchun was your nephew?"

"Yes, yes," responded Thérèse, now thoroughly alarmed, and approaching as close to Mr. Rufe Jimson as the dividing rail would permit, "What of him, please?"

He turned again to discharge an accumulation of tobacco juice into a thick border of violets, and resumed.

"You see a hot-blooded young feller, ez wouldn't take no more 'an give no odds, stranger or no stranger in the town, he couldn't ixpect civil treatment; leastways not from Colonel Bill Klayton. Ez I said to Tozier—"

"Please tell me as quickly as possible what has happened," demanded Thérèse with trembling eagerness, steadying herself with both hands on the railing before her.

"You see it all riz out o' a little altercation 'twixt him and Colonel Klayton in the colonel's store. Some says he'd ben drinkin'; others denies it. Howsomever they did hev words risin' out o' the colonel addressing your nephew under the title o' 'Frenchy'; which most takes ez a insufficient cause for rilin'."

"He's dead?" gasped Thérèse looking at the dispassionate Texian[2] with horrified eyes.

"Wall, yes," an admission which he seemed not yet willing to leave unqualified; for he went on, "It don't do to alluz speak out open an' above boards, leastways not thar in Cornstalk. But I'll 'low to you, it's my opinion that the colonel acted hasty. It's true 'nough, the young feller hed drawed, but ez I said to Tozier, thet's no reason to persume it was his intention to use his gun."

So Grégoire was dead. She understood it all now. The manner of his death was plain to her as if she had seen it, out there in some disorderly settlement. Killed by the hand of a stranger with whom perhaps the taking of a man's life counted as little as it had once counted with his victim. This flood of sudden and painful intelligence staggered her, and leaning against the column she covered her eyes with both hands, for a while forgetting the presence of the man who had brought the sad tidings.

But he had never ceased his monotonous unwinding. "Thar hain't no manner o' doubt, marm," he was saying, "thet he did hev the sympathy o' the intire community—ez far ez they was free to express it—barrin' a few. Fur he was a likely young chap, thar warn't no two opinions o' that. Free with his money—alluz ready to set up fur a friend. Here's a bit o' writin' thet'll larn you more o' the pertic'lars," drawing a letter from his pocket, "writ by the Catholic priest, by name of O'Dowd. He 'lowed you mought want proyer meetin's and sich."

"Masses," corrected Thérèse, holding out her hand for the letter. With the other hand she was wiping away the tears that had gathered thick in her eyes.

"Thar's a couple more little tricks thet he sont," continued Rufe Jimson, apparently dislocating his joints to reach the depths of his trouser pocket, from which he drew a battered pocket book wrapped around with an infinity of string. From the grimy folds of this receptacle he took a small paper parcel which he placed in her hand. It was partly unfastened, and as she opened it fully, the pent-up tears came blindingly—for before her lay a few curling rings of soft brown hair, and a pair of scapulars,[3] one of which was pierced by a tell-tale bullet hole.

"Won't you dismount?" she presently asked again, this time a little more kindly.

"No, marm," said the Texian, jerking his hitherto patient pony by the bridle till it performed feats of which an impartial observer could scarcely have suspected it.

"Don't reckon I could make Colfax before dark, do you?"

"Hardly," she said, turning away, "I'm much obliged to you, Mr. Jimson, for having taken this trouble—if the flat is on the other side, you need only call for it."

"Wall, good day, marm—I wish you luck," he added, with a touch of gallantry which her tears and sweet feminine presence had inspired. Then turning, he loped his horse rapidly forward, leaning well back in the saddle and his elbows sawing the air.

XIII

MELICENT HEARS THE NEWS

It was talked about and wept about at Place-du-Bois, that Grégoire should be dead. It seemed to them all so unbelievable. Yet, whatever hesitancy they had in accepting the fact of his death, was perforce removed by the convincing proof of Father O'Dowd's letter.

None could remember but sweetness and kindness of him. Even Nathan, who had been one day felled to earth by a crowbar in Grégoire's hand, had come himself to look at that deed as not altogether blamable in light of the provocation that had called it forth.

Fanny remembered those bouquets which had been daily offered to her forlornness at her arrival; and the conversations in which they had understood each other so well. The conviction that he was gone away beyond the possibility of knowing him further, moved her to tears. Hosmer, too, was grieved and shocked, without being able to view the event in the light of a calamity.

No one was left unmoved by the tidings which brought a lowering cloud even upon the brow of Aunt Belindy, to rest there the whole day. Deep were the mutterings she hurled at a fate that could have been so short-sighted as to remove from earth so bright an ornament as Grégoire. Her grief further spent much of itself upon the inoffensive Betsy, who, for some inscrutable reason was for twenty-four hours debarred entrance to the kitchen.

Thérèse, seated at her desk, devoted a morning to the writing of letters, acquainting various members of the family with the unhappy intelligence. She wrote first to Madame Santien, living now her lazy life in Paris, with eyes closed to the duties that lay before her and heart choked up with an egoism that withered even the mother instincts. It was very difficult to withhold the reproach which she felt inclined to deal her; hard to refrain from upbraiding a selfishness which for a life-time had appeared to Thérèse as criminal.

It was a matter less nice, less difficult, to write to the brothers—one up on the Red River plantation living as best he could; the other idling on the New Orleans streets. But it was after all a short and simple story to tell. There was no lingering illness to describe; no moment even of consciousness in which harrowing last words were to be gathered and recorded. Only a hot senseless quarrel to be told about; the speeding of a bullet with very sure aim, and— quick death.

Of course, masses must be said.[1] Father O'Dowd was properly instructed. Père Antoine in Centreville was addressed on the subject. The Bishop of Natchitoches, respectfully asked to perform this last sad office for the departed soul. And the good old priest and friend at the New Orleans Cathedral, was informed of her desires. Not that Thérèse held very strongly to this saying of masses for the dead; but it had been a custom holding for generations in the family and which she was not disposed to abandon now, even if she had thought of it.

The last letter was sent to Melicent. Thérèse made it purposely short and pointed, with a bare statement of facts—a dry, unemotional telling, that sounded heartless when she read it over; but she let it go.

Melicent was standing in her small, quaint sitting-room, her back to the fire, and her hands clasped behind her. How handsome was this Melicent! Pouting now, and with eyes half covered by the dark shaded lids, as they gazed moodily out at the wild snowflakes that were hurrying like crazy things against the warm window pane and meeting their end there. A loose tea-gown clung in long folds about her. A dull colored thing, save for the two broad bands of sapphire plush hanging straight before, from throat to toe. Melicent was plainly dejected; not troubled, nor sad, only dejected, and very much bored; a condition that had made her yawn several times while she looked at the falling snow.

She was philosophizing a little. Wondering if the world this morning were really the unpleasant place that it appeared, or if these conditions of unpleasantness lay not rather within her own mental vision; a train of thought that might be supposed to have furnished her some degree of entertainment had she continued in its pursuit. But she chose rather to dwell on her causes of unhappiness, and thus convince herself that that unhappiness was indeed outside of her and around her and not by any possibility to be avoided or circumvented. There lay now a letter in her desk from David, filled with admonitions if not reproof which she felt to be not entirely unjust, on the disagreeable subject of Expenses. Looking around the pretty room she conceded to herself that here had been temptations which she could not reasonably have been expected to withstand. The temptation to lodge herself in this charming little flat; furnish it after her own liking; and install that delightful little old poverty-stricken English woman as keeper of Proprieties,[2] with her irresistible white starched caps and her altogether delightful way of inquiring daily after that "poor, dear, kind Mr. Hosmer." It had all cost a little more than she had foreseen. But the worst of it, the very worst of it was, that she had already begun to ask herself if, for instance, it were not very irritating to see every day, that same branching palm, posing by the window, in that same yellow *jardinière*.[3] If those draperies that confronted her were not becoming positively offensive in the monotony of their solemn folds. If the cuteness and quaintness of the poverty-stricken little English woman were not after all a source of entertainment that she would willingly forego on occasion. The answer to these questions was a sigh that ended in another yawn.

Then Melicent threw herself into a low easy chair by the table, took up her visiting book,[4] and bending lazily with her arms resting on her knees, began to turn over its pages. The names which she saw there recalled to her mind an entertainment at which she had assisted on the previous afternoon. A progressive euchre party; and the remembrance of what she had there endured now filled her soul with horror.

She thought of those hundred cackling women—of course women are never cackling, it was Melicent's exaggerated way of expressing herself—packed into those small overheated rooms, around those twenty-five little tables; and how by no chance had she once found herself with a congenial set. And how that Mrs. Van Wycke had cheated! It was plain to Melicent that she had taken advantage of having fat Miss Bloomdale for a partner, who went to euchre parties only to show her hands and rings. And little Mrs. Brinke playing against her. Little Mrs. Brinke! A woman who only the other day had read an original paper entitled: "An Hour with Hegel" before her philosophy class; who had published that dry mystical affair "Light on the Inscrutable in Dante."[5] How could such a one by any possibility be supposed to observe the disgusting action of Mrs. Van Wycke in throwing off on her partner's trump and swooping down on the last trick with her right bower? Melicent would have thought it beneath her to more than look her contempt as Mrs. Van Wycke rose with a triumphant laugh to take her place at a higher table, dragging the plastic Bloomdale with her. But she did mutter to herself now, "nasty thief."

"Johannah," Melicent called to her maid who sat sewing in the next room.

"Yes, Miss."

"You know Mrs. Van Wycke?"

"Mrs. Van Wycke, Miss? the lady with the pinted[6] nose that I caught a-feeling of the curtains?"

"Yes, when she calls again I'm not home. Do you understand? not at home."

"Yes, Miss."

It was gratifying enough to have thus summarily disposed of Mrs. Van Wycke; but it was a source of entertainment which was soon ended. Melicent continued to turn over the pages of her visiting book during which employment she came to the conclusion that these people whom she frequented were all very tiresome. All, all of them, except Miss Drake who had been absent in Europe for the past six months. Perhaps Mrs. Manning too, who was so seldom at home when Melicent called. Who when at home, usually rushed down with her bonnet on, breathless with "I can only spare you a moment, dear. It's very sweet of you to come." She was always just going to the "Home" where things had got into such a muddle whilst she was away for a week. Or it was that "Hospital" meeting where she thought certain members were secretly conniving at her removal from the presidency which she had held for so many years. She was always reading minutes at assemblages which Melicent knew nothing about; or introducing distinguished guests to Guild[7] room meetings. Altogether Melicent saw very little of Mrs. Manning.

"Johannah, don't you hear the bell?"

"Yes, Miss," said Johannah, coming into the room and depositing a gown on which she had been working, on the back of a chair. "It's that postman," she said, as she fastened her needle to the bosom of her dress. "And such a one as he is, thinking that people must fly when he so much as touches the bell, and going off a writing of 'no answer to bell,' and me with my hand on the very door-knob."

"I notice that always happens when I'm out, Johannah; he's ringing again."

It was Thérèse's letter, and as Melicent turned it about and looked critically at the neatly written address, it was not without a hope that the reading of it might furnish her a moment's diversion. She did not faint. The letter did not "fall from her nerveless clasp." She rather held it very steadily. But she grew a shade paler and looked long into the fire. When she had read it three times she folded it slowly and carefully and locked it away in her desk.

"Johannah."

"Yes, Miss."

"Put that gown away; I shan't need it."

"Yes, Miss; and all the beautiful passmantry[8] that you bought?"

"It makes no difference, I shan't use it. What's become of that black camel's-hair that Mrs. Gauche spoiled so last winter?"

"It's laid away, Miss, the same in the cedar chest as the day it came home from her hands and no more fit, that I'd be a shame meself and no claims to a dress-maker. And there's many a lady that she never would have seen a cent, let alone making herself pay for the spiling of it."

"Well, well, Johannah, never mind. Get it out, we'll see what can be done with it. I've had some painful news, and I shall wear mourning[9] for a long, long time."

"Oh, Miss, it's not Mr. David! nor yet one of those sweet relations in Utica? leastways not I hope that beautiful Miss Gertrude, with such hair as I never see for the goldness of it and not dyed, except me cousin that's a nun, that her mother actually cried when it was cut off?"

"No, Johannah; only a very dear friend."

There were a few social engagements to be canceled; and regrets to be sent out, which she attended to immediately. Then she turned again to look long into the fire. That crime for which she had scorned him, was wiped out now by expiation. For a long time—how long she could not yet determine—she would wrap herself in garb of mourning and move about in sorrow-ing—giving evasive answer to the curious who questioned her. Now might she live again through those summer months with Grégoire—those golden afternoons in the pine woods—whose aroma even now came back to her. She might look again into his loving brown eyes; feel beneath her touch the softness of his curls. She recalled a day when he had said, "Neva to see you— my God!" and how he had trembled. She recalled—strangely enough and for the first time—that one kiss, and a little tremor brought the hot color to her cheek.

Was she in love with Grégoire now that he was dead? Perhaps. At all events, for the next month, Melicent would not be bored.

XIV

A Step Too Far

Who of us has not known the presence of Misery? Perhaps as those fortunate ones whom he has but touched as he passed them by. It may be that we see but a promise of him as we look into the prophetic faces of children; into the eyes of those we love, and the awfulness of life's possibilities pressed into our souls. Do we fly him? hearing him gain upon us panting close at our heels, till we turn from the desperation of uncertainty to grapple with him? In close scuffle we may vanquish him. Fleeing, we may elude him. But what if he creep into the sanctuary of our lives, with his subtle omnipresence, that we do not see in all its horror till we are disarmed; thrusting the burden of his companionship upon us to the end! However we turn he is there. However we shrink he is there. However we come or go, or sleep or wake he is before us. Till the keen sense grows dull with apathy at looking on him, and he becomes like the familiar presence of sin.

Into such callousness had Hosmer fallen. He had ceased to bruise his soul in restless endeavor of resistance. When the awful presence bore too closely upon him, he would close his eyes and brave himself to endurance. Yet Fate might have dealt him worse things.

But a man's misery is after all his own, to make of it what he will or what he can. And shall we be fools, wanting to lighten it with our platitudes?

My friend, your trouble I know weighs. That you should be driven by earthly needs to drag the pinioned spirit of your days through rut and mire. But think of the millions who are doing the like. Or is it your boy, that part of your own self and that other dearer self, who is walking in evil ways? Why, I know a man whose son was hanged the other day; hanged on the gibbet;[1] think of it. If you be quivering while the surgeon cuts away that right arm, remember the poor devil in the hospital yesterday who had both his sawed off.

Oh, have done, with your mutilated men and your sons on gibbets! What are they to me? My hurt is greater than all, because it is my own. If it be only that day after day I must look with warm entreaty into eyes that are cold. Let it be but that peculiar trick of feature which I have come to hate, seen each morning across the breakfast table. That recurrent pin-prick: it hurts. The blow that lays the heart in twain: it kills. Let be mine which will; it is the one that counts.

If Misery kill a man, that ends it. But Misery seldom deals so summarily with his victims. And while they are spared to earth, we find them usually sustaining life after the accepted fashion.

Hosmer was seated at table, having finished his breakfast. He had also finished glancing over the contents of a small memorandum book, which he replaced in his pocket. He then looked at his wife sitting opposite him, but turned rather hastily to gaze with a certain entreaty into the big kind eyes of the great shaggy dog who stood—the shameless beggar—at his side.

"I knew there was something wrong," he said abruptly, with his eyes still fixed on the dog, and his fingers thrust into the animal's matted wool, "Where's the mail this morning?"

"I don't know if that stupid boy's gone for it or not. I told him. You can't depend on any one in a place like this."

Fanny had scarcely touched the breakfast before her, and now pushed aside her cup still half filled with coffee.

"Why, how's that? Sampson seems to do the right thing."

"Yes, Sampson; but he ain't here. That boy of Minervy's been doing his work all morning."

Minvervy's boy was even now making his appearance, carrying a good sized bundle of papers and letters, with which he walked boldly up to Hosmer, plainly impressed with the importance of this new rôle.

"Well, colonel; so you've taken Sampson's place?" Hosmer observed, receiving the mail from the boy's little black paws.

"My name's Major, suh. Maje; dats my name. I ain't tuck Sampson's place: no, suh."

"Oh, he's having a day off—" Hosmer went on, smiling quizzingly at the dapper little darkey, and handing him a red apple from the dish of fruit standing in the center of the table. Maje received it with a very unmilitary bob of acknowledgement.

"He yonda home 'cross de riva, suh. He ben too late fu' kotch de flat's mornin'. And he holla an' holla. He know dey warn't gwine cross dat flat 'gin jis' fu' Sampson."

Hosmer had commenced to open his letters. Fanny with her elbows on the table, asked the boy—with a certain uneasiness in her voice—"Ain't he coming at all to-day? Don't he know all the work he's go to do? His mother ought to make him."

"Don't reckon. Dat away Sampson: he git mad he stay mad," with which assurance Maje vanished through the rear door, towards the region of the kitchen, to seek more substantial condiments than the apple which he still clutched firmly.

One of the letters was for Fanny, which her husband handed her. When he had finished reading his own, he seemed disposed to linger, for he took from the fruit dish the mate to the red apple he had given Maje, and commenced to peel it with his clasp-knife.

"What has our friend, Belle Worthington, to say for herself?" he inquired good humoredly. "How does she get on with those Creoles down there?"

"You know as well as I do, Belle Worthington, ain't going to mix with Creoles. She can't talk French if she wanted to. She says Muddy-Graw[2] don't begin to compare with the Veiled Prophets. It's just what I thought—with their 'Muddy-Graw'," Fanny added, contemptuously.

"Coming from such high authority, we'll consider that verdict a final clincher," Hosmer laughed a little provokingly.

Fanny was looking again through the several sheets of Belle Worthington's letter. "She says if I'll agree to go back with her, she'll pass this way again."

"Well, why don't you? A little change wouldn't hurt."

"'Tain't because I want to stay here, Lord knows. A God-forsaken place like this. I guess you'd be glad enough," she added, with voice shaking a little at her own boldness.

He closed his knife, placed it in his pocket, and looked at his wife, completely puzzled.

The power of speech had come to her, for she went on, in an unnatural tone, however, and fumbling nervously with the dishes before her. "I'm fool enough about some things, but I ain't quite such a fool as that."

"What are you talking about, Fanny?"

"That woman wouldn't ask anything better than for me to go to St. Louis."

Hosmer was utterly amazed. He leaned his arms on the table, clasping his hands together and looked at his wife.

"That woman? Belle Worthington? What *do* you mean, any way?"

"I don't mean Belle Worthington," she said excitedly, with two deep red spots in her cheeks. "I'm talking about Mrs. Laferm."

He thrust his hands into his pockets and leaned back in his chair. No amazement now, but very pale, and with terrible concentration of glance.

"Well, then, don't talk about Mrs. Lafirme," he said very slowly, not taking his eyes from her face.

"I will talk about her, too. She ain't worth talking about," she blurted incoherently. "It's time for somebody to talk about a woman passing herself off for a saint, and trying to take other women's husband's—"

"Shut up!" cried Hosmer maddened with sudden fury, and rising violently from his chair.

"I won't shut up," Fanny cried excitedly back at him; rising also. "And what's more I won't stay here and have you making love under my very eyes to a woman that's no better than she ought to be."

She meant to say more, but Hosmer grasped her arm with such a grasp, that had it been her throat she would never have spoken more. The other hand went to his pocket, with fingers clutching the clasp knife there.

"By heaven—I'll—kill you!" every word weighted with murder, panted close in her terrified face. What she would have uttered died upon her pale lips, when her frightened eyes beheld the usually calm face of her husband distorted by a passion of which she had not dreamed.

"David," she faltered, "let go my arm."

Her voice broke the spell that held him, and brought him again to his senses. His fingers slowly relaxed their tense hold. A sigh that was something between a moan and a gasp came with his deliverance and shook him. All the horror now was in his own face as he seized his hat and hurried speechless away.

Fanny remained for a little while dazed. Hers was not the fine nature that would stay cruelly stunned after such a scene. Her immediate terror being past, the strongest resultant emotion was one of self-satisfaction at having spoken out her mind.

But there was a stronger feeling yet, moving and possessing her; crowding out every other. A pressing want that only Sampson's coming would relieve, and which bade fair to drive her to any extremity if it were not appeased.

XV

A Fateful Solution

osmer passed the day with a great pain at his heart. His hasty and violent passion of the morning had added another weight for his spirit to drag about, and which he could not cast off. No feeling of resentment remained with him; only wonder at his wife's misshapen knowledge and keen self-rebuke of his own momentary forgetfulness. Even knowing Fanny as he did, he could not rid himself of the haunting dread of having wounded her nature cruelly. He felt much as a man who in a moment of anger inflicts an irreparable hurt upon some small, weak, irresponsible creature, and must bear regret for his madness. The only reparation that lay within his power—true, one that seemed inadequate—was an open and manly apology and confession of wrong. He would feel better when it was made. He would perhaps find relief in discovering that the wound he had inflicted was not so deep—so dangerous as he feared.

With such end in view he came home early in the afternoon. His wife was not there. The house was deserted. Even the servants had disappeared. It took but a moment for him to search the various rooms and find them one after the other, unoccupied. He went out on the porch and looked around. The raw air chilled him. The wind was blowing violently, bringing dashes of rain along with it from massed clouds that hung leaden between sky and earth. Could she have gone over to the house? It was unlikely, for he knew her to have avoided Mrs. Lafirme of late, with a persistence that had puzzled him to seek its cause, which had only fully revealed itself in the morning. Yet, where else could she be? An undefined terror was laying hold of him. His sensitive nature, in exaggerating its own heartlessness, was blindly overestimating the delicacy of hers. To what may he not have driven her? What hitherto untouched chord may he not have started into painful quivering? Was it for him to gauge the endurance of a woman's spirit? Fanny was not now the wife whom he hated; his own act of the morning had changed her into the human being, the weak creature whom he had wronged.

In quitting the house she must have gone unprepared for the inclement weather, for there hung her heavy wrap in its accustomed place, with her umbrella beside it. He seized both and buttoning his own great coat about him, hurried away and over to Mrs. Lafirme's. He found that lady in the sitting-room.

"Isn't Fanny here?" he asked abruptly, with no word of greeting.

"No," she answered looking up at him, and seeing the evident uneasiness in his face. "Isn't she at home? Is anything wrong?"

"Oh, everything is wrong," he returned desperately, "But the immediate wrong is that she has disappeared—I must find her."

Thérèse arose at once and called to Betsy who was occupied on the front veranda.

"Yas, um," the girl answered to her mistress' enquiry. "I seed ma'am Hosma goin' to'ads de riva good hour 'go. She mus' crost w'en Nathan tuck dat load ova. I yain't seed 'er comin' back yit."

Hosmer left the house hastily, hardly reassured by Betsy's information. Thérèse's glance—speculating and uneasy—followed his hurrying figure till it disappeared from sight.

The crossing was an affair of extreme difficulty, and which Nathan was reluctant to undertake until he should have gathered a "load" that would justify him in making it. In his estimation, Hosmer did not meet such requirement, even taken in company with the solitary individual who had been sitting his horse with Egyptian patience for long unheeded moments, the rain beating down upon his back, while he waited the ferryman's pleasure. But Nathan's determination was not proof against the substantial inducements which Hosmer held out to him; and soon they were launched, all hands assisting in the toilsome passage.

The water, in rising to an unaccustomed height, had taken on an added and tremendous swiftness. The red turbid stream was eddying and bulging and hurrying with terrific swiftness between its shallow banks, striking with an immensity of power against the projection of land on which stood Marie Louise's cabin, and rebounding in great circling waves that spread and lost themselves in the seething turmoil. The cable used in crossing the unwieldy flat had long been submerged and the posts which held it wrenched from their fastenings. The three men, each with his long heavy oar in hand began to pull up stream, using a force that brought the swelling veins like iron tracings upon their foreheads where the sweat had gathered as if the day were midsummer. They made their toilsome way by slow inches, that finally landed them breathless and exhausted on the opposite side.

What could have been the inducement to call Fanny out on such a day and such a venture? The answer came only too readily from Hosmer's reproaching conscience. And now, where to seek her? There was nothing to guide him; to indicate the course she might have taken. The rain was falling heavily and in gusts and through it he looked about at the small cabins standing dreary in their dismantled fields. Marie Louise's was the nearest at hand and towards it he directed his steps.

The big good-natured negress had seen his approach from the window, for she opened the door to him before he had time to knock, and entering he saw Fanny seated before the fire holding a pair of very wet smoking feet to dry. His first sensation was one of relief at finding her safe and housed. His next, one of uncertainty as to the kind and degree of resentment which he felt confident must now show itself. But this last was soon dispelled, for turning, she greeted him with a laugh. He would have rather a blow. That laugh said so many things—too many things. True, it removed the dread which had been haunting him all day, but it shattered what seemed to have been now his last illusion regarding this woman. That unsounded chord which he feared he had touched was after all but one in harmony with the rest of her common nature. He saw too at a glance that her dominant passion had been leading and now controlled her. And by one of those rapid trains of thought in which odd and detached fancies, facts, impressions and observations form themselves into an orderly sequence leading to a final conviction—all was made plain to him that before had puzzled him. She need not have told him her reason for crossing the river, he knew it. He dismissed at once the attitude with which he had thought to approach her. Here was no forgiveness to be asked of dulled senses. No bending in expiation of faults comitted. He was here as master.

"Fanny, what does this mean?" he asked in cold anger; with no heat now, no passion.

"Yaas, me tell madame, she goin' fur ketch cole si she don' mine out. Dat not fur play dat kine wedder, no. Teck chair, M'sieur; dry you'se'f leet beet. Me mek you one cup coffee."

Hosmer declined the good Marie Louise's kind proffer of coffee, but he seated himself and waited for Fanny to speak.

"You know if you want a thing done in this place, you've got to do it yourself. I've heard you say it myself, time and time again about those people at the mill," she said.

"Could it have been so urgent as to call you out on a day like this, and with such a perilous crossing? Couldn't you have found some one else to come for you?"

"Who? I'd like to know. Just tell me who? It's nothing to you if we're without servants, but I'm not going to stand it. I ain't going to let Sampson act like that without knowing what he means," said Fanny sharply.

"Dat Sampson, he one leet dev'," proffered Marie Louise, with laudable design of shifting blame upon the easy shoulders of Sampson, in event of the domestic jar which she anticipated. "No use try do nuttin' 'id Sampson, M'sieur."

"I had to know something, one way or the other," Fanny said in a tone which carried apology, rather by courtesy than by what she considered due.

Hosmer walked to the window where he looked out upon the dreary, desolate scene, little calculated to cheer him. The river was just below; and from this window he could gaze down upon the rushing current as it swept around the bend further up and came striking against this projection with a force all its own. The rain was falling still; steadily, blindingly, with wild clatter against the shingled roof so close above their heads. It coursed in little swift rivulets down the furrows of the almost perpendicular banks. It mingled in a demon dance with the dull, red water. There was something inviting to Hosmer in the scene. He wanted to be outside there making a part of it. He wanted to feel that rain and wind beating upon him. Within, it was stifling, maddening; with his wife's presence there, charging the room with an atmosphere of hate that was possessing him and beginning to course through his veins as it had never down before.

"Do you want to go home?" he asked bluntly, turning half around.

"You must be crazy," she replied, with a slow, upward glance out the window, then down at her feet that were still poised on the low stool that Marie Louise had placed for her.

"You'd better come." He could not have said what moved him, unless it were recklessness and defiance.

"I guess you're dreaming, or something, David. You go on home if you want. Nobody asked you to come after me any way. I'm able to take care of myself, I guess. Ain't you going to take the umbrella?" she added, seeing him start for the door empty handed.

"Oh, it doesn't matter about the rain," he answered without a look back as he went out and slammed the door after him.

"M'sieur look lak he not please," said Marie Louise, with plain regret at the turn of affairs. "You see he no lak you go out in dat kine wedder, me know dat."

"Oh, bother," was Fanny's careless reply. "This suits me well enough; I don't care how long it lasts."

She was in Marie Louise's big rocker, balancing comfortably back and forth with a swing that had become automatic. She felt "good," as she would have termed it herself; her visit to Sampson's hut having not been without results tending to that condition. The warmth of the room was very agreeable in contrast to the bleakness of out-doors. She felt free and moved to exercise a looseness of tongue with the amiable old negress which was not common with her. The occurrences of the morning were gradually withdrawing themselves into a distant perspective that left her in the attitude of a spectator rather than that of an actor. And she laughed and talked with Marie Louise, and rocked, and rocked herself on into drowsiness.

Hosmer had no intention of returning home without his wife. He only wanted to be out under the sky; he wanted to breathe, to use his muscles again. He would go and help cross the flat if need be; an occupation that promised him relief in physical effort. He joined Nathan, whom he found standing under a big live-oak, disputing with an old colored woman who wanted to cross to get back to her family before supper time.

"You didn' have no call to come ova in de fus' place," he was saying to her, "You womens is alluz runnin' back'ards an for'ards like skeard rabbit in de co'n fiel'."

"I don' stan' no sich talk is dat f'om you. Ef you kiant tin' to yo' business o' totin' folks w'en dey wants, you betta quit. You done cheat Mose out o' de job, anyways; we all knows dat."

"Mine out, woman, you gwine git hu't. Jis' le'me see Mose han'le dat 'ar flat onct: Jis' le'me. He lan' you down to de Mouf 'fo' you knows it."

"Let me tell you, Nathan," said Hosmer, looking at his watch, "say you wait a quarter of an hour and if no one else comes, we'll cross Aunt Agnes anyway."

"Dat 'nudda t'ing ef you wants to go back, suh."

Aunt Agnes was grumbling now at Hosmer's proposal that promised to keep her another quarter of an hour from her expectant family, when a big lumbering creaking wagon drove up, with its load of baled cotton all covered with tarpaulins.[1]

"Dah!" exclaimed Nathan at sight of the wagon, "ef I'd a' listened to yo' jawin'—what?"

"Ef you'd listen to me, you'd 'tin' to yo' business betta 'an you does," replied Aunt Agnes, raising a very battered umbrella over her grotesquely apparelled figure, as she stepped from under the shelter of the tree to take her place in the flat.

But she still met with obstacles, for the wagon must needs go first. When it had rolled heavily into place with much loud and needless swearing on the part of the driver who, being a white man, considered Hosmer's presence no hindrance, they let go the chain, and once again pulled out. The crossing was even more difficult now, owing to the extra weight of the wagon.

"I guess you earn your money, Nathan," said Hosmer, bending and quivering with the efforts he put forth.

"Yas, suh, I does; an' dis job's wuf mo' 'an I gits fu' it."

"All de same you done lef' off wurking crap sence you start it," mumbled Aunt Agnes.

"You gwine git hu't, woman; I done tole you dat; don' wan' listen," returned Nathan with halting breath.

"Who gwine hu't me?"

Whether from tardy gallantry or from pre-occupation with his arduous work, Nathan offered no reply to this challenge, and his silence left Aunt Agnes in possession of the field.

They were in full mid-stream. Hosmer and the teamster were in the fore end of the boat; Nathan in the rear, and Aunt Agnes standing in the center between the wagon and the protecting railing, against which she leaned her clasped hands that still upheld the semblance of umbrella.

The ill-mated horses stood motionless, letting fall their dejected heads with apathetic droop. The rain was dripping from their glistening coats, and making a great patter as it fell upon the tarpaulins covering the cotton bales.

Suddenly came an exclamation: "Gret God!" from Aunt Agnes, so genuine in its amazement and dismay, that the three men with one accord looked quickly up at her, then at the point on which her terrified gaze was fixed. Almost on the instant of the woman's cry, was heard a shrill, piercing, feminine scream.

What they saw was the section of land on which stood Marie Louise's cabin, undermined—broken away from the main body and gradually gliding into the water. It must have sunk with a first abrupt wrench, for the brick chimney was shaken from its foundation, the smoke issuing in dense clouds from its shattered sides, the house toppling and the roof caving. For a moment Hosmer lost his senses. He could but look, as if at some awful apparition that must soon pass from sight and leave him again in possession of his reason. The leaning house was half submerged when Fanny appeared at the door, like a figure in a dream; seeming a natural part of the awfulness of it. He only gazed on. The two negroes uttered loud lamentations.

"Pull with the current!" cried the teamster, first to regain his presence of mind. It had needed but this, to awaken Hosmer to the situation.

"Leave off," he cried at Nathan, who was wringing his hands. "Take hold that oar or I'll throw you overboard." The trembling ashen negro obeyed on the instant.

"Hold fast—for God's sake—hold fast!" he shouted to Fanny, who was clinging with swaying figure to the door post. Of Marie Louise there was no sign.

The caved bank now remained fixed; but Hosmer knew that at any instant it was liable to disappear before his riveted gaze.

How heavy the flat was! And the horses had caught the contagion of terror and were plunging madly.

"Whip those horses and their load into the river," called Hosmer, "we've got to lighten at any price."

"Them horses an' cotton's worth money," interposed the alarmed teamster.

"Force them into the river, I say; I'll pay you twice their value."

"You 'low to pay fur the cotton, too?"

"Into the river with them or I'll brain you!" he cried, maddened at the weight and delay that were holding them back.

The frightened animals seemed to ask nothing more than to plunge into the troubled water; dragging their load with them.

They were speeding rapidly towards the scene of catastrophe; but to Hosmer they crawled—the moments were hours. "Hold on! hold fast!" he called again and again to his wife. But even as he cried out, the detached section of earth swayed, lurched to one side—plunged to the other, and the whole mass was submerged—leaving the water above it in wild agitation.

A cry of horror went up from the spectators—all but Hosmer. He cast aside his oar—threw off his coat and hat; worked an instant without avail at his wet clinging boots, and with a leap was in the water, swimming towards the spot where the cabin had gone down. The current bore him on without much effort of his own. The flat was close up with him; but he could think of it no longer as a means of rescue. Detached pieces of timber from the ruined house were beginning to rise to the surface. Then something floating softly on the water: a woman's dress, but too far for him to reach it.

When Fanny appeared again, Hosmer was close beside her. His left arm was quickly thrown about her. She was insensible, and he remembered that it was best so, for had she been in possession of her reason, she might have struggled and impeded his movements. He held her fast—close to him and turned to regain the shore. Another horrified shriek went up from the occupants of the flat-boat not far away, and Hosmer knew no more—for a great plunging beam struck him full upon the forehead.

When consciousness came back to him, he found that he lay extended in the flat, which was fastened to the shore. The confused sound of many voices mingled with a ringing din that filled his ears. A warm stream was trickling down over his cheek. Another body lay beside him. Now they were lifting him. Thérèse's face was somewhere—very near, he saw it dimly and that it was white—and he fell again into insensibility.

XVI

To Him Who Waits

The air was filled with the spring and all its promises. Full with the sound of it, the smell of it, the deliciousness of it. Such sweet air; soft and strong, like the touch of a brave woman's hand. The air of an early March day in New Orleans. It was folly to shut it out from nook or cranny. Worse than folly, the lady thought who was making futile endeavors to open the car window near which she sat. Her face had grown pink with the effort. She had bit firmly into her red nether lip, making it all the redder; and then sat down from the unaccomplished feat to look ruefully at the smirched finger tips of her Parisian gloves. This flavor of Paris was well about her; in the folds of her graceful wrap that set to her fine shoulders. It was plainly a part of the little black velvet toque[1] that rested on her blonde hair. Even the umbrella and one small valise which she had just laid on the seat opposite her, had Paris written plain upon them.

These were impressions which the little grey-garbed conventional figure, some seats removed, had been noting since the striking lady had entered the car. Points likely to have escaped a man, who—unless a minutely observant one,—would only have seen that she was handsome and worthy of an admiration that he might easily fancy rising to devotion.

Beside herself and the little grey-garbed figure was an interesting family group at the far end of the car. A husband, but doubly a father, surrounded and sat upon by a small band of offspring. A wife—presumably a mother—absorbed with the view of the outside world and the elaborate gold chain that hung around her neck.

The presence of a large valise, an overcoat, a cane and an umbrella disposed on another seat, bespoke a further occupant, likely to be at present in the smoking car.

142

The train pushed out from the depôt. The porter finally made tardy haste to the assistance of the lady who had been attempting to open the window, and when the fresh morning air came blowing in upon her, Thérèse leaned back in her seat with a sigh of content.

There was a full day's journey before her. She would not reach Place-du-Bois before dark, but she did not shrink from those hours that were to be passed alone. She rather welcomed the quiet of them after a visit to New Orleans full of pleasant disturbances. She was eager to be home again. She loved Place-du-Bois with a love that was real; that had grown deep since it was the one place in the world which she could connect with the presence of David Hosmer. She had often wondered—indeed was wondering now—if the memory of those happenings to which he belonged would ever grow strange and far away to her. It was a trick of memory with which she indulged herself on occasion, this one of retrospection. Beginning with that June day when she had sat in the hall and watched the course of a white sunshade over the tops of the bending corn.

Such idle thoughts they were with their mingling of bitter and sweet—leading nowhere. But she clung to them and held to them as if to a refuge which she might again and again return to.

The picture of that one terrible day of Fanny's death, stood out in sharp prominent lines; a touch of the old agony always coming back as she remembered how she had believed Hosmer dead too—lying so pale and bleeding before her. Then the parting which had held not so much of sorrow as of awe and bewilderment in it: when sick, wounded and broken he had gone away at once with the dead body of his wife; when the two had clasped hands without words that dared to be uttered.

But that was a year ago. And Thérèse thought many things might come about in a year. Anyhow, might not such length of time be hoped to rub the edge off a pain that was not by its nature lasting?

That time of acute trouble seemed to have thrown Hosmer back upon his old diffidence. The letter he wrote her after a painful illness which prostrated him on his arrival in St. Louis, was stiff and formal, as men's letters are apt to be, though it had breathed an untold story of loyalty which she had felt at the time, and still cherished. Other letters—a few—had gone back and forth between them, till Hosmer had gone away to the sea-shore with Melicent, to recuperate, and June coming, Thérèse had sailed from New Orleans for Paris, whither she had passed six months.

Things had not gone well at Place-du-Bois during her absence, the impecunious old kinsman whom she had left in charge, having a decided preference for hunting the *Gros-Bec*[2] and catching trout in the lake to supervising the methods of a troublesome body of blacks. So Thérèse had had much to engage her thoughts from the morbid channel into which those of a more idle woman might have drifted.

She went occasionally enough to the mill. There at least she was always sure to hear Hosmer's name—and what a charm the sound of it had for her. And what a delight it was to her eyes when she caught sight of an envelope lying somewhere on desk or table of the office, addressed in his handwriting. That was a weakness which she could not pardon herself; but which staid with her, seeing that the same trifling cause never failed to awaken the same unmeasured delight. She had even trumped up an excuse one day for carrying off one of Hosmer's business letters—indeed of the dryest in substance, and which, when half-way home, she had torn into the smallest bits and scattered to the winds, so overcome was she by a sense of her own absurdity.

Thérèse had undergone the ordeal of having her ticket scrutinized, commented upon and properly punched by the suave conductor. The little conventional figure had given over the contemplation of Parisian styles and betaken herself to the absorbing pages of a novel which she read through smoked glasses. The husband and father had peeled and distributed his second outlay of bananas amongst his family. It was at this moment that Thérèse, looking towards the door, saw Hosmer enter the car.

She must have felt his presence somewhere near; his being there and coming towards her was so much a part of her thoughts. She held out her hand to him and made place beside her, as if he had left her but a half hour before. All the astonishment was his. But he pressed her hand and took the seat she offered him.

"You knew I was on the train?" he asked.

"Oh, no, how should I?"

Then naturally followed question and answer.

Yes, he was going to Place-du-Bois.

No, the mill did not require his presence; it had been very well managed during his absence.

Yes, she had been to New Orleans. Had had a very agreeable visit. Beautiful weather for city dwellers. But such dryness. So disastrous to the planters.

Yes—quite likely there would be rain next month: there usually was in April. But indeed there was need of more than April showers for that stiff land—that strip along the bayou, if he remembered? Oh, he remembered quite well, but for all that, he did not know what she was talking about. She did not know herself. Then they grew silent; not from any feeling of the absurdity of such speech between them, for each had but listened to the other's voice. They became silently absorbed by the consciousness of each other's nearness. She was looking at his hand that rested on his knee, and thinking it fuller than she remembered it before. She was aware of some change in him which she had not the opportunity to define; but this firmness and fullness of the hand was part of it. She looked up into his face then, to find the same change there, together with a new content. But what she noted beside was the dull scar on his forehead, coming out like a red letter when his eyes looked into her own. The sight of it was like a hurt. She had forgotten it might be there, telling its story of pain through the rest of his life.

"Thérèse," Hosmer said finally, "won't you look at me?"

She was looking from the window. She did not turn her head, but her hand went out and met his that was on the seat close beside her. He held it firmly; but soon with an impatient movement he drew down the loose wristlet of her glove and clasped his fingers around her warm wrist.

"Thérèse," he said again; but more unsteadily, "look at me."

"Not here," she answered him, "not now, I mean." And presently she drew her hand away from him and held it for a moment pressed firmly over her eyes. Then she looked at him with brave loving glance.

"It's been so long," she said, with the suspicion of a sigh.

"Too long," he returned, "I couldn't have borne it but for you—the thought of you always present with me; helping me to take myself out of the past. That was why I waited—till I could come to you free.[3] Have you an idea, I wonder, how you have been a promise, and can be the fulfillment of every good that life may give to a man?"

"No, I don't know," she said a little hopelessly, taking his hand again, "I have seen myself at fault in following what seemed the only right. I feel as if there were no way to turn for the truth. Old supports appear to be giving way beneath me. They were so secure before. It commenced, you remember—oh, you know when it must have begun. But do you think, David, that it's right we should find our happiness out of that past of pain and sin and trouble?"

"Thérèse," said Hosmer firmly, "the truth in its entirety isn't given to man to know—such knowledge, no doubt, would be beyond human endurance. But we make a step towards it, when we learn that there is rottenness and evil in the world, masquerading as right and morality—when we learn to know the living spirit from the dead letter. I have not cared to stop in this struggle of life long enough to question. You, perhaps, wouldn't dare to alone. Together, dear one, we will work it out. Be sure there is a way—we may not find it in the end, but we will at least have tried."

XVII

CONCLUSION

One month after their meeting on the train, Hosmer and Thérèse had gone together to Centreville where they had been made one, as the saying goes, by the good Père Antoine; and without more ado, had driven back to Place-du-Bois: Mr. and Mrs. Hosmer. The event had caused more than the proverbial nine days' talk.[1] Indeed, now, two months after, it was still the absorbing theme that occupied the dwellers of the parish: and as such it promised to remain till supplanted by something of sufficient dignity and importance to usurp its place.

But of the opinions, favorable and other, that were being exchanged regarding them and their marriage, Hosmer and Thérèse heard little and would have cared less, so absorbed were they in the overmastering happiness that was holding them in thralldom. They could not yet bring themselves to look at it calmly—this happiness. Even the intoxication of it seemed a thing that promised to hold. Through love they had sought each other, and now the fulfillment of that love had brought more than tenfold its promise to both. It was a royal love; a generous love and a rich one in its revelation. It was a magician that had touched life for them and changed it into glory. In giving them to each other, it was moving them to the fullness of their own capabilities. Much to do in two little months; but what cannot love do?

"Could it give a woman more than this?" Thérèse was saying softly to herself. Her hands were clasped as in prayer and pressed together against her bosom. Her head bowed and her lips touching the intertwined fingers. She spoke of her own emotion; of a certain sweet turmoil that was stirring within

146

her, as she stood out in the soft June twilight waiting for her husband to come. Waiting to hear the new ring in his voice that was like a song of joy. Waiting to see that new strength and courage in his face, of whose significance she lost nothing. To see the new light that had come in his eyes with happiness. All gifts which love had given her.

"Well, at last," she said, going to the top of the steps to meet him when he came. Her welcome was in her eyes.

"At last," he echoed, with a sigh of relief; pressing her hand which she held out to him and raising it to his lips.

He did not let it go, but passed it through his arm, and together they turned to walk up and down the veranda.

"You didn't expect me at noon, did you?" he asked, looking down at her.

"No; you said you'd be likely not to come; but I hoped for you all the same. I thought you'd manage it some way."

"No," he answered her, laughing, "my efforts failed. I used even strategy. Held out the temptation of your delightful Creole dishes and all that. Nothing was of any avail. They were all business and I had to be all business too, the whole day long. It was horribly stupid."

She pressed his arm significantly.

"And do you think they will put all that money into the mill, David? Into the business?"

"No doubt of it, dear. But they're shrewd fellows: didn't commit themselves in any way. Yet I could see they were impressed. We rode for hours through the woods this morning and they didn't leave a stick of timber unscrutinized. We were out on the lake, too, and they were like ferrets into every cranny of the mill."

"But won't that give you more to do?"

"No, it will give me less: division of labor, don't you see? It will give me more time to be with you."

"And to help with the plantation," his wife suggested.

"No, no, Madame Thérèse," he laughed, "I'll not rob you of your occupation. I'll put no bungling hand into your concerns. I know a sound piece of timber when I see it; but I should hardly be able to tell a sample of Sea Island cotton[2] from the veriest low middling."

"Oh, that's absurd, David. Do you know you're getting to talk such nonsense since we're married; you remind me sometimes of Melicent."

"Of Melicent? Heaven forbid! Why, I have a letter from her," he said, feeling in his breast pocket. "The size and substance of it have actually weighted my pocket the whole day."

"Melicent talking of weighty things? That's something new," said Thérèse, interested.

"Is Melicent ever anything else than new?" he enquired.

They went and sat together on the bench at the corner of the veranda, where the fading Western light came over their shoulders. A quizzical smile came into his eyes as he unfolded his sister's letter—with Thérèse still holding his arm and sitting very close to him.

"Well," he said, glancing over the first few pages—his wife following—"she's given up her charming little flat and her quaint little English woman: concludes I was right about the expense, etc., etc. But here comes the gist of the matter," he said, reading from the letter—'I know you won't object to the trip, David, I have my heart so set on it. The expense will be trifling, seeing there are four of us to divide carriage hire, restaurant and all that: and it counts.

"If you only knew Mrs. Griesmann I'd feel confident of your consent. You'd be perfectly fascinated with her. She's one of those highly gifted women who knows everything. She's very much interested in me. Thinks to have found that I have a quick comprehensive intellectualism (she calls it) that has been misdirected. I think there is something in that, David; you know yourself I never did care really for society. She says it's impossible to ever come to a true knowledge of life as it is—which should be every one's aim—without studying certain fundamental truths and things.'"

"Oh," breathed Thérèse, overawed.

"But wait—but listen," said Hosmer, "'Natural History and all that—and we're going to take that magnificent trip through the West—the Yosemite and so forth. It appears the flora of California is especially interesting and we're to carry those delicious little tin boxes strapped over our shoulders to hold specimens. Her son and daughter are both, in their way, striking. He isn't handsome; rather the contrary; but so serene and collected—so intensely bitter—his mother tells me he's a pessimist. And the daughter really puts me to shame, child as she is, with the amount of her knowledge. She labels all her mother's specimens in Latin. Oh, I feel there's so much to be learned. Mrs. Griesmann thinks I ought to wear glasses during the trip. Says we often require them without knowing it ourselves—that they are so restful. She has some theory about it. I'm trying a pair, and see a great deal better through them than I expected to. Only they don't hold on very well, especially when I laugh.

"Who do you suppose seized on to me in Vandervoort's the other day, but that impertinent Mrs. Belle Worthington! Positively took me by the coat and commenced to gush about dear sister Thérèse. She said: 'I tell you what, my dear—' called me my dear at the highest pitch, and that odious Mrs. Van

Wycke behind us listening and pretending to examine a lace handkerchief. 'That Mrs. Lafirme's a trump,' she said—'too good for most any man. Hope you won't take offense, but I must say, you brother David's a perfect stick—it's what I always said.' Can you conceive of such shocking impertinence?'

"Well; Belle Worthington does possess the virtue of candor," said Hosmer amused and folding the letter. "That's about all there is, except a piece of scandal concerning people you don't know; that wouldn't interest you."

"But it would interest me," Thérèse insisted, with a little wifely resentment that her husband should have a knowledge of people that excluded her.

"Then you shall hear it," he said, turning to the letter again. "Let's see—'conceive—shocking impertinence—' oh, here it is.

"'Don't know if you have learned the horrible scandal; too dreadful to talk about. I shall send you the paper. I always knew that Lou Dawson was a perfidious creature—and Bert Rodney! You never did like him, David; but he was always so much the gentleman in his manners—you must admit that. Who could have dreamed it of him. Poor Mrs. Rodney is after all the one to be pitied. She is utterly prostrated. Refuses to see even her most intimate friends. It all came of those two vile wretches thinking Jack Dawson out of town when he wasn't; for he was right there following them around in their perambulations. And the outcome is that Mr. Rodney has his beauty spoiled they say forever; the shot came very near being fatal. But poor, poor Mrs. Rodney!

"'Well, good-bye, you dearest David mine. How I wish you both knew Mrs. Griesmann. Give that sweet sister Thérèse as many kisses as she will stand for me.

'Melicent.'"

This time Hosmer put the letter into his pocket, and Thérèse asked with a little puzzled air: "What do you suppose is going to become of Melicent, anyway, David?"

"I don't know, love, unless she marries my friend Homeyer."

"Now, David, you are trying to mystify me. I believe there's a streak of perversity in you after all."

"Of course there is; and here comes Mandy to say that 'suppa's gittin' cole.'"

"Aunt B'lindy 'low suppa on de table gittin' cole," said Mandy, retreating at once from the fire of their merriment.

Thérèse arose and held her two hands out to her husband.

He took them but did not rise; only leaned further back on the seat and looked up at her.

"Oh, supper's a bore; don't you think so?" he asked.

"No, I don't," she replied. "I'm hungry, and so are you. Come, David."

"But look, Thérèse, just when the moon has climbed over the top of that live-oak? We can't go now. And then Melicent's request; we must think about that."

"Oh, surely not, David," she said, drawing back.

"Then let me tell you something," and he drew her head down and whispered something in her pink ear that he just brushed with his lips. It made Thérèse laugh and turn very rosy in the moonlight.

Can that be Hosmer? Is this Thérèse? Fie, fie. It is time we were leaving them.

FIGURES

CHOPIN FAMILY BURIAL PLOT,
ST. LOUIS, MISSOURI. PHOTO BY
DAVID J. CAUDLE. 1999.

KATE CHOPIN HOUSE, CLOUTIERVILLE, LOUISIANA.
PHOTO BY SUZANNE DISHEROON GREEN. 2000.

Kate Chopin's headstone. Photo by
Suzanne Disheroon Green. 1999.

Melrose Plantation. This home is a good example of
southern plantations of the late nineteenth century.
Photo by Anitra Kinder. 2000.

[Right] Grave marker of Robert McAlpin, alleged to be the model for the character Simon Legree, in Harriet Beecher Stowe's *Uncle Tom's Cabin*. Photo by Anitra Kinder. 2000.

[Left] Grave marker of a McAlpin slave, alleged to be the model for the character Uncle Tom, in Harriet Beecher Stowe's *Uncle Tom's Cabin*. Photo by Suzanne Disheroon Green. 2000.

Former slave quarters, Natchitoches Parish, Louisiana. Photo by Charles L. Green. 2000.

St. Augustine Catholic Church, Isle Brevelle,
Natchitoches Parish, Louisiana. Photo by Charles
L. Green. 2000.

Maps

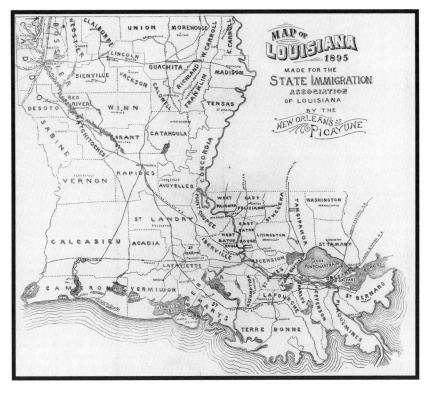

Louisiana, 1895. Special Collections, Tulane University Libraries, New Orleans, Louisiana. Reprinted by permission.

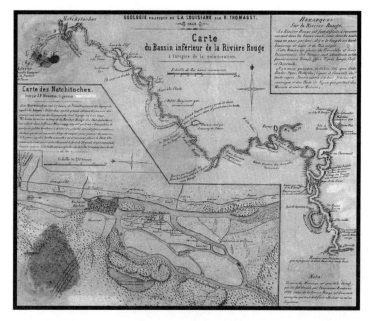

Lower Red River Basin, 1859. Folder 1, Watson Collection, Cammie G. Henry Research Center, Watson Memorial Library, Northwestern State University of Louisiana, Natchitoches. Reprinted by permission.

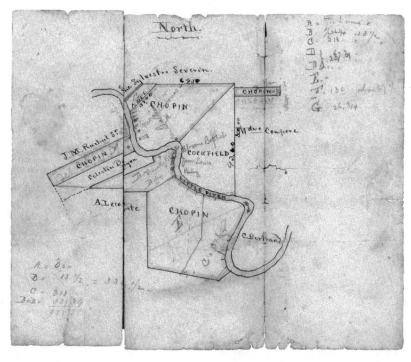

Route of Texas and Pacific Railroad, 1882. Reprinted by permission of the Office of Graduate Studies and Research, Northwestern State University of Louisiana.

[Opposite page bottom]: Chopin family land holdings in Natchitoches Parish. Cammie G. Henry Research Center, Watson Memorial Library, Northwestern State University of Louisiana, Natchitoches. Reprinted by permission.

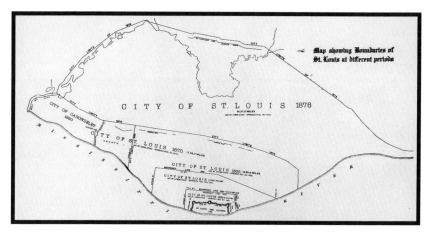

Boundaries of St. Louis at different periods. Reprinted by permission of Missouri Historical Society, St. Louis.

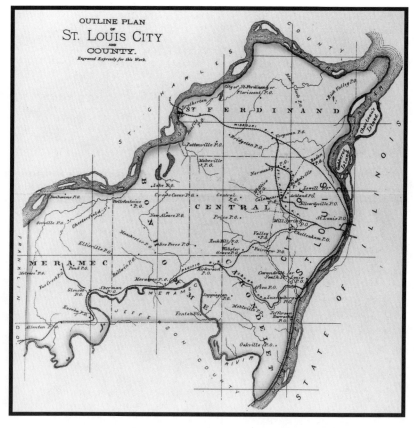

Outline plan of St. Louis City and County. Reprinted by permission of Missouri Historical Society, St. Louis.

BACKGROUNDS
AND CONTEXTS

he following selections are intended to provide a thorough background for appreciating Kate Chopin's *At Fault*. These readings address aspects of the narrative and the Louisiana cultural milieu that may be unfamiliar to those new to Chopin's writing.

The state of Louisiana is distinguished from the remainder of the South by historical, cultural, religious, and ethnic differences. Many of the state's unique characteristics derive from its early years as a colony, first of France and then of Spain. It was not until Louisiana had been under European control for nearly two hundred years that she came under American governance. Prior to the Louisiana Purchase in 1803 and the imposition of American law, citizens of Louisiana experienced a way of life different from that of people in America's former British colonies. They were accustomed to governance by a king's appointed representative rather than by democratically elected officials; they spoke a variety of languages other than English; they practiced Catholicism rather than Protestantism; and they embraced a tripartite racial caste system that was utterly foreign to the one that held sway in the remainder of the slave-holding states. Even in the postbellum period—sixty years following the Louisiana Purchase and the beginning of American control—the effects of the long period of colonization by France and Spain continued to influence all levels of the culture.

The regional flavor of Chopin's novel is derived from these unique aspects of Louisiana culture. Therefore, an understanding of these and other cultural differences is necessary to appreciate fully the nuances of *At Fault*. The selections that follow attempt to provide a brief overview of some major aspects of Louisiana culture, law, race and gender roles, and economic development that are relevant to the understanding of Chopin's novel.

CONTEMPORARY REVIEWS

This segment contains the extant reviews of *At Fault*. The reviews are generally positive, praising the way in which Chopin captures the local culture and landscape, but none of the reviewers seems to view her as a writer of serious literature. Instead, the impression that the reviewers leave with readers is that Chopin is a member of the class of women writers whose sentimental domestic fiction and pieces of local color, while popular at the time, were not to be classed with the more serious literary efforts of the late nineteenth century.

SPECTATOR (Oct. 4 1890)

Among the many bright women in St. Louis that have during the last decade published books Mrs. Kate Chopin will now be enrolled. A copy of her story *At Fault,* lies upon my desk after having been carefully read from first to last. No inclination was felt to use the reviewer's privilege of skipping. The story is so concisely and gracefully told that each part is necessary to the other. The scene opens at a cotton plantation in Nacogdoche [*sic*] Parish, La., its situation so retired that there is little change in the state of society since the war. The negroes cultivate the soil, looking as of yore to the whites for guidance and protection. The lady of the manor is Therese Lafirme, a young creole widow with the charms of her peculiar race apparent in both appearance and character. David Hosmer, a lumber merchant from St. Louis, comes to Place-du-Bois plantation and rents land from its mistress upon which he builds a saw mill and engages in lucrative trade. A natural interest between these parties deepens into warm affection and David declares his love. Simultaneous with

---

"Review of *At Fault*" in *St. Louis Spectator,* October 4, 1890.

this Thérèse learns that he has a divorced wife living. Possessed with the Roman Catholic idea that the marriage tie is indissolvable she uses her great influence to induce David to remarry his wife and bring her to Place-du-Bois. Fanny, the wife, is unworthy, yet in spite of her frivolity, selfishness and habit of taking stimulants, there is a vein of pity in the contempt she inspires, such natures being to some extent irresponsible. The story gets its incidents from rural southern life. The young "cajun" (Arcadian) Grégoire may seem exaggerated to such as have no experience of that phase of character, but is by no means an impossible type. The negroes are very well drawn and the scene where Pierson describes Grégoire's spree to Uncle Hiram and Aunt Belindy, particularly the comments of the latter upon it, inimitable. Their [sic] is a weird horror in the burning of the mill and the struggle of old Morico to save his wretched son, Joçint. With the cry "Mon Fils, Mon garçon?" he ends his life, a falling timber engulfing him with the dead burden and consigning both to a fiery grave. The book ends with a sweet picture of happiness, when David and Thérèse, after the death of the unfortunate Fanny, are made husband and wife, with a reign of joy likely to continue many years on the old plantation. There are other characters and incidents which give a pleasing variety to the book. Mrs. Chopin is to be congratulated on the interest her book is sure to produce among the lovers of sprightly and refined literature. Mrs. Chopin's book *At Fault* is put out by the St. Louis firm, Nixon & Jones.

ST. LOUIS POST-DISPATCH (OCTOBER 5, 1890)

Part of the Scenes Are in St. Louis and the Characters St. Louisans—
The New Webster International Dictionary—Some of the Latest Books—
Literary News and Gossip—The Magazines.

The most recent plunge into fiction by a local writer is that of Mrs. Kate Chopin, several of whose short stories have been published in the SUNDAY POST-DISPATCH. Her initial effort as a novelist is entitled *At Fault,* and a great deal of the domestic drama set forth in it has St. Louis as its stage setting. Many of its allusions are local, and several of the principal characters are St. Louisans, so that the story is essentially a local one, and will thus prove of unusual interest to residents of the city. The action of *At Fault* turns upon a mistaken idea. David Hosmer, who hails from St. Louis, is a rugged and strong-willed but high-strung and nervous man, who has made an unfortunate marriage, lured

---

Review of Kate Chopin, *At Fault,* in "A St. Louis Novelist. *At Fault,* Mrs. Kate Chopin's New Novel." *St. Louis Post-Dispatch,* October 5, 1890.

thereto by a bundle of feminine weaknesses which by so many strong men are mistaken for indications of womanly character. After several years of wedded misery, during which his wife took to drink, he was forced, or thought he was forced, to separate from her. When she sued for a divorce he interposed no obstacle, and doubled the alimony which was granted her. He plunges into business, which absorbs his whole attention. In furtherance of one of his projects he goes South, where he meets Mrs. Thérèse Lafirme, a widow of five years—a woman in every respect the opposite of his former wife, highly bred, cultivated, with a knowledge of the world and of affairs seldom possessed by woman, tempered withal by womanly dignity and refinement of character—all uniting to attract a man of Hosmer's stamp in maturity of his character, and to whom he was a figure of unusual interest. He declares his love and tells his story, but loving him as only such a woman can love, she bids him go back to his wife and reclaim her. He rejects her arguments, but does her bidding, because to obey her is the dearest privilege of his life. He remarries his wife and takes her to the Louisiana plantation, where Thérèse befriends her. But she cannot be reclaimed. Weak, vulgar, commonplace, she resents the friendship of the better woman and soon falls into her old ways. Hosmer's life is more miserable than ever, and Thérèse's is not less so on seeing the misery she has wrought by her injudicious efforts at duty doing. But Fanny's life is brought to a sudden close, her death being the direct consequence of her thirst for liquor.

Mrs. Chopin has shown in this, her first venture as a novelist, that she has the qualities of a successful fictionist. She has avoided the temptations which beset the path even of experienced writers, and has made herself a place in the literature of the West. Setting out to write a novel, she has written it with no other purpose apparently than to tell the story well. The story suggests its own moral. Mrs. Chopin exhibits more than usual consideration for the reader in keeping her own opinions in the background and letting the situation depend upon its own eloquence for its moral effect. She does not always succeed, but her opinions must be sought in the dialogue, not in the narrative. It is not apparent that she is animated by anything but a deep interest in a deeply interesting situation. It does not appear that she wants to point a moral or indicate a "tendency," but she has cleverly succeeded in displaying a human group charged with suggestion and meaning. And she is equally happy in the management of the plot. It works itself out by the force of its own vitality. With true artistic instinct Mrs. Chopin has kept her hands off the sequence. The procession of events is the natural and necessary outcome of circumstance and character. Even in compassing Fanny's death—the point where under a less clever hand, nature might have been supplanted by mechanism, there is nothing artificial. Indeed, this episode in its preparation and accomplishment is the cleverest exhibition of ARTISTIC SKILL in the whole book.

In the fortunes of Gregoire and the whims of Melicent are found materials for a parallel thread, which is woven skillfully into the thread of the main story. These two characters, one a nephew of Mrs. Lafirme, the other Hosmer's sister, are charming in their unaffected naturalness. And there are delightful gleams of plantation life. Happily there is not much dialect, but there is enough to give a relish to the story. Only an instructive and unconscious observer could portray the negro characteristics so faithfully and vividly. Full of humor are the conversations of the darky servants who serve Thérèse so devotedly—a humor not always perceptible, broad as it is, to the ordinary Northern observer. And the burning of the mill, with its attendant accessories of superstition and death, is a good example of realistic and dramatic power.

The author in *At Fault* does not believe in making people over, sadly in need though they may be of a regenerating process. Indeed, her matter of fact way of taking things and people as they are is sometimes exasperating to a reader who has got into the habit of dreaming of things as he would like to have them. One shudders at hearing Hosmer tell his wife to "shut up," and we protest against Melicent's five engagements. If she really was engaged five times it ought not to be mentioned. We have no objection to realism when applied to Belle Worthington and Lou Dawson, but in the name of an effete prejudice we object to a man like Hosmer saying "shut up."

Altogether Mrs. Chopin has produced a novel which St. Louis can be proud of. The faults of detail which now and then crop out, are not owing to lack of natural skill, but to a want of cunning of hand, which comes with practice, and even these faults are trivial. The story is interesting for itself. To those who like to moralize there is a pretty question of morality put in the remarriage of a divorced couple under the influence of a mistaken sense of duty. Thérèse acknowledged that her judgment was at fault and before the end comes sees clearly enough that duty cannot be so well defined [*sic*] by a procrustean code as by individual intelligence applied to individual needs, that moral conditions do not result from good intentions unless the good intentions are rationalized by a good intelligence. In this feature Mrs. Chopin has offered her readers food for speculation—perhaps without intending it. But with whatever mind the book is read it cannot fail to interest, and St. Louis people may be congratulated on having one among them who promises to rival the fame of Miss Murfree.

[*At Fault,* BY KATE CHOPIN. NIXON AND JONES, ST. LOUIS.]

Natchitoches Enterprise (DECEMBER 1890)

A novel with the scene laid out in the valley of Cane River is in itself quite a novelty. Catherine Cole sketched in a charming manner that section of Natchitoches Parish and so have occasional local writers, but it required the pen of a St. Louis lady to weave the customs and traditions of its people into a romance. The old McAlpine [*sic*] plantation, now owned by Mr. Lami [*sic*] Chopin, is the chosen spot, and whiskey interwoven with love is the foundation of the story.

The plot of the novel is full of interest and opens with the death of Mr. LaFirme and a realistic discription [*sic*] of the place at the time that the Texas Pacific Railway was constructed. Then follows the acquaintance of Widow Lefirme [*sic*] also called Thirese [*sic*] with Mr. Hosmer a divorced man from St. Louis—his pleasant reception, his employment on the Saw Mill and his final love making with Thirese. He seperated [*sic*] from his wife because she was addicted to the liquor habit and found sympathy with Thirese who advises him to take her back. Meanwhile he had made love to Thirese; upon his re-marriage to his divorced wife which is done quite suddenly, he returns and finds that a lingering affection still existed between himself and Thirese. His wife continues in her old ways and while seeking for a colored boy whom she had sent after her liquor, she tarries at a negro cabin which caves in the stream and she is drowned despite her husband's efforts to save her life. The tender feeling long cultivated between Hosmer and Thirese, now fully developed, culminates in their marriage and the novel ends with that event. There are, however, other interesting incidents. Hosmer's sister and Gregoire—an uneducated Creole—appear to be quite in love with each other, but his want of culture and the murder of an incendiary by him ruptures the match and she returns to St. Louis.

While we have nothing but praise for the delineation of her characters and for the literary merits of the work—though at times the style is apparently swollen and high-sounding—we find that the love or love-making which existed and was somewhat continuous between Thirese and Hosmer, to be out of place, or in other words improper. Such a feeling between the parties seems to mar the beauty of their lives which rests upon such a pure

---

Review of Kate Chopin, *At Fault,* in *Natchitoches (La.) Enterprise*, December 4, 1890. Available in Kate Chopin Vertical File, Cammie G. Henry Research Center, Watson Memorial Library, Northwestern State University of Louisiana, Natchitoches, Louisiana. Transcribed from original for Vertical File by Heather Kirk Thomas.

and high plane. In fact there is a contradiction between their lives when separated and when together. The denouncement [*sic*] is a relief and a satisfactory solution of the situation.

The character of Gregoire is a type of the uninstructed Creole and the language and expressions put in his mouth are true to nature. His canoe-ride with Melicent on Lake du Bois is a delightful description of such pastimes in Louisiana, but the scene at McFarland's grave is rather highly colored and hardly probable in parties so newly acquainted.

The negro character [*sic*] are exceedingly well reproduced and the authoress traces with a mistress' hand the peculiarities of the Africans [*sic*] dialect. Pierson describes in the natural Etheopian [*sic*] style Gregoire's spree in Cloutierville and the light and shade thrown in by Belinda's remarks are perfect specimens of negro mannerism. Marie Louise and Morico form exquisite pictures of the old time darkies and remind the writer of the race and characteristics of his old nurse and yard-servant of the long ago.

An effective dramatic situation is that of poor old Morico who amid his lamentations expires over the dead body of his son. Another thrilling incident is that of the caving bank with Mrs. Hosmer and the rescue of her lifeless body by the almost super-human efforts of her husband. Here the authoress forgot to drop a tear over Marie Louise's watery grave. Mrs. Hosmer who is the one "At Fault," and ostensibly the heroine of the story, leads the life of a drunken sot, and her manoeuvers [*sic*] and devices in securing her liquor form an ingenious by-play. Mr. Duplan and family, Creoles of the neighborhood, pay Thirese a visit and their elegant manners and quaint english [*sic*] give the authoress much latitude for her discriptive [*sic*] powers which makes this chapter one of the most readable in the book.

The characters introduced from St. Louis are people of leisure, except the Drummer, of whom we frequently hear and read and their fashionable lives terminate finally in a scandel [*sic*]. This portion of the novel is indited [*sic*] in the reportorial [*sic*] style and is a valuable auxiliary to the story.

There are other characters and incidents in the plot and the connections are well kept up throughout. The authoress indulges in brief philosophical reflections to which we refer the reader.

The perusal of the work afforded us much pleasure and we hope that Mrs. Kate Chopin will again favor us with another. Upon the whole, 'tis our humble opinion that while we cannot accord genius to the fair authoress we are willing to admit that she is a lady who possesses talents of no common order.

FLORA

Kate Chopin Replies (December 1890)

Saint Louis, December 9, 1890

To the Editor of *The Enterprise:*

While thanking your reviewer for the many agreeable and clever things said of my story *At Fault*, kindly permit me to correct a misconception. Fanny is not the heroine. It is charitable to regard her whole existence as a misfortune. Therese Lafirme, the heroine of the book is the one who was at fault—remotely, and immediately. Remotely—in her blind acceptance of an undistinguishing, therefore unintelligent code of righteousness by which to deal out judgments. Immediately—in this, that unknowing of the individual needs of *this* man and *this* woman, she should yet constitute herself not only as a mentor, but an instrument in reuniting them.

Their first marriage was an unhappy mistake; their reunion was a crime against the unwritten moral law. Emerson says: "Morals is [*sic*] the science of substances, not of shows. It is the *what* and not the *how*. . . . It were an unspeakable calamity if anyone should think he has the right to impose a private will on others. That is a part of a striker, an assassin."

Towards the close of the story, Therese acknowledges her error, and Hosmer reads her a brief lecture upon the "living spirit." the "dead letter," etc.

I ask to straighten this misconception—of Fanny having been "at fault," because it is one, which if accepted by the reader is liable to throw the story entirely out of prospective [*sic*].

Yours very truly,

Kate Chopin

Saint Louis Republic (October 1890)

"At Fault; a Novel." By Kate Chopin. St. Louis: Nixon-Jones Printing Co.

A clever romance of Louisiana life, the French Creole accent, when speaking English, being well caught. The heroine, Therese Lafirme, is, through the

---

Kate Chopin, "*At Fault:* A Correction," *Natchitoches (La.) Enterprise,* December 18, 1890. Available in Kate Chopin Vertical File, Cammie G. Henry Research Center, Watson Memorial Library, Northwestern State University of Louisiana, Natchitoches, Louisiana. Transcribed from original for Vertical File by Heather Kirk Thomas.

Review of Kate Chopin, *At Fault,* in "Literary News and New Books," *Saint Louis (Mo.) Republic,* October 18, 1890.

whole book, except at its very close, in love with another woman's husband. She raves to herself of the bliss it would be:

> "If it were her right instead of another's to watch for his coming and rejoice at it! Hers to call him husband and lavish on him the love that awoke so strongly when she permitted herself, as she was doing now, to invoke it! She felt what capability lay within her of rousing the man to new interests in life. She pictured the dawn of an unsuspected happiness coming to him: broadening; illuminating; growing in him to answer to her own bigheartedness."

Indeed, the women who love other women's husbands and the men who love other men's wives always do feel that way; as bachelors' children are always admirably reared, they could always make the beloved one happy. This is her history:

> "When Jerome Lafirme died, his neighbors awaited the results of his sudden taking off with indolent watchfulness. It was matter of unusual interest to them that a plantation of 4,000 acres had been left unincumbered to the disposal of a handsome, inconsolable, childless Creole widow of 30. A betise of some sort might safely be looked for. But time passing, the anticipated folly failed to reveal itself; and the only wonder was that Therese Lafirme so successfully followed the methods of her departed husband.
>
> Therese was of a roundness of figure suggesting a future of excessive fulness [sic] if not judiciously guarded; and she was fair, with a warm whiteness that a passing thought could deepen into color. The waving blonde hair, gathered in an abundant coil on top of her head, grew away with a pretty sweep from the temples, the low forehead and nape of the white neck that showed above a frill of soft lace. Her eyes were blue, as certain gems are: that deep blue that lights, and glows, and tells things of the soul."

The man she falls so desperately in love with is a Northerner who buys the right to erect a saw-mill in some woods on her plantation. A visit is thus described:

> Hardly had the clerk gone with his letters than a light footstep sounded on the narrow porch; the quick tap of a parasol was heard on the door-sill: a pleasant voice asking: "Any admission except on business?" and Therese crossed the small room and seated herself beside Hosmer's desk before giving him time to arise.

> She laid her hand and arm—bare to the elbow—across his work, and said, looking at him reproachfully:
>
> "Is this the way you keep a promise?"
>
> "A promise?" he questioned, smiling awkwardly and looking furtively at the white arm, then very earnestly at the ink-stand beyond.
>
> "Yes. Didn't you promise to do no work after 5 o'clock?"
>
> "But this is merely pastime," he said, touching the paper, yet leaving it undisturbed beneath the fair weight that was pressing it down. "My work is finished."

Hosmer's wife, Fanny, is a fatal terror; she "guesses," she drinks to excess of whiskey, she steals from an old darkey's cabin, and uses slang that gives one shivers; but as the fair author herself, in the narrative portion of the volume, speaks of a railway station as a "depot" and a shop as a "store"—mistakes that might do in the mouth of one of the characters, who many of them use "aint" for is not, but mar the value of the book when used in the narrative portion— she may have made Fanny worse than she intended.

They kill off the wife, and Hosmer and Therese marry and are happy ever after.

Some of the secondary characters are particularly well drawn, and the local color is excellent.

NEW ORLEANS DAILY PICAYUNE (OCTOBER 1890)

At Fault by Kate Chopin. St. Louis: Nixon Jones Printing Company.
New Orleans: Book and News Company.

The author of this interesting novel is the widow of the late Oscar Chopin, commission merchant in New Orleans, and lived here ten years—from 1870 to 1880. She afterwards resided on a plantation in Natchitoches Parish, where the main incidents of the story occur. The life of a handsome Creole widow of 30 is charmingly related in the book.

SAINT LOUIS LIFE (OCTOBER 1890)

A new book that has been very favorably reviewed by several St. Louis journals, and which richly deserves all the good things that have been said of it, is

---

Review of Kate Chopin, *At Fault,* in "Recent Publications," *New Orleans Daily Picayune,* October 12, 1890.

Review of Kate Chopin, *At Fault,* in *Saint Louis (Mo.) Life,* October 11, 1890.

that of Mrs. Kate Chopin, "At Fault," just from the press of Nixon and Jones. It is a pleasing story, exceptionally well-told, and proves that Mrs. Chopin possesses a talent that should prove a source of pleasure to the public and profit to herself. Lack of space prevents an extended criticism of the book in the columns of *Life,* but many more ambitious books have afforded less pleasure in the reading than this charming story of life on a Louisiana bayou. Mrs. Chopin seems to possess an intuitive perception of what is fitting and artistic. Without any apparent effort or labored description she brings before the mental vision of the readers pictures of places and persons that at once strike us as true to life. Her characters say always the right thing, and are witty, tender, or commonplace, just as she means them to be. Such art as Mrs. Chopin's is the result of long familiarity with the best literature combined with natural talent trained in the best schools. The finish of her work is in marked contrast to the crudity of the majority of first books. The book will have a wide circulation if it receive its deserts.

THE NATION (1 OCTOBER 1890)

. . . It is not quite clear who is cast for the title-role in *At Fault,* since all the characters have valid pretensions to the part. There is the lady who drinks and the gentleman who gets a divorce from her, the widow who loves and is beloved by him, but who persuades him to remarry his divorced partner and bring her to the Louisiana plantation, where she (the widow) may have a fostering care of the two and help them do their duty to each other. There is also the young lady of many engagements, the negro who commits arson, the young gentleman who shoots him, the Colonel who shoots the young gentleman, the St. Louis lady who goes to matinées and runs off with the matinée-going gentleman. It may not be amiss, in deciding who is "At Fault," to consider as well the claims of the author, the publisher, and the reader. The reverse side to all this is a graphic description of life on a cotton plantation, an aptitude for seizing dialects of whites and blacks alike, no little skill in perceiving and defining character, and a touch which shows that the array of disagreeables was born rather of literary crudity than of want of refinement.

Georgios Drosines, "Amaryllis" [review of Kate Chopin, *At Fault*], *The Nation* 53 (1890): 264.

LITERARY SOURCES

ate Chopin was a well-read literary critic and translator of French literature. Therefore, she held strong opinions as to the merits—or lack thereof—of her literary peers. In both of her novels, Chopin expresses subtle disdain for a number of her critically acclaimed colleagues. This literary disdain appears to have been mutual, given opinions expressed in numerous letters, such as those from Nathaniel Hawthorne to his friends William Ticknor and James C. Fields, which are excerpted here.

The selection from Ralph Waldo Emerson's essay "Spiritual Laws" illustrates his writing style, a style that Chopin describes as little more than a sedative to several of her characters. Emerson was one of the most prominent and influential thinkers of the Unitarian church, and *At Fault's* Melicent embraces his religious views. Chopin also shows Belle Worthington using volumes of Emerson's and John Ruskin's essays as anchors for dry goods being aired out on a rooftop.

Despite the fact that his works are used as ballast in Chopin's novel, Ruskin was one of the most influential critics of art and society during the late nineteenth century. The Ruskin selections illustrate his disdain for the *nouveau riche* of his era, a view seemingly shared by Chopin herself, in light of her depiction of Fanny's St. Louis friends.

A number of literary selections which illuminate these and other aspects of Chopin's novel are included in this section. The brief selection from *Hamlet* supplies the context for Melicent's remark about Hosmer's "pale cast of thought." Alice Dunbar Nelson's short story, "The Goodness of St. Roque," provides insight into Louisiana's Creole culture and beliefs. Grégoire and Thérèse are members of this culture, and it is familiar to Chopin because of the time she spent in both New Orleans and Natchitoches Parish. Dunbar

Nelson's story also demonstrates the ways in which Catholicism and voodoo have become intertwined in much of Louisiana's culture.

The selection from *Uncle Tom's Cabin* is especially close to Chopin's personal experience in northwestern Louisiana. The model for Simon Legree is identified through local legend, folklore, and even legal documentation as Robert McAlpin, a close neighbor of Kate Chopin and her husband Oscar. McAlpin is also the man from whom Oscar's father purchased much of his land. The affidavits and documentary included here describe Harriet Beecher Stowe's visit to McAlpin's plantation and its summary termination after the owner discovered that she had been interviewing his slaves. Although some debate continues as to the source of Stowe's characters, this legal document and excerpts from D. B. Corley's *A Visit to Uncle Tom's Cabin* strongly support the local legend, to this day circulated by the residents of Natchitoches Parish.

Nathaniel Hawthorne on Women Writers (1852 and 1855)

Liverpool, Jany 19th, '55.

Dear Ticknor,

. . . I shall spend a year on the Continent, and then decide whether to go back to the Wayside, or to stay abroad and write books. But I had rather hold this office two years longer; for I have not seen half enough of England, and there is the germ of a new Romance in my mind, which will be all the better for ripening slowly. *Besides, America is now wholly given over to a d——d mob of scribbling women, and I should have no chance of success while the public taste is occupied with their trash—and should be ashamed of myself if I did succeed.* What is the mystery of these innumerable editions of the Lamplighter, and other books neither better nor worse?—worse they could not be, and better they need not be, when they sell by the 100,000.

Your friend,

Nathl Hawthorne

Selections from Nathaniel Hawthorne, *Letters of Hawthorne to William D. Ticknor, 1851–1864* (Newark, N.J.: Carteret Book Club, 1910; reprinted, Washington D.C.: Bruccoli-Clark, 1972), 75; and Nathaniel Hawthorne, *The Letters, 1843–1853*, p. 624, ed. Thomas Woodson, L. Neal Smith, and Norman Holmes Pearson (Columbus: Ohio State University Press, 1985), 624.

Concord, Decr 11th 1852

Dear Fields,

As a less aukward mode of doing the business, I have preferred rather to acknowledge Mrs. Crosland's books, in a note to yourself, than to her. You will find it enclosed; and if it meet your approbation, please to forward it. I really don't know that I have said any more than truth, in a good-humored mood, will warrant; but, nevertheless, I can very well conceive of a person's tossing the books aside as tedious twaddle. My favorable opinion of the book has evaporated, in the process of writing it down. *All* women, as authors, are feeble and tiresome. I wish they were forbidden to write, on pain of having their faces deeply scarified with an oyster-shell. . . .

Truly yours,

Nathl Hawthorne.

(Don't make a mistake, and send this note to Mrs. Crosland!)

Spiritual Laws
Ralph Waldo Emerson

In like manner, our moral nature is vitiated by any interference of our will. People represent virtue as a struggle, and take to themselves great airs upon their attainments, and the question is everywhere vexed, when a noble nature is commended, whether the man is not better who strives with temptation. But there is no merit in the matter. Either God is there, or he is not there. . . .

If we look wider, things are all alike; laws, and letters, and creeds and modes of living, seem a travestie of truth. Our society is encumbered by ponderous machinery which resembles the endless aqueducts which the Romans built over hill and dale, and which are superseded by the discovery of the law that water rises to the level of its source. . . .

A little consideration of what takes place around us every day would show us, that a higher law than that of our will regulates events; that our painful labors are unnecessary, and fruitless; that only in our easy, simple, spontaneous action are we strong, and by contenting ourselves with obedience we become divine. Belief and love,—a believing love will relieve us of a vast load

Selections from Ralph Waldo Emerson, "Spiritual Laws," in *The Essays of Ralph Waldo Emerson* (Philadelphia: H. Altemus, 1896), 77–96.

of care. O my brothers, God exists. There is a soul at the centre of nature, and over the will of every man, so that none of us can wrong the universe. It has so infused its strong enchantment into nature, that we prosper when we accept its advice, and when we struggle to wound its creatures, our hands are glued to our sides, or they beat our own breasts. The whole course of things goes to teach us faith. We need only obey. There is guidance for each of us, and by lowly listening we shall hear the right word. . . .

The same reality pervades all teaching. The man may teach by doing, and not otherwise. If he can communicate himself, he can teach, but not by words. He teaches who gives, and he learns who receives. There is no teaching until the pupil is brought into the same state or principle in which you are; a transfusion takes place: he is you, and you are he; then is a teaching, and by no unfriendly chance or bad company can he ever quite lose the benefit. But your propositions run out of one ear as they ran in at the other. . . .

Human character evermore publishes itself. The most fugitive deed and word, the mere air of doing a thing, the intimated purpose, expresses character. If you act, you show character; if you sit still, if you sleep, you show it. You think because you have spoken nothing, when others spoke, and have given no opinion on the times, on the church, on slavery, on marriage, on socialism, on secret societies, on the college, on parties and persons, that your verdict is still expected with curiosity as a reserved wisdom. Far otherwise; your silence answers very loud. You have no oracle to utter, and your fellow men have learned that you cannot help them; for, oracles speak. Doth not wisdom cry, and understanding put forth her voice? . . .

The lesson which these observations convey is, Be, and not seem. Let us acquiesce. Let us take our bloated nothingness out of the path of the divine circuits. Let us unlearn our wisdom of the world. Let us lie low in the Lord's power, and learn that truth alone makes rich and great. . . .

. . . Let the great soul incarnated in some woman's form, poor and sad and single, in some Dolly or Joan, go out to service, and sweep chambers and scour floors, and its effulgent daybeams cannot be muffled or hid, but to sweep and scour will instantly appear supreme and beautiful actions, the top and radiance of human life, and all people will get mops and brooms; until, lo, suddenly the great soul has enshrined itself in some other form, and done some other deed, and that is now the flower and head of all living nature.

Thoughts on the Degradation of Labour
John Ruskin

The Stones of Venice

It is verily this degradation of the operative into a machine, which, more than any other evil of the times, is leading the mass of the nations everywhere into vain, incoherent, destructive struggling for a freedom of which they cannot explain the nature to themselves. Their universal outcry against wealth, and against nobility, is not forced from them either by the pressure of famine, or the sting of mortified pride. These do much, and have done much in all ages; but the foundations of society were never yet shaken as they are at this day. It is not that men are ill fed, but that they have no pleasure in the work by which they make their bread, and therefore look to wealth as the only means of pleasure. It is not that men are pained by the scorn of the upper classes, but they cannot endure their own; for they feel that the kind of labour to which they are condemned is verily a degrading one, and makes them less than men. Never had the upper classes so much sympathy with the lower, or charity for them, as they have at this day, and yet never were they so much hated by them: for, of old, the separation between the noble and the poor was merely a wall built by law; now it is a veritable difference in level of standing, a precipice between upper and lower grounds in the field of humanity, and there is pestilential air at the bottom of it.

Pre-Raphaelitism

It may be proved, with much certainty, that God intends no man to live in this world without working: but it seems to me no less evident that He intends every man to be happy in his work. It is written, 'in the sweat of thy brow,' but it was never written, 'in the breaking of thine heart,' thou shalt eat bread: and I find that, as on the one hand, infinite misery is caused by idle people, who both fail in doing what was appointed for them to do, and set in motion various springs of mischief in matters in which they should have had no concern, so on the other hand, no small misery is caused by overworked and unhappy people, in the dark views which they necessarily take up themselves, and force upon others, of work itself. Were it not so, I believe the fact of their being unhappy is in itself a violation of divine law, and a sign of some kind of folly or sin in their way of life. Now in order that people may be happy in their work, these three things are needed:

Selections from John Ruskin, *The Stones of Venice* (London: Smith, Elder & Co., 1853), vol. 2, chap. 6, 162–72.

Selections from John Ruskin, "Work," in *Pre-Raphaelitism* (New York: J. Wiley, 1851), 7–41.

They must be fit for it: They must not do too much of it: and they must have a sense of success in it—not a doubtful sense, such as needs some testimony of other people for its confirmation, but a sure sense, or rather knowledge, that so much work has been done well, and fruitfully done, whatever the world may say or think about it. So that in order that a man may be happy, it is necessary that he should not only be capable of his work, but a good judge of his work.

FORS CLAVIGERA

I had to go to Verona by the afternoon train. In the carriage with me were two American girls with their father and mother, people of the class which has lately made so much money, suddenly, and does not know what to do with it: and these two girls, of about fifteen and eighteen, had evidently been indulged in everything (since they had had the means) which western civilization could imagine. And here they were, specimens of the utmost which the money and invention of the nineteenth century could produce in maidenhood,—children of its most progressive race,—enjoying the full advantages of political liberty, of enlightened philosophical education, of cheap pilfered literature, and of luxury at any cost. Whatever money, machinery, or freedom of thought could do for these two children, had been done. No superstition had deceived, no restraint degraded them:—types, they could not but be, of maidenly wisdom and felicity, as conceived by the forwardest intellects of our time.

And they were travelling through a district which, if any in the world, should touch the hearts and delight the eyes of young girls. Between Venice and Verona! Portia's villa perhaps in sight upon the Brenta, Juliet's tomb to be visited in the evening,—blue against the southern sky, the hills of Petrarch's home. Exquisite midsummer sunshine, with low rays, glanced through the vine-leaves; all the Alps were clear, from the Lake of Garda to Cadore, and to farthest Tyrol. What a princess's chamber, this, if these are princesses, and what dreams might they not dream, therein!

But the two American girls were neither princesses, nor seers, nor dreamers. By infinite self-indulgence, they had reduced themselves simply to two pieces of white putty that could feel pain. The flies and the dust stuck to them as to clay, and they perceived, between Venice and Verona, nothing but the flies and the dust. They pulled down the blinds the moment they entered the carriage, and then sprawled, and writhed, and tossed among the cushions of it, in vain contest, during the whole fifty miles, with every miserable sensation of bodily affliction that could make time intolerable.

Selection from John Ruskin, "Benediction," in *Fors Clavigera: Letters to the Workmen and Labourers of Great Britain* (New York: J. Wiley, 1872), letter 20, August 1872, 345–46.

"To Be or Not To Be?"
William Shakespeare

To be, or not to be—that is the question:
Whether 'tis nobler in the mind to suffer
The slings and arrows of outrageous fortune
Or to take arms against a sea of troubles,
And by opposing end them. To die—to sleep—
No more; and by a sleep to say we end
The heartache, and the thousand natural shocks
That flesh is heir to. 'Tis a consummation
Devoutly to be wish'd. To die—to sleep.
To sleep—perchance to dream: ay, there's the rub!
For in that sleep of death what dreams may come
When we have shuffled off this mortal coil,
Must give us pause. There's the respect
That makes calamity of so long life.
For who would bear the whips and scorns of time,
Th' oppressor's wrong, the proud man's contumely,
The pangs of despis'd love, the law's delay,
The insolence of office, and the spurns
That patient merit of th' unworthy takes,
When he himself might his quietus make
With a bare bodkin? Who would these fardels bear,
To grunt and sweat under a weary life,
But that the dread of something after death—
The undiscover'd country, from whose bourn
No traveller returns—puzzles the will,
And makes us rather bear those ills we have
Than fly to others that we know not of?
Thus conscience does make cowards of us all,
And thus the native hue of resolution
Is sicklied o'er with *the pale cast of thought*,
And enterprises of great pith and moment
With this regard their currents turn awry
And lose the name of action.

William Shakespeare, *Hamlet,* Act III, Scene 1, lines 56–88.

UNCLE TOM'S CABIN
HARRIET BEECHER STOWE

CHAPTER 10: THE PROPERTY IS CARRIED OFF

The February morning looked gray and drizzling through the window of Uncle Tom's cabin. It looked on downcast faces, the images of mournful hearts. The little table stood out before the fire, covered with an ironing-cloth; a coarse but clean shirt or two, fresh from the iron, hung on the back of a chair by the fire, and Aunt Chloe had another spread out before her on the table. Carefully she rubbed and ironed every fold and every hem, with the most scrupulous exactness, every now and then raising her hand to her face to wipe off the tears that were coursing down her cheeks.

Tom sat by, with his Testament open on his knee, and his head leaning upon his hand;—but neither spoke. It was yet early, and the children lay all asleep together in their little rude trundle-bed.

Tom, who had, to the full, the gentle, domestic heart, which woe for them! has been a peculiar characteristic of his unhappy race, got up and walked silently to look at his children.

"It's the last time," he said.

Aunt Chloe did not answer, only rubbed away over and over on the coarse shirt, already as smooth as hands could make it; and finally setting her iron suddenly down with a despairing plunge, she sat down to the table, and "lifted up her voice and wept."

"S'pose we must be resigned; but oh Lord! How ken I? If I know'd anything whar you's goin', or how thay'd sarve you! Missis says she'll try an 'deem ye, in a year or two; but Lor! nobody never comes up that goes down thar! They kills 'em! I've hearn 'em tell how dey works 'em up on dem ar plantations."

"There'll be the same God there, Chloe, that there is here."

"Well," said Aunt Chloe, "s'pose dere will; but de Lord lets dreful things happen, sometimes. I don't seem to get no comfort dat way."

"I'm in the Lord's hands," said Tom; "nothin' can go no furder than he lets it;—and thar's *one* thing I can thank him for. It's *me* that's sold and going down, and not you nur the chil'en. Here you're safe;—what comes will come only on me; and the Lord, he'll help me,—I know he will."

Selections from Harriet Beecher Stowe, *Uncle Tom's Cabin; or, Life Among the Lowly* (Philadelphia: John C. Winston and Company, 1897), chapters 10, 30, and 41.

Ah, brave, manly heart,—smothering thine own sorrow, to comfort thy beloved ones! Tom spoke with a thick utterance, and with a bitter choking in his throat,—but he spoke brave and strong.

"Let's think on our marcies!" he added, tremulously, as if he was quite sure he needed to think on them very hard indeed.

"Marcies!" said Aunt Chloe; "don't see no marcy in't! 'tan't right! tan't right it should be so! Mas'r never ought ter left it so that ye *could* be took for his debts. Ye've arnt him all he gets for ye, twice over. He owed ye yer freedom, and ought ter gin't to yer years ago. Mebbe he can't help himself now, but I feel it's wrong. Nothing can't beat that ar out o' me. Sich a faithful crittur as ye've been,—and allers sot his business 'fore yer own every way,—and reckoned on him more than yer own wife and chil'en! Them as sells heart's love and heart's blood, to get out thar scrapes, de Lord'll be up to 'em!"

"Chloe! now, if ye love me, ye won't talk so, when perhaps jest the last time we'll ever have together! And I'll tell ye, Chloe, it goes agin me to hear one word agin Mas'r. Wan't he put in my arms a baby?—it's natur I should think a heap of him. And he couldn't be spected to think so much of poor Tom. Mas'rs is used to havin' all these yer things done for 'em, and nat'lly they don't think so much on't. They can't be spected to, no way. Set him 'longside of other Mas'rs—who's had the treatment and livin' I've had? And he never would have let this yer come on me, if he could have seed it aforehand. I know he wouldn't."

"Wal, any way, thar's wrong about it *somewhar*," said Aunt Chloe, in whom a stubborn sense of justice was a predominant trait; "I can't jest make out whar't is, but thar's wrong somewhar, I'm *clar* o' that."

"Yer ought ter look up to the Lord above—he's above all—thar don't a sparrow fall without him."

"It don't seem to comfort me, but I spect it orter," said Aunt Chloe. "But dar's no use talkin'; I'll jes wet up de corn-cake, and get ye one good breakfast, 'cause nobody knows when you'll get another."

CHAPTER 31: THE MIDDLE PASSAGE

On the lower part of a small, mean boat, on the Red river, Tom sat,—chains on his wrists, chains on his feet, and a weight heavier than chains lay on his heart. All had faded from his sky,—moon and star; all had passed by him, as the trees and banks were now passing, to return no more. Kentucky home, with wife and children, and indulgent owners; St. Clare home, with all its refinements and splendors; the golden head of Eva, with its saint-like eyes; the proud, gay, handsome, seemingly careless, yet ever-kind St. Clare; hours of ease and indulgent leisure,—all gone! and in place thereof, *what* remains?

It is one of the bitterest apportionments of a lot of slavery, that the negro, sympathetic and assimilative, after acquiring, in a refined family, the tastes and feelings which form the atmosphere of such a place, is not the less liable to become the bond-slave of the coarsest and most brutal,—just as a chair or table, which once decorated the superb saloon, comes, at last, battered and defaced, to the bar-room of some filthy tavern, or some low haunt of vulgar debauchery. The great difference is, that the table and chair cannot feel, and the *man* can; for even a legal enactment that he shall be "taken, reputed, adjudged in law, to be a chattel personal," cannot blot out his soul, with its own private little world of memories, hopes, loves, fears, and desires.

Mr. Simon Legree, Tom's master, had purchased slaves at one place and another, in New Orleans, to the number of eight, and driven them, handcuffed, in couples of two and two, down to the good steamer Pirate, which lay at the levee, ready for a trip up the Red river.

Having got them fairly on board, and the boat being off, he came round, with that air of efficiency which ever characterized him, to take a review of them. Stopping opposite to Tom, who had been attired for sale in his best broadcloth suit, with well-starched linen and shining boots, he briefly expressed himself as follows:

"Stand up."

Tom stood up.

"Take off that stock!" and, as Tom, encumbered by his fetters, proceeded to do it, he assisted him, by pulling it, with no gentle hand, from his neck, and putting it in his pocket.

Legree now turned to Tom's trunk, which, previous to this, he had been ransacking, and, taking from it a pair of old pantaloons and dilapidated coat, which Tom had been wont to put on about his stable-work, he said, liberating Tom's hands from the handcuffs, and pointing to a recess in among the boxes,

"You go there, and put these on."

Tom obeyed, and in a few moments returned.

"Take off your boots," said Mr. Legree.

Tom did so.

"There," said the former, throwing him a pair of coarse, stout shoes, such as were common among the slaves, "put these on."

In Tom's hurried exchange, he had not forgotten to transfer his cherished Bible to his pocket. It was well he did so; for Mr. Legree, having refitted Tom's handcuffs, proceeded deliberately to investigate the contents of his pockets. He drew out a silk handkerchief, and put it into his own pocket. Several little trifles, which Tom had treasured, chiefly because they had amused Eva, he looked upon with a contemptuous grunt, and tossed them over his shoulder into the river.

Tom's Methodist hymn-book, which, in his hurry, he had forgotten, he now held up and turned over.

"Humph! pious, to be sure. So, what's yer name,—you belong to the church, eh?"

"Yes, Mas'r," said Tom, firmly.

"Well, I'll soon have *that* out of you. I have none o' yer bawling, praying, singing niggers on my place; so remember. Now, mind yourself," he said, with a stamp and fierce glance of his gray eye, directed at Tom, "*I'm* your church now! You understand,—you've got to be as *I* say."

Something within the silent black man answered *No!* and, as if repeated by an invisible voice, came the words of an old prophetic scroll, as Eva had often read them to him,—"Fear not! for I have redeemed thee. I have called thee by name. Thou art MINE!"

But Simon Legree heard no voice. That voice is one he never shall hear. He only glared for a moment on the down-cast face of Tom, and walked off. He took Tom's trunk, which contained a very neat and abundant wardrobe, to the forecastle, where it was soon surrounded by various hands of the boat. With much laughing, at the expense of niggers who tried to be gentlemen, the articles very readily were sold to one and another, and the empty trunk finally put up at auction. It was a good joke, they all thought, especially to see how Tom looked after his things, as they were going this way and that; and then the auction of the trunk, that was funnier than all, and occasioned abundant witticisms.

This little affair being over, Simon sauntered up again to his property.

"Now, Tom, I've relieved you of any extra baggage, you see. Take mighty good care of them clothes. It'll be long enough 'fore you get more. I go in for making niggers careful; one suit has to do for one year, on my place."

CHAPTER 40: THE MARTYR

The escape of Cassy and Emmeline irritated the before surly temper of Legree to the last degree; and his fury, as was to be expected, fell upon the defenceless head of Tom. When he hurriedly announced the tidings among his hands, there was a sudden light in Tom's eye, a sudden upraising of his hands, that did not escape him. He saw that he did not join the muster of the pursuers. He thought of forcing him to do it; but, having had, of old, experience of his inflexibility when commanded to take part in any deed of inhumanity, he would not, in his hurry, stop to enter into any conflict with him.

Tom, therefore, remained behind, with a few who had learned of him to pray, and offered up prayers for the escape of the fugitives.

When Legree returned, baffled and disappointed, all the long-working hatred of his soul towards his slave began to gather in a deadly and desperate form. Had not this man braved him,—steadily, powerfully, resistlessly,—ever since he bought him? Was there not a spirit in him which, silent as it was, burned on him like the fires of perdition?

"I *hate* him!" said Legree, that night, as he sat up in his bed; "I *hate* him! And isn't he MINE? Can't I do what I like with him? Who's to hinder, I wonder?" And Legree clenched his fist, and shook it, as if he had something in his hands that he could rend in pieces.

But, then, Tom was a faithful, valuable servant; and, although Legree hated him the more for that, yet the consideration was still somewhat of a restraint to him. . . .

The hunt was long, animated, and thorough, but unsuccessful; and, with grave, ironic exultation, Cassy looked down on Legree, as, weary and dispirited, he alighted from his horse.

"Now, Quimbo," said Legree, as he stretched himself down in the sitting-room, "you jest go and walk that Tom up here, right away! The old cuss is at the bottom of this yer whole matter; and I'll have it out of his old black hide, or I'll know the reason why!"

Sambo and Quimbo, both, though hating each other; were joined in one mind by a no less cordial hatred of Tom. Legree had told them, at first, that he had bought him for a general overseer, in his absence; and this had begun an ill will, on their part, which had increased, in their debased and servile natures, as they saw him becoming obnoxious to their master's displeasure. Quimbo, therefore, departed, with a will, to execute his orders.

Tom heard the message with a forewarning heart; for he knew all the plan of the fugitives' escape, and the place of their present concealment;—he knew the deadly character of the man he had to deal with, and his despotic power. But he felt strong in God to meet death, rather than betray the helpless.

He sat his basket down by the row, and, looking up, said, "Into thy hands I commend my spirit! Thou hast redeemed me, oh Lord God of truth!" and then quietly yielded himself to the rough, brutal grasp with which Quimbo seized him.

"Ay, ay!" said the giant, as he dragged him along; "ye'll cotch it, now! I'll boun' Mas'r's back's up *high!* No sneaking out, now! Tell ye, ye'll get it, and no mistake! See how ye'll look, now, helpin' Mas'r's niggers to run away! See what ye'll get!"

The savage words none of them reached that ear!—a higher voice there was saying, "Fear not them that kill the body, and, after that, have no more than they can do." Nerve and bone of that poor man's body vibrated to those words, as if touched by the finger of God; and he felt the strength of a thousand souls in one. As he passed along, the trees and bushes, the huts of his servitude, the whole scene of his degradation, seemed to whirl by him as the landscape by the rushing ear. His soul throbbed,—his home was in sight,— and the hour of release seemed at hand.

"Well, Tom!" said Legree, walking up, and seizing him grimly by the collar of his coat, and speaking through his teeth, in a paroxysm of determined rage, "do you know I've made up my mind to KILL you?"

"It's very likely, Mas'r," said Tom, calmly.

"I *have*," said Legree, with a grim, terrible calmness, "*done—just—that— thing,* Tom, unless you'll tell me what you know about these yer gals!"

Tom stood silent.

"D'ye hear?" said Legree, stamping, with a roar like that of an incensed lion. "Speak!"

"*I han't got nothing to tell, Mas'r,*" said Tom, with a slow, firm, deliberate utterance.

"Do you dare to tell me, ye old black Christian, ye don't *know?*" said Legree. Tom was silent.

"Speak!" thundered Legree, striking him furiously. "Do you know anything?"

"I know, Mas'r; but I can't tell anything. *I can die!*"

Legree drew in a long breath; and, suppressing his rage, took Tom by the arm, and, approaching his face almost to his, said, in a terrible voice, "Hark'e, Tom!—ye think, 'cause I've let you off before, I don't mean what I say; but, this time, *I've made up my mind,* and counted the cost. You've always stood it out again' me: now, *I'll conquer ye, or kill ye!*—one or t'other. I'll count every drop of blood there is in you, and take 'em, one by one, till ye give up!"

Tom looked up to his master, and answered, "Mas'r, if you was sick, or in trouble, or dying, and I could save ye, I'd *give* ye my heart's blood; and, if taking every drop of blood in this poor old body would save your precious soul, I'd give 'em freely, as the Lord gave his for me. O, Mas'r! don't bring this great sin on your soul! It will hurt you more than't will me! Do the worst you can, my troubles'll be over soon; but, if ye don't repent, yours won't *never* end!"

Like a strange snatch of heavenly music, heard in the lull of a tempest, this burst of feeling made a moment's blank pause. Legree stood aghast, and looked at Tom; and there was such a silence, that the tick of the old clock could be heard, measuring, with silent touch, the last moments of mercy and probation to that hardened heart.

It was but a moment. There was one hesitating pause,—one irresolute, relenting thrill,—and the spirit of evil came back, with seven-fold vehemence; and Legree, foaming with rage, smote his victim to the ground.

Scenes of blood and cruelty are shocking to our ear and heart. What man has nerve to do, man has not nerve to hear. What brother-man and brother-Christian must suffer, cannot be told us, even in our secret chamber, it so harrows the soul! And yet, oh my country! these things are done under the shadow of thy laws! O, Christ! thy church sees them, almost in silence!

But, of old, there was One whose suffering changed an instrument of torture, degradation and shame, into a symbol of glory, honor, and immortal life; and, where His spirit is, neither degrading stripes, nor blood, nor insults, can make the Christian's last struggle less than glorious.

Was he alone, that long night, whose brave, loving spirit was bearing up, in that old shed, against buffeting and brutal stripes?

Nay! There stood by him ONE,—seen by him alone,—"like unto the Son of God."

The tempter stood by him, too,—blinded by furious, despotic will,—every moment pressing him to shun that agony by the betrayal of the innocent. But the brave, true heart was firm on the Eternal Rock. Like his Master, he knew that, if he saved others, himself he could not save; nor could utmost extremity wring from him words, save of prayers and holy trust.

"He's most gone, Mas'r," said Sambo, touched, in spite of himself, by the patience of his victim.

"Pay away, till he gives up! Give it to him!—give it to him!" shouted Legree. I'll take every drop of blood he has, unless he confesses!"

Tom opened his eyes, and looked upon his master. "Ye poor miserable critter!" he said, "there ain't no more ye can do! I forgive ye, with all my soul!" and he fainted entirely away.

"I b'lieve, my soul, he's done for, finally," said Legree, stepping forward, to look at him. "Yes, he is! Well, his mouth's shut up, at last,—that's one comfort!"

Yes, Legree; but who shall shut up that voice in thy soul? that soul, past repentance, past prayer, past hope, in whom the fire that never shall be quenched is already burning!

Yet Tom was not quite gone. His wondrous words and pious prayers had struck upon the hearts of the imbruted blacks, who had been the instruments of cruelty upon him; and, the instant Legree withdrew, they took him down, and in their ignorance, sought to call him back to life,—as if *that* were any favor to him.

"Sartin, we's been doin' a drefful wicked thing!" said Sambo; "hopes Mas'r'll have to 'count for it, and not we."

They washed his wounds,—they provided a rude bed, of some refuse cotton, for him to lie down on; and one of them, stealing up to the house, begged a drink of brandy of Legree, pretending that he was tired, and wanted it for himself. He brought it back, and poured it down Tom's throat.

"O, Tom!" said Quimbo, "we's been awful wicked to ye!"

"I forgive ye, with all my heart!" said Tom, faintly.

"O, Tom! do tell us who is *Jesus*, anyhow?" said Sambo,—"Jesus, that's been a standin' by you so, all this night!—Who is he?"

The word roused the failing, fainting spirit. He poured forth a few energetic sentences of that wondrous One,—his life, his death, his everlasting presence, and power to save.

They wept,—both the two savage men.

"Why didn't I never hear this before?" said Sambo; "but I do believe!—I can't help it! Lord Jesus, have mercy on us!"

"Poor critters!" said Tom, "I'd be willing to bar' all I have, if it'll only bring ye to Christ! O, Lord! give me these two more souls, I pray!"

That prayer was answered!

AFFIDAVIT OF AUGUSTUS L. GROW (1892)

STATE OF LOUISIANA
PARISH OF GRANT

BEFORE ME the undersigned authority personally came and appeared AUGUSTUS L. GROW, a native of the State of Vermont and a resident of the Parish of Grant, State of Louisiana, who after being by me first duly sworn deposes and says:

That in the summer of 1867 I taught school in the Town of Cloutierville, Parish of Natchitoches, Louisiana, where I met Dr. S. O. Scruggs, a practicing physician, a resident of said Town of Cloutierville.

That I boarded at the residence of said Dr. S. O. Scruggs for five months during said year 1867. Dr. Scruggs appeared to be at least fifty years of age. I

This document is available in Misc. No. 3, 1-4-4, La Croix Collection, Cammie G. Henry Research Center, Watson Memorial Library, Northwestern State University of Louisiana, Natchitoches, Louisiana. Obvious typographical errors have been corrected.

think Dr. Scruggs told me that he had resided at the said Town of Cloutierville for twenty-seven years up to the year 1867.

We had many conversations relative to the happenings and conditions of this section of country prior to the war of 1860–66. We were intimately associated together during the time I was at his residence.

One evening during said time of my said residence at Dr. Scruggs' residence, we were in conversation and the work written by Mrs. Harriet Beecher Stowe entitled "Uncle Tom's Cabin or Life Among the Lowly" was brought up and he asked me if I knew one of the principal characters of said work resided within a few miles of Cloutierville.

On my asking him who it was he told me it was the character of Simon Legree. That he lived on the place then owned by Dr. Chopin (1867), now owned by his son the present Mr. Chopin, and that the name of the person filling said character of Legree was Robert McAlpin.

He stated that when Mrs. Stowe was getting up material for her said work that she came up Red River in company with a young lady and a young gentleman who was stated to have been a nephew of Mrs. Stowe's.

That Mrs. Stowe's party stopped as guests a few days at the residence of the said Robt. McAlpin.

That he, Dr. Scruggs, practiced medicine at McAlpin's place and became acquainted with Mrs. Stowe and party there.

That he was very much fascinated with them and asked them to pay him a long visit before they left the country.

After they had been a few days at McAlpin's, he, McAlpin, discovered that a mulatto woman who was his housekeeper was in the habit of going to the room occupied by Mrs. Stowe and holding long conversations with her in the night.

When McAlpin made this discovery, he unceremoniously put the whole party out of his house.

That they, the Stowe party, all came to the residence of Dr. Scruggs and remained as his guest for several weeks or a long visit. This was before 1850. Just a year or two previous to the publication of "Uncle Tom's Cabin or Life Among the Lowly."

Dr. Scruggs also told me that McAlpin (alias Legree) was a very cruel man to his slaves and was looked upon as rather a bad man by his neighbors. That he had no wife, but a mulatto housekeeper.

Dr. Scruggs told me Mrs. Stowe paid the trick McAlpin played them in ejecting them from his residence by giving him the character of Legree.

Dr. Scruggs stated to me that he did not know when he had been so taken with anyone as he did with Mrs. Stowe and her party.

Said that their stay with him was an intellectual treat to him, that they discussed science, literature, art, religion, politics, government, etc. and that they were okay in everything.

Affiant further said Dr. S. O. Scruggs died some years ago, and that when Dr. Scruggs and myself had the above mentioned conversation of 1867, Robt. McAlpin had been dead some years.

Signed: A. L. Grow

Sworn to and subscribed before me at Colfax, La. This 11th day of July, 1892.

Signed: W. L. Shackelford
Clerk District Court

A VISIT TO UNCLE TOM'S CABIN (1892)

Late in the month of August, 1892, I decided to make a visit to the old plantation in Natchitoches Parish, Louisiana, where I knew the original "Uncle Tom's Cabin" was still standing, just as it stood the day that the old slave died the tragic death that has been accorded him. And knowing that it was situated in the Southern portion of the parish, some twenty miles from the parish site Natchitoches, I decided to go first to that place and ascertain from the Records of Deeds and whatever else I could find, something more of the authenticity of the "story," it being my purpose, in case I could establish the fact that it was the real cabin, to make such terms as might be made with the owner of it, and then remove it to Chicago, Ill., where it would be placed upon exhibition during the World's Fair to be held in that city in 1892 and 1893. . . .

Shortly after my arrival, I called upon the clerk of the parish at the courthouse, whom I found to be a very estimable gentleman and possessed of the information I was in search of. He told me at once that the Legree plantation was situated in the lower portion of the parish, and that while the name "Legree" had been given to the public as the cruel slave-holder in the story of "Uncle Tom's Cabin," that in reality his name was Robert McAlpin. He further gave it as his opinion that the fictitious name "Legree" was used by the

Selections from D. B. Corley, *A Visit to Uncle Tom's Cabin* (Chicago: Baird & Lee, 1892). Available in Bound Volume 80, Melrose Collection, Cammie G. Henry Research Center, Watson Memorial Library, Northwestern State University of Louisiana, Natchitoches, Louisiana, 3–78. Reprinted by permission of Watson Memorial Library, Northwestern State University of Louisiana.

authoress of "Uncle Tom's Cabin" to prevent him, Robert McAlpin, from laying a suit for slander or defamation of character against her if he should choose to do so.

The clerk also gave me a kind of abstract of the tract of land upon which the "cabin" stood. He said that it was granted by the government to Richard McAlpin, who lived at that time, he thought, somewhere in New England; that he never came out to that country at all, and that after his death his nephew, Robert McAlpin, fell heir to a portion of the tract of land and came forward and settled upon it, and afterward bought up the interest his brothers and sisters had in it, and shortly became sole owner of it. There were 4,800 acres originally in the grant and that he Robert McAlpin, alias "Simon Legree," lived there until his death, which occurred in 1852, at which time J. B. Chopin, the father of the present owner, bought it at administrator's sale. After the death of J. B. Chopin the tract was subdivided among his children, and that the old negro cabins and McAlpin's residence fell to his son, L. Chopin, the present owner. The records of his office show these facts. . . .

Acting upon this plan I started out along the aforementioned unstraightened street; nor had I proceeded very far before noticing an old man sitting at a state of rest upon a long bench under a mulberry tree in front of a saloon. Drawing near I saluted him, and taking my seat upon the other end of the bench proceeded to engage in conversation with the old gentleman. After we had exchanged a few words, which led me to the conclusion that he would engage in conversation with me . . .

"Well, well," said I, "you are truly a historic character and I am glad to have met you. You say you settled in this town in 1835 and that you have lived here ever since; you must have known something of the cruel slave-holder, 'Simon Legree,' who was written up in a little book called 'Uncle Tom's Cabin.' The book appeared about 1852, I believe. And the whole scene was laid on the Red river here in your parish. Do you remember such a man?"

"I guess I do, and I not only remember the man, but I remember him as the meanest man that I ever knowed in my life. Why, he lived in the lower part of this parish right on the bank of the river, and was the terror of the whole country. But say, how come that woman up North who wrote that book to get his name wrong? His name was not 'Legree,' it was old Bob McAlpin. She got the house and the locality and even the circumstances, as far as I know, all correct, but she missed the name. That was old Bob McAlpin. I knew him well. He was the worst man in the whole country. That woman did not tell one-half of his meanness. He sewed up a nigger in a sack and drowned him in the river.

"His chief delight was to torture his own negroes, even unto death. And he done it as often as his hellish spirit prompted him to do it. Yes; he did live and die there, as she wrote, but he was a heap meaner man than she ever made him out to be. Oh, he was bitter, he was so severe, and then he would drink so much, and all this seemed to enrage him the more. Yes, he was an old bachelor. I knew him well; he died drunk, just as she said, and was buried there on the plantation on a hill. I think that he come to this country from one of the New England states, but I could not tell you which one. I could come nearer guessing where he went to from this country than I could where he come from, if the Bible is true." . . .

Soon, however, I found myself engaged in conversation with another old timer of that section. It was L. Charleville this time, and a merchant of Cloutierville, La. He was a fluent talker and conversed freely with me upon the subject. He said that he knew the "Legree" of "Uncle Tom's Cabin" well, and that his name was Robert McAlpin; that he had lived right there in that section all of his life; that he had served in the Mexican War under Gen. Taylor, and in the Confederate army under Gen. Lee; that he believed Robert McAlpin was among the cruelest, if not the cruelest, slave-holder he ever knew. He had read the book of "Uncle Tom's Cabin," and said Mrs. Stowe did not tell of one-half his meanness. That he was notoriously cruel to his slaves. That at times they would despair and kill themselves.

He remembered one case in particular, where at his grandfather's sale some negroes were being sold and that Robert McAlpin bid upon one of them, whereupon the negro (a man) spoke out and said to McAlpin, "If you buy me I will kill myself before night. I will not try to live with such a man as you are." That upon such a positive statement McAlpin ceased to bid and the negro was struck off to some one else. That McAlpin died in a drunken spree in 1852 and was buried on a hill on the plantation near his residence. That he knew well where the grave was, and had seen it often.

Mr. Charleville further stated that it was his opinion that Mrs. Stowe was at Robert McAlpin's house in 1850 or '51. Anyway, he says that there was a lady there at the time and accounts for Mrs. Stowe's accurate description of the place in this way. That if she was not personally present and an eye-witness of some of these things, that the lady who was there furnished her with a full description of the house, etc. This latter portion of his surmise as to its being another woman is most likely to be a correct one, for it would be a great strain for us to imagine for a moment that a lady of Mrs. Stowe's refined feelings and ladylike culture would have ever taken refuge or shelter at all under the roof of such a man as Robert McAlpin, alias "Simon Legree." . . .

Approaching the door of the cabin, we noticed that it was securely fastened with hasp and staple, made in the olden times by hand. Lifting the lock from its hold, we slowly swung back the shutter upon rudely hand-made hinges that had held it in place since 1825. We entered—all was still; the black, smoked logs with here and there a two-inch auger hole bored into their inside face into which pins or pegs were once used as supports for shelves, were plainly visible. From these it could be seen that a number of these shelves once ranged around the room. I looked and wondered which one of these "Tom" kept his Bible on. But which one it was, I could not tell. Yet, that it was one of this number there is no mistake.

We next cast an upward glance at the roof which appeared to be in good shape, when we consider its great age, though it was plainly visible that at places it did "let in the sunshine and the rain"; and while gazing through these apertures at the blue sky beyond, we wondered if the spirit of "Tom," still accompanied by that of the gentle "Eva" did not at times gaze down through them upon the hard bed he once occupied there—thinking that possibly it might be so. At least

> "It is a beautiful belief,
> That ever round our head
> Are hovering, on angel wings,
> The spirits of the dead."

The floor was perfectly sound and all in place, save three or four planks that were missing from the south side of the room. This vacancy extended clear across, exposing the joist below, which appeared to have been sawed. The opening in the end wall for the fire-place was all perfectly intact, the chimney having been removed many years ago, there being only a few bricks left scattered around over the hearth-site.

Oh, thought I, could a phonograph of modern build have been placed within this room when these walls were first erected, and have recorded the successive silence and sounds that have prevailed and broken forth here in the wretched ages that have passed and gone since they were first reared, what a tale it could now tell, of sighs and sobs and sorrows; of prayers and pitiful pleadings. But we will not trace this theme further; for if it were so we might hear, reproduced, sobbing sounds of a "mother as she kissed her baby—gave it laudanum—held it to her bosom while it breathed its young life away," rather than see it grow up and follow in the miserable and wretched footsteps of her degradation; and I would not now, for all the world's present wealth, have these repeated.

Noticing that the entire house was built of heart cypress, the most durable of all woods, and that the clapboards with which it had been covered were handriven, and of the same material and nailed on with hand-made nails, we began to feel that we were in possession of all the knowledge we were seeking, and that we were now ready for our departure. So passing out through the doorway we closed and clasped its shutter and then departed from the place. Near by stands the old overseer's house, built about the same time, though not occupied during Legree's life by a white overseer. His negro drivers, "Sambo" and "Quimbo," evidently resided there during the time they acted in that capacity. And afterward it was occupied by Legree's successors, successively ever since up to the late war. It is now occupied by an intelligent colored man and his family. It is a part of this man's daily business to watch and protect the "cabin" against the raids of relic hunters. And he told me that between the combined effort of himself and wife, his children and his dog, that he had succeeded wonderfully well.

We will next notice a small brick building standing between the "cabin" and Legree's residence, but near the latter. This building has a shed in front of it and was the kitchen built there at the time the other buildings were erected. From some unknown cause the public has for the last fifteen years understood that this house was "Uncle Tom's Cabin," and in consequence of this understanding they have pretty well pulled down and carried the shed away as relics of it. . . .

We slowly climbed up the hill to where its top takes a ridge shape and is covered with tall trees, from every branch and limb of which hangs in great profusion long tapering bunches of greenish looking moss, about one hundred yards, to where the ridge widens out a little, and we came to the grave of Robert McAlpin, alias "Simon Legree." His remains lie there beneath a brick tomb, that was originally built to the average height, but which has by long neglect and exposure been reduced until it does not now stand more than a foot above the level. Around it and covering nearly the entire little flat mentioned are a number of other graves. These, we were told, were all the graves of negroes, many of whom he had cruelly put to death in his lifetime, he being the only white person buried there. . . .

The deep gulch passes from this swamp close to the quarters, thence near the house of Legree, and thence to the river. Its position upon the ground, and its relation to both quarters and residence, is conclusive proof that the authoress of "Uncle Tom's Cabin" either viewed it once in person, or else got her information from one who had made a careful survey of it. After crossing over the bridge we turned up the gulch on the opposite side from where the "cabin" stands, about a hundred and fifty yards, to the little church. As we approached it, Eugenie commenced again: "Now, just see that little church; well, my papa gave a lease to the ground for this church for ninety-nine years for five cents a year, and he built the church for them besides, and it is so nice. I love to come here to church and see and hear the negroes shout. You see they are all Methodists, and they do shout and carry on so! I am so glad to see them have a church right here so close to 'Uncle Tom's Cabin.' Old Legree would not let his negroes have any church or books either. I hate to read about that man, he was so fearfully cruel." . . .

Being now thoroughly satisfied as to the identity of the plantation as that of the Legree of Mrs. Stowe's narrative of "Uncle Tom's Cabin," I closed a trade with Mr. Chopin by which he gave me a lease on the cabin for the purposes of exhibiting it at the World's Fair at Chicago, and such other places as I might deem fit to exhibit it afterward.

Testimonial of L. Chopin (1892)

State of Louisiana

Parish of Natchitoches

My name is L. Chopin. I am forty-two years old and was born and raised in Natchitoches Parish, Louisiana. In the year 1852 my father bought at public sale the Robert McAlpin plantation, situated on Red river in the southern portion of the parish, and moved upon the place shortly afterward. The occasion of the plantation being sold was on account of McAlpin's death. He being a bachelor the estate was wound up and the proceeds distributed among distant relatives.

Outside of a few years spent in Europe at school, I have lived on the plantation all my life, and until the Texas and Pacific railroad run through the place I lived in the old McAlpin residence. A portion of the old residence was torn down by the railroad, and the roadbed now runs through it, the balance of the building being used as a section house.

When my father first moved on the place, or at least a few years afterward, he had one of the two rows of China trees in front of the house cut down because it obstructed the view and made too much of shade. I still remember, although a child at the time, the great time we children had helping the negroes

Selection from D. B. Corley, *A Visit to Uncle Tom's Cabin* (Chicago: Baird & Lee, 1892). Available in Bound Volume 80, Melrose Collection, Cammie G. Henry Research Center, Watson Memorial Library, Northwestern State University of Louisiana, Natchitoches, Louisiana, 41–43. Reprinted by permission of Watson Memorial Library, Northwestern State University of Louisiana.

pull on the ropes which were fastened to the tops of the trees being cut down to prevent them falling over and damaging those that were to be kept.

After the war my father commenced tearing down the cabins from the negro quarters and scattering them over the plantation, as the negroes objected to living in the old "quarters." It "looked too much like slavery," so they said.

After I assumed the control of the place at my father's death, I continued tearing down and moving the cabins, and there is now standing on the grounds where the negro quarters were located only the cabin known as Uncle Tom's cabin. This I never moved, and have religiously kept ever since on account of the tradition connected with it, which makes it the cabin that "Uncle Tom" occupied on the Legree plantation.

Tradition has it that McAlpin was the Legree of Mrs. Stowe's book. From all reports of white and black he was a very cruel master to his slaves, and when drunk would abuse them dreadfully and is said to have caused the death of several of them. He was a very hard drinker and died from the effects of drink. He was buried on a little hill near the residence, and his grave can still be seen there, although very much dilapidated. His is the only white man's grave there; the place has always and is still used as a plantation burial ground, and quite a number of negroes are buried around his grave.

When quite young I knew the place as the Legree plantation and the cabin as Uncle Tom's, and it is well known as "Uncle Tom's" cabin and believed to be so, not only here, but all over the country, as I have at several times received letters from the different states asking for pieces of boards from the cabin to be kept as relics.

For years I have kept the cabin just for the sake of its association with Mrs. Stowe's book, without any thought of its ever being of any money value and without a thought of its ever being moved from the plantation, but lately I have been approached by parties from Chicago and New York who have offered to buy the cabin with the view of bringing it to the World's Fair at Chicago. Those offers I refused, and refused at first to entertain any idea of its being moved from the place even temporarily, but have finally consented to its being moved to Chicago for the World's Fair, after repeated representations were made me that such a cabin, so closely connected with such a well-known book as Uncle Tom's Cabin, was in a manner public property and the opportunity should be given to everybody to see it.

L. Chopin

Sworn to and subscribed before me this 15th Oct., 1892.

[SEAL]   Jno. A. Barlow,
D. Clk. 10th D.C.

The Goodness of Saint Rocque
Alice Dunbar Nelson

Manuela was tall and slender and graceful, and once you knew her the lithe form could never be mistaken. She walked with the easy spring that comes from a perfectly arched foot. To-day she swept swiftly down Marais Street, casting a quick glance here and there from under her heavy veil as if she feared she was being followed. If you had peered under the veil, you would have seen that Manuela's dark eyes were swollen and discoloured about the lids, as though they had known a sleepless, tearful night.

There had been a picnic the day before, and as merry a crowd of giddy, chattering Creole girls and boys as ever you could see boarded the ramshackle dummy-train that puffed its way wheezily out wide Elysian Fields Street, around the lily-covered bayous, to Milneburg-on-the-Lake. Now, a picnic at Milneburg is a thing to be remembered for ever. One charters a rickety-looking, weather-beaten dancing-pavilion, built over the water, and after storing the children—for your true Creole never leaves the small folks at home—and the baskets and mothers downstairs, the young folks go upstairs and dance to the tune of the best band you ever heard. For what can equal the music of a violin, a guitar, a cornet, and a bass viol to trip the quadrille to at a picnic?

Then one can fish in the lake and go bathing under the prim bath-houses, so severely separated sexually, and go rowing on the lake in a trim boat, followed by the shrill warnings of anxious mamans. And in the evening one comes home, hat crowned with cool gray Spanish moss, hands burdened with fantastic latanier baskets woven by the brown bayou boys, hand in hand with your dearest one, tired but happy.

At this particular picnic, however, there had been bitterness of spirit. Theophilé was Manuela's own especial property, and Theophilé had proven false. He had not danced a single waltz or quadrille with Manuela, but had deserted her for Claralie, blonde and petite. It was Claralie whom Theophilé had rowed out on the lake; it was Claralie whom Theophilé had gallantly led to dinner; it was Claralie's hat that he wreathed with Spanish moss, and Claralie whom he escorted home after the jolly singing ride in town on the little dummy-train.

Not that Manuela lacked partners or admirers. Dear no! she was too graceful and beautiful for that. There had been more than enough for her. But Manuela loved Theophilé, you see, and no one could take his place. Still, she had tossed her head and let her silvery laughter ring out in the dance, as though she were the happiest of mortals, and had tripped home with Henri, leaning on his arm, and looking up into his eyes as though she adored him.

Alice Dunbar Nelson, *The Goodness of Saint Rocque and Other Stories* (New York: Dodd, Mead and Company, 1899), 3–16.

This morning she showed the traces of a sleepless night and an aching heart as she walked down Marais Street. Across wide St. Rocque Avenue she hastened. "Two blocks to the river and one below—" she repeated to herself breathlessly. Then she stood on the corner gazing about her, until with a final summoning of a desperate courage she dived through a small wicket gate into a garden of weed-choked flowers.

There was a hoarse, rusty little bell on the gate that gave querulous tongue as she pushed it open. The house that sat back in the yard was little and old and weather-beaten. Its one-story frame had once been painted, but that was a memory remote and traditional. A straggling morning-glory strove to conceal its time-ravaged face. The little walk of broken bits of brick was reddened carefully, and the one little step was scrupulously yellow-washed, which denoted that the occupants were cleanly as well as religious.

Manuela's timid knock was answered by a harsh "Entrez."

It was a small sombre room within, with a bare yellow-washed floor and ragged curtains at the little window. In a corner was a diminutive altar draped with threadbare lace. The red glow of the taper lighted a cheap print of St. Joseph and a brazen crucifix. The human element in the room was furnished by a little, wizened yellow woman, who, black-robed, turbaned, and stern, sat before an uncertain table whereon were greasy cards.

Manuela paused, her eyes blinking at the semi-obscurity within. The Wizened One called in croaking tones:

"An' fo' w'y you come here? Assiez-là, ma'amzelle."

Timidly Manuela sat at the table facing the owner of the voice.

"I want," she began faintly; but the Mistress of the Cards understood: she had had much experience. The cards were shuffled in her long grimy talons and stacked before Manuela.

"Now you cut dem in t'ree part, so—un, deux, trois, bien! You mek' you' weesh wid all you' heart, bien! Yaas, I see, I see!"

Breathlessly did Manuela learn that her lover was true, but "dat light gal, yaas, she mek' nouvena in St. Rocque fo' hees love."

"I give you one lil' charm, yaas," said the Wizened One when the séance was over, and Manuela, all white and nervous, leaned back in the rickety chair. "I give you one lil' charm fo' to ween him back, yaas. You wear h'it 'roun' you' wais', an' he come back. Den you mek prayer at St. Rocque an' burn can'le. Den you come back an' tell me, yaas. Cinquante sous, ma'amzelle. Merci. Good luck go wid you."

Readjusting her veil, Manuela passed out the little wicket gate, treading on air. Again the sun shone, and the breath of the swamps came as healthful sea-breeze unto her nostrils. She fairly flew in the direction of St. Rocque.

There were quite a number of persons entering the white gates of the cemetery, for this was Friday, when all those who wish good luck pray to the saint, and wash their steps promptly at twelve o'clock with a wondrous mixture to guard the house. Manuela bought a candle from the keeper of the little lodge at the entrance, and pausing one instant by the great sun-dial to see if the heavens and the hour were propitious, glided into the tiny chapel, dim and stifling with heavy air from myriad wish-candles blazing on the wide table before the altar-rail. She said her prayer and lighting her candle placed it with the others.

Mon Dieu! how brightly the sun seemed to shine now, she thought, pausing at the door on her way out. Her small finger-tips, still bedewed with holy water, rested caressingly on a gamin's head. The ivy which enfolds the quaint chapel never seemed so green; the shrines which serve as the Way of the Cross never seemed so artistic; the baby graves, even, seemed cheerful.

Theophilé called Sunday. Manuela's heart leaped. He had been spending his Sundays with Claralie. His stay was short and he was plainly bored. But Manuela knelt to thank the good St. Rocque that night, and fondled the charm about her slim waist. There came a box of bonbons during the week, with a decorative card all roses and fringe, from Theophilé; but being a Creole, and therefore superstitiously careful, and having been reared by a wise and experienced maman to mistrust the gifts of a recreant lover, Manuela quietly thrust bonbons, box, and card into the kitchen fire, and the Friday following placed the second candle of her nouvena in St. Rocque.

Those of Manuela's friends who had watched with indignation Theophilé gallantly leading Claralie home from High Mass on Sundays, gasped with astonishment when the next Sunday, with his usual bow, the young man offered Manuela his arm as the worshippers filed out in step to the organ's march. Claralie tossed her head as she crossed herself with holy water, and the pink in her cheeks was brighter than usual.

Manuela smiled a bright good-morning when she met Claralie in St. Rocque the next Friday. The little blonde blushed furiously, and Manuela rushed post-haste to the Wizened One to confer upon this new issue.

"H'it ees good," said the dame, shaking her turbaned head. "She ees 'fraid, she will work, mais you' charm, h'it weel beat her."

And Manuela departed with radiant eyes.

Theophilé was not at Mass Sunday morning, and murderous glances flashed from Claralie to Manuela before the tinkling of the Host-Bell. Nor did Theophilé call at either house. Two hearts beat furiously at the sound of every passing footstep, and two minds wondered if the other were enjoying the beloved one's smiles. Two pair of eyes, however, blue and black, smiled on others, and their owners laughed and seemed none the less happy. For your Creole girls are proud, and would die rather than let the world see their sorrows.

Monday evening Theophilé, the missing, showed his rather sheepish countenance in Manuela's parlour, and explained that he, with some chosen spirits, had gone for a trip—"over the Lake."

"I did not ask you where you were yesterday," replied the girl, saucily.

Theophilé shrugged his shoulders and changed the conversation.

The next week there was a birthday fête in honour of Louise, Theophilé's young sister. Everyone was bidden, and no one thought of refusing, for Louise was young, and this would be her first party. So, though the night was hot, the dancing went on as merrily as light young feet could make it go. Claralie fluffed her dainty white skirts, and cast mischievous sparkles in the direction of Theophilé, who with the maman and Louise was bravely trying not to look self-conscious. Manuela, tall and calm and proud-looking, in a cool, pale yellow gown was apparently enjoying herself without paying the slightest attention to her young host.

"Have I the pleasure of this dance?" he asked her finally, in a lull of the music.

She bowed assent, and as if moved by a common impulse they strolled out of the dancing-room into the cool, quaint garden, where jessamines gave out an overpowering perfume, and a caged mocking-bird complained melodiously to the full moon in the sky.

It must have been an engrossing tête-a-tête, for the call to supper had sounded twice before they heard and hurried into the house. The march had formed with Louise radiantly leading on the arm of papa. Claralie tripped by with Leon. Of course, nothing remained for Theophilé and Manuela to do but to bring up the rear, for which they received much good-natured chaffing.

But when the party reached the dining-room, Theophilé proudly led his partner to the head of the table, at the right hand of maman, and smiled benignly about at the delighted assemblage. Now you know, when a Creole young man places a girl at his mother's right hand at his own table, there is but one conclusion to be deduced therefrom.

If you had asked Manuela, after the wedding was over, how it happened, she would have said nothing, but looked wise.

If you had asked Claralie, she would have laughed and said she always preferred Leon.

If you had asked Theophilé, he would have wondered that you thought he had ever meant more than to tease Manuela.

If you had asked the Wizened One, she would have offered you a charm.

But St. Rocque knows, for he is a good saint, and if you believe in him and are true and good, and make your nouvenas with a clean heart, he will grant your wish.

LEGAL, HISTORIC, AND
ECONOMIC INFLUENCES

The rapid rise and expansion of the railroads were both a manifestation and a byproduct of the economic boom that accompanied the end of the Civil War and the industrialization that followed. Even rural areas, such as northwestern Louisiana, could not escape these influences and the changes that they brought. Lisa Abney's essay, "The Milieu of the Timber Industry and Chopin's *At Fault,*" addresses the growth of railroads in rural Louisiana and the rise of the timber industry that this growth made possible.

At Fault's Thérèse Lafirme felt strong trepidation regarding the arrival of the railroad and the often unsavory characters who took advantage of the new mobility it afforded. In two articles excerpted here, Gilles Vandal illuminates these factors, which explain the community's reaction to Grégoire's summary execution of Joçint. Vandal's work also explains the lack of legal consequences when Grégoire himself is murdered in Texas.

The Temperance Movement, which ultimately succeeded in passing a constitutional amendment banning the production and sale of alcoholic beverages in the United States, had its origins in the early nineteenth century. By Chopin's time, the movement had gathered considerable force. Its influence is reflected in the novel, as characters speak of "taking the pledge" to abstain from alcohol and as Hosmer ends his first marriage to Fanny when he comes home and finds her intoxicated. The texts presented in this section articulate official positions of the organized temperance movement.

The 1904 World's Fair, celebrating the centennial of the Louisiana Purchase, was a major economic and social event for the city of St. Louis. A series of similar exhibitions was held around the country and in St. Louis itself prior to this spectacular event. The excerpts from *Louisiana and the*

Fair and *"Indescribably Grand"* illustrate the crowds and the excitement that Hosmer encounters when he returns to St. Louis to remarry Fanny. He seeks to escape from his dismal domestic situation by walking the streets, but he finds the excitement of the fair-goers too upbeat for his depressed emotional state.

THE TIMBER INDUSTRY AND CHOPIN'S *AT FAULT*
LISA ABNEY

Louisiana's timber industry reached its peak during the time in which Kate Chopin wrote her novella, *At Fault.* Chopin clearly was aware of Louisiana's rapidly changing social and industrial conditions. The fact that one of the protagonists of *At Fault,* Mrs. Lafirme, revels in the natural beauty that surrounds her and eschews the rapidly advancing technology is no accident. In the following passage, Thérèse Lafirme studies the advance of the railroad and the increasing numbers of outsiders, contrasting them with the natural landscape surrounding the station:

> Thérèse loved to walk the length of the wide veranda. . . . Then her gaze swept from cabin to cabin; from patch to patch; up to the pine-capped hills, and down to the station which squatted a brown and ugly intruder within her domain.
>
> She had made pouting resistance to this change at first, opposing it step by step with a conservatism that yielded only to the resistless. She pictured a visionary troop of evils coming in the wake of the railroad, which, in her eyes no conceivable benefits could mitigate. The occasional tramp, she foresaw as an army; and the travelers whom chance deposited at the store that adjoined the station, she dreaded [as] an endless procession of intruders forcing themselves upon her privacy.[1]

In *At Fault,* Chopin illustrates the struggle between the economic stability that the indiscriminate clear-cutting of timber could yield and the preservation of nature, which most people of the era, unlike Mrs. Lafirme, ignored.

The timber industry in Louisiana has roots which extend to the 1700s. Early colonials logged cypress trees and marketed them in the French West Indies.[2] By the 1820s, domestic demand for the trees had increased, and the

---

Lisa Abney is the director of the Louisiana Folklife Center at Northwestern State University, Natchitoches. This essay was prepared especially for this volume.

foreign market had grown less important. Early Louisianians consumed huge quantities of the easily worked, durable cypress, using it to construct homes, shops, and other buildings. Sawmill owners and vendors, in advertisements of the era, called cypress the "wood eternal."[3] The demand for cypress and, similarly, for pine remained steady through most of the nineteenth century and well into the early years of the twentieth century.

In the late 1800s and early 1900s, clear-cutting of the virgin cypress and pine timber stands became commonplace. Cypress became an integral part of the Louisiana economy, yet cypress cutting proved to be a difficult task. More often than not, cypress grew in swamps and wetlands—as it does today, in parts of Louisiana and Florida—and loggers of the eighteenth, nineteenth, and early twentieth centuries had none of the sophisticated logging equipment that timber harvesters employ today. Most were forced to stand in water, sometimes chest high, to cut the cypress with crosscut saws. These early loggers worked in pairs, using the expansive saws to bisect the trunk of the massive cypress trees. Cypress trees of the period could be as wide as thirty feet and as tall as one hundred feet. Wedges were inserted after the tree was half-sawed to allow the team to move the blade. Sometimes, spring or staging boards were constructed against the trunks of the trees, and the loggers stood on these as they sawed. These timber cutters earned around seventy-five cents for each tree that they cut, and that small amount usually had to be split between the two loggers. As most of these individuals lived by hunting, fishing, and subsistence farming, logging was one of the few industries which yielded steady pay. Not only was the rise of the timber industry attractive to the loggers and their families, but the industry also fueled Louisiana's economy and spurred the construction of railroad systems and urban development.[4]

Cypress trees, because of their wetland habitat, were hard to transport. Early loggers learned that the easiest and most economical manner of moving trees to mills was to float them down through bayous, streams, or rivers. Once at the sawmill, they were cut into planks and sold. Cypress logs were tall and wide, and floating them was no easy task. Often, the logs were too heavy and would sink. Loggers began to look for ways to lighten the logs, and some chose to girdle trees by cutting a one-foot-wide band about two inches deep into the tree. Girdling allowed the sap to drain from the green trees, which made floating the logs easier; it also aided in cutting and transporting the cypress trees. Log floating remained a constant activity, since pine, like cypress, also was floated down the many streams and bayous of Louisiana.

As log floating developed and traffic on these waterways increased, lumberboats came into existence to guide the flotilla downstream to the mill.

Usually the lumberboats would push the logs, but some served as tugboats and pulled them downstream.

In the middle of the nineteenth century, the Age of the Railroad dawned in Louisiana, and railroad tracks began to cover the state, connecting backwater towns to sawmill towns. An overhead railroad log-skidder—a system for transporting logs using cables and rail cars—was invented; thus the process of transporting logs eased somewhat. Overland accessibility remained limited in some cases, however, and even after rail expansion occurred, both marine and land transport methods coexisted for many years, for there was enough timber business to bring profits to every participant.

While cypress logging indeed was dangerous because of the swamps and wetlands in which the trees grew, the virgin pine stands, found predominantly in northwestern and western Louisiana, posed their own set of challenges. Louisiana's western pine district spanned a triangular zone which extended north from Alexandria to Many, and then south to Lake Charles. These longleaf pines, rarer today than in the past, towered above the ground to some one hundred feet and generally had a diameter of three feet or larger. Virgin longleaf pines were so great that their canopy of foliage kept the light from reaching the ground.[5] Opinions of those who encountered these virgin pines varied; some called the stands serene and peaceful, while others found them to be depressing and oppressive.[6]

European settlers in this area of Louisiana had to contend with this dense tree growth. For many, the task of clearing land for a farm was daunting, as they had no power saws or heavy equipment to push down the trees. Thus, when loggers approached farmers about buying timber, the small farmers of the region quickly took the opportunity to earn a good sum of money and to have someone else clear away the trees. For many in the region, timber was "found money"; it was a resource which was handily exploited and, like cypress, not carefully managed.

Some of the early settlers cleared their own timber, hauled the logs, drifted them downriver, cut firewood for locomotives and steamboats, and worked in the many emerging sawmills of the state. Many of these residents left farming completely in order to profit from the timber industry. As with early cypress logging, pine logs were floated in the deep streams of Sabine and other parishes. Later, after the Civil War ended and Reconstruction began, railroads in Louisiana again grew in importance as transportation for people and timber. Timber supplies in other parts of the United States had been depleted prior to the war, due to clear-cutting. Thus, Louisiana was left in a prime position for the timber industry to blossom. Foreign investors and northerners brought large sums of money into the economy of the state, and a new, wealthy Louisianian, the timber baron, emerged. Chopin modeled David Hosmer after the timber barons of her time. Hosmer, like many of his ilk, traveled the United States following virgin timber.

Because the federal government did not regulate timber cutting in its early years, almost no restrictions existed regarding the harvest of timber and sale of lumber. Hence, the timber barons held vast amounts of power and attendant wealth. Many of these men, the pine loggers in particular, were unscrupulous. They not only cut timber on private land adjoining government land, but they also made forays into government holdings and took tremendous amounts of timber from these parcels as well. This illegal timber then was floated to secret mills where it was cut, mixed with legal timber, and sold. Behavior such as this did not go unnoticed, and many of today's timber laws stem from these early timber barons' activities.

While the timber barons clear-cut the virgin longleaf pines and cypress, ambitious sawmill owners and lumber companies began to open mills throughout the region. In many instances, these companies opened mills in extant towns and cities; for the most part, though, they preferred to open mills in underdeveloped areas and then build a town around the mill. The mill companies controlled these towns and profited not only from the timber milled there, but also from the workers and their families, who lived in company houses and bought on credit at company stores. These sawmill towns were highly functional entities, and, like many other elements of the timber industry, within only a few decades, their success had led to their demise.

While the timber boom brought huge profits to investors, sawmill owners, loggers, and landowners, the spoils were relatively short-lived. By 1925, the large-scale industrial timber industry had done its job so well that there was no longer any timber left to harvest. All the large stands of cypress had been ravaged.[7] In 1913, when more than one billion board feet was produced, cypress milling peaked.[8] By 1980, only a few sawmills processed cypress, and cypress production amounted to less than 240 million board feet.

Because of the careful management of second-growth forests, cypress slowly is making a return in the wetlands of Louisiana. The pine forests of northwestern and western Louisiana, too, have become carefully managed entities; longleaf pines, however, have not rebounded in the manner of the virgin stands that reigned in the region during the earlier half of the twentieth century.

Chopin's *At Fault,* which is set against a backdrop of these early timber clearing activities, makes several environmental and social statements regarding the industry. Chopin offers thinly veiled criticism of the sawmill culture and the conditions in which its workers (who were poor whites or recently emancipated African Americans) were immersed. Characters such as Joçint, who are swallowed up by this culture of greed, illustrate in miniature the difficulties endured by sawmill workers. These sawmill workers exemplify the social ills brought by this new industry, while Mrs. Lafirme's dedication to her land makes a strong statement regarding the importance of preserving the environment. Ultimately, like the forward-thinking Mrs. Lafirme, the timber industry of today must balance economic exploitation and development with conservation of natural areas and processes.

CRIME IN POST–CIVIL WAR RURAL LOUISIANA
GILLES VANDAL

The Civil War brought not only the emancipation of slaves, but a new land of economic ruin and social disruption. An increasing number of rural inhabitants, unable to adjust to the post-War conditions, lived off robbery and marauding. While tensions between planters and freedmen were an individual matter in most cases, a minority of whites and blacks turned to crime and joined gangs of outlaws and robbers which plundered the countryside. Consequently, petty thefts, robbery, burglary and other property offenses reflect more than simply the activity of common criminals acting alone or in groups. These particular criminal activities revealed the deep social contradictions, conflicts and disequilibrium of the post–Civil War Southern society. . . .

It is impossible to pick up a country paper from mid–nineteenth century Louisiana without noticing the epidemic nature of crimes of all types and grades, particularly burglaries and robberies, that were committed. Property crimes became so frequent after the War that many local papers stopped reporting petty thefts and mentioned other property offenses only of an aggravated nature. Still, a quick look at local newspapers under the headings of "District Court" or "Local Items" and the several congressional, district attorney and penitentiary reports, reveals numerous cases of indictments for arson, breaking into stores and houses, burglary, embezzlement, forgery, fraud, larceny, petty theft, robbery, etc., that regularly afflicted most country parishes. . . .

. . . Arson became one of the most serious crimes in post–Civil War Louisiana. It was usually committed at night and although it aroused the whole

---

Selections from Gilles Vandal, "Property Offenses, Social Tension and Racial Antagonism in Post–Civil War Rural Louisiana," *Journal of Social History* 31 (1997): 127–54. Reprinted by permission of *Journal of Social History*.

community the perpetrators were rarely caught. Rural society appeared defenseless in the face of arsonists. When a suspicious fire erupted in a particular town, village or parish, protective associations or vigilance committees were set up to discover the arsonist and to prevent the repetition of such acts. When an arsonist was caught by the law, he was usually sentenced to the state penitentiary for life, if he had not previously suffered at the hands of a vigilance committee. Still, arson, like other property offenses represented an important manifestation of the aggressiveness and social tension that prevailed in rural Louisiana.

Although blacks were charged by whites with being responsible for most larcenies, robberies and arsons, the present data show that whites had a greater propensity to commit property crimes than blacks. Whites composed only 38% of the rural population, but committed 60% of all property offenses in countryside parishes (Table [1]). Moreover, black thievery differed from white in the nature of the offenses. Blacks were more often charged with petty thefts and stealing cattle, horses, hogs and mules for food consumption, while whites were more often charged with violent and aggravated property crimes. Finally, people who robbed did not come only from the lower classes of society. Some of them went around after having committed their villainous deeds sporting a cane as any ordinary gentlemen.

Confronted with white violence, blacks did resort occasionally to violence as a way to correct wrongs committed against them. In these cases, violence was used either to obtain a just settlement for sale of crops or to rescue blacks arrested and charged with stealing. But destruction of property and

Table [1]

RACIAL DISTRIBUTION OF PEOPLE INVOLVED IN
CRIMES AGAINST PROPERTY, 1866 TO 1876

TYPE OF OFFENSE	NUMBER	% WHITES	WHITE PROPENSITY
Robbery and murder	228	62.7	2.7
Robbery and personal violence	293	89.0	13.7
Arson or destruction of property	52	80.7	6.8
Robbery, burglary or breaking and entering	163	73.6	4.6
Bribery, embezzlement, forgery or fraud	26	57.7	2.2
Horse stealing	127	43.3	1.2
Cattle, mule, hog stealing	64	26.5	-1.7
Petty theft and larceny	634	46.2	1.4
Total and average	1587	59.6	2.4

arson became the preferred response of blacks. Not only did arson provide a complete revenge, but blacks felt less liable to retaliation as arsonists were rarely caught. Still, arson represented a two-edged sword as white conservatives often used it as a means to intimidate black and white Republicans.

In rural Louisiana, stealing, robberies and petty thefts were often committed by several people acting together in ephemeral associations which periodically yielded gangs of outlaws and robbers. The development of outlaw bands was favored by a series of independent factors: the prevailing frontier spirit of some regions, the ease of finding refuge, or the authorities' inability to maintain law and order. Louisiana also suffered from more particular conditions: the economic destruction caused by the War, social dislocation generated by emancipation and post–Civil War political turmoil. These factors created conditions favorable for the proliferation of criminal activities in Louisiana and in some other southern states such as Texas. Consequently, although bands of outlaws were fairly common before the Civil War, they posed an even greater problem afterward. The large number of outlaw bands reflected the prevailing economic conditions. . . .

. . . As Federal authorities did not have enough troops in Louisiana to maintain law and order in rural areas, these gangs were largely responsible for the general atmosphere of lawlessness that prevailed in the Pelican state after the War; they rode around the countryside, whipping and robbing freedmen and defying the military and civil authorities before retreating to the swamps which offered a secure hiding place. . . .

Robberies, murders and other depredations committed by gangs and individual thieves created a general atmosphere of suspicion and fear in rural areas. When a band of robbers appeared in a region or moved to a new area and began to operate its villainous trade, the most improbable stories about them arose and became exaggerated. Rumors could swell the size of a five-member band to fifty, describing the thieves as armed to the teeth and eager to perpetrate any act of violence. The whole country would then become worked up to a pitch of excitement. People were warned to become more watchful, to "sleep with one eye on watch, have a good-barrell gun, well loaded with sixteen, whistlers in each barrels [*sic*] always at your bed side and don't bother the judiciary with an investigation." Many papers advised rural people to keep their guns fully loaded and to resort to summary punishments whenever a thief was caught stealing. . . .

. . . Crimes against property were considered by district attornies [*sic*] and judges to be the most heinous offenses, and burglars, forgers, highway robbers and petty thieves were not only promptly tried and convicted but also

Table [2]

DISTRIBUTION OF SENTENCING FOR CRIMES AGAINST
PROPERTY IN RURAL LOUISIANA, 1866 TO 1876

	(1)	(2)	(3)	(4)	(5)	(6)	(7)	(8)	Total
No action	196	291	53	113	22	60	35	323	1093
Acquitted	3	2	1	1	0	0	32	40	79
Escapees	14	1	1	0	0	3	1	1	21
Liberated on bonds	16	24	24	—	—	—	—	—	65
Found guilty	11	1	57	5	13	6	36	88	217
To pay a fine	0	0	1	0	1	0	3	9	14
Less than a month	0	0	0	0	0	1	2	2	5
1 to 6 months	0	1	1	6	6	3	4	4	25
6 months to 1 year	0	0	0	3	1	2	0	0	6
1 to 2 years	17	56	1	67	18	81	14	14	268
2 to 5 years	0	0	0	83	5	77	10	10	185
6 to 10 years	0	0	2	19	0	0	0	0	21
11 to 20 years	2	1	7	10	0	0	0	0	20
More than 20 years	0	0	0	1	0	0	0	0	1
Hard labor for life	15	0	1	4	0	0	0	0	20
Death sentence	16	0	0	0	0	0	0	0	16
Lynched	4	0	0	0	0	2	3	3	12
Total	294	377	149	312	66	235	140	494	2067

Key:

(1) Robbery and murder
(2) Robbery and personal violence
(3) Arson or destruction of property
(4) Robbery, burglary or breaking and entering

(5) Bribery, embezzlement, forgery or fraud
(6) Horse stealing
(7) Cattle, mule, hog stealing
(8) Petty theft and larceny

more severely punished than those convicted of violent crimes against a person. Still, in spite of the efforts of local law enforcement officers in apprehending robbers and the severity of the court, most people who committed property crimes escaped the heavy hand of the law (Table [2]).

It was fashionable during the period to blame the state administration and its law enforcement officers for this unfortunate state of affairs. Newspapers all over the state complained about the inefficiency of the authorities in arresting and prosecuting thieves and burglars. The Democratic press asserted that filling civil offices with "unprincipled vagabonds and ignorant negroes" was the first cause for the general atmosphere of lawlessness. But the problem was more complex. Louisiana lacked the coherent centralized police force to repress banditry and brigandage in the countryside that Texas and most other states had. The state militia rarely operated outside of New Orleans, and local law enforcement officers were at the mercy of whatever local support they could muster to repress outlaws. The lax state of affairs hampering law enforcement was further complicated by the unwillingness of whites to sit with blacks on juries. The judicial system was also disrupted by legal technicalities which allowed many criminals to escape justice. Moreover, corruption overrode the selection of jurors in criminal trials. Social and pecuniary influences were brought to bear on jurors by influential offenders. Finally, the fear of reprisal by desperate criminals influenced many jurors. Few people were willing to lay charges against criminals who, as a consequence, were allowed to go free. The detention, trial and punishment of offenders became more and more farcical and uncertain. Although robberies and murders were regularly committed, most people doubted that the perpetrators of those deeds could be brought to justice.

Moreover, various parish newspapers and grand juries noted that the notorious inadequacies of the local jails and prisons throughout the state were an important factor in the inability of officials to cope with crime. Men indicted for arson, burglary, larceny, horse stealing, and even murder, often escaped trial by breaking out of jails. However, the reluctance of country residents to pay higher taxes for larger and more secure jails made the task of keeping offenders who awaited trial almost impossible.

Faced with the inability of state and local authorities to put an end to theft and other crimes committed by gangs of robbers in the countryside, vigilance committees were organized as a last resort. The rumor that a band of robbers was operating in a region was often enough to generate the formation of preventive vigilance committees before any crimes had been committed. Consequently, associations of citizens periodically formed vigilance committees or protective associations all over the state to hold in check robbers and other property offenders.

. . . Some law officers did occasionally try to resist vigilance committees or lynching mobs, but the plain truth is that lynching was usually endorsed by local notables and occurred with the compliance of law officials.

Meanwhile, following emancipation, lynching and other forms of summary executions became a disturbing feature of race relations in Louisiana and in the South, as blacks were no longer protected by their market value. Many blacks were caught and brutally murdered by vigilance committees for allegedly stealing chickens, hogs, horse [sic] or cattle, and others were killed for such trivial reasons as stealing an onion or an apple from the planter's gar-den, stealing meat from a smokehouse or simply for going into the smokehouse, or being accused of stealing a box of sardines. But the lynching of blacks for alledged [*sic*] stealing or arson was not limited to offenses against white prop-erty. On one occasion, a black reputed to be a notorious thief was lynched after a summary trial for stealing a cow from another black. In another instance, a black in Ascension Parish was brutally murdered in 1875 by "white ruffians" for refusing to confess complicity in a robbery with which it was later learned that he had nothing to do. But lynching to protect property was not only a brutal and summary way to administer justice, it was also an important tool in converting Louisiana into a white man's territory.

White Violence Against Blacks in Caddo Parish
Gilles Vandal

Violence has always been an important component of Louisiana history and culture. Even before the Civil War, Louisiana was infamous for its frequent feuds, street fights, duels, whiskey brawls, vigilance committees and outbursts of violence. In Reconstructed Louisiana, violence reached new highs as it took on racial and political overtones. . . .

For Caddo Parish the end of the Civil War did not bring peace. For years after the war, the parish had little or no law and witnessed within its borders some of the most atrocious murders ever recorded. In July 1870, the *Jefferson State Register* declared that disorderly ruffians had given Caddo an unenviable reputation. This view was echoed by the *Donaldsonville Chief* which asserted in March 1875 that Caddo was living up to its name and rightly deserved to be called "Bloody Caddo." It went on to say that human life was held so cheaply there that scarcely a week passed without bringing news of some horrible new crime. Moreover, three congressional committees concluded that "Bloody Caddo" merited its epithet, as the worst men known to any civilized country lived within the limits of that parish.

Reconstructed Louisiana was indeed notorious for its unenviable record of violence. . . . [O]ur data not only confirm that Caddo parish was a very violent area, but also show, when compared with other areas, that Caddo had

Selections from Gilles Vandal, "'Bloody Caddo': White Violence Against Blacks in a Louisiana Parish, 1865–1876," *Journal of Social History* 25 (1991): 373–88. Reprinted by permission of *Journal of Social History*.

a homicide rate well above the state level, in a state where violence went beyond any reasonable standard even for the period. . . .

. . . Caddo and the surrounding parishes constituted the only region in Louisiana that was spared by the war. As the parish did not live through the terror, famine and others sufferings brought by the war, no rebuilding, no repair or reconstruction needed to be done there. Moreover, the war had brought great prosperity to the parish, as Shreveport became the capital of Confederate Louisiana after the fall of New Orleans. As the region escaped invasion and was occupied only after the surrender of the Southern armies, white people there did not feel they had been vanquished. As a consequence, the white community in Caddo was periodically dominated by a class of daring, brave and utterly reckless men who stubbornly opposed the federal government and its reconstruction policy and who strongly resented the presence of federal troops, particularly when those occupying forces were composed of black regiments. These men firmly resisted the changes brought by the war, and did not shrink from anything, even from murder. Violence, consequently, became the ultimate instrument in coercing blacks into submissiveness and in maintaining Caddo as a white-man's country. . . .

When violence reached a paroxysm, as it did in 1868 and again in 1874, even the most moderate whites could not disagree with the conservative policies of intimidation and violence. . . . Indeed, our data show that no less than 379 whites in Caddo were involved in killing blacks. This meant that no less than 30% of whites in Caddo between the ages of 18 and 45 were involved in those homicides. This percentage was ten times higher than the one for the state as a whole. No less significant, however, is the fact that 123 whites (32%) were involved in more than one homicide (Table [3]). Moreover, data on the occupation and social profile of the whites involved in the killing of blacks show that these people represented the best class of Caddo community (Table [4]). Indeed, violence originated from the top of the white social stratum. . . .

. . . Caddo Parish was unique in Louisiana in the intensity and high level of its racial violence. Our statistics show that political issues in Caddo pervaded all conflicts and lay at the root of most violence that occurred in that parish. Indeed, the situation in Caddo was particularly difficult as the parish came out of the war undamaged, without suffering any devastation. As a result, whites there did not feel vanquished and resented more strongly the changes brought by the war. This factor made post–Civil War adjustment in Caddo more difficult than in any other region of Louisiana, and underlined the greater political and social turmoil that troubled the parish at the time.

Table [3]

INVOLVEMENT OF WHITES IN KILLING BLACKS

NUMBER OF HOMICIDES	CADDO	%	LOUISIANA	%
At least one	256	67.5	1361	65.2
Two	34	8.9	182	8.7
Three to five	64	16.8	305	14.6
Six to ten	12	3.1	174	8.3
More than ten	13	3.4	64	3.0
Total	379	99.7	2086	99.8

Table [4]

OCCUPATIONS OF WHITES INVOLVED IN KILLING BLACKS

NUMBER OF HOMICIDES	CADDO	%	LOUISIANA	%
Public officials	17	14.2	29	5.4
Liberal professions	9	7.5	62	11.6
Businessmen	1	0.8	14	2.6
Planters	52	43.7	177	33.2
Farmers	25	21.0	142	26.6
Small professionals	3	2.5	23	4.3
Small businessmen	3	2.5	12	2.2
Skilled workers	1	0.8	20	3.7
Laborers	2	1.6	26	4.9
Farm Laborers	1	0.8	20	3.7
Students	3	2.5	8	1.5
Others	2	1.6	5	0.9
Total	119	99.8	533	99.9

POCKET CYCLOPEDIA OF TEMPERANCE (1891)

Temperance—The true definition of temperance would be "moderation in the use of everything good, abstinence from the use of everything bad."

Temptation—The liquor interests say that the prohibitionists are forgetful of the biblical statement that "Temptation must needs come," but, in the words of Dr. Clarence True Wilson, they forget the other part of the declaration, "But woe to him by whom temptation cometh." The liquor press frequently

Clarence True Wilson, ed., *The Pocket Cyclopedia of Temperance* (Topeka, Kansas: Temperance Society of the M.E. Church, 1891), 312, 317–18.

speaks of alcohol as a "selective force" which eliminates the weaklings from the race and therefore contributes to the average strength of character and body. . . . It is true that alcohol contributes somewhat to "the survival of the fittest"—*those that are fittest for survival only.* Instead of removing the weaklings from the race it frequently removes such men as Robert Burns, Edgar Allen [*sic*] Poe, and others whose names will occur to any student of history.

DOCUMENTS OF THE AMERICAN TEMPERANCE SOCIETY (1835)

The greatest improvement of modern times consists in the discovery that alcohol, as a beverage, is poison for the mind, as well as the body; and the greatest invention of our day is, that of constructing those moral machines, called Temperance Societies. They as far exceed steam-engines, railways, cotton-spinning machines, &c. as the mind is superior to matter; and the bodies and souls of mankind, are of more consequence than money, and merchandise. We hope, therefore, that the time will soon arrive, when all the inhabitants of the United States will compose a Temperance Society; of which every man, woman and child, who has arrived at years of discretion, will be a member.

Multitudes now believe, that they cannot continue even to use ardent spirit, without the commission of known and aggravated sin; or furnish it for others, without being accessory to the ruin, temporal and eternal, of their fellow men. Hundreds of ministers of the gospel, thousands and tens of thousands of professed Christians, and hundreds of thousands of distinguished and philanthropic men, have become convinced, that the traffic in ardent spirit, as an article of luxury or diet, is inconsistent with the Christian religion, and ought to be abandoned throughout the world.

When great changes take place in the natural or moral world, many are anxious to know the cause; and the means by which those changes were effected. This is now the case with regard to the Temperance Reformation. Numerous inquiries have been made, during the past year, in this and other countries, with regard to the origin of the American Temperance Society; and the reasons which led its friends to adopt *abstinence from the use of ardent spirit,* as the first grand principle of their operations.

These inquiries the Committee are disposed to answer; both as a testimony to the divine goodness, and an encouragement to all who are disposed,

---

Selections from *Temperance Documents of the American Temperance Society* (Boston: Seth Bliss and Perkins, Marvin, 1835), 1:6–7, 1:11.

in dependence on divine aid, and in the use of suitable means, to attempt to do all for the benefit of man which needs to be done.

About seventeen years ago, a communication was made by a member of this Committee, on the evils of using intoxicating liquors at funerals; and reasons were presented, why this practice, which had become common in some parts of the country, should be done away. One reason was, the tendency of this practice to prevent the benefit that might otherwise be derived from providences, and the religious exercises of funeral occasions. The effect showed that such labors are not in vain in the Lord. The practice declined, and was soon, in a great measure, done away.

Not long after, he made another communication on the evils of furnishing ardent spirit as an article of entertainment, especially to ministers of the gospel; a practice which was also common, and was thought by many to be a suitable expression of respect and kindness toward the ministerial office. The effect of this also was strongly marked; and some persons from that time adopted the plan of not using ardent spirit on any occasion. The benefits of abstinence were striking; facts were collected, and arrangements made for a more extended exhibition of this subject. Men were found who had been led by their own reflections, in view of the evil which it occasions, to renounce the use of this poison; and others who had never used it. Yet, as a body, they enjoyed better health than those who continued to use it, were more uniform and consistent in their deportment, and more ready for every good word and work.

In 1822, a teamster, partially intoxicated, by using what some persons, for less, probably, than twenty-five cents, had given him, fell under the wheels of his wagon, and was crushed to death. Another man, tending a coal-pit, became partially intoxicated, fell asleep, on some straw, and was burnt to death. These events occasioned the delivery of two discourses, viz. one on the wretchedness of intemperate men, and another on the duty of preventing sober men from becoming intemperate; that, when the present race of drunkards should be removed, the whole land might be free. The means of doing this, the sure means, and the only means, were shown to be, *abstinence from the use of intoxicating liquors.* This was shown, by facts, to be both practicable and expedient, and was urged as the indispensable duty of all men; a duty which they owed to God, to themselves, their children, their country, and the world.

This doctrine appeared to many to be strange; excited great attention, occasioned much conversation, and, through the blessing of the Lord, produced great results. It was again and again enforced. A conviction of the duty of abstinence was fastened on many consciences; and it became evident from facts, that this doctrine is adapted to commend itself to every man's conscience in the sight of God. . . .

What shall be done to banish intemperance from the United States?

After prayer for divine guidance, and consultation on the subject, the . result was, a determination to attempt the formation of an American Temperance Society, whose grand principle should be, *abstinence from strong drink;* and its object, by light and love, to change the habits of the nation, with regard to the use of intoxicating liquors. Some of the reasons of this determination were:

1. Ardent spirit, which is one of the principal means of drunkenness, is not needful, and the use of it is, to men in health, always injurious.
2. It is adapted to form intemperate appetites; and while it is continued, the evils of intemperance can never be done away.
3. The use of this liquor is causing a general deterioration of body and mind; which, if the cause is continued, will continue to increase.
4. To remove the evils, we must remove the cause; and to remove the cause, efforts must be commensurate with the evil, and be continued till it is eradicated.
5. We never know what we can do by wise, united, and persevering efforts, in a good cause, till we try.
6. If we do not try to remove the evils of intemperance, we cannot free ourselves from the guilt of its effects.

GERARDI'S PROJECTED HOTEL (1891)

In real estate circles the week's business, and practically the business of the new year, opened up with a lively inquiry for choice residence property yesterday morning, which resulted in the consummation of several small sales. Judging by the amount of inquiry and the confidence shown by speculators, the dealers have no hesitancy in predicting an active January market, and from the inquiry yesterday it is predicted that there will be some heavy transactions in real estate during the week.

The new Union Depot has occasioned quite a movement in property in the vicinity of Olive street, between Fifteenth and Twenty-second, and offers of what would a short time ago have appeared fabulous prices for property in this section are daily refused. An offer of $100,000 for the northeast corner of Twelfth and Olive streets was made yesterday by the Ohio Real Estate Company. The

---

Selections from "Gerardi's Projected Hotel at Grand Avenue and Olive Street," article in *St. Louis (Mo.) Republic,* January 6, 1891, p. 8.

corner is 100 x 100 feet square and is owned by the Turner estate. The offer was a fair one, but it is very probable that it will not be entertained, as Twelfth street is one of the districts which will doubtless be greatly altered by the location of the new depot. Twelfth street, it has been predicted by some of the leading real estate dealers, foremost among whom is Mr. Frank Obear, will be made the great centre for all the street railways in the city. From the inquiry and the number of deals that have taken place in the vicinity of the new depot, it is evident that Olive street property is in greatest demand.

Gerardi's Scheme

Mr. Joseph Gerardi, the caterer and former proprietor of the Planters' House, has leased the Lincoln flats at the northeast corner of Grand avenue and Olive street, opposite the Hotel Boers, and will start a West End hotel. This was the rumor in real estate row yesterday, and it is said to have emanated from Mr. Gerardi himself. The Lincoln flats occupy 100 x 150 feet of ground fronting on Grand avenue and Olive street, the 150 feet front being on Olive street. The building is a three-story brick structure, built by Grable & Webber, the architects, for Mr. Rosenblatt. It is said that Mr. Gerardi will have the building raised three stories, making it a six-story structure, and will have the interior arrangements changed and remodelled. Mr. Gerardi has also secured a lease on two of the three vacant stores in the Odd-Fellows' Temple, east of the Bank of the Republic, and between it and J. T. McCasland's new office, and will open a first-class restaurant there.

Louisiana and the 1904 World's Fair

Louisiana was represented by exhibits in nine buildings: Agriculture, Horticulture, Forestry, Fish, and Game, Anthropology, Transportation, Education, Liberal Arts, and Mines and Minerals. In agriculture special exhibits were made of the three great staples of Louisiana, viz.: sugar, rice, and cotton. A complete sugar house with a cane field, field implements, a train of cars, and all the products of the sugar house and refinery, were to be seen.

In the rice department a field of growing rice; implements for preparing the soil, seeding, harvesting, and threshing machines; a complete irrigation

Selections from J. W. Buel, ed., *Louisiana and the Fair: An Exposition of the World, Its People and Their Achievements* (St. Louis, Mo.: World's Progress Publishing Company, 1905), 3691–3694. Available as Item F351B93, vol. 10, Rare Book Collection, Cammie G. Henry Research Center, Watson Memorial Library, Northwestern State University of Louisiana, Natchitoches, Louisiana.

plant; complete rice-mill; warehouses; cars and locomotives with several variet-
ies of rice in all of its forms, were to be seen. In the cotton exhibit were fifteen
bales of cotton, wrapped in silk and bound with brass bands, surmounted by the
"Carnival King" in cotton; cotton gins and presses and a complete cotton seed
oilmill; samples of cotton in large quantities; growing cotton, products of the
oilmills, etc., were also exhibited.

In the other agriculture exhibits were samples of corn, wheat, oats, bar-
ley, rye, grasses, forage crops, clover, alfalfa, tespedeza, etc., and vegetables of
all kinds, both fresh and in wax. Fiber plants and their products were also
exhibited, including ramie in all forms from the stalk to the finished garments.
There were also handsome displays of field and vegetable seeds, canned foods
of every description, and sauces, including the famous "Fabas co Pepper." A
topographical map of the State, nine feet by ten feet, showed the areas devoted
to the different crops.

In horticulture a large and fine collection of pecans was to be seen. Oranges, mandarins, and grape fruit were exhibited from Louisiana's cebrous
groves. Apples, pears, plums, peaches, figs, and pomegranates were also presented. Besides the above, handsome specimens of all Louisiana fruits were
shown in wax. In the conservatory of the Horticulture Building was a carload
of rare and excellent plants, including palms, bananas, pineapples, tea, olives,
magnolia tuscala, oranges, pomegranates, etc.

In forestry, the woods of Louisiana's extensive forests, with planks from
the same, together with products of every kind made from these woods were
to be seen, also finished specimens of furniture, doors, windows, mantel-pieces,
bric-a-brac, made from oak, gum, cypress, and pine. A topographical map of
the State, eight by ten, showed the forest areas of the State. In fish and game
were exhibited many kinds of fish and wild animals of the State.

In anthropology many valuable Indian relics and a number of baskets
made by the Indian tribes of the State were displayed.

In Transportation Building [*sic*] was shown transportation on the Mississippi River, past and present. Beginning with the Indian canoe every style of
craft was shown up to the present ocean liner, capable of carrying 28,000 bales
of cotton. Excellent specimens of saddlery were also exhibited, an industry
that is growing rapidly in Louisiana.

In education, the public, private, and religious schools of the State were
all represented. The Industrial School, the State University, Tulane University, and the Colored State and Denominational Universities all made handsome displays. The larger cities of the State had also fine exhibits of the works
of their high schools.

In liberal arts excellent topographical maps of New Orleans in 1803 and 1903, a splendid topographical map of the levees of the State, thirty-five by four, and a model of the large United States dock in New Orleans, were shown. Besides these there were more than 200 maps of the Louisiana coast, from 1500 to the present time, and a number of rare old books exhibited by Mr. Wm. Beer of the Howard Library of New Orleans.

In mines and minerals were interesting figures of the "Devil" in sulphur and "Lot's Wife" in salt, also sixty specimens of crude and refined petroleums, and many samples of marble, sandstone, artificial stones, pressed brick, clay, iron ore, coal, etc. The exhibit was enclosed in a wall made of sulphur and salt bricks. There was also a topographical map of the State, showing its geological and mineralogical features.

Recollections of the 1904 World's Fair
Sam P. Hyde

Trouble had begun early on the Pike. A thousand pedestrians thronged the great thoroughfare beneath ten thousand electric lights, whilst the din of cow bells, whistles, megaphones, the infernal yelling of the barkers mingled with the boom of cannon in the sham battle shows,[1] and every body making all the noise they could with every conceivable device that would produce discord upon general principles rendered a pandemonium that I don't expect to hear again this side of Hades. Troops of young men joining hands would worm through the crowd in a string and coming on to some poor fellow walking sweetly with his girl they would quickly encircle the unsuspecting couple, dance around them yelling like fiends incarnate and close in till all were involved in a human maelstrom and indescribable confusion. Then they would break away and scatter as quickly as they came, leaving the bewildered swain to pull themselves together, pick up their hats and their dignity, shake out their ruffled garments, take their bearings and move on. Serpentine[2] shot through the air like meteors of varied hue and confetti rained in torrents. Every stiff hat was a target for the inflated bladder.[3] No respect was shown to age or dignity, no mercy to starch and feathers, it was an all round go as you please and if you didn't like it you could get off the Pike.

One of the most popular noise-making schemes and perhaps the most effective in results was the dragging of several tin cans by a string over the

Selections from Sam P. Hyde, "Recollections of the Fair," in *"Indescribably Grand": Diaries and Letters from the 1904 World's Fair,* ed. Martha R. Clevenger (St. Louis: Missouri Historical Society Press, 1996), 142–43. Reprinted by permission of Missouri Historical Society.

cobblestones. The carnival spirit prevailed however and no body got mad however severe the punishment. But it was getting late in the season and many of the shows had resorted to showing some of their best stock on a platform at the door between the performances. Females were conspicuous of course. Spanish, French and Russian dancing girls. Esquimos, Scandinavians and Hottentots. And the shorter their skirts the bigger the crowd that gathered to hear the barker tell what wonderful stunts they would do.

Performance to begin "right away." I was taking in these free shows and studying the faces from a scientific point of view. Repulsively vile, most of them and I thought it would take no prophet to detect "the mark of the beast" on their foreheads. Poor girls perhaps it was rather their misfortune than their fault that they were there. I noticed the disappointment on the face of the professor sometimes when the crowd instead of thronging to the ticket box after his talk would all march off to the next free show. "The Great Creation" "Under and Over the Sea" "Mysterious Asia" "The Girls of Madrid" were ringing on the ear, whilst ever and anon rose a deep voice "Hagenback Hagenback"[4] and here would come a great camel down the crowded thoroughfare with a girl in oriental costume on its back.

I drew up at last in front of a platform on which sat some half dozen of as vile looking creatures as ever bore the name of woman.

A well dressed young man mounted the box and presented the merits of his show in something like these words. Remember however that this speech is not as I recall it after four years, but copied verbatim from a memorandum I made the next day. I have not drawn on my imagination nor substituted expressions. These are his words not mine.

"Now gentlemen we have a hot show in here and I would not advise spinsters from the church sewing societies to come in, it is no place for prudes and old maid missionaries. I am candid with you when I say it's a warm entertainment, and boys if you bring your sweethearts in here you can call their attention to the fresco on the ceiling when the temperature gets too high and while they are looking aloft you watch the stage and you'll catch it all.

"Some people go out of here saying 'it's awful, it ought not to be allowed' others say 'it's fine and it's all right.' Now as I say we have an all round warm show but you are not obliged to remain if it's uncomfortably warm. Some people think it has been bad before this, but these are lively girls and it's hard to hold them down. And as this is Thanksgiving night we have turned the girls loose and it's hotter than ever. Now come right in the performance begins right away. Some folks say it is going too far while others would like to see it carried further, but we will admit it is the limit. We have put the price down to one dime, only ten cents pass right in and get your money's worth one dime pays the bill."

You might supposed that after hearing this statement in plain English that the show was not decent, the crowd would have turned away with one accord. On the contrary there was rush for the ticket window. Men and women and young fellows with nice looking girls on their arms bought their tickets and passed in. If this was the spirit of the Pike it was an unclean spirit. But they were on a lark and had some curiosity to see what "the limit" was. And yet it was a holiday and my last chance, I had spent very little on Pike shows, why should not I be a little bad just for once. No said I, when I want to be bad I won't be bad that way, and I put the dime back in my pocket and dropped out of line. I believe if the Pike had been a mile longer it would have led to hell.

Religious Influences

eligious devotion played an important role in nineteenth-century Louisiana. Much of the action in *At Fault* is motivated by the religious convictions of Thérèse and Melicent. Hosmer's remarriage to Fanny is a direct result of the Catholic prohibition on divorce. A practicing Catholic like Thérèse would have committed a mortal sin, leading to eternal damnation, by marrying a divorced man. The Catholic faith also addressed issues such as intemperance in regard to the use of alcohol and the use of violence in defense of life and property. Selections from the *Catholic Catechism* which clarify these issues are presented below.

Unitarianism, a belief system that was foreign to both the Catholic Creoles and the fundamentalist African Americans of the Cane River region, is seen in Melicent's articulate and outspoken denial of the doctrine of hellfire and everlasting suffering. Melicent's religious convictions lead her to reject Grégoire after he murders Joçint. Readers will find below relevant selections from the *Unitarian Catechism,* addressing these doctrinal issues.

A Catholic Catechism

242. How do we sin against our own life?

We sin against our own life when we:
1. Take our life;
2. Risk it without sufficient reason;
3. Ruin our health by excesses.

Selections from Rev. James Groenings, *A Catholic Catechism for the Parochial and Sunday Schools of the United States,* trans. Very Rev. James Rockliff (New York: Benziger Brothers, 1900), 70–71.

243. How do we most frequently injure our health?

We most frequently injure our health by eating or drinking too much. (Intemperance.)

He is intemperate who eats or drinks too much or too greedily.

244. How do we injure the soul of another?

We injure the soul of another when we:
1. Purposely teach him to commit sin; (Seduction.)
2. Lead him to sin by bad example. (Scandal.)

278. What evil is meant from which we should decline?

The evil from which we should decline is sin.

279. What is sin?

Sin is an offence against God.

280. When do we commit sin?

We commit sin when we wilfully [*sic*] disobey God.

281. How do we commit sin?

We commit sin:
1. By evil thoughts and desires; (Inwardly.)
2. By evil words and deeds; (Outwardly.)
3. By not doing our duty. (Omission.)

282. When do we commit a grievous sin?

We commit a grievous sin when we wilfully [*sic*] disobey God in an important matter.

Grievous sin consists in disobeying God:
1. In an important matter;
2. With clear knowledge of the evil;
3. With full and free consent of the will.

It is also called *Mortal Sin*.

283. Why is grievous sin called mortal sin?

Grievous sin is called mortal sin, because it destroys the supernatural life of the soul and causes eternal death.

319. What are the most important moral virtues?

The most important virtues are Prudence, Justice, Temperance, and Fortitude.

322. What is the virtue of Temperance?

Temperance is the virtue that keeps us from all excess in the enjoyment of lawful pleasure.

456. With whom can a Catholic not contract a valid marriage?

A Catholic cannot contract a valid marriage with:
1. One who is already married;
2. One who is not baptized;
3. A near relative;
4. One who is spiritually related to him.

457. When is a Catholic not allowed to marry?

A Catholic is NOT ALLOWED to marry if:
1. He has taken a vow to remain single;
2. He has promised marriage to another party;
3. The banns have not been published three times in the church;
4. He intends to marry a non-Catholic. (Mixed marriage.)

458. Why does the Church so strictly forbid mixed marriages?

The Church strictly forbids mixed marriages:
1. Because the non-Catholic party usually believes in divorce;
2. Because the Catholic party is in danger of losing his faith or growing lukewarm in it;
3. Because the children mostly receive a poor Catholic education or none at all.

CATHOLIC MORALITY
REV. BERNARD J. KELLY

Intoxication: When immoderation in eating or—as is more usual—in drinking is of such a kind as to deprive a person of the use of reason it is known as intoxication.[1] It is a grave sin to intoxicate oneself completely—that is to say, to be so immoderate in the use of intoxicating food[2] or drink as to deprive onself completely of the use of reason, even for a time. Intoxication is sufficiently complete to constitute a grave sin if it causes a person to act in an altogether untoward manner, to be unable to distinguish right from wrong, etc., even though it does not reduce him to total unconsciousness.

Selections from Rev. Bernard J. Kelly, *Apologetics and Catholic Doctrine, Part 3: Catholic Morality* (Dublin, Ireland: Gill & Son, 1951), 306–7, 261–62, 283–87. Reprinted by permission of Holy Ghost Congregation.

When intoxication is partial it constitutes, of itself, a venial sin.

It is necessary to consider the effects of intoxication before passing judgment on any particular instance of it. For though partial intoxication is only a venial sin in itself it may easily involve mortal sin through consequent neglect of one's family, through exposing oneself to temptation, through frequenting bad company, through weakening one's power to resist temptation, etc.

Total Abstinence: Alcoholic liquor is not bad in itself. Like all the works of God's hands it is good and can serve good purposes. But for reasons such as those outlined above it may be harmful to certain people. For them it is prudent, or even necessary, to restrict their use of alcohol and even to abstain totally from it. Total abstinence may be practised also as a form of self-denial by people for whom alcohol constitutes no real danger. Finally, it may be practised in a spirit of reparation to God for all the sins committed against Him, especially those committed through drunkenness. God, Who is so good, deserves that reparation be made to Him. Besides, reparation brings down His blessings on men. Hence, those who are willing to make reparation by the practice of total abstinence, or in any other way, perform a truly Christian work as well as giving good example of respect for the virtue of temperance. . . .

Having spoken already of the relations between father (and mother) and children, it remains now only to speak of those between husband and wife. The husband is the head, or superior of the wife, entitled to obedience within the limits of his authority: "Let women be subject to their husbands as to the Lord: Because the husband is the head of the wife as Christ is head of the Church." His authority has, however, limits: the wife is a partner, not a servant. She has the same right to his love and affection that he has to hers. On the other hand the husband has the right and duty to control the course of family life; he has the right and duty to see that his wife performs her household offices; he has the right and duty to supervise the education of his children; and finally he has the right and duty to administer the family goods (except those which the wife possesses in her own right).

Hence a wife would sin:

(a) If she were disobedient to her husband's reasonable commands in matters which pertain to his sphere of authority.

(b) If without sufficient cause—such as the husband's neglect or incapacity—she were to take control of the family purse or possessions.

(c) If she were to injure her husband in word or deed.

A husband would sin gravely:

(a) By injuring his wife seriously by word or deed.

(b) By striking her violently.

(c) By neglecting to provide for her needs.

(d) By wasting the family possessions.

It is clear from the above that the subjection of the wife to the husband is in no sense a form of slavery. Those who claim the so-called emancipation of women, aim, perhaps in ignorance of the consequences of their claim, at tearing her violently from the environment and way of life in which she can best reach her full perfection and development. It is true that some women do not get from their husbands and family the love and support to which they are entitled. Such cases show that family life—like every other gift of God's—can be abused. But the gift is itself good: married life, and all that goes to make it up, is good and holy. Besides, the wife who bears her cross for the love of God, and out of respect for the duties of her married life, earns for herself a high place in the unending happiness of Heaven. The same is true, also, for the husband, in cases in which he is the party treated unjustly. . . .

Killing in Self-defence:[3] Since God has given us our lives to spend them in His service, He gives us the right to defend them when they are in danger. If the danger is caused by a man, we are entitled to defend ourselves, even by doing him some injury. But, that our action be justified, we must inflict no more than is required for self-defence. Thus, if we can ward off the danger by inflicting a slight injury, we may not inflict a grave one, and if a grave one will do, we may not kill the aggressor. If, however, there is no other way of saving our lives, we have the right to kill him. The following conditions should be realised before one has the right to kill in self-defence:

(a) The evil intention of the aggressor must be certain.

(b) The act of aggression must have begun, at least morally. A man has not the right to kill here and now, another man who, he knows, intends to murder him later in the day.

Not only one's life, but also one's members, one's virtue, or even a very large sum of money may be defended in this way. If, however, the injury has been done already—as for example, if the aggressor has done bodily harm, and is now departing—it is not allowed to attack him, as that would be no longer self-defence but rather revenge.

When availing of this right to defend oneself by doing violence to an aggressor it is most necessary not to exceed what is required for the purpose of self-defence. It would be gravely sinful—in short, it would be murder—to kill an aggressor who could easily be disposed of in another way. In the case of attempted robbery, if the robber is identified and redress can, therefore, be obtained through the civil courts, it would not be allowable to safeguard one's goods by inflicting serious injury on him. It would, however, be permissible to do him some slight injury if that sufficed for the purpose. For example, owners of orchards who catch children stealing their apples are entitled to administer some slight punishment. When the attack is on one's life or person, if it can be warded off safely by flight, it is not permissible to inflict a serious injury on the aggressor. . . .

Murder: By murder is meant the direct and intentional killing of an innocent person. It is a grave sin. Not even the state could legalise the execution of an innocent person, even if his death would avert a great danger: for example, the state could not decree the execution (by poisoning or other means) of citizens sick with dangerous and infectious disease.

Though it is never permissible to kill an innocent person directly, it is permissible to do or omit something from which the death of an innocent person may follow indirectly—provided always that there is a sufficiently good reason for the action or omission, and that it is not itself sinful. . . .

Scandal: The sin of *scandal,* consists in saying or doing something which is either wrong, or appears to be wrong, and thereby occasioning the sin of another or others. Scandal inflicts harm on the soul of one's neighbour much the same as physical violence inflicts harm on his body.

It should be noted that scandal can be given not only by words or actions which are sinful, but even by those which have no more than the appearance of sin. For example, a person dispensed from the law of abstinence could give scandal by eating meat on a Friday in a place in which he was known to be a Catholic, but not known to be dispensed.

Note, also, that scandal-giving does not mean to cause horror or amazement. It consists essentially in causing the spiritual ruin of others by leading them into sin. In the example given just now, the scandal given consists in the likelihood that others not dispensed from the law, would take meat also if they saw one whom they knew to be a Catholic taking it;

The following principles show the different kinds of scandal and their respective guilts:

(a) Scandal given precisely in order to cause another to sin, is a sin against both charity and the virtue to which the sin in question is opposed. For example, scandal given to lead another to sin against chastity, is a sin against both charity and chastity. If scandal is given to lead another to commit a grave sin, the sin of scandal so committed is mortal. If it be given to lead another to commit a venial sin, or if it is only remotely an incitement to mortal sin, the sin of scandal committed is venial. As an example to illustrate the last point, we may take a person who, of set purpose, irritates another slightly, with the unexpected result that the other gets into a very great rage and utters a number of blasphemies. Since the great rage and the blasphemies were neither intended nor foreseen, the sin of scandal committed is venial only.[4]

UNITARIAN CATECHISM

DEATH AND AFTER.

1. Q. What is death?
   A. It is the ceasing of our bodily life.
2. Q. Is it a punishment for sin?
   A. No: it existed among the lower animals before there were any men to do wrong.
3. Q. Why did it come into the world?
   A. It is the law of all organized creatures that they must die as well as be born.
4. Q. Is it an evil?
   A. No: as things are in this world, it would be much worse if there were no death.
5. Q. Does it take away from the world's happiness?
   A. No: there is much more happiness with it.
6. Q. How is this?
   A. If there were no death, the world would soon be crowded with all sorts of creatures as well as with men.
7. Q. Then what?
   A. No more could be born, and so no more could experience the joy of living. Life is like a feast. If the first tableful sat there forever, no more could come.
8. Q. What makes people dread death?
   A. Largely the old teachings about the next world.

Selections from Minot Judson Savage, *Unitarian Catechism,* rev. ed. (Boston: Press of George II. Ellis, 1891).

9. Q. What else?

A. The sickness and pain connected with it.

10. Q. Anything else?

A. Yes: the separation from friends.

11. Q. Are these any real part of dying?

A. No: the fears of the future are chiefly imaginary. The pain and illness need not exist when people learn to live rightly; and the separation is only for a little while.

12. Q. What ought death, then, to be?

A. A happy rebirth into another life when through with this.

13. Q. Ought so many people to die so soon?

A. No: it is because we do not know or keep the laws of health.

14. Q. Can we hope that so much illness, pain, and early dying may be outgrown?

A. We may.

15. Q. Then what will dying be?

A. Like going to sleep when one has grown tired.

16. Q. Is death the end?

A. No: we believe it is only another kind of birth.

17. Q. Does death change one's character?

A. No: no more than a night's sleep does.

18. Q. Are there special places called heaven and hell?

A. No: each soul is happy or unhappy according to character.

19. Q. Can one find happiness after death except by being and doing right?

A. No: this is the only way.

20. Q. Where do those who die, go?

A. Probably not far away.

21. Q. Is there some special planet for their home?

A. Probably not. The spiritual world may be very near us; and perhaps its inhabitants can go from place to place as duty or pleasure lead.

22. Q. Do spirits have forms or bodies?

A. Probably: only of a kind that we know little or nothing of as yet.

23. Q. Why do we not know?

A. Knowledge is limited by experience; and as yet we have had no experience to teach us these things.

24. Q. What do these spiritual beings do?

A. Study and live their own lives as we do here. They may also serve, influence, and help us in many ways, though we do not see them.

25. Q. Ought we to dread dying, then?

A. No: after we have learned what earth has to teach us, we ought to anticipate going on and up to this higher life.

26. Q. Whom shall we find there?

A. All the great and noble of all past ages. Also, our own loved ones who have gone.

27. Q. Death, then, is not a sign of God's anger with us?

A. No: it is one of God's gifts to his children.

28. Q. Have we, then, nothing to fear in dying?

A. Only the natural consequences of our actions, the same as here.

29. Q. Will it be better with some when they die than with others?

A. Yes: it will be best for those who have lived best here.

30. Q. Why?

A. Just as it is best, on going out into life, for that boy or girl who has made the best preparation for it.

31. Q. What, then, is the chief end of man?

A. To learn to live rightly; for this means good in this world and in all worlds.

CREOLE LANGUAGE, CUSTOMS, AND SOCIETY; RACIAL CODES

E specially for those not intimately familiar with Louisiana culture, finding an unambiguous and uncontested definition of the word *Creole* can be challenging, if not impossible. Part of the problem is that the term has changed over time, making historical context critical in determining a precise definition. Perhaps more important, at least in the present time, is the fact that two distinct groups have attempted to lay claim to exclusive use of the term. One group, concentrated in New Orleans and its surrounding area, consists of the white descendants of the state's French and Spanish colonial settlers. The other, centered in the Isle Brevelle area of Natchitoches Parish near Kate Chopin's Cloutierville home, is a group with a unique cultural history—the "Creoles of Color." The material included in this section should help the reader understand this complicated cultural issue.

In the selections below from two essays by Joseph P. Tregle Jr., "Early New Orleans Society: A Reappraisal" and "On That Word 'Creole' Again: A Note," the author argues that, in the nineteenth century, the term *Creole* was used to designate any person or thing indigenous to the Louisiana territory. Interestingly, one of the few annotations in the first edition of *At Fault* is a note written by Chopin defining the word *Creole* in a manner consistent with Tregle's argument.

The selections from Gary Mills's *The Forgotten People: Cane River's Creoles of Color* examine the history of this unique culture and its relationship to Louisiana's other ethnic and social groups. Michelle Pichon's original and insightful sketch, "This, That, and the Others," offers a view of *At Fault* from the perspective of a member of the Isle Brevelle community. This essay demonstrates the passion with which those who self-identify as Creole define the term and defend their community.

Finally, we include selections from Louisiana's Black Code—a code enacted by the French but pointedly readopted by the Spanish when Louisiana was handed over to them forty years prior to the Louisiana Purchase. Though this colonial document lost its legal force after the Louisiana Purchase in 1803, its contents reflect the prevailing social customs and attitudes throughout the antebellum period. Sadly, many of the attitudes implicit in this code survived the Civil War and Reconstruction and deeply affected the course of Louisiana society for many years following the end of Reconstruction.

Early New Orleans Society
Joseph G. Tregle Jr.

Most of the South has been content with one Lost Cause, one romantic memory of a time gone by in which it has been possible to linger with mixed emotions of pride in the perfection of the past and regret for its passing. But in that most distinct of southern states, Louisiana, where loyalties have so often been confused, even the Confederacy has been unable to dominate the nostalgia of the people, and, indeed, the commiseration felt by Louisianians for the death of the ante-bellum South has been as nothing compared to their mourning over the fate of the Creole.

A veritable cult of the Creole has grown over the years, propagated by historians as well as by journalists, by scholars as well as by the often pathetic present-day representatives of this supposed tradition, confused but happy in their knowledge that once their kind had ruled these lands along the Mississippi with a grace and charm long since lost to the modern world. For those who look so longingly to the past, these old Latin ways and forms have taken on the character of a superior culture, doomed to be crushed in the eventual day of Anglo-Saxon uniformity....

... There are few things clung to so tenaciously or taught so vehemently in New Orleans as the doctrine of the Creole, which might be summed up as the religious belief that all those who bore that name were Louisianians born to descendants of the French and Spanish, that they were almost uniformly genteel and cultured aristocrats, above the lure of money, disdainful of physical labor, and too sensitive to descend into the dirty business of political and monetary struggle with the crude *Américains,* though they were influential

Selections from Joseph G. Tregle Jr., "Early New Orleans Society: A Reappraisal," *Journal of Southern History* 18, no. 1 (Feb. 1952): 20–36. Reprinted by permission of the Managing Editor, Southern Historical Association, Pittsburgh, Pennsylvania.

enough to engulf the barbarism of the latter and give social and artistic tone to the city.

Nothing so infuriates the apostles of the Creole myth as the widespread belief in some outland quarters that the term implies a mixture of white and Negro blood, and they insist with an air of finality and aggressiveness that no Creole has ever been anything but a native white Louisianian descended from the Latin colonial stock. Even the descendants of the Acadian migrants from Canada are ruled out of this select society—they may be Cajuns, but never Creoles, for who has ever heard of a lowly Creole? Poor, perhaps, but never lowly. Only on one point is there any compromise, and that is in the willingness of the elect to admit that "Creole" may be legitimately used as an adjective to classify any number of things as native to the state, so that one may speak correctly of a slave as a "Creole Negro," for example, if never simply as a "Creole." Some latitudinarians will even concede a place to those such as the scions of the German settlers who came into Louisiana under John Law, or to post-Purchase French migrants, since all these eventually became identified with the Gallic culture of the community. But the more frequent insistence is on the narrower definition. . . .

Their great accomplishment, we are told, was to know how to live. Not for them the rush and greed of the grasping American, whose god was the dollar and who had little time or inclination for the joys of the theater or the appreciation of beauty. It was breeding, never money, which counted with the Creole of tradition, and family pride made it impossible for him even to consider an economic pursuit which required the removal of his coat or the laborious use of his hands. He could be a banker, of course, which was eminently respectable, a professional man, a planter, or even a merchant, if on a large enough scale. But it should occasion no surprise that he fell farther and farther behind in the economic race with the Yankee—no man of his sensibilities could be expected to care enough for mere money to chase it with the almost frightening determination of a John McDonogh, or to allow the bothersome details of business to interfere with the serious things of life such as the theater, the opera, the ball, or the hunt. One could not be expected always to have an eye on the Americans! Thus life for the traditional Creole had few sharp edges— he moved in the circles of his society with gentility of manner and an awareness of all the subtleties of good living which could only have come from his noble lineage. Paragon of style, judge of good wine and fine food, connoisseur of handsome women, he was to the manner [*sic*] born.[1]

The only serious fault with this hallowed doctrine of the Creole is that it does demonstrable violence to historical truth. It is abundantly clear that in the 1820s and 1830s "Creole" was generally used in Louisiana to designate any person native to the state, be he white, black, or colored, French, Spanish, or Anglo-American, and used not as an adjective but as a noun. Thus the terms "Creole" and "native" were interchangeable, and if one wished to speak only of those Latin Louisianians who could trace their ties to the soil back to colonial days, the only precise form for so doing was that of the *ancien population.*" It is true, of course, that since the great preponderance of Creoles were of this original stock it was not at all unusual to find "Creole" being used as a more convenient term than *"ancien population,"* especially when one considers that the Anglo-American Creoles were neither numerous enough nor generally old enough in the 1820s and 1830s to make necessary the more limited and accurate terminology during the heated racial conflicts in the community, and certainly it was realized that no one would think of considering the Negro as being at all involved in any of these factional distinctions among white men. Moreover, the *ancien population* almost universally insisted upon identifying their interests as those common to all *native* Louisianians, and they deliberately embraced the non-Latin native as one of themselves. There could be no question, therefore, of denying him the title of Creole. It follows naturally that the Acadians were likewise full-fledged members of this group, and there was certainly never any attempt in the press or the hustings to consider them in any other light. . . .

It was as a native Louisianian, as a matter of fact, that the Latin Creole primarily thought of himself, for he saw in that powerful and mystical bond which ties most men to the soil of their birth the principal justification for his determination not to become a forgotten man in his own land. The danger of that eventuality coming to pass was by no means slight in the 1820s and 1830s. For two other major groups in New Orleans and throughout the state had gradually come to dominate the affairs of the community to the growing exclusion of all others: the Anglo-Americans and the so-called "foreign French."[2]

The Americans, of course, were of all kinds and from all places. They had come down into Louisiana principally after the Purchase to seek their fortunes in the rich acres of the new territory and in its markets, banks, courts, and thriving trading centers. There had been other Americans in New Orleans before 1803, to be sure, and they had generally been of a breed that was not easy to forget. Rough, violent, profane, and brawling, the floating adventurers, the river bullies, and the backwoods denizens come to market had made the American and Kentuckian names things to be feared and often detested among the citizens of the great port, who welcomed the trade but regretted the traders. One did not need the pride of the Creole of tradition to decide that he would have little to do with men such as these.

Louisiana folklore has, unfortunately, too greatly stressed this vulgarity and barbarism of the early Americans in Louisiana, and a part of the Creole myth would have it that for many decades the Creoles held aloof from the newcomers, confident of their own evident superiority, keeping alive the social, artistic, and cultural traditions of the community while the Yankee changed money in the temple. Nothing could be further from the truth, for it is a misrepresentation of both the Latin Creole and the Anglo-American types.

The plain truth of the matter is that the *ancien population* of the early nineteenth century, the Latin Creoles, were hardly the same sort of people met with so delightfully in the Creole myth. That they were charming in their way can hardly be denied, but theirs was a charm springing from simplicity, from a natural, sensate joy in life, and from the fervid and mercurial emotionalism of their temperaments, rather than the charm of a highly cultured or accomplished people. Many of them unquestionably possessed the courtliness of manner which had sprung from the days of the greatness of France and Spain, but the form had long outlived the substance of any aristocratic heritage. Illiteracy among the Latin Creoles was appalling, for example, and was certainly not limited to the less fortunate of their members. Even such men as Jacques Villeré and Bernard Marigny were notoriously limited in education, though both had spent time in France and were unquestionably among the elite of Creole society. At one time both of these men were charged, not by Anglo-Americans but by other Latin Creoles, with being unable to write a simple sentence. Marigny, indeed, the so-called "Creole of Creoles," is reliably reported to have eaten with his fingers instead of the more customary knife and fork.[3]

. . . Provincial in outlook, style, and taste, the typical Latin Creole was complaisant, unlettered, unskilled, content to occupy his days with the affairs of his estate or the demands of his job, for it should be obvious that the average Creole was no more wealthy than the average man anywhere and worked where work was to be had. He lived in sensation rather than reflection, enjoying the balls and dances, betting heavily at table, or perhaps at the cockpit, endlessly smoking his inevitable cigar, whiling away hours over his beloved dominoes, busying himself with the many demands of his close-knit family life. . . .

And so we must take the Creole as he actually was, rather than as some would give him to us: a provincial whose narrow experience and even narrower education left him pitifully unprepared to compete for leadership with the Anglo-Americans and foreign French. He could surpass them in nothing but numbers. Generally illiterate, almost always politically naïve, genuinely uninterested in intellectual or artistic concerns, and not unduly fastidious in his theatrical tastes, the Creole was basically a simple man averse to change. He was no more an aristocrat than he was an Ottoman Turk.

But he was human, and he could not help but resent the Anglo-Americans and the foreign French, because they represented in many ways everything that the Latin Creole was not. . . .

It was inevitable that the Latin Creole should rapidly react toward these newcomers with feelings of envy, jealousy, and an overwhelming sense of inferiority. He naturally resented the Anglo-American assumption that the natives were too backward to understand the nature of republican government; he bridled when English was made the legal language of the community; and he fumed at the staid New England propriety which insisted he was headed straight for hell because he managed to enjoy himself on Sundays. He knew full well his own limitations in this struggle for supremacy, and he finally in desperation sought help from those who were closer to him in blood, language, and heritage—the foreign French—though these too he hated and feared for their superiority and their condescending manner. There was little else which he could do, however. Very few, indeed, were the Creoles who were leaders at the bar, and fewer still were those able to fill the important editorial chairs which so influenced public opinion—for such important tasks the natives were forced to depend on foreign talent.[4]

The foreign French were not at all loathe to make a bid for power in the state. Like the Americans they were generally men of at least some education and training, with initiative enough to have triumphed over disaster or misfortune in their original homes and with stamina sufficient to have brought them to this new world for the fashioning of new careers. . . .

They had been coming into Louisiana ever since the early days of the French Revolution, fugitives from the continental Terror, victims of Napoleonic oppression, émigrés from the conservative strictures of the Bourbon Restoration, escapees from the nightmare of slave insurrection in Santo Domingo. In Louisiana they found not only a safe refuge but a society with which they had much in common, including language, religion, mores, and law, and from the very beginning they had become a major force in their new community.[5] It was evident, however, that they had failed to endear themselves to the Louisianians. Conscious of their general superiority, they had been quite free in their ridicule of Creole provincialism, criticizing local styles and deploring native backwardness. Never blind to their own advantage, most of them readily accepted United States citizenship, with loud avowals of loyalty,[6] and yet they had more cause even than the Creole to hate the new Anglo-American settlers. For not only did these latter threaten a disruption of those Gallic forms and ways of life which the refugee had good reason to cherish, they were also the major competitors for that mastery of the affairs of the state which the foreign French were determined to enjoy themselves. . . .

The other major foreign elements in the city's population, such as the numerous Irish and Germans, lacked the cohesion and leadership which made the foreign French such a power in the community. . . .

The free persons of color were no less unrestrained and enjoyed a status in Louisiana probably unequaled in any other part of the South.[7] Members of this class were often to be found as owners of cabarets and especially of gaming houses where slaves and free Negroes might consort without interference from the authorities, even after the curfew gun.[8] Many were artisans, barbers, and shopkeepers, and became so prosperous as to own slaves of their own and to acquire large holdings of real property in the Quarter.

ON THAT WORD CREOLE AGAIN
JOSEPH G. TREGLE JR.

Almost thirty years ago I argued in "Early New Orleans Society: A Reappraisal" (*Journal of Southern History,* February 1952), that the supposed imprecision of the term "creole" derived largely from the historian's ignoring of documentary evidence demonstrating how contemporaries of various periods used the word in their habitual communication. The emphasis in that particular piece was on the 1803–1860 antebellum era, unquestionably the reputed heyday of a traditional "creole aristocracy" in the state. It was further suggested that whatever confusion surrounded "creole" was largely the consequence of post–Civil War and twentieth-century extension into the prewar years of later racial, ethnic, and class prejudices which insisted variously on all-white, all-French, all-Spanish, all-European, mixed French and Spanish, "upper class," or "non-Acadian" requirements for membership in the "creole" community. Finally, it was indicated that this confusion, sadly, was only compounded by largely irrelevant excursions into etymological derivations or citations of usage elsewhere in the world. . . .

Selections from Joseph G. Tregle Jr., "On That Word 'Creole' Again: A Note," *Louisiana History* 23 (1982): 193–98. Reprinted by permission of the Louisiana Historical Association, Lafayette, Louisiana.

In renewed but probably misplaced optimism, therefore, there are appended herewith a number of more recently discovered instances of usage of the term as found in letters, newspapers, and official records of the antebellum period, all supporting the "Early New Orleans Society" thesis that Louisianians, in the 1803–1860 period at least, used the word *primarily* to designate *anyone native to Louisiana,* regardless of race, ethnic origin, language, or social position. They go far to confirm what is still the most accurate *historical* definition for the antebellum years, that of Joseph H. Ingraham in *The Quadroone* of 1841:

> The term *creole* will be used throughout this work in its simple Louisianian acceptation, *viz.,* as the synonym for *native.* It has no reference whatever to African descent, and means nothing more nor less than *native.* . . . The children of northern parents, if born in Louisiana, are "Creoles." The term, however, is more peculiarly appropriated by those who are of French descent.

Similarly, the fact that all Acadians were creoles but not all creoles were Acadians accommodated any need for greater specificity of terminology, as when the Spanish in a 1794 general census of the Attakapas militia classified its members under "nationality" as "creole," "Acadian," or "American" (*Attakapas Gazette,* XVI [1981]: 56–63). But even if one argues for an implicit restrictiveness in these examples, it is more than offset by the extensively broader antebellum practice evidenced in the following illustrations:

1. As to the general definition—

> "Creole."—A most singular, and we think preposterous and absurd definition of this word, is contained in the *Emporium* of Wednesday last; namely, that none are creoles but such as are born of *European parents.* I have always been called, and so consider myself, a *creole,* notwithstanding my father and my father's father were called *creoles.* We have also called the slaves born in the country *creoles.* . . . [The word is one by which] we have ever been distinguished from those who have emigrated to the state. . . . [It is also used] to signify such as have been born in the country, whether white, yellow, or black; whether the children of French, Spanish, English, or Dutch, or of any other nation . . . (New Orleans *Louisiana Courier,* October 28, 1831).

> Understand, good reader, that Creole is a word signifying "native," and applies to all kinds of men and things indigenous to New Orleans. (A. Oakey Hall, *The Manhattaner in New Orleans,* p. 17).

2. As to Anglo-American creoles—

> I would be very happy to do away the distinction [between Anglo-
> American and French Louisianians]. But this cannot be done, until
> our children all become creoles of Louisiana. (Josiah Stoddard
> Johnston to Isaac L. Baker, December 24, 1823, Johnston Papers).

During the debates of the Constitutional Convention of 1845, the "two leading candidates" for governor were described as being both creoles. One was William de Buys, Whig, the other Isaac Johnson, Florida-parish champion of the Anglo-American Democracy (*Debates in the Convention of Louisiana* [1845], p. 87 [New Orleans Sessions]). As noted previously in "Early New Orleans Society," Johnson himself had long claimed this creole identity: he once told Edward Douglas White, "I am a creole. . . . I had considered myself a creole in the ordinary acceptation of the term," by which he meant "native-born" (New Orleans *Mercantile Advertiser*, July 1, 1834).

In the same 1845 convention proceedings, another delegate completely identified with Anglo-American political and cultural dominance, James F. Brent of Rapides, assured his colleagues: "I am a native of Louisiana, but I would be the last one to secure a monopoly for creoles." (*Debates,* p. 91).

Timothy Flint, author of the well-known books on early Louisiana and the Mississippi valley, himself a Massachusetts Yankee, referred thus to his Louisiana-born son:

> Mrs. Johnston will have seen my rustic son. He is a very good lad, &
> only wants a few months of teaching, under her eye and example, to
> make a tolerable concern, for a creole. (Flint to Josiah Stoddard
> Johnston, November 21, 1827, Johnston Papers).

> Some of ye Americans [in Louisiana] are Creoles of ye country.
> (John Gurley to Francis Granger, July 14, 1803, Thomas Jefferson
> Papers, Manuscript Division, Library of Congress).

3. As to Acadians as creoles—
Thomas Curry assured Josiah Stoddard Johnston in the 1832 Congressional campaign that their Clayite associate Henry A. Bullard was sure to beat the "Potent Creole"—the Acadian Alexander Mouton. (Curry to Johnston, May 6, 1832, Johnston Papers)

Edmund Vaughn Davis, of opposite political persuasion, praised Mouton to Levi Woodbury as a "high-soul'd creole." (Davis to Woodbury, September 25, 1836, Levi Woodbury Papers, Manuscript Division, Library of Congress)

A newspaper clipping in the University of Southwestern Louisiana Mouton Collection, clearly from the 1842 campaign period, hails the Acadian candidate as "the Creole of the Prairies."

4. As to blacks as creoles—

W. H. Overton advertises for sale his plantation near Alexandria, "with or without Fifty Prime Negroes, principally creoles." (New Orleans *Louisiana Advertiser*, November 12, 1823)

Isaac McCoy advertises that he will offer for sale on January 20, 1824, at the Exchange Coffee House: "the Negress Louies [*sic*], a creole." (New Orleans *Louisiana Advertiser,* January 20, 1824)

Joseph Ducayet proposes to put at auction on March 31, 1824, at Elkins' Coffee House, "a very likely faithful mulatto Boy, aged about 17, named Louis, a creole of this city." (New Orleans *Louisiana Advertiser,* March 23, 1824)

Mossy et Alpuente advise that on Monday, April 26, 1824, "sera vendu à la bourse d'Elkins . . . Leon, negre âgé de 19 ans, créole" (New Orleans *Louisiana Advertiser,* April 6, 1824)

Isaac L. McCoy offers to sell at auction, April 21, 1827, "Fanny, aged 26 years, a creole" (New Orleans *Louisiana Advertiser,* April 20, 1827).

> To be known by everyone who sees this letter that I Don Juan Bautista Poeyfarre, neighbor of this City, grant that I have really sold to Don Pedro Bailly, free mulatto of this neighborhood a piece of land of my own. . . . P[edro] Bailly Senior being sworn . . . deposeth . . . that he is a creole of this Country. . . . (Depositions in case files, Morgan *vs.* Livingston, 1818, Archives of the Supreme Court of Louisiana, Earl K. Long Library, University of New Orleans)

Finally, "Early New Orleans Society" challenged the traditionalist view of a "creole aristocracy" as being essentially a myth, arguing that generally the American newcomers to early Louisiana tended to dismiss the *ancienne population* as backward, ignorant, and innocent of the sophistications of the modern world. That interpretation is reinforced by these last citations:

Writing to a friend from Dutch Settlement near Berwick Bay, Abner Nash observed:

> the Society is not of such people as we have been accustomed to, the creolds [*sic*] of the country are a mixture of Dutch and French that are most egregiously ignorant though they are kind and wealthy. (To William P. Graham, July 7, 1831, William P. Graham

Collection, Southern Historical Collection, University of North Carolina at Chapel Hill)

In applying for appointment as Superintendent of the Live Oak Timber Agency, John F. H. Claiborne observed that:

> It would give me the opportunity of patrolling the state, and of securing that large & peculiar class of indigenous people who are born, vegetate & die on the insulated bayous & shell islands of Louisiana, without ever leaving their homes, scarcely ever seeing a stranger, wholly uneducated, and interfering no more with public affairs than if they resided in China. It is estimated that there are 1500 individuals of this class of creoles who have never voted. (To James Bryce, March 18, 1845, Polk Papers)

Writing to his brother from their family plantation in 1828, Hore Browse Trist reported:

> The dull, inert leaven of the yeomanry here, is not easily set to work as with you [in Virginia]. The people of Ascension, you know, swore that they would not vote for Adams, at the last election, because he had, through negligence, suffered his levee to break, inundating their lands, & subjected them to a heavy parish tax— meaning *Ned* Adams. But I must not "médine" of my constituency. (To Nicholas P. Trist, May 12, 1828, Nicholas P. Trist Papers, Manuscript Division, Library of Congress)

Indeed, it was "American" impatience with this perceived ignorance, provincialism, and backwardness of the Latin creole which was largely responsible for the division of the city of New Orleans in 1836.

In short, however some amongst our own generation may wish to define "creole," they have no fight to impose their contemporary usage upon the past.

CANE RIVER'S CREOLES OF COLOR
GARY B. MILLS

Cane River's Creoles of color were, despite their unique and separate way of life, a component of a larger social order which was a confraternity peculiar to Louisiana. Known as *gens de couleur libre,* the men and women of this society

---

Selections from Gary B. Mills, *The Forgotten People: Cane River's Creoles of Color* (Baton Rouge: Louisiana State University Press, 1977), xiii–xv, xviii–xix, xxvi–xxvii, 192, 193–98, 199, 200, 247–48. Reprinted by permission of Louisiana State University Press.

were neither black nor white. They successfully rejected identification with any established racial order and achieved recognition as a distinct ethnic group. From the diverse cultures which spawned them was developed a unique ideology, conceived of necessity, nurtured by hope, and jealously guarded against changing mores of society. The status which they enjoyed, however, was not entirely of their own making. The growth of this singular people was fostered by the attitude of a society not common to North America.

The fact that most free men or women of color bore some degree of white blood was of little consequence in most of the United States. By law and social custom, the Negro and the part-Negro, whether slave or free, were usually relegated to the same social status and frequently displayed the same life-style and personal philosophy. The primary exception to this general rule was found in Louisiana.

From the time of the introduction of African slaves into the Louisiana colony, a distinctive and complex caste system existed for Creoles of African descent. Special terminology denoted the ratio of Negro blood to Caucasian blood which each nonwhite possessed. The classifications most commonly found in colonial and antebellum records of Louisiana are:

Negro	applied usually to one of full Negro blood
Sacatra	7/8 Negro—1/8 white
Griffe	3/4 Negro—1/4 white
Mulatto	1/2 Negro—1/2 white
Quadroon or Quarteron	1/4 Negro—3/4 white
Octoroon or sang-mele	1/8 Negro—7/8 white

The degree of privilege or degradation which a nonwhite, whether slave or free, was accorded by society in general was frequently dependent upon that individual's placement upon this caste scale.

The racial philosophy of the white Creoles who dominated Louisiana society also contained a counterpoint to this caste system. Upon obtaining freedom, a nonwhite classified as sacatra or above entered into a separate but complementary racial category, an intermediate class between white and black that was seldom recognized outside Louisiana. Under the title of *gens de couleur libre,* free part-white Creoles were accorded special privileges, opportunities, and citizenship not granted to part-Negroes in other states.

Preservation of this third racial class in Louisiana society was contingent upon strict adherence to the caste system by its members. Just as the whites entertained feelings of superiority to Negroes, so did Louisiana's *gens de couleur libre*. Often possessing more white blood than black, and quite often on good terms with and publicly recognized by their white relatives, most members of this third caste in Louisiana were reared to believe that they were a race apart from the blacks, who occupied the lowest stratum of society. Countless testimonials reveal their inherent pride in their French or Spanish heritage and their identification with the white rather than the black race.

Into this complex caste system still another factor injected itself: economic status. Louisiana's legal code provided a wider berth of economic opportunities to free people of color than could be found in any of the other states. As is the case with any given society, the *gens de couleur libre* displayed varying degrees of initiative, industry, and aptitude. The extent to which individual members of this third class utilized their opportunities often determined their degree of social acceptability in society as a whole.

As a consequence of these factors, this third class in Louisiana advanced socially, economically, and politically to a level unknown among nonwhites in North American society. Yet few efforts have been made to examine the depth of their success or the scope of the factors which produced it. As early as 1917 Alice Dunbar-Nelson lamented, "There is no state in the Union, hardly any spot of like size on the globe, where the man of color has lived so intensely, made so much progress, been of such historical importance and yet about whom so comparatively little is known." . . .

The main difficulty encountered in a thorough study of this Cane River colony was occasioned by the nature of the people themselves. The social uncertainty which members of this third caste have felt, and especially the events and attitudes that have prevailed since the emancipation of all people of color, have produced a closely knit and closemouthed society. Betrayals by those they considered to be their friends quite naturally have left them suspicious of the motives of all "outsiders." Many of the people are hesitant to talk to writers for fear they may be misrepresented or that their statements may be misquoted in such a way as to offend their family and friends. A few, apparently, are still afraid that whites in their area may take offense at suggestions of close friendship or even a blood relationship between their ancestors.

Still others among Cane River's Creoles of color shun the whites who come among them for a much more personal reason: they dislike hearing themselves referred to by the terms which are indiscriminately applied to people of their racial origins, specifically *Negro* and *mulatto*. As will be seen, these people have consistently refused to identify themselves as Negro, and the term *mulatto* is particularly detested by many of them, despite the fact that it has been a universally applied term from the time the first children of mixed ancestry appeared in the colonies. Since the word *mulatto* is a derivative of the French and Spanish words for mule, its connotation is especially offensive. . . .

While the issue of terminology is being discussed, it should be noted that considerable disagreement exists regarding the exact definition of the term *Creole* and the elements of Louisiana society to which this term should be applied, . . . the term is used to signify any person born in the colony of French or Spanish descent (with the sole exclusion of the Acadian exiles—popularly called Cajuns—who settled in south Louisiana and maintained a distinct ethnic identity). *Creole* will not be limited herein to Louisianians of pure-white descent, to the wealthy aristocracy of the state, or to the residents of the New Orleans–Baton Rouge area exclusively, as has often been the restrictive usage. . . .

According to the legend, the Cane River colony owes its beginnings to a woman known as Marie Thérèze, or Coincoin. Of African origins, she was from her childhood a slave in the household of the commandant of the Natchitoches post, Sieur Louis Juchereau de St. Denis. The legendary Coincoin was outstanding even as a slave; her natural intelligence, her loyalty, and her devotion to duty soon made her a favored servant in the St. Denis household. Ultimately, these qualifications were to earn for her the one thing she most desired: freedom.

Supposedly the event which gave her the chance to break the bonds of slavery and take the first step toward becoming the founder of this unique society was the illness of her mistress. Mme. de St. Denis was in bad health, and the local physician could find no cure. Others were brought in from New Orleans, Mexico, and even France; their efforts were to no avail. The family was counseled to accept the will of God. But one member of the household refused to despair. Marie Thérèze, who had gained from her African parents a knowledge of herbal medicines, begged for an opportunity to save the dying mistress whom she loved deeply. In desperation the family yielded to her entreaties, and to the bafflement of the educated physicians she accomplished her purpose. In appreciation the St. Denis family rewarded her with the ultimate gift a slave can receive.

The gratitude of the St. Denis family, according to the legend, did not end with Marie Thérèze's manumission. Through their influence, she applied for and received a grant of land which contained some of the most fertile soil in the colony. With two slaves given to her by the family and many more whom she was to purchase later, this African woman carved from the wilderness a magnificent plantation. . . .

With astute planning and diligent application of their talents, Cane River's Creoles of color acquired wealth and culture. In their best years they ranked financially in the highest levels of Natchitoches society. They possessed a superior education and set excellent examples in both refinement and religious devotion. They had overcome the handicaps posed by slavery, poverty, illiteracy, and illegitimacy, but they were still *gens de couleur libre*. The most formidable difficulty they faced remains to be examined: the exercise of the rights of citizenship. . . .

Clearly, the laws of the antebellum United States accorded no special privileges to a nonwhite simply because he possessed some measure of white blood. In general, the privileges of citizenship were granted on an all-or-nothing basis. By contrast, America's neighbors in the New World (excepting Canada) have traditionally recognized the third caste and have accorded it a special role in society. In comparing the United States to one South American country, Degler notes that in the latter "the mulatto or mixed blood in general, occupies a special place intermediate between white and black; he is neither black or white. No such place is reserved for the so-called mixed blood in the United States; a person is either a black or a white."[1]

The French-Spanish, Roman Catholic heritage of Louisiana produced an entirely different set of racial concepts from that which developed in the predominantly Anglo-Saxon Protestant societies of the other American colonies. Consequently, when Creole Louisiana was inducted into the American states, the immediate result was a clash of racial concepts and ideals. Several decades of ideological conflict followed, but inevitably "English attitudes and institutions . . . triumphed over Spanish-French resistance, and Anglo American ideals and prejudices were superimposed on Latin Louisiana."[2] Those who lost the most in the conflict were the members of the third caste. The people of Isle Brevelle and their counterparts at New Orleans, Opelousas, East Baton Rouge, and thousands more scattered throughout the rural areas of the state lost their political and social "escape hatch."

An analysis of the legal status of the colony and the interracial relationships which affected them shows clearly the unusual role which Louisiana's third caste played, in contrast to the situation in other regions. In 1715, for example, the state of Maryland enacted a law permitting quite indiscriminate arrest of free nonwhites; those who were unable to prove satisfactorily that they were not runaways were returned to their last master or sold into servitude to pay the costs of their detention and trial.[3] By contrast, as long as the free man of color in French colonial

Louisiana "complied with the rather mild regulations governing their conduct, they enjoyed the same economic and legal privileges as White persons."[4]

While Virginia in 1757 prohibited free Negroes or part-Negroes from bearing arms in the state militia,[5] Louisiana not only outfitted two complete units of free men of color in New Orleans[6] and permitted free nonwhites at the other posts to join local units, but she went so far as to arm slaves and gave them the opportunity to defend the territory in exchange for their freedom.[7]

By 1793 Virginia had on her statute books a law prohibiting free people of color from entering the state.[8] At this same time, Spanish Louisiana welcomed all settlers, regardless of color, and made generous grants to all free heads of households who sought them, whether they were white, black, or *gens de couleur libre.* It was this lenient policy of the colonial Louisiana government which enabled Marie Thérèze and her children to accumulate their initial holdings in land. Had they been forced to labor until they had saved sufficient cash to purchase the 5,753 acres which the Spanish government allowed them, it is doubtful that the family would have achieved any significant foothold in society.

Although the racial policies of colonial Louisiana were extremely tolerant in comparison to those in the other North American colonies, it is not be assumed that they were completely indiscriminatory. On the contrary, interracial marriages were flatly prohibited, and the Spanish ordinances went so far as to forbid women of the slightest color to show excessive attention to their dress. Such items popular among stylish Creole ladies as feathers, jewelry, caps, and mantillas were specifically proscribed for free women of color. Their heads, in fact, were required to be bound at all times in a handkerchief, or *tignon.*[9]

In general, colonial Louisiana accorded the free man of color most rights of citizenship but drew the line at full social equality. This was the society into which the Cane River colony was born and the society to which they tenaciously clung. Long after Louisiana had become a part of the United States, they continued to refer to themselves as "French citizens."

With the transfer of Louisiana to the United States, the position of the free man of color became increasingly restricted. The Americans were exceedingly apprehensive over the existence of a "large, wealthy, *armed* free colored community." To them it was "painful and perplexing" to envision "the formidable aspect of the armed Blacks and Mulattoes officered and organized."[10] Despite at least one recommendation that it was "worth the consideration of the government [that free people of color] be made good citizens," the new regime proceeded to revise Louisiana's black code in order to align it more closely with those of the other American states.[11]

In 1806, the first American revisions in the black code appeared, limiting the privileges of all men of color, slave or free. Strict immigration laws were passed to prevent an influx of more free people of color from the French West Indies. Those already in Louisiana were required to appear before authorities and give proof of their freedom or be classed as runaway slaves. Any free people of color carrying guns were required to carry also their freedom papers.[12]

In 1808 the territorial legislature decreed that all public documents referring to free people of color must contain the words "free man of color" or "free woman of color" or the appropriate abbreviation after the surname of the individual. In 1812, when Louisiana was granted statehood, suffrage was limited to whites. During the next half-century many additional restrictions were placed upon the free Creole of color, denying him such rights of citizenship as military and jury service and taking from him various social and economic privileges.[13]

Such changes were not always readily accepted, even by the white Creole population. According to one authority, "When the ancient customs and traditions conflicted with the [new American] code, there were many in Louisiana who sought to evade and nullify the law." Indeed, the conflict between French tradition and American law became so serious that at one point a judge was forced to rule that the *"decisions of the courts of France"* were no longer legally binding in Louisiana.[14] Obviously, the people of Isle Brevelle were not alone when they continued to regard themselves as "French citizens."

Creoles of color enjoyed several important advantages, even under the Americanized black code, that were frequently denied to free people of color in other states. According to one judicial decision, "as far as it concerns everything, except political rights, free people of color appear to possess all other rights of persons, whether absolute or relative.... They ... may take and hold property by purchase, inheritance or donation; they may marry, and as a consequence, exercise parental authority over their children; they may be witnesses; they may stand in judgement, and they are responsible under the general designation of 'persons' for crimes."[15]

One of the basic advantages which the free man of color held in Louisiana was the presumption of freedom versus presumption of bondage. In direct contrast to the rulings in Georgia and in most other states that a man of color was considered to be a slave until he proved himself to be free, the supreme court of Louisiana ruled in 1810: "Considering how much probability there is in favor of the liberty of these persons, they ought not to be deprived of it upon mere presumption."[16] As late as 1845 this ruling was upheld by the same court: "Ever since the case of *Adelle vs. Beauregard* it has been the settled doctrine here, that persons of color are presumed to be free. . . . The presumption is in favor of freedom, and the burden of proof is on him who claims the colored person as a slave."[17]

A second privilege not usually accorded to American nonwhites that the *gens de couleur libre* occasionally enjoyed was the right to bear arms in defense of their country. In the War of 1812, for example, the free men of color in Louisiana were allowed to form militia units, as their ancestors had done in colonial days, to assist in the defense of New Orleans against the British. Special authorization of the governor was given the Creoles of color in Natchitoches Parish to form an auxiliary unit of no more than eighty-four men, provided that they furnished their own arms and horses. Only those who possessed property worth at least one hundred dollars were allowed to participate in this enterprise. Since the Metoyer colony on Isle Brevelle represented 45 percent of the households headed by free people of color in the parish and 73 percent of the property owners in this category, it is reasonable to assume that they also made up a large percentage of the patriots who formed this militia unit.[18]

Between 1824 and 1832 free nonwhites in Maryland were entirely denied the privilege of owning firearms.[19] Other states adopted measures that were almost as drastic. One early-twentieth-century study of Louisiana's *gens de couleur libre* asserts that they suffered the same restriction. A later study, however, contends that they were able to own weapons but were not permitted to carry them unless they also carried their freedom papers. . . . [20]

Another onerous restriction which was placed on the free nonwhites throughout the United States did definitely apply to Louisiana's *gens de couleur libre*. The South Carolina appeals court ruling that free nonwhites "belong to a degraded caste [and] ought by law to be compelled to demean themselves as inferiors"[21] had its counterpart in the Americanized black code of Louisiana: "Free People of Color ought never to insult or strike white people, nor presume to conceive themselves equal to the white, but on the contrary, they ought to yield to them in every occasion, and never speak or answer to them but with respect, under the penalty of imprisonment, according to the nature of the offense."[22]

The people of Isle Brevelle were keenly aware of this discriminatory clause in the law. They fought it with the best weapons that their wealth and relative independence afforded them: quiet dignity and strict formality in their dealings with whites. One less well-to-do relative of theirs, the "handsome, light coloured young barber" whom Olmsted interviewed on board the steamship *Dalmau,* offered the following insight into their personality and attitude: "They rather avoided white people. . . . They were uncertain of their position with them, and were afraid, if they were not reserved, they would be thought to be taking liberties, and would be subject to insults, which they could not very well resent."[23] On the other hand, the relative indicated that there were some whites whom the people knew quite well and with whom they were very much at ease. . . . [24]

One of the most serious rights of citizenship that were denied free non-whites, not only in the South but in much of the North as well, was the privilege of testifying in court against a white man. They were, in fact, prohibited from even instituting a suit against a white in most states before the Civil War.[25] By contrast, the Creole of color was permitted free access to the courts of law in Louisiana. Not only was he entitled to defend himself in court against whites, but he could bring charges against whites as well. His testimony was accepted in every type of legal case.[26] As late as 1850 the supreme court of Louisiana pointed out that in many areas of the state the free men of color were "respectable from [sic] their intelligence, industry, and habits of good order. Many . . . are enlightened by education and . . . [are] large property holders." The word of such people, the court decreed, should be accepted without hesitation by any court or jury. . . . [27]

Throughout the remainder of the nineteenth century Cane River's Creoles of color suffered economic deprivation and increasing social degradation. They were soon abandoned by all but their closest white friends, and with the passing of years even these relationships withered. Moreover, the establishment of a church on the plantation of a white planter of the Côte Joyeuse drew away the whites from the Chapel of St. Augustine. The contacts of the people became almost exclusively limited to the confines of their own society.

Only a small number out of this group emerged from the Civil War in comfortable circumstances. These few, including such men as Emanuel Dupre, who was by far the wealthiest member of the colony in 1870, became the new leaders of the community. For even these men, however, the passing of years brought a steady diminution of fortunes. Each new generation resulted in a further division of property holdings until many families owned no more than narrow strips of land. Large plantation homes were lost along with the land on which they stood. Those members of the colony who managed to hold their land but could not afford the upkeep on their large houses moved into the cabins formerly occupied by their slaves. The "mansion houses" were torn down, and the bricks and lumber sold for whatever they would bring. The expensive furniture and other inherited heirlooms were the last vestiges of earlier wealth to be parted with. The huge four-poster beds and ceiling-high armoires literally filled the rooms of the little cabins, but not until all other resources were exhausted did the people succumb to the clamor of the eager collectors who coveted these items.

The decline of the colony's economy and status was accompanied by a similar decline in educational opportunities. The children of the Isle did not deign to go to school with the blacks who attended the new public institutions after the war. Their parents could ill afford to send them to the private academies which their upper-class white neighbors supported; nor could they afford private tutors any longer. The Daughters of the Cross reopened their convent on the Isle at the close of the war and continued to operate it for many decades, with only one lapse of several years. Education in the church-sponsored school, however, covered only the primary grades. The general level of education within the colony fell sharply.

With each new reversal, the Cane River colony became more and more a society within a society. More than ever its members withdrew into themselves, insisting upon self-reliance and group solidarity as a defense against the ambivalence of outsiders. Indeed, one organization, the *Societé des amis unis de L'Ile Brevelle,* was formed in 1889 for the specific purpose of providing mutual succor and of raising the morale of its membership.

As the parish moved rapidly toward Americanization, the colony clung tenaciously to its French heritage, to the Creole culture that was for all practical purposes the last remaining tie between their postwar society and the life they had once known. But throughout their tribulations, the people never lost their pride. "It's blood that counts," they taught their children, and parents instructed the young ones concerning the virtue, integrity, and superiority of the blood they had inherited from their genteel ancestors.

By the arrival of the twentieth century, younger members of the colony had begun to disperse, hoping to find more opportunity in the industrial cities than they could find on the small tracts of land that barely supported their parents. Many settled in the larger cities of Louisiana. A number went to the industrial areas of the North and the West Coast. A few, whose complexions and predilections were already white, assimilated into the white population, but the majority of migrants settled together in the cities and founded small colonies there. Yet, regardless of where the people lived or worked, Isle Brevelle was still their home. Ties to the Isle and to the families there remained strong, and many of those who died in distant places expressed a last wish to be buried on the Isle.

THIS, THAT, AND THE OTHERS
MICHELLE PICHON

Hidden among the most prominent stories of Louisiana is another that is not as familiar. It is a story of a people, my people, a family if you will, whose variations and differences are what unite us. We are the offspring of the marriage of the Old World and the New. We are from neither here nor there. We are in and of ourselves, and we have lived our entire lives blending into all the worlds that surround us. We are the Creoles of Louisiana. We are the misunderstood, misrepresented, misinterpreted mysteries of yesterday and today. In a world so accustomed to seeing her children in black or white, the Creoles remain the Others.

When Americans began to populate Louisiana, they were shocked to see so many Creoles, people of color, living freely. Before the Americans came, Europeans (Spanish and French) and Creoles lived openly together without much incident. They socialized together, interbred, and sometimes even intermarried. American settlers who came to Louisiana from other parts of the country brought with them their prejudices and strong beliefs in racial separation and place. Creoles, once free, were now restrained. Laws were passed by new governing forces that forbade anyone of African blood to marry Whites or even to congregate as a group. While Creoles were not slaves, they were still not entirely free. Whites, for the most part, saw Creoles as being beneath them. Creoles were perceived by some as the freakish offspring of immoral unions and by others as mysterious and intriguing legends.

These viewpoints add to the misunderstanding of Creoles, and therefore to the misrepresentation of them in literature. Their unique appearance and language were objects of curiosity to those unfamiliar with them. Because of their mysterious African and/or Haitian ties, they served many authors as superstitious fools or conjuring evildoers. They were stereotypically depicted as mammies, rebels, or mysterious old people.

Kate Chopin subscribes to these stereotypes in her first novel, *At Fault*. The narration has a very pretentious tone and refers to Creoles in limited and derogatory ways. The Creoles she includes in her story come across as amusing little pets or as pests. Of course, there is the mammy, Marie Louise; the

---

Michelle Pichon was born and raised in Isle Brevelle, Natchitoches Parish, Louisiana. Ms. Pichon is a graduate student in English and a researcher for the Creole Heritage Center at Northwestern State University, Natchitoches, Louisiana. Her essay was prepared especially for this volume.

rebellious and mischievous Joçint; and the mysterious old Morico. Their only purpose is to serve, entertain, or cause trouble for the main characters, upper-class Whites. Many writers have used Creoles as stock characters, usually placing them in roles such as these. There is rarely any mention that some Creoles were able to live independent lives and earn wages in ways other than serving Whites.

Even today Creoles are viewed in the same limited ways. Tours of Creole plantations are very popular in Louisiana. What is not so popular is making it known that the history of Creole people extends beyond the plantation. In many instances, Creoles owned the plantations currently open for tours. Many Creoles were also wealthy landowners, artists, or business people. They formed their own communities and were self-sufficient, relying more on each other than they did on White society. They were not allowed to be an equal part of White society under law, but Blacks, free and slave, did not feel Creoles were part of their world either. Therefore, Creoles had a strong bond with one another and had to create their own world. This is the world that is too often neglected or misrepresented or misunderstood in literature. Novels such as *At Fault,* and others like it, only celebrate the misunderstanding of Creole people.

As a Creole person in today's society, I feel it is important to present other perspectives on Creole life, past and present. It is necessary that Creoles be represented in a more accurate and fair way. One way to ensure an accurate representation is for Creoles finally to tell their own stories. There is not just one Creole people or history. We are composed of many ethnic groups, including African, French, Haitian, Indian, Irish, Spanish, West Indian, and even Chinese. With such a wide array of possibilities, there should be no need for stereotypes. Among this diversity of people who have come to be known as Creole, there are many stories. These are the stories that need to be told, and these are the perspectives from which they should come.

Kate Chopin's *At Fault* represents an outdated view of Creoles in literature, along with the confusion and distortion of Creoles that is so often found in literature. The future of the real Creoles in literature depends on the real Creoles of today. We must correct the literary misimpressions from the past and represent ourselves in a more accurate, true light. We must tell the tales of the Creole and say for ourselves: This is who we are; this is who I am.

BLACK CODE OF THE FRENCH (1724)

BLACK CODE

ART. 1.

Decrees the expulsion of the Jews from the colony.

ART. 2.

Makes it imperative on masters to impart religious instructions to their slaves.

ART. 3.

Permits the exercise of the Roman Catholic creed only. Every other mode of worship is prohibited.

ART. 4.

Negroes placed under the direction or supervision of any other person than a Catholic, are liable to confiscation.

ART. 5.

Sundays and holydays are to be strictly observed. All negroes found at work on these days are to be confiscated.

ART. 6.

We forbid our white subjects, of both sexes, to marry with the blacks, under the penalty of being fined and subjected to some other arbitrary punishment. We forbid all curates, priests, or missionaries of our secular or regular clergy, and even our chaplains in our navy, to sanction such marriages. We also forbid all our white subjects, and even the manumitted or free-born blacks, to live in a state of concubinage with slaves. Should there be any issue from this kind of intercourse, it is our will that the person so offending, and the master of the slave, should pay each a fine of three hundred livres. Should said issue be the result of the concubinage of the master with his slave, said master shall not only pay the fine, but be deprived of the slave and of the children, who shall be adjudged to the hospital of the locality, and said slaves shall be forever incapable of being set free. But should this illicit intercourse have existed between a free black and his slave, when said free black had no legitimate wife, and should said black marry said slave according to the forms prescribed by the church, said slave shall be thereby set free, and the children shall also become free and legitimate; and in such a case, there shall be no application of the penalties mentioned in the present article.

Selections from Charles Gayarré, *History of Louisiana: The French Domination,* 3rd ed. (New Orleans: Armand Hawkins, 1885), 1:531–40.

ART. 7.

The ceremonies and forms prescribed by the ordinance of Blois, and by the edict of 1639, for marriages, shall be observed both with regard to free persons and to slaves. But the consent of the father and mother of the slave is not necessary; that of the master shall be the only one required.

ART. 8.

We forbid all curates to proceed to effect marriages between slaves without proof of the consent of their masters; and we also forbid all masters to force their slaves into any marriage against their will.

ART. 9.

Children, issued from the marriage of slaves, shall follow the condition of their parents, and shall belong to the master of the wife and not of the husband, if the husband and wife have different masters.

ART. 10.

If the husband be a slave, and the wife a free woman, it is our will that their children, of whatever sex they may be, shall share the condition of their mother, and be as free as she, notwithstanding the servitude of their father; and if the father be free and the mother a slave, the children shall all be slaves.

ART. 11.

Masters shall have their Christian slaves buried in consecrated ground.

ART. 12.

We forbid slaves to carry offensive weapons or heavy sticks, under the penalty of being whipped, and of having said weapons confiscated for the benefit of the person seizing the same. An exception is made in favor of those slaves who are sent a hunting or a shooting by their masters, and who carry with them a written permission to that effect, or are designated by some known mark or badge.

ART. 20.

Slaves who shall not be properly fed, clad, and provided for by their masters, may give information thereof to the attorney-general of the Superior Council, or to all the other officers of justice of an inferior jurisdiction, and may put the written exposition of their wrongs into their hands; upon which information, and even *ex officio,* should the information come from another quarter, the attorney-general shall prosecute said masters without charging any costs to the complainants. It is our will that this regulation be observed in all accusations for crimes or barbarous and inhuman treatment brought by slaves against their masters.

ART. 27.

The slave who, having struck his master, his mistress, or the husband of his mistress, or their children, shall have produced a bruise, or the shedding of blood in the face, shall suffer capital punishment.

ART. 28.

With regard to outrages or acts of violence committed by slaves against free persons, it is our will that they be punished with severity, and even with death, should the case require it.

ART. 29.

Thefts of importance, and even the stealing of horses, mares, mules, oxen, or cows, when executed by slaves or manumitted persons, shall make the offender liable to corporal, and even to capital punishment, according to the circumstances of the case.

ART. 38.

We also forbid all our subjects in this colony, whatever their condition or rank may be, to apply, on their own private authority, the rack to their slaves, under any pretense whatever, and to mutilate said slaves in any one of their limbs, or in any part of their bodies, under the penalty of the confiscation of said slaves; and said masters, so offending, shall be liable to a criminal prosecution. We only permit masters, when they shall think that the case requires it, to put their slaves in irons, and to have them whipped with rods or ropes.

ART. 39.

We command our officers of justice in this colony to institute criminal process against masters and overseers who shall have killed or mutilated their slaves, when in their power and under their supervision, and to punish said murderer according to the atrocity of the circumstances; and in case the offense shall be a pardonable one, we permit them to pardon said masters and overseers without its being necessary to obtain from us letters patent of pardon.

ART. 40.

Slaves shall be held in law as movables, and as such, they shall be part of the community of acquests between husband and wife; they shall not be liable to be seized under any mortgage whatever; and they shall be equally divided among the co-heirs without admitting from any one of said heirs any claim founded on preciput or right of primogeniture, or dowry.

ART. 43.

Husbands and wives shall not be seized and sold separately when belonging to the same master; and their children, when under fourteen years of age, shall not be separated from their parents, and such seizures and sales shall be null and void. The present article shall apply to voluntary sales, and in case such sales should take place in violation of the law, the seller shall be deprived of the slave he has illegally retained, and said slave shall be adjudged to the purchaser without any additional price being required.

Art. 44.
Slaves, fourteen years old, and from this age up to sixty, who are settled on lands and plantations, and are at present working on them, shall not be liable to seizure for debt, except for what may be due out of the purchase money agreed to be paid for them, unless said grounds or plantations should also be distressed, and any seizure and judicial sale of a real estate, without including the salves of the aforesaid age who are part of said estate, shall be deemed null and void.

Art. 54.
We grant to manumitted slaves the same rights, privileges, and immunities which are enjoyed by free-born persons. It is our pleasure that their merit in having acquired their freedom, shall produce in their favor, not only with regard to their persons, but also to their property, the same effects which our other subjects derive from the happy circumstance of their having been born free.

In the name of the king.

BIENVILLE, DE LA CHAISE.

Fazende, Bruslé, Perry,

March, 1724

Social Classes and Roles in Southern Society

![A] *t Fault* is set in the late nineteenth century, a period in American history often referred to as the "Gilded Age." In the aftermath of the Civil War, American society experienced an unprecedented period of economic expansion and urbanization, along with the social difficulties which are inherent in this type of rapid change.

Thorstein Veblen, a contemporary of Chopin's and a scholar at Yale University, noted these changes and produced an economic theory to account for them, a theory that in many respects is still highly regarded. The excerpts below from Veblen's *The Theory of the Leisure Class* provide a broad historical and economic overview of late nineteenth century American society. Veblen addresses equally the upper classes, as noted in his book's title; the newly emerging middle class; and those lower in the socioeconomic hierarchy. His observations are relevant to *At Fault,* particularly as he contrasts rural society with urban and analyzes those urban "professional time wasters" whom Chopin describes so disdainfully.

Catherine Clinton's essay, "The Plantation Mistress: Her Working Life," peeks behind the mask of southern gentility, exploding the myth of the languid southern belle. Clinton provides a detailed and realistic description of the daily lives of plantation owners' wives, such as Thérèse. Her portrait of the sometimes harsh reality of daily chores and responsibilities contrasts strikingly with the romanticized myth of the delicate and pampered southern woman of leisure.

Another aspect of southern mythology is explored through excerpts from John Blassingame's collection of slave testimony and from interviews with former slaves, collected during the Great Depression by the Works Progress Administration (WPA), a federal government agency. While some

253

slave owners developed close relationships with their slaves, and especially with their household servants, owners and employers like Thérèse, who lived up to the ideal of *noblesse oblige* espoused by the southern aristocracy, were the exception rather than the rule. The often harsh treatment afforded the servant class, both black and white, is suggested by works such as *The Young Lady's Friend,* which admonishes employers to treat their servants fairly and as fellow human beings. The WPA slave narratives also illuminate the implicitly unbalanced relationships between slaves or former slaves and their owners and employers.

The formal period of mourning is a social custom which the twentieth century reader is unlikely to appreciate. However, when we meet Thérèse, we know that she is in deepest mourning because she is draped in crepe. Later in the novel, Melicent adopts a formal period of mourning, though her relationship with Grégoire does not require such an act. The significance of this gesture would not have been lost on Chopin's contemporaries, but the intricacies of such customs seem foreign to us a century later. Accordingly, brief discussions from etiquette manuals such as *Decorum*, *Etiquette,* and Lou Taylor's *Mourning Dress,* give a sense of the obligations, in terms of both behavior and manner of dress, imposed upon those who had lost a family member.

THE THEORY OF THE LEISURE CLASS
THORSTEIN VEBLEN
CONSPICUOUS LEISURE

The vicarious leisure performed by housewives and menials, under the head of household cares, may frequently develop into drudgery, especially where the competition for reputability is close and strenuous. This is frequently the case in modern life. Where this happens, the domestic service which comprises the duties of this servant class might aptly be designated as wasted effort, rather than as vicarious leisure. But the latter term has the advantage of indicating the line of derivation of these domestic offices, as well as of neatly suggesting the substantial economic ground of their utility; for these occupations are chiefly useful as a method of imputing pecuniary reputability to the master or to the household on the ground that a given amount of time and effort is conspicuously wasted in that behalf.

Thorstein Veblen, *The Theory of the Leisure Class: An Economic Study of Institutions* (New York: Macmillan, 1899), 59–62, 65–66, 76–78, 84–88, 96–97, 170–73, 179–82.

In this way, then, there arises a subsidiary or derivative leisure class, whose office is the performance of a vicarious leisure for the behoof of the reputability of the primary or legitimate leisure class. This vicarious leisure class is distinguished from the leisure class proper by a characteristic feature of its habitual mode of life. The leisure of the master class is, at least ostensibly, an indulgence of a proclivity for the avoidance of labour and is presumed to enhance the master's own well-being and fulness of life; but the leisure of the servant class exempt from productive labour is in some sort a performance exacted from them, and is not normally or primarily directed to their own comfort. The leisure of the servant is not his own leisure. So far as he is a servant in the full sense, and not at the same time a member of a lower order of the leisure class proper, his leisure normally passes under the guise of specialised service directed to the furtherance of his master's fulness of life. Evidence of this relation of subservience is obviously present in the servant's carriage and manner of life. The like is often true of the wife throughout the protracted economic stage during which she is still primarily a servant—that is to say, so long as the household with a male head remains in force. In order to satisfy the requirements of the leisure-class scheme of life, the servant should show not only an attitude of subservience, but also the effects of special training and practice in subservience. The servant or wife should not only perform certain offices and show a servile disposition, but it is quite as imperative that they should show an acquired facility in the tactics of subservience—a trained conformity to the canons of effectual and conspicuous subservience. Even to-day it is this aptitude and acquired skill in the formal manifestation of the servile relation that constitutes the chief element of utility in our highly paid servants, as well as one of the chief ornaments of the well-bred housewife.

The first requisite of a good servant is that he should conspicuously know his place. It is not enough that he knows how to effect certain desired mechanical results; he must, above all, know how to effect these results in due form. Domestic service might be said to be a spiritual rather than a mechanical function. Gradually there grows up an elaborate system of good form, specifically regulating the manner in which this vicarious leisure of the servant class is to be performed. Any departure from these canons of form is to be deprecated, not so much because it evinces a shortcoming in mechanical efficiency, or even that it shows an absence of the servile attitude and temperament, but because, in the last analysis, it shows the absence of special training. Special training in personal service costs time and effort, and where it is obviously present in a high degree, it argues that the servant who possesses it, neither is nor has been habitually engaged in any productive occupation. It is *prima facie* evidence of a vicarious leisure extending far back in the past. So that trained service has utility, not only as gratifying the master's instinctive liking for good and skillful workmanship and his propensity for conspicuous dominance over those whose lives are subservient to his own, but it has utility also as putting in evidence a much larger consumption of human service than would be shown by the mere present conspicuous leisure performed by an untrained person. It is a serious grievance if a gentleman's butler or footman performs his duties about his master's table or carriage in such unformed style as to suggest that his habitual occupation may be ploughing or sheep-herding. Such bungling work would imply inability on the master's part to procure the service of specially trained servants; that is to say, it would imply inability to pay for the consumption of time, effort, and instruction required to fit a trained servant for special service under an exacting code of forms. If the performance of the servant argues lack of means on the part of his master, it defeats its chief substantial end; for the chief use of servants is the evidence they afford of the master's ability to pay. . . .

The proximate reason for keeping domestic servants, for instance, in the moderately well-to-do household of to-day, is (ostensibly) that the members of the household are unable without discomfort to compass the work required by such a modern establishment. And the reason for their being unable to accomplish it is (1) that they have too many "social duties," and (2) that the work to be done is too severe and that there is too much of it. These two reasons may be restated as follows: (1) Under a mandatory code of decency, the time and effort of the members of such a household are required to be ostensibly all spent in a performance of conspicuous leisure, in the way of calls, drives, clubs, sewing-circles, sports, charity organisations, and other like social functions. Those persons whose time and energy are employed in these matters privately avow that all these observances, as well as the incidental attention to dress and other conspicuous consumption, are very irksome but altogether unavoidable. (2) Under the requirement of conspicuous consumption of goods, the apparatus of living has grown so elaborate and cumbrous, in the way of dwellings, furniture, bric-a-brac, wardrobe and meals, that the consumers of these things cannot make way with them in the required manner without help. Personal contact with the hired persons whose aid is called in to fulfill the routine of decency is commonly distasteful to the occupants of the house, but their presence is endured and paid for, in order to delegate to them a share in this onerous consumption of household goods. The presence of domestic servants, and of the special class of body servants in an eminent degree, is a concession of physical comfort to the moral need of pecuniary decency.

Conspicuous Consumption

As wealth accumulates, the leisure class develops further in function and structure, and there arises a differentiation within the class. There is a more or less elaborate system of rank and grades. This differentiation is furthered by the inheritance of wealth and the consequent inheritance of gentility. . . . Those who stand near the higher and the highest grades of the wealthy leisure class, in point of birth, or in point of wealth, or both, outrank the remoter-born and the pecuniarily weaker. These lower grades, especially the impecunious, or marginal, gentlemen of leisure, affiliate themselves by a system of dependence or fealty to the great ones; by so doing they gain an increment of repute, or of the means with which to lead a life of leisure, from their patron. They become his courtiers or retainers, servants; and being fed and countenanced by their patron they are indices of his rank and vicarious consumers of his superfluous wealth. Many of these affiliated gentlemen of leisure are at the same time lesser men of substance in their own right; so that some of them are scarcely at all, others only partially, to be rated as vicarious consumers. So many of them, however, as make up the retainers and hangers-on of the patron may be classed as vicarious consumers without qualification. Many of these again, and also many of the other aristocracy of less degree, have in turn attached to their persons a more or less comprehensive group of vicarious consumers in the persons of their wives and children, their servants, retainers, etc.

Throughout this graduated scheme of vicarious leisure and vicarious consumption the rule holds that these offices must be performed in some such manner, or under some such circumstance or insignia, as shall point plainly to the master to whom this leisure or consumption pertains, and to whom therefore the resulting increment of good repute of right inures. The consumption and leisure executed by these persons for their master or patron represents an investment on his part with a view to an increase of good fame. As regards feasts and largesses this is obvious enough, and the imputation of repute to the host or patron here takes place immediately, on the ground of common notoriety. Where leisure and consumption is [*sic*] performed vicariously by henchmen and retainers, imputation of the resulting repute to the patron is effected by their residing near his person so that it may be plain to all men from what source they draw. . . .

. . . The leisure class stands at the head of the social structure in point of reputability; and its manner of life and its standards of worth therefore afford the norm of reputability for the community. The observance of these standards, in some degree of approximation, becomes incumbent upon all classes lower in the scale. In modern civilized communities the lines of demarcation between social classes have grown vague and transient, and wherever this happens the norm of reputability imposed by the upper class extends its coercive influence with but slight hindrance down through the social structure to the lowest strata. The result is that the members of each stratum accept as their ideal of decency the scheme of life in vogue in the next higher stratum, and bend their energies to live up to that ideal. On pain of forfeiting their good name and their self-respect in case of failure, they must conform to the accepted code, at least in appearance.

The basis on which good repute in any highly organised industrial community ultimately rests is pecuniary strength; and the means of showing pecuniary strength, and so of gaining or retaining a good name, are leisure and a conspicuous consumption of goods. Accordingly, both of these methods are in vogue as far down the scale as it remains possible; and in the lower strata in which the two methods are employed, both offices are in great part delegated to the wife and children of the household. . . .

. . . It appears that the utility of both [conspicuous leisure and consumption] alike for the purposes of reputability lies in the element of waste that is common to both. In the one case it is a waste of time and effort, in the other it is a waste of goods. Both are methods of demonstrating the possession of wealth, and the two are conventionally accepted as equivalents. . . .

The modern organisation of industry works in the same direction also by another line. The exigencies of the modern industrial system frequently place individuals and households in juxtaposition between whom there is little contact in any other sense than that of juxtaposition. One's neighbours, mechanically speaking, often are socially not one's neighbours, or even acquaintances; and still their transient good opinion has a high degree of utility. The only practicable means of impressing one's pecuniary ability on these unsympathetic observers of one's everyday life is an unremitting demonstration of ability to pay. In the modern community there is also a more frequent attendance at large gatherings of people to whom one's everyday life is unknown; in such places as churches, theatres, ballrooms, hotels, parks, shops, and the like. In order to impress these transient observers, and to retain one's self-complacency under their observation, the signature of one's pecuniary strength should be written in characters which he who runs may read. It is evident, therefore, that the present trend of the development is in the direction of heightening the utility of conspicuous consumption as compared with leisure.

It is also noticeable that the serviceability of consumption as a means of repute, as well as the insistence on it as an element of decency, is at its best in those portions of the community where the human contact of the individual is widest and the mobility of the population is greatest. Conspicuous consumption claims a relatively larger portion of the income of the urban than of the rural population, and the claim is also more imperative. The result is that, in order to keep up a decent appearance, the former habitually live hand-to-mouth to a greater extent than the latter. So it comes, for instance, that the American farmer and his wife and daughters are notoriously less modish in their dress, as well as less urbane in their manners, than the city artisan's family with an equal income. It is not that the city population is by nature much more eager for the peculiar complacency that comes of a conspicuous consumption, nor has the rural population less regard for pecuniary decency. But the provocation to this line of evidence, as well as its transient effectiveness, are more decided in the city. This method is therefore more readily resorted to, and in the struggle to outdo one another the city population push [sic] their normal standard of conspicuous consumption to a higher point, with the result that a relatively greater expenditure in this direction is required to indicate a given degree of pecuniary decency in the city. The requirement of conformity to this higher conventional standard becomes mandatory. The standard of decency is higher, class for class, and this requirement of decent appearance must be lived up to on pain of losing caste. . . .

Throughout the entire evolution of conspicuous expenditure, whether of goods or of services or human life, runs the obvious implication that in order to effectually mend the consumer's good fame it must be an expenditure of superfluities. In order to be reputable it must be wasteful. No merit would accrue from the consumption of the bare necessaries of life, except by comparison with the abjectly poor who fall short even of the subsistence minimum; and no standard of expenditure could result from such a comparison, except the most prosaic and unattractive level of decency. A standard of life would still be possible which should admit of invidious comparison in other respects than that of opulence; as, for instance, a comparison in various directions in the manifestation of moral, physical, intellectual, or aesthetic force. Comparison in all these directions is in vogue to-day; and the comparison made in these respects is commonly so inextricably bound up with the pecuniary comparison as to be scarcely distinguishable from the latter. This is especially true as regards the current rating of expressions of intellectual and aesthetic force or proficiency; so that we frequently interpret as aesthetic or intellectual a difference which in substance is pecuniary only.

DRESS AS AN EXPRESSION OF THE PECUNIARY CULTURE

. . . Simple conspicuous waste of goods is effective and gratifying as far as it goes; it is good *prima facie* evidence of pecuniary success, and consequently *prima facie* evidence of social worth. But dress has subtler and more far-reaching possibilities than this crude, first-hand evidence of wasteful consumption only. If, in addition to showing that the wearer can afford to consume freely and uneconomically, it can also be shown in the same stroke that he or she is not under the necessity of earning a livelihood, the evidence of social worth is enhanced in a very considerable degree. Our dress, therefore, in order to serve its purpose effectually, should not only be expensive, but it should also make plain to all observers that the wearer is not engaged in any kind of productive labour. . . . It goes without saying that no apparel can be considered elegant, or even decent, if it shows the effect of manual labour on the part of the wearer, in the way of soil or wear. The pleasing effect of neat and spotless garments is chiefly, if not altogether, due to their carrying the suggestion of leisure—exemption from personal contact with industrial processes of any kind. Much of the charm that invests the patent-leather shoe, the stainless linen, the lustrous cylindrical hat, and the walking-stick, which so greatly enhance the native dignity of a gentleman, comes of their pointedly suggesting that the wearer cannot when so attired bear a hand in any employment that is directly and immediately of any human use. Elegant dress serves its purpose of elegance not only in that it is expensive, but also because it is the insignia of leisure. It not only shows that the wearer is able to consume a relatively large value, but it argues at the same time that he consumes without producing.

The dress of women goes even further than that of men in the way of demonstrating the wearer's abstinence from productive employment. It needs no argument to enforce the generalisation that the more elegant styles of feminine bonnets go even farther towards making work impossible than does the man's high hat. The woman's shoe adds the so-called French heel to the evidence of enforced leisure afforded by its polish; because this high heel obviously makes any, even the simplest and most necessary manual work extremely difficult. The like is true even in a higher degree of the skirt and the rest of the drapery which characterises woman's dress. The substantial reason for our tenacious attachment to the skirt is just this: it is expensive and it hampers the wearer at every turn and incapacitates her for all useful exertion. The like is true of the feminine custom of wearing the hair excessively long.

But the woman's apparel not only goes beyond that of the modern man in the degree in which it argues exemption from labour; it also adds a peculiar and highly characteristic feature which differs in kind from anything habitually practised by the men. This feature is the class of contrivances of which the corset is the typical example. The corset is, in economic theory, substantially a mutilation, undergone for the purpose of lowering the subject's vitality and rendering her permanently and obviously unfit for work. It is true, the corset impairs the personal attractions of the wearer, but the loss suffered on that score is offset by the gain in reputability which comes of her visibly increased expensiveness and infirmity. It may broadly be set down that the womanliness of woman's apparel resolves itself, in point of substantial fact, into the more effective hindrance to useful exertion offered by the garments peculiar to women. The difference between masculine and feminine apparel is here simply pointed out as a characteristic feature.

. . . In dress construction this norm works out in the shape of divers contrivances going to show that the wearer does not and, as far as it may conveniently be shown, can not engage in productive labour. Beyond these two principles there is a third of scarcely less constraining force, which will occur to any one who reflects at all on the subject. Dress must not only be conspicuously expensive and inconvenient; it must at the same time be up to date. . . . Obviously, if each garment is permitted to serve for but a brief term, and if none of last season's apparel is carried over and made further use of during the present season, the wasteful expenditure on dress is greatly increased. . . .

. . . In woman's dress there is an obviously greater insistence on such features as testify to the wearer's exemption from or incapacity for all vulgarly productive employment. This characteristic of woman's apparel is of interest, not only as completing the theory of dress, but also as confirming what has already been said of the economic status of women, both in the past and in the present.

. . . It has in the course of economic development become the office of the woman to consume vicariously for the head of the household; and her apparel is contrived with this object in view. It has come about that obviously productive labour is in a peculiar degree derogatory to respectable women, and therefore special pains should be taken in the construction of women's dress, to impress upon the beholder the fact (often indeed a fiction) that the wearer does not and can not habitually engage in useful work. Propriety requires respectable women to abstain more consistently from useful effort and to make more of a show of leisure than the men of the same social classes. It grates painfully on our nerves to contemplate the necessity of any well-bred woman's earning a livelihood by useful work. It is not "woman's sphere." Her sphere is within the household, which she should "beautify," and of which she should be the "chief ornament." The male head of the household is not currently spoken of as its ornament. This feature taken in conjunction with the other fact that propriety requires more unremitting attention to expensive display in the dress and other paraphernalia of women, goes to enforce the view already implied in what has gone before. By virtue of its descent from a patriarchal past, our social system makes it the woman's function in an especial degree to put in evidence her household's ability to pay. According to the modern civilised scheme of life, the good name of the household to which she belongs should be the special care of the woman; and the system of honorific expenditure and conspicuous leisure by which this good name is chiefly sustained is therefore the woman's sphere. In the ideal scheme, as it tends to realise itself in the life of the higher pecuniary classes, this attention to conspicuous waste of substance and effort should normally be the sole economic function of the woman.

At the stage of economic development at which the women were still in the full sense the property of the men, the performance of conspicuous leisure and consumption came to be part of the services required of them. The women being not their own masters, obvious expenditure and leisure on their part would redound to the credit of their master rather than to their own credit; and therefore the more expensive and the more obviously unproductive the women of the household are, the more creditable and more effective for the purpose of the reputability of the household or its head will their life be. So much so that the women have been required not only to afford evidence of a life of leisure, but even to disable themselves for useful activity.

It is at this point that the dress of men falls short of that of women, and for a sufficient reason. Conspicuous waste and conspicuous leisure are reputable because they are evidence of pecuniary strength; pecuniary strength is reputable or honorific because, in the last analysis, it argues success and superior force; therefore the evidence of waste and leisure put forth by any individual in his own behalf cannot consistently take such a form or be carried to such a pitch as to argue incapacity or marked discomfort on his part; as the exhibition would in that case show not superior force, but inferiority, and so defeat its own purpose. So, then, wherever wasteful expenditure and the show of abstention from effort is normally, or on an average, carried to the extent of showing obvious discomfort or voluntarily induced physical disability, there the immediate inference is that the individual in question does not perform this wasteful expenditure and undergo this disability for her own personal gain in pecuniary repute, but in behalf of some one else to whom she stands in a relation of economic dependence; a relation which in the last analysis must, in economic theory, reduce itself to a relation of servitude.

To apply this generalisation to women's dress, and put the matter in concrete terms: the high heel, the skirt, the impracticable bonnet, the corset, and the general disregard of the wearer's comfort which is an obvious feature of all civilised women's apparel, are so many items of evidence to the effect that in the modern civilised scheme of life the woman is still, in theory, the economic dependent of the man,—that, perhaps in a highly idealised sense, she still is the man's chattel. The homely reason for all this conspicuous leisure and attire on the part of women lies in the fact that they are servants to whom, in the differentiation of economic functions, has been delegated the office of putting in evidence their master's ability to pay.

There is a marked similarity in these respects between the apparel of women and that of domestic servants, especially liveried servants. In both there is a very elaborate show of unnecessary expensiveness, and in both cases there is also a notable disregard of the physical comfort of the wearer. But the attire of the lady goes farther in its elaborate insistence on the idleness, if not on the physical infirmity of the wearer, than does that of the domestic. And this is as it should be; for in theory, according to the ideal scheme of the pecuniary culture, the lady of the house is the chief menial of the household.

THE PLANTATION MISTRESS: HER WORKING LIFE
CATHERINE CLINTON

While visiting the home of an ante-bellum Southern planter, one visitor was charmed by the grace and hospitality of the mistress. She was warm, gentle and refined in her manner. He found her a genial hostess and a model of what he expected "the Southern lady" to be. Having gained the permission of his host to stroll around the plantation alone during his visit, the stranger one day spied his host's wife hard at work. The matron was considerably disarrayed; hoops removed from her skirt, she was bent over a salting barrel, up to her elbows in brine. As he was about to approach her, the gentleman realized he faced a delicate situation. To fail to greet her might seem rude, but to acknowledge her would put the woman in an awkward position. He had essentially caught his hostess behind the scenes, accidentally violating the rules by wandering backstage. Thus he ambled by without a direct glance. This would have been an insult in the normal course of events, but as an acceptable outcome it reveals the absurdity of the myth-ridden South. A guest passes by the mistress of the plantation, paying her less attention than he would a slave. Exalted imagery and an unwillingness to cope with reality when it conflicted with the ideal created this eccentric world.

Within the perimeters of the Cotton Kingdom, planters created their own moral and political universe, a biracial slave society whose symbols and values were vastly different from those of the North. First and foremost, manual labor and physical work were disdained. The Southern lady was a symbol of gentility and refinement for plantation culture, designed to fill the requisites of chauvinist stereotype by embracing those qualities slave owners wished to promote, even though the practical needs of plantation life cast her in quite a different role. The clash of myth and reality was monumental.

The stately, pillared mansion at the end of a winding, tree-lined road was another symbol of the plantation South. In addition to the Big House, most Southern estates also included extensive outbuildings: barns, stables, workshops and warehouses. Slave cabins were built at a convenient distance from the master's home. The Big House often had a detached kitchen, and on larger estates separate smokehouses and storehouses were erected. The "household" thus extended far beyond the walls of the Big House and required upkeep and daily work as well as the care and feeding of all those, both black and white, who lived and worked on the plantation. This was the plantation mistress's domain.

The planter's wife was in charge not merely of the two- or three-story mansion but of the entire spectrum of domestic operations throughout the estate, from food and clothing to the physical and spiritual care of both her white family and her husband's slaves. The borders of her domain might extend from the mansion's locked pantry to the slave-quarter hospital and the slaughtering pen for the hogs. Very little escaped the attention of the white mistress, and most plantation problems were brought to her unless, being crop-related, they fell within the sphere of the overseer.

And, generally, the larger the plantation, the more extensive the household cares and responsibilities that devolved upon the mistress. Most women began their careers as plantation mistresses in profound ignorance. Parents lectured daughters during their adolescent years on the necessity of being good housekeepers, but as young girls, Southern women were seldom trained to keep house; education at home and in academies instead emphasized intellectual and artistic accomplishments. When females were taught such rudimentary skills as sewing, they concentrated their efforts on samplers and other ornamental needlework rather than on the practical application of such

ladylike accomplishments. One planter wrote to his recently married daughter: "You will have to study housekeeping. You are too young to have learnt
much of it. . . . It is a fault in female education housekeeping is not made
more a part of it; book learning is not sufficient: the kitchen and dairy must
be attended to as well as the drawing room."

The ante-bellum plantation mistress shared common work patterns with
many other women of her era. Like all married women, she was subject to the
demands of her husband on her time and energies. Like all mothers, she performed long and arduous tasks connected with child care. As a housekeeper,
the plantation mistress undertook numerous chores similar to those of her
Northern or urban or impoverished sister. Like her New England counterpart, the planter's wife managed a large household.

Even without the work created by their husbands' slave owning, the
numerous tasks of ante-bellum housekeeping kept plantation mistresses busy:
gardening, dairy activities, salting pork, preserving fruits and vegetables, mixing medicines, making candles, soap, rugs, pillows, linen, bedding and so on.
Women believed that their work was never done, and their assiduous daily
activity, begun most often at dawn, testified in favor of such claims. Complaints flowed freely in family letters. Many women felt that plantation labors
combined with family demands drove them to a state of near-collapse. One
woman confessed: "I do not know if I have any positive disease, but I have my
own proper share of nervousness, weakness, swimming in the head and a dull
sleepy sensation. . . . My family claims untiring attention." Women's only
respite came on the Sabbath; for six days of the week, a ceaseless stream of
household activities overwhelmed them.

Care of slaves was the plantation mistress's constant chore. She distributed
dairy foods and grain produced under her direction, often supervising the fields
that supplied the Big House pantry and the storeroom for slave food. Even if the
overseer supervised these plots, the final responsibility for feeding all those on
the plantation still rested with the plantation mistress. Gardens were a major
source of food for white and black, and women worked the family plots of fruits
and vegetables diligently. Even though slaves tended their own gardens on many
plantations, the planters were responsible for staples; their wives doled out milk,
pork and corn to slaves in much the same way that they parceled out their own
daily household supplies from the family storeroom.

Most plantations supported an extensive dairy operation. The mistress
supervised all stock kept for food (as opposed to work animals). As few plantations boasted an ice house, the processing of dairy products was a constant
and delicate operation.

Many women kept detailed records of their planting. Eliza Person Mitchell's gardening diary for 1834 contains 51 entries. Her listing for May gives some idea of the plantation mistress's agenda:

> May 4th planted out cabbage plants, 6th Strawberries for tea, 16th at night a killing frost, corn, cimbelines, cotton, snaps and everything killed, 17th planted early snaps, planted salsafa planted cimbelines, 22nd planted sugar beets planted snaps, 23rd Manured the Black Raspberry vines with Woodpile Manure, 23rd Strawberries dressed over grass and weeds taken out, 23rd the Weather very dry indeed, everything burning up in Garden.

In addition to growing the food, the plantation mistresses were preoccupied during summer and fall with preserving and pickling their gardens' yields.

The winter months were equally taxing. As one woman lamented in January, 1833: "I will not weary you by recounting all my solitary troubles, you can well imagine them if you will recall that hateful season to all housekeepers (the putting up of Pork)." December was the month set aside for hog killing. The mistress supervised the long and complicated series of jobs that the process entailed and actually performed certain tasks herself.

First, the animal was hit over the head with an ax to stun it, and its throat was slit. The hog was then hoisted up and dipped into a kettle of scalding water, after which the bristles were scraped off and saved for making brushes, and the carcass hung head down from a tree, to be disemboweled and halved. Male slaves did the dirty work of the slaughter; the mistress would take little part in these preliminary activities.

Once the carcass was prepared, however, the mistress took over. She emptied and scraped clean the small intestines, which were later stuffed with sausage. She processed the fat into lard, and chopped and seasoned the back meat, funneling it into skins for smoking. The ham shoulders and bacon flanks went into a barrel of brine to be corned. Thus the mistress processed each portion of the hog, down to the chitlings (intestines), into food. One plantation mistress complained that after salting meat for hours "all the skin was nearly off my hands"—a far cry from the privileged "lily-white hands" celebrated in plantation legend. ▪

Candlemaking and soapmaking were time-consuming chores for the Southern housekeeper. Although slaves occasionally participated in the soapmaking, plantation mistresses thought the dipping of candles was too complex to trust to anyone but themselves. A skillful woman could produce in a day's work 30 dozen candles, which would provide a month's supply of candlelight. Mistresses spun the down from milkweed pods into wicks. Frugality led women to store their candles in boxes kept under lock and key.

Although many planters were able to purchase goods such as furniture, crystal, cutlery and lamps, many of the home furnishings and household necessities were handmade by the plantation mistress. A young wife commented in 1829: "Two years ago I commenced the mighty job of making a carpet—a rag carpet, without being at all aware of the difficulties of the task. It is the most unseemly object imaginable." Another homemaker exulted to a friend: "I have made an excellent Mattress which I am proud of, as being so much the work of my own hands, also made all my Pickles and catsup, preserves and different kinds and drying Peaches in different ways and such like things." In early autumn, geese were killed and plucked. Women sorted the feathers—large ones for beds and small ones for pillows—then fashioned the quills into pens and the birds into Sunday dinners.

Though it surprises us to think of "sheltered" women grappling with such heavy burdens, women in agricultural societies throughout time have generally been charged with food production. The plantation may have been an expanded, near-industrial operation, but planters still expected women to fulfill this role. Despite wealth and status, plantation mistresses followed the tradition of their colonial forebears; almost all females isolated on rural farms learned to be inventive and thrifty, developing uses for everything and seeing that nothing was wasted. Planters constantly voiced their financial worries and looked to women to reduce them through efficient and innovative management.

With so many duties to perform and a multiplicity of roles to fulfill, the plantation mistress could easily be overwhelmed by responsibilities when she took up housekeeping. Mother and sisters often supplied goods as well as advice to the novice homemaker. A matron wrote to her newlywed sister:

> I believe I forgot to tell you that I should give you two pairs of my linen pillowcases. You will find them with the beds. Supposing that a trunk might be useful to you I put the blankets up in one. Phill will give you the key. I put a dimity counterpane in it too. You will receive a box of candles, a box of hard soap, twelve hams, half a dozen brooms, and one of my low posted bedsteads.

Most young plantation mistresses depended upon their female relatives for actual assistance, as well. Mothers and aunts, more experienced housekeepers, paid visits to novice plantation mistresses to help them "settle in." Their help and encouragement proved invaluable. Friends and neighbors might also give aid, but an aunt's visit during the summer months when jars needed filling for the winter ahead, or a mother's help during the hog killing, rescued many a young housekeeper from dreadful straits.

Housecleaning was an unpleasant series of tasks. Although she had a staff of house slaves, sometimes headed by a black steward or housekeeper, the plantation mistress regularly inspected all activities that she did not herself supervise or perform. Wives of Southern planters did not participate in such basic tasks as laundering or dishwashing, but they took on other menial chores. Wives with husbands in business also supervised the care of their husbands' offices in town. An exasperated housekeeper reported: "It was a hard day's work for myself and three other servants, the dusting and sweeping of books, papers, inkstands, etc. etc."

In addition to furnishing and maintaining their homes, women supplied their own families and others on the plantation with clothing. Although mothers taught their daughters ornamental sewing as girls, few brides were accomplished seamstresses. Matrons soon learned from female relatives to knit and sew for their husbands and children, as well as their slaves. The production of linen, counterpanes and quilts was women's responsibility. Although the quilting bee afforded an entertaining diversion for the plantation mistress, it was but one of her many sewing activities in the midst of numerous domestic projects. The lament of the overworked seamstress was a common theme in letters. A North Carolina woman confided to her sister in 1837: "I have about two months sewing to do. I never was so tired of sewing in my life. My fingers are worn out."

Shoes and socks were less troublesome to produce than clothing. If slave artisans did not make shoes on the plantation, mistresses ordered footwear from local merchants for their husband's slaves. Mistresses rarely purchased stockings, and instead knit them themselves. Virginia mistress Ann Cocke described her activities to her mother in 1811: "My hands are as full as possible. We have completed 25 out of the number of 40 pair of socks which are necessary for the crop hands." The Southern woman most often carried on her knitting at intervals during her many daily activities. A stocking took 185 stitches per row, on the average, and most plantation mistresses could manage to fit in 150 rows per day when knitting at a steady pace. At that rate, a single sock took six days; a housewife could complete a pair of stockings every two weeks. At the very least, each slave required one pair of stockings a year.

If a woman was mistress of a plantation with 30 slaves, she was able to manage all the knitting for her family and slaves herself, working at a relaxed pace. But if her husband owned more than 30 slaves, the mistress had to concentrate on knitting for prolonged periods of time or train the black women in the house to knit their own stockings and those of other slaves.

The recipe books left by Southern women reflect the industriousness of their lives. The record of Martha B. Eppes demonstrates her varied activities: included are how to make scarlet dye, the number of blankets distributed to slaves and recipes for grape wine and "instantaneous beer." Eliza Person Mitchell's housekeeping book contains 20 pages of recipes, notes on pickling and preserving, a record of soapmaking, a formula for furniture polish and instruction on the making of paint. But even more striking, all recipe books included, side by side with directions for mixing cakes and puddings, medical remedies.

On large plantations, certain areas were designated as hospitals and nurseries. Elderly slave women served as nurses and attendants. As the recipe books tell us, the plantation mistress had to assume responsibility as ministering physician as well as housekeeper. She made daily rounds to the cabins of sick slaves or to the buildings set aside for the invalid and infant members of the slave community. Women frequently commented on and complained about the trouble of slave illnesses in their correspondence. They doctored the slaves both as humane plantation mistresses, seeing to the needs of their black charges, and in their capacity as slaveowners' wives, looking out for their husbands' property interests.

During the post-Revolutionary era, many planters elected to political office or forced to travel extensively on business confidently left the management of their estates to their wives, as well as to overseers. Although they continued to supervise plantation finances—at home or from abroad—many planters allowed their wives total discretion in business affairs during their absence. Even when masters maintained control over planting, crops and other concerns through postal directives, the daily decisions and business of farming were of necessity left in capable women's hands when planters were called away. A variety of sources suggest that plantation mistresses were familiar with all the facets of farm management. Without the interim management of females, Southern plantations would have suffered irreparable damage. Men expected and depended upon women's abilities.

A few women resisted the responsibilities shifted onto them by their absent husbands. Subjected to long periods of isolation on her husband's Louisiana plantation, Diana Dunbar made her own decisions about farming operations but did not shy away from expressing her complaints:

I am sorry you do not find my letters so pretty as they used to be; but if you knew, my love, how I am vex and plagu'd with a set of worthless servents you woul'd not be surprised at it, but I will make you uneasy with my complaints: I have told you already about the plantation & the Tobacco. Indeed my love there is too much to do for the few people you left. As I thought it woul'd be too long before I could get an answer from you, concerning hiring a hand to help in making up the Tobacco, I have hired one today.

Dunbar vacillated between anger at her husband's demands and the desire to please him with an efficient job:

> You seem, my Dear, to expect we have a deal of time upon our hands, to do everything necessary about the plantation. I would not have you expect too much for fear you may be disappointed; tho' my love, if you will consider everything rightly I don't think you will complain. . . . I would willingly follow your advice and not go in the sun if I could avoid it, but there is many things to do about a place that you men don't think of.

The plantation mistress was often burdened by a husband's numerous directives, while being admonished not to exert herself. Most women accepted the inherent tensions of their role and struggled when necessary to manage successfully both the household and the plantation overall.

During the master's absence, financial concerns added to the burden of planting and often posed a more serious threat to the mistress's ability to cope. Most wives sent a list of questions as well as a flurry of complaints to their absent husbands, and it is clear that, despite their varying degrees of ability, many suffered a lack of confidence in their business acumen, particularly when questions involved areas outside the perimeters of the plantation itself. Law and social custom reinforced these psychological constraints. Socialization from birth trained women to defer to males; decision making outside the domestic sphere proved difficult for plantation mistresses. Some dealt masterfully, such as a matron who won her husband's approval in 1806: "What you mention concerning the purchase of pork and other matters meet with my approbation as indeed your transactions have always done." But more often the strain provoked husbands to discourage their wives from financial transactions during the master's absences.

If forced by circumstances, women could manage internal plantation affairs without the advice or consent of males. Daughters who inherited estates from their fathers or widows who were left to run plantations alone seemed to survive on the land without male intervention.

But even a mistress who demonstrated a clear ability to manage her plantation as a discrete economic unit and make it pay was not permitted by law to handle personal or business affairs in the public sphere. Women's inadequacies, real or perceived, were a direct result of the "sheltering" system that designated women as dependents, under the protection—and at the mercy—of men. While this system failed to keep women from exercising authority and demonstrating capability in daily routines, it effectively shackled them in any external dealing beyond plantation boundaries.

As a result, women rightly felt vulnerable in the world of legal finance. They held no power before the law, which provided for man's total control over woman: her property, her behavior, her very person.

All women in Southern society recognized the important financial and legal handicap under which they lived, and most accepted the limitations imposed by society as unalterable. Women did not resist as much as resent dependency. The psychological tensions—exacerbated by the enormous strain of physical chores—created depression, melancholy and a whole range of debilities for women. These women did not inhabit mythical estates, but rather productive working plantations: the routine was grueling, life was harsh. No wonder they complained of being themselves enslaved. The plantation mistress found herself trapped within a system over which she had no control, one from which she had no means of escape. Cotton was King, white men ruled, and both white women and slaves served the same master.

SLAVE TESTIMONY

My mother was cook in the house for about twenty-two years. She cooked for from twenty-five to thirty-five, taking the family and the slaves together. The slaves ate in the kitchen. After my mistress's death, my mother was the only woman kept in the house. She took care of my master's children, some of whom were then quite small, and brought them up. One of the most trying scenes I ever passed through, when I would have laid down my life to protect her if I had dared, was this: after she had raised my master's children, one of his daughters, a young girl, came into the kitchen one day, and for some trifle about the dinner, she struck my mother, who pushed her away, and she fell on the floor. Her father was not at home. When he came, which was while the slaves were eating in the kitchen, she told him about it. He came down, called my mother out, and, with a hickory rod, he beat her fifteen or twenty strokes, and then called his daughter and told her to take her satisfaction of her, and she did beat her until she was satisfied. Oh! it was dreadful, to see the girl whom my poor mother had taken care of from her childhood, thus beating her, and I must

Selections from John Blassingame, ed., *Slave Testimony: Two Centuries of Letters, Speeches, Interviews and Autobiography* (Baton Rouge: Louisiana State University Press, 1977), 132–33.

stand there, and did not dare to crook my finger in her defence. My mother's labor was very hard. She would go to the house in the morning, take her pail upon her head, and go away to the cow-pen, and milk fourteen cows. She then put on the bread for the family breakfast, and got the cream ready for churning, and set a little child to churn it, she having the care of from ten to fifteen children, whose mothers worked in the field. After clearing away the family breakfast, she got breakfast for the slaves; which consisted of warm corn bread and buttermilk, and was taken at twelve o'clock. In the meantime, she had beds to make, rooms to sweep, &c. Then she cooked the family dinner, which was simply plain meat, vegetables, and bread. Then the slaves' dinner was to be ready at from eight to nine o'clock in the evening. It consisted of corn bread, or potatoes, and the meat which remained of the master's dinner, or one herring apiece. At night she had the cows to milk again. There was little ceremony about the master's supper, unless there was company. This was her work day by day. Then in the course of the week, she had the washing and ironing to do for her master's family, (who, however, were clothed very simply,) and for her husband, seven children and herself.

OKLAHOMA SLAVE NARRATIVE: MRS. MATTIE LOGAN

My mother belonged to Mistress Jennie who thought a heap of her, and why shouldn't she? Mother nursed all Miss Jennie's children because all of her young ones and my mammy's was born so close together it wasn't no trouble at all for mammy to raise the whole kaboodle of them. I was born about the same time as the baby Jennie. They say I nursed on one breast while that white child, Jennie, pulled away at the other!

That was a pretty good idea for the Mistress, for it didn't keep her tied to the place and she could visit around with her friends most any time she wanted 'thout having to worry if the babies would be fed or not.

Mammy was the house girl and account of that and because her family was so large, the Mistress fixed up a two room cabin right back of the Big House and that's where we lived. The cabin had a fireplace in one of the rooms, just like the rest of the slave cabins which was set in a row away from the Big House. In one room was bunk beds, just plain old two-by-fours with holes bored through the plank so's ropes could be fastened in and across for to hold the corn-shuck mattress.

Selections from "Oklahoma Narratives: Mrs. Mattie Logan," in *Slave Narratives: A Folk History of Slavery in the United States from Interviews with Former Slaves* (Washington, D.C.: Library of Congress, 1936–38), Reel 9.

My brothers and sisters was allowed to play with the Master's children, but not with the children who belonged to the field Negroes. We just played yard games like marbles and tossing a ball. I don't rightly remember much about games, for there wasn't too much fun in them days even if we did get raised with the Master's family. We wasn't allowed to learn any reading or writing. They say if they catched a slave learning them things they'd pull his finger nails off! I never saw that done, though.

THE YOUNG LADY'S FRIEND
H. O. WARD

Let us try to make the service of private families more desirable, not by extravagant wages, but by justice and kindness, and a liberal consideration of the convenience and pleasure of those who do the drudgery of our houses. Let us attach them to us by a sincere sympathy in their feeling, interests, and concerns; if we make them see that we are not selfishly bent on getting all the service we can for our wages, but that their happiness is a large item in the account, they will in return consult our interest and convenience, and we shall have the willing labor of love, instead of reluctant eye-service.

In much of the fault-finding that is heard about domestics, may be traced the influence of aristocratic feeling, and that spirit of domination which invariably accompanies a state of society, in which domestics are numerous, and labor can be commanded at a cheap rate; and though it is long since this was the state of things in the northern and eastern States of America, the feeling is transmitted, and ladies often talk as if they were living in olden times, and had a right to govern with absolute sway those whom they hire. They talk of the contracts made with house servants, as if the obligations were all on one side, and as if in consideration of the wages paid, the hired persons were to lose all free agency; to hold every moment at the command of their employers; to have no will but theirs; to perform the same round of duties, month after month, without relief or variety; to seek no amusements; to gain no further knowledge; but be content to drudge on thus to the end of their days. . . .

When they find their comfort provided for in the family arrangements, and that their employers are willing to make occasional sacrifices of convenience to their special enjoyment, they become considerate and generous in their turn; and instead of encroaching upon this kindness, they avail themselves of it very scrupulously. Nothing so entirely vulgarizes a household as a tone of hostility

Selections from H. O. Ward, *The Young Lady's Friend* (Philadelphia: Porter & Coates, 1880), 201.

between servants and employers. A mistress should remember that the best servants she can get are not faultless, but are liable to the same errors, temptations, and passions as their employers. She will endeavor to correct their faults, and not to provoke them; above all, she will treat them, and encourage her children to treat them, with uniform kindness and civility, remembering that service is a relationship of employer and employed, and not of master and slave. One can never overestimate the effect of sympathy in dealing with a class of inferior rank to our own.

DECORUM: A PRACTICAL TREATISE

PERIOD OF MOURNING.

On this subject we quote from a modern writer who says:

"Those who wish to show themselves strict observers of etiquette keep their houses in twilight seclusion and sombre with mourning for a year, or more, allowing the piano to remain closed for the same length of time. But in this close observance of the letter of the law its spirit is lost entirely.

"It is not desirable to enshroud ourselves in gloom after a bereavement, no matter how great it has been. It is our duty to ourselves and to the world to regain our cheerfulness as soon as we may, and all that conduces to this we are religiously bound to accept, whether it be music, the bright light of heaven, cheerful clothing or the society of friends.

"At all events, the moment we begin to chafe against the requirements of etiquette, grow wearied of the darkened room, long for the open piano and look forward impatiently to the time when we may lay aside our mourning, from that moment we are slaves to a law which was originally made to serve us in allowing us to do unquestioned what was supposed to be in true harmony with our gloomy feelings.

"The woman who wears the badge of widowhood for exactly two years to a day, and then puts it off suddenly for ordinary colors, and who possibly has already contracted an engagement for a second marriage during these two years of supposed mourning, confesses to a slavish hypocrisy in making an ostentatious show of a grief which has long since died a natural (and shall we not say a desirable?) death.

"In these respects let us be natural, and let us moreover, remember that, though the death of friends brings us real and heartfelt sorrow, yet it is still a time for rejoicing for their sakes."

Selections from *Decorum: A Practical Treatise on Etiquette and Dress of the Best American Society* (New York and Chicago: J. A. Ruth, 1879), 260–61, 289.

ETIQUETTE: WHAT TO DO AND HOW TO DO IT
LADY CONSTANCE HOWARD

The time that people now-a-days continue in mourning, is regulated very much more than it was formerly by the affection people bear for the memory of those deceased.

Formerly a hard and fast rule was laid down for the period of mourning to be observed, according to the relationship of the survivors to the person for whom they were in mourning.

But in the present day, the deepest mourning, and the strictest seclusion are often observed, for *friends* only, while the period of mourning and the extent of it is materially curtailed when it is a question of *relations.*

Although universal '*humbug*' is the rule, alas! rather than the exception, in the matter of mourning, people have gained, rather than lost, in honesty and sincerity; and generally do not put on 'outward and visible' signs of woe, when their hearts are not in mourning likewise.

In this age of '*shams,*' something has thereby been gained that those who are 'true,' need not be ashamed of.

The correct time to mourn for a mother or father is *not* less than a year; where children are very devoted to their parents' memory, eighteen months or two years would not be a day too long, although a year is the generally accepted period; but in mourning, as in all else, 'circumstances alter cases,' and personal, individual feeling must, and should be, the *only* guide.

No one ought ever to wear mourning for so short a time as *six* months, where the mourning is for a parent, the very shortest time being nine months; and this short period would be the visible acknowledgment of a lack of *affection,* almost amounting to *indifference,* on the part of the son or daughter observing it.

Widows do not, as a rule, mourn for less than two years; eighteen months and a year being unusual; but *here,* perhaps, more than in any other case of mourning, individual feeling reigns paramount.

Where widows have lost all this world holds for them of love and happiness, by the death of their husbands, they very often mourn and wear 'widows' weeds' to the end of their lives, and quite right that it should be so.

Equally right is it, that where the death of husband or wife is a blessing much to be desired by the survivor, that then the survivor should only comply in the extent and period of his or her mourning with the demands of society and

Selections from Lady Constance Howard, *Etiquette: What to Do, and How to Do It* (London: F. V. White, 1885).

etiquette—that is to say, eighteen months, or even a year, and not outwardly feign grief for the loss of the man or woman, whose decease has given them the priceless boon of *peace,* and probably happiness—at any rate, freedom from eternal rows and worries.

The same applies to widowers, their feelings *alone* should regulate the period of their mourning.

MOURNING DRESS
Lou Taylor

Recommended lengths of family mourning 1876–97
TAKEN FROM CONTEMPORARY SOURCES

	First Mourning	Second Mourning	Ordinary Mourning	Half-Mourning	Total
Widow for Husband	1 year 1 day in bombazine and heavy plain crape	9 months with less crape	3 months in black silk with ribbon and jet	6 months min. in half-mourning colours	2 1/2 years
Widower for Wife	3 months in black suit, with black watch chain, buttons and tie			None	3 months
Mother for Child	6 months in bombazine and crape		3 months in black silk	3 months in half-mourning colors	1 year
Child for Parent	Black or white crape for 6 months		3 months	3 months	1 year
Wife for Her Parents	18 months mantle in paramatta and crape		3 months	3 months	2 years
Wife for Mother-In-Law	18 months mantle in paramatta and crape		3 months	3 months	2 years
For Brother and Sister			2 months	1 month	6 months
Niece for Aunt or Uncle	None		3 to 6 months depending on how remote the relationship		Usually 3 months
First Cousin	None		3 weeks 3 weeks Or stretching to 3 months		6 weeks to 3 months
Grand-Daughter for Grandparents	6 months in crape		2 to 3 months	1 to 3 months	6 to 9 months
Mothers for Parents-In-Law of Their Married Children	None		6 weeks black without crape		6 weeks
Second Wife for Husband's Frist Wife's Parents			3 months		3 months
Servants Mourning	Same as their employers but in cheap, tougher fabrics, and black and white only for half-mourning.				

Selection from Lou Taylor, *Mourning Dress: A Costume and History* (London: George Allen and Unwin, 1983), 303–4.

Chronology of
Kate Chopin's Life

February 8, 1850	Born in St. Louis, Missouri.
Fall 1855	Enters Academy of the Sacred Heart in St. Louis. Attends sporadically for next thirteen years.
November 1, 1855	Death of father, Thomas O'Flaherty, in railroad accident.
January 16, 1863	Death of great-grandmother, Victoire Verdon Charleville.
June 29, 1868	Graduation from Academy of the Sacred Heart.
June 9, 1870	Marries Oscar Chopin at Holy Angels Church, St. Louis.
June–September 1870	Honeymoon in Europe. Couple settles in New Orleans.
May 22, 1871	Son Jean Baptiste born.
October 28, 1874	Son George Francis born.
January 26, 1876	Son Frederick born.
January 8, 1878	Son Felix Andrew born.
December 31, 1879	Daughter Marie Laïza (Lélia) born.
December 10, 1882	Death of Oscar Chopin.
1884	Kate Chopin returns to St. Louis.
June 28, 1885	Death of mother, Eliza O'Flaherty.
January 10, 1889	First literary publication, the poem "If It Might Be."

September 1890   *At Fault* published.

March 24, 1894   Short story collection *Bayou Folk* published.

November 1897   Short story collection *A Night in Acadie* published.

April 22, 1899   *The Awakening* published.

February 1900   Publisher rejects short story collection *A Vocation and a Voice.*

August 22, 1904   Dies two days after suffering cerebral hemorrhage at St. Louis World's Fair.

1991   *A Vocation and a Voice* published posthumously.

NOTES

INTRODUCTION

1. Emily Toth, *Kate Chopin: A Life of the Author of* The Awakening (New York: William Morrow and Co., 1990), 35.

2. Toth, *Kate Chopin,* 26.

3. Business agents known as factors served plantation owners of the American South in the eighteenth and nineteenth centuries. In addition to providing the normal services expected of a commodities broker for crops such as cotton and tobacco, these agents also maintained accounts for planters that allowed them to borrow funds against the sale of future crops. They additionally arranged for the purchase and transportation of goods, especially imports such as fine home furnishings, that could not be manufactured on the largely self-sufficient plantations or procured in the often isolated local economies of the southern states. Most factors also speculated in commodities futures markets, which provided the opportunity to make or lose large sums of money rapidly.

4. Toth, *Kate Chopin,* 161.

5. In addition to the abundance of propaganda produced in the late nineteenth century by the temperance movement itself, many works of fiction dealt with the effects of alcohol abuse. Most noteworthy is the work of Frank Norris, a contemporary of Chopin's, many of whose novels and works of short fiction present an even darker and more striking take on this theme than does *At Fault.* Norris is much more graphic than Chopin in depicting the physical abuse, societal degradation, and random violence which often accompany alcohol abuse. For a more thorough discussion of this topic, especially as it relates to gender and class issues, see David J. Caudle, "The Fall and Rise of Kate Chopin and Her Works," in *Kate Chopin: An Annotated Bibliography of Critical Works,* ed. Suzanne Disheroon Green and David J. Caudle (Westport, Conn.: Greenwood Press, 1999).

6. Toth, *Unveiling Kate Chopin* (Jackson: Univ. Press of Mississippi, 1999), 166.

7. Martha R. Clevenger, *Indescribably Grand: Diaries and Letters from the 1904 World's Fair* (St. Louis: Missouri Historical Society Press, 1996).

8. J. W. Buel, ed., *Louisiana and the Fair: An Exposition of the World, Its People and Their Achievements* (St. Louis: World's Progress Pub. Co., 1905). Watson

Memorial Library, Cammie G. Henry Research Center, Rare Book Collection, F351B93, vol. 10.

9. Bertram Wyatt-Brown, *Southern Honor: Ethics and Behavior in the Old South* (Oxford: Oxford Univ. Press, 1982).

10. Chopin wrote a third novel, *Young Dr. Gosse and Théo,* in 1890, but destroyed the manuscript after numerous failed attempts to find a publisher. Nonetheless, a friend of Chopin's called it her "very strongest work" (Toth, *Kate Chopin,* 189).

11. Larzer Ziff, *The American 1890s: Life and Times of a Lost Generation* (New York: Viking, 1966), 298.

12. Robert D. Amer, "Landscape Symbolism in Kate Chopin's *At Fault,*" *Louisiana Studies* 9 (1970): 142–53.

13. William Warkin, "Fire, Light, and Darkness in Kate Chopin's *At Fault,*" *Kate Chopin Newsletter* 1, no. 2 (1975): 17–27.

14. Lewis Leary, "Kate Chopin's Other Novel," *Southern Literary Journal* 1, no. 1 (1968): 60–74.

15. Thomas Bonner Jr., "Kate Chopin's *At Fault* and *The Awakening:* A Study in Structure," *Markham Review* 7 (1977):10–14.

16. Jo Ridgley, *Nineteenth Century Southern Literature* (Lexington: Univ. Press of Kentucky, 1980).

17. The myth of the southern lady and the expectations of southern womanhood have been well described by a variety of critics of southern literature, culture, and history. Most notably, see Anne Goodwyn Jones, *Tomorrow Is Another Day: The Woman Writer in the South 1859–1936*; Kathryn Lee Seidel, *The Southern Belle in the American Novel*; Elizabeth Fox-Genovese, *Within the Plantation Household*; and Barbara Ewell, "Changing Places: Women, the Old South; Or, What Happens When Local Color Becomes Regionalism," *Amerikastudien: American Studies* 42, no. 2 (1997): 159–79.

18. Donald A. Ringe, "Cane River World: Kate Chopin's *At Fault* and Related Stories," *Studies in American Fiction* 3 (1975):157–66.

19. Bert Bender, "The Teeth of Desire: *The Awakening* and *The Descent of Man,*" in *Critical Essays on Kate Chopin,* ed. Alice Hall Petry (New York: G. K. Hall, 1996).

20. Thomas Bonner Jr., "Christianity and Catholicism in the Fiction of Kate Chopin," in *Old New Orleans,* ed. W. Kenneth Holditch (Jackson: Univ. Press of Mississippi, 1983).

21. Jane Hotchkiss, "Confusing the Issue: Who's *At Fault?*" *Louisiana Literature* 2, no. 1 (1994): 31–43.

22. Barbara Ewell, *Kate Chopin,* New York: Ungar Publishing Company, 1986.

23. Doris Crow Grover, "Kate Chopin and the Bayou Country," *Journal of the American Studies Association of Texas* 15 (1984): 29–34.

24. Pamela Glenn Menke, "Fissure as Art in Kate Chopin's *At Fault,*" *Louisiana Literature* 2, no. 1 (1994): 44–58.

25. Pamela Glenn Menke, "The Catalyst of Color and Women's Regional Writing: *At Fault, Pembroke,* and *The Awakening," Southern Quarterly* 37 (1999): 9–20.

26. Philip Tarpley, "Kate Chopin's Sawmill: Technology and Change in *At Fault,"* *Proceedings of the Red River Symposium,* ed. Norman A. Dolch and Karen Douglas (Baton Rouge: Louisiana State Univ. Press, 1986). (The author's name appears as "Tapley" in both the article and the periodical databases).

27. Violet Harrington Bryan, *The Myth of New Orleans in Literature: Dialogues of Race and Gender* (Knoxville: Univ. of Tennessee Press, 1993).

28. Thomas Bonner Jr., "Kate Chopin: Tradition and the Moment," *Southern Literature in Transition: Heritage and Promise,* ed. Philip Castille and William Osborne (Memphis: Memphis State Univ. Press, 1983).

29. Sandra Gunning, "Kate Chopin's Local Color Fiction and the Politics of White Supremacy," *Arizona Quarterly* 52, no. 3 (1995): 61–86.

30. Jean Bardot, "French Creole Portraits: The Chopin Family from Natchitoches Parish," in *Kate Chopin Reconsidered: Beyond the Bayou,* ed. Lynda S. Boren and Sara deSaussure Davis (Baton Rouge: Louisiana State Univ. Press, 1992).

31. Winfried Fluck, "Kate Chopin's *At Fault:* The Usefulness of Louisiana French for the Imagination," in *Transatlantic Encounters: Studies in European-American Relations, Presented to Winfried Herget,* ed. Udo J. Hebel and Karl Ortsiefen (Trier, Germany: W.V.T. Wissenshaftlicher Verlag Trier, 1995).

32. Christopher Benfy, *Degas in New Orleans: Encounters in the Creole World of Kate Chopin and George Washington Cable* (New York: Knopf, 1998).

At Fault

Part I

In the text, parenthetical comments and notes indicated by the symbol * are Chopin's notes as they appeared in the first edition of *At Fault.* Translations from the French should be assumed to be standard French rather than Creole French unless otherwise indicated. French translations are provided by Marie François Conin-Jones, University of North Texas, Denton.

Chapter I. The Mistress of Place-Du-Bois

1. *Bêtise:* A blunder, a stupid action.

2. Southern conventions in the late nineteenth century dictated that once African Americans—especially those who worked closely with the family—reached an advanced age, men were referred to as "Uncle" and women as "Aunt" or "Auntie."

3. *Cambric:* A kind of fine linen, originally made at Cambray, in Flanders. Also an imitation made of hard-spun cotton yarn.

4. For further discussion of conventions surrounding the mourning of the dead, and the ways in which these conventions influenced the lives of both men and

women, see the selections on *Decorum, Etiquette,* and *Mourning Dress* in the "Backgrounds and Contexts" section of this book.

5. The theft of cottonseed was a common criminal act during this era. For further discussion of this type of criminal activity, see "Property Offenses, Social Tension and Racial Antagonism in Post–Civil War Rural Louisiana" in the "Backgrounds and Contexts" section of this book.

6. *Place-Du-Bois:* Place name meaning "The Wooded Place."

7. *Lac-du-Bois:* Place name meaning "The Wooded Lake."

8. *Bayou:* In the southern United States, a stream or channel with little current, often forming an inlet or outlet to a river or lake.

9. *Rod:* A measure of length equal to 5 1/2 yards or 16 1/2 feet.

10. *Section House:* A structure occupied by those responsible for maintaining a section of railway.

11. Creole architecture was based upon traditional French designs, adapted for the rain and long summers of Louisiana. According to Frank W. Masson, the typical Creole dwelling, regardless of size, was "rectangular, usually of two stories, and the rooms opened onto one another without halls. The first story was built entirely of stuccoed brick and was used for utility purposes; the second story was of *colombage* [a heavy timber building frame brought from France] filled with brick or *boullizage* [a mixture of mud and moss or straw] and covered on the outside with stucco or wide shiplapped boards. . . . Access to the second floor was by exterior stairs under the sheltering gallery roofs. . . . Ceilings on the principal [second] floor were generally high (10 to 12 feet) to allow the summer heat to rise so that cross-ventilation could carry it out of the house." The resulting high, sloping roofs allowed easy drainage during the rainy season and provided a large, sheltered verandah for summertime living space. See Charles Reagan Wilson and William Ferris, eds., *Encyclopedia of Southern Culture* (Chapel Hill: Univ. of North Carolina Press, 1989), 68.

12. *Cottonade:* A heavy, coarsely woven cloth of cotton or cotton mixture used for sport or work clothes. See Mary Brooks Picken, *The Language of Fashion: A Dictionary of Fabric, Sewing, and Dress* (New York: Funk and Wagnall's, 1939), 37.

Chapter II. At the Mill

1. *Cypresse Funerall:* Literally, in Creole French, "mournful cypress." Its relevance to the burgeoning timber industry in late-nineteenth-century Louisiana is discussed in Lisa Abney's essay, "The Milieu of the Timber Industry and Chopin's *At Fault,*" in the "Backgrounds and Contexts" section of this book.

2. For discussions of reform movements, see selections entitled *The Pocket Cyclo-pedia of Temperance* and *Temperance Documents of the American Temperance Society,* in the "Backgrounds and Contexts" section of this book.

3. *Pirogue:* A "small canoe-like dugout and planked craft used by the Acadians to carry them through the shallow waters of the swamps and bayous. It could hold one or two people and was propelled by paddling or poling." See Thomas Bonner Jr., *The Kate Chopin Companion* (Westport, Conn.: Greenwood Press, 1988).

4. See John Ruskin's "The Stones of Venice" and his "Pre-Raphaelitism," excerpted in "Literary Sources" in the "Backgrounds and Contexts" section of this book

CHAPTER III. IN THE PIROGUE

1. Chopin's use of the offensive term *nigger* in this context is indicative not only of its usage in the nineteenth century, but of an implicit, three-caste social hierarchy that Louisianians tacitly understood. For further discussion of the racial system in Louisiana, see the selections relating to Creole Society in the "Backgrounds and Contexts" section of this book.

2. See the "Illustrations" section for contemporary maps of the Red River region.

3. During the late nineteenth century, *vail* and *veil* were used interchangeably. The 1899 *Funk and Wagnall's Dictionary* indicates that both spellings were in common usage. Isaac K. Funk, ed., *A Standard Dictionary of the English Language,* 2 vols. (New York: Funk and Wagnall's, 1899).

4. As in our era, during Chopin's time *gray* and *grey* were interchangeable. The 1899 *Funk and Wagnall's Dictionary* indicates this by bracketing the two spellings and providing the same phonetic pronunciation and definitions for the two words.

5. Local legend holds that the evil Simon Legree and the saintly Uncle Tom, characters in Harriet Beecher Stowe's famous novel, *Uncle Tom's Cabin,* are based upon residents of Natchitoches Parish. Robert McAlpin, who owned the plantation land that Oscar Chopin's father, J. B. Chopin, purchased, alleg-edly was the model for Legree. For further discussion of the Legree-McAlpin connection, see the selections from *Uncle Tom's Cabin,* the "Affidavits," and the selections from *A Visit to Uncle Tom's Cabin* among "Literary Sources" in the "Backgrounds and Contexts" section of this book.

6. The Santien boys represent one of several families of repeating characters in Chopin's fiction. For an exhaustive list of repeating elements in Chopin's fiction, see Bonner, *Kate Chopin Companion.* For critical discussions of Chopin's repeat-ing characters, see Donald Ringe, "Cane River World: Kate Chopin's *At Fault* and Related Stories," *Studies in American Fiction* 3 (1975): 157–66; and Sylvia Bailey Shurbutt, "The Cane River Characters and Revisionist Mythmaking in the Work of Kate Chopin," *Southern Literary Journal* 25, no. 2 (1993): 14–23.

CHAPTER IV. A SMALL INTERRUPTION

1. *De pied en cap:* From head to foot, from top to toe.
2. *En-quire', en-quir' er, en-quir' y:* Alternative forms of *inquire,* etc. The latter spellings are now more common, though *enquire* and *enquiry* (meaning "to ask a question" or "a question") remain in frequent use. *En-* was the common spelling in Middle English and the corresponding Old French; it was derived from the Latin *in-* (*Funk and Wagnall's Dictionary,* 1899).
3. *Sinecure:* Any office or position which has no work or duties attached to it, especially one which yields some stipend or emolument.
4. Forms of address such as "Miss T'rèse" or "Miss Melicent" were common means of both conveying respect for the person being spoken to and implying a hierarchical relationship understood to exist between servants and employers. Such forms of address are still commonly used in many Southern towns, where children are admonished never to address adults by their first names.

CHAPTER V. IN THE PINE WOODS

1. Morico's reference to Melicent as the "American lady" demonstrates the clear distinction that Louisianians saw between those indigenous to Louisiana who were of European heritage, especially French, and those from outside the Louisiana territory, who were referred to, often somewhat derisively, as Americans.
2. In the nineteenth century, the term *safe* referred to an early form of icebox. *Garde manger* is the French equivalent, literally meaning "meat safe."
3. Meaning *time* [Chopin's note in first edition].
4. *Wiggles:* The larvae of mosquitoes. Their presence would have been the sign of a poorly maintained and perhaps contaminated well or cistern.

CHAPTER VI. MELICENT TALKS

1. *Toilet:* The action or process of dressing. Also sometimes used to refer to the implements used in dressing.
2. *Piny* is a variant of *piney* (*Funk and Wagnall's Dictionary,* 1899).

CHAPTER VII. PAINFUL DISCLOSURES

1. For a further discussion of Catholic beliefs, especially those pertaining to marriage and divorce, see the selections under "Religious Influences" in the "Backgrounds and Contexts" section of this book.
2. *Truck* (verb): To give in exchange; to sell or trade petty articles or garden produce. *Truck* (noun): Garden produce intended for market; as, "He raises truck" (*Funk and Wagnall's Dictionary,* 1899).
3. *Inveigled:* To persuade into some unwise act by deceptive arts of flattery; lead astray by hoodwinking; wheedle; entice. Example: "After vainly trying

to inveigle Locke into a fault, the government resolved to punish him without one" (*Funk and Wagnall's Dictionary*, 1899).

4. *Mésalliance:* Occurs when a person of the upper classes marries below his or her rank, class, or fortune.

Chapter VIII. Treats of Melicent

1. *Properly:* Twentieth-century grammatical conventions indicate that the form should be *proper.* However, in 1899, *proper,* when used as an adverb, was considered "vulgar" ("prop' er, adv. [vulgar], properly; also, very; extremely" (*Funk and Wagnall's Dictionary*, 1899).

2. *Paris green:* A vivid, light-green pigment composed of aceto-arsinite of copper, and commonly used as an insecticide.

3. *Paean:* A song of praise or thanksgiving; a song of triumph.

4. For information on Unitarian beliefs, see the "Religious Influences" section in the "Backgrounds and Contexts" section of this book.

Chapter IX. Face to Face

1. *Exposition:* See selections from *Louisiana and the Fair* and *Indescribably Grand* in this volume.

2. *Flat:* A multi-story apartment unit. This type of housing, a growing necessity for the rapidly expanding St. Louis metropolitan area, was new during Chopin's lifetime.

Chapter X. Fanny's Friends

1. *Nottingham curtains:* Nottingham, England has been known for its production of delicate laces, silks, and netting since the early 18th century. By the 19th century, Tambour lace was a popular product of the region, and its production was facilitated by the technology to make laces and netting by machine. A Nottingham curtain would have been made from Nottingham lace, which is described as "any flat lace made by machine . . . [including] curtain laces." Imported lace curtains would be yet another sign of the wealth and ostentation of the St. Louis "professional time-wasters." For more on Nottingham curtains, see Picken, *Language of Fashion,* 89.

2. *Ain't:* Colloquial term pronounced —ênt. Am not; are not; also illiterate for is not, has not, and have not (*Funk and Wagnall's Dictionary*, 1899). Chopin uses the spelling '*aint* in Part 1 of *At Fault,* and *ain't* in Part 2. We have regularized the spelling so that it conforms with twentieth-century slang conventions.

3. *Avoir-dupois:* The normal French spelling is *avoir du poids*, meaning "to be heavy, to weigh a lot." Metaphorically, the term means to have power or influence. Also, the apothecary scale of weight measurement.

4. *Patchouly:* An odoriferous plant native to Silhat, Penang, and the Malay Peninsula; it yields an essential oil, from which the scent is derived. *Jockey-club:* A brand of cologne.

5. Perhaps a reference to Cicero's remark that "A room without books is as a body without a soul."

6. John Ruskin (1819–1900) was a British author, art critic, and social reformer. Excerpts of his works are included under "Literary Sources" in the "Backgrounds and Contexts" section of this book.

   Arthur Schopenhauer (1788–1860) was a German Romantic philosopher, noted for his pessimism, who eventually came to espouse Buddhism.

   Ralph Waldo Emerson (1803–1882) was an American essayist, poet, and Unitarian minister. Excerpts of Emerson's works are included in the "Literary Sources" section of this book.

7. *Sacred Heart Convent:* Convent housing the Academy of the Sacred Heart, a primary and secondary school for girls in St. Louis, which Chopin attended.

8. *Forest Park:* A large St. Louis park which hosted many expositions and fairs in the late nineteenth century, culminating with the 1904 World's Fair.

9. *Taken the pledge:* To have taken a formal, often written, pledge to abstain from alcoholic beverages.

10. *Poke* (verb): To urge by a push or thrust; incite; as, . . . [poke him up] (*Funk and Wagnall's Dictionary,* 1899). See also Eric Partridge, *A Dictionary of Slang and Unconventional English* (New York: Macmillan, 1966); or John S. Farmer and W. E. Henley, *Slang and Its Analogues: Past and Present* (London: Printed in 7 volumes for subscribers only, 1890–1904; reprint, New York: Kraus Reprint Corp., 1965).

11. *Partie-carrée:* Normally a wife-swapping party, but here double-date probably would be closer to what Chopin meant. This term may be an example of an archaic or highly unusual usage. Given the denouement of the novel, however, it is also possible that a bit of liberated sexual behavior could be taking place.

12. *Tête-à-tête:* A private conversation or a date.

CHAPTER XI. THE SELF-ASSUMED BURDEN

1. See outline map of St. Louis streets, circa 1890, in this book (Map 5).

2. So-called "blue laws" were enforced throughout the United States from colonial times, and in some locales well into the twentieth century. These statutes, designed to encourage church attendance by limiting other options, generally prohibited the operation of most businesses, especially retail and entertainment establishments, on Sunday. Some jurisdictions prohibited other non-religious activities as well.

3. Chopin's reference to the "brace of strong-minded girls walking" is reminiscent of her own habit of walking unaccompanied in the streets of New Orleans and St. Louis. This habit, along with her habit of smoking Cuban

cigarettes (see Toth, *Kate Chopin,* 20), caused a good deal of gossip about the author. For more on Chopin's personal habits, see Toth, *Kate Chopin;* Emily Toth, *Unveiling Kate Chopin* (Jackson: Univ. Press of Mississippi, 1999); and Per Seyersted, *The Complete Works of Kate Chopin,* 2 vols. (Baton Rouge: Louisiana State Univ. Press, 1969).

4. This is perhaps an ironic allusion to the work of the German Romantic philosopher Friedrich Nietzsche, who discussed the 'all-powerful I Am' in the context of the "Will to Power."

CHAPTER XII. SEVERING OLD TIES

1. *Wrapper pattern:* A sewing pattern for making a wrapper; a garment, especially for indoor use, designed for enveloping the whole (or nearly whole) figure; a loose robe or gown.

2. *Sylph:* A slender graceful woman or girl.

3. *Rep:* A textile fabric having a corded surface of wool, cotton, or silk, or of silk and wool [Cor. of rib, N.] (*Funk and Wagnall's Dictionary,* 1899). This material often was used for women's skirts and suits, and for men's and boy's clothing.

4. St. Lawrence the martyr was one of seven deacons in charge of helping the poor and the needy in Rome. According to Catholic beliefs, after the execution of Pope Sixtus, Lawrence was ordered by the prefect of Rome to bring him the church's extensive fortune that he suspected was hidden away. Lawrence's response was to bring all of the poor and sick that the church supported before the prefect, telling him that they were the church's treasure. The prefect became so enraged at his insolence that he sentenced Lawrence to be placed "on top of an iron grill over a slow fire that roasted his flesh little by little, but Lawrence was burning with so much love of God that he almost did not feel the flames. In fact, God gave him so much strength and joy that he even joked. 'Turn me over. I'm done on this side!' Just before he died, he said, 'It's cooked enough now.'" See "St. Lawrence martyr," in *Catholic Saints Online, 1997,* saints.catholic.org/saints/lawrencemartyr, Feb. 25, 2000.

5. *Coup d'œil:* literally, a glance.

6. *Dutch cocktails:* The appellation "Dutch" was often attached to a word or phrase to indicate derision, often as an allusion to the supposed drinking habits of Dutch and German immigrants. Examples: *Dutch courage:* A reference to alcoholic beverages or the false courage derived from their consumption. *Dutch treat:* An outing, especially a lunch or dinner date, in which each party pays her or his own expenses. *Dutch uncle:* An unduly harsh critic or superior.

7. In poker, *drawing to the middle* refers to, for example, holding a 2 and a 6 and then drawing a 3, 4, and 5 after opening bets have been placed. Such a hand is referred to as a straight, and, although the odds of drawing to the middle of a straight are impossible to calculate precisely in the absence of more information about the particular hand, such odds would be astronomical, probably

several hundred thousand to one, against. A truism among experienced poker players is "Never try to draw to an inside straight." Since drawing a straight is more than seven times less likely than drawing three of a kind, three aces is usually a very powerful hand, and Jack likely would have bet heavily on such a hand. To leave a game after winning under these circumstances without allowing the losers a chance to recover their losses is considered bad form, at best, and many players would take such an act as at least a possible sign of cheating.

Part II

Chapter I. Fanny's First Night at Place-Du-Bois

1. *Andiron:* A horizontal bar, one of a pair, sustained on short feet, with an upright pillar, usually ornamental, in front, placed at each side of the hearth to support burning wood.

2. *Bromide:* A primary compound of bromine with an element or an organic radical; often used medicinally.
   Valerian: Any of the various species of herbaceous plants belonging to the genus *valerius* which have been used medicinally as stimulants and anti-spasmodics.

Chapter II. "Neva To See You!"

1. *Toilette* is an alternate spelling of toilet. See part 1, chapter 6, note 1.

Chapter III. A Talk Under the Cedar Tree

1. Native products are called "Creole" in Louisiana: Creole chickens, Creole eggs, Creole butter, Creole ponies, etc. [Chopin's note in first edition].

2. *Fricassée:* Poultry or meat cut up and stewed in gravy (from Old French *fricasser,* fry).

3. *Wrapt:* Past tense or past participle of *wrap* (also *wrapped,* but *wrapt* was acceptable in 1899) (*Funk and Wagnall's Dictionary,* 1899).

4. *Satyr:* One of a class of woodland gods or demons, in form part human and part bestial, supposed to be the companions of Bacchus; also, figuratively, indicative of a type of lustfulness. Satyriasis is the male equivalent of nymphomania.

5. *Mater Dolorosa:* A painting of the Virgin of Sorrows by Titian (1554) that now hangs in the Prado Museum in Madrid.

6. The reference to David's "pale cast of thought" is borrowed from *Hamlet.* See excerpt from Shakespeare's tragedy in the "Literary Sources" segment of the "Backgrounds and Contexts" section of this book.

7. *Bedlam:* A state of wild uproar and confusion. The term is derived from the name of the Hospital of St. Mary of Bethlehem, an asylum for the mentally ill

in southeastern London. In Middle English, *bedlem* was an alternative form for Bethlehem.

8. *Focus him:* Melicent intends to photograph Morico as he makes his fans.

Chapter IV. Thérèse Crosses the River

1. *Crib:* A barred receptacle for fodder.

2. *Grosse tante:* Big Auntie.

3. *Volante:* In Creole French, a loose calico dress.

4. *Tignon:* In Creole French, a bun or chignon; a hair style.

5. *Quo faire to pas voulez rentrer, Tite maîtresse?* In Creole French, "Won't you come in, Little Mistress?"

6. *Croquignoles:* In Creole French, cookies.

7. *Ces néges Américains:* In Creole French, "Those Black Americans."

8. *Chef de cuisine:* Head gourmet cook.

9. In Chopin's fictional Cane River community, Lucien Santien is the patriarch of the Santien family. His sons populate Chopin's fiction: Grégoire, seen in *At Fault* and "In Sabine," among other stories; Hector, an infamous New Orleans gambler, seen in "In and Out of Old Natchitoches"; and Placide, the spurned lover of Euphrasie in "A No Account Creole."

10. *Eau sédative:* Sedative water. A medication for migraine headaches.

11. *Père Antoine:* Father Francis Antonio Ildefonso Moreno y Arze (1748–1829) was born in Sedella, Granada, Spain. He was a member of the Capuchin Order and was appointed assistant vicar-general, pastor, superior of the Spanish Capuchins, and assistant ecclesiastical judge in New Orleans. He also was appointed Commissary of the Holy Inquisition in Louisiana in 1787. He was much beloved among his parishioners as a pious and charitable priest and especially as a friend to the poor and to children. He was less loved by his superiors in the ecclesiastical hierarchy and by the Spanish governors of the Louisiana colony. He feuded with them constantly. Members of the colony's religious and secular elites viewed him as insubordinate and rebellious, and his performance of his official duties was deemed both scandalous and abusive, reducing the Church in Louisiana to its "lowest ebb." Père Antoine's legendary status throughout Louisiana was no doubt familiar to Chopin, perhaps influencing her decision to create a character of the same name, who shares some of his noble attributes. He also appears in Chopin's short story, "Love on the Bon Dieu." Roger Baudier, *The Catholic Church in Louisiana* (New Orleans: Public Library Section, Louisiana Public Library Association, 1939).

12. *Breakdown:* A riotous dance popular among nineteenth-century African Americans.
Juba: A breakdown often performed on plantations in the Southern United States, accompanied by repeated cries of "Juba."

Chapter V. One Afternoon

1. *Pis aller:* Last resort, makeshift.
2. *Tenez madame; goutez un peu; ça va vous faire du bien:* "Here madam, drink some of this. You'll feel better."
3. *Je vous assure madame, ça ne peut pas vous faire du mal:* "Believe me, madam, that won't hurt you."
4. All-Saint's—Halloween. [Chopin's note in first edition]
5. *Sacré imbécile:* "You dumb fool!"

Chapter VI. One Night

1. *Staid:* Imperative and past participle of *stay* (verb); stay [stayed or staid; staying]; to continue to be in a specified place, remain in, with, at, away (*Funk and Wagnall's Dictionary,* 1899).
2. *Reeking:* Intransitive—reek—to emit vapor; be full of fumes; steam; smoke; now usually implying a disagreeable odor, as to reek of filth (*Funk and Wagnall's Dictionary,* 1899).
3. *Demoniac:* One possessed of a demon; a lunatic, as formerly supposed to be so possessed. Also, one possessed of superior or supernatural intelligence (*Funk and Wagnall's Dictionary,* 1899).
4. *Furies:* One of the avenging deities of classical mythology (in female form, with serpents twined in their hair). In later accounts, three in number: Alecto, Megaera, Tisiphone.
5. *Mon fils! mon garçon!:* "My son! My boy!"

Chapter VIII. With Loose Rein

1. An allusion to Jason "Jay" Gould (1836–1892), who became a self-made multimillionaire through manipulation of railroad stocks and the gold market. His speculation in gold, while making him a substantial fortune in 1869, instigated one of America's worst financial panics. By 1890, he controlled more than 13,000 miles of railroad, including the Missouri-Pacific system. The Missouri-Pacific Railway was also the company for which Chopin's father worked.

Chapter IX. The Reason Why

1. This spelling of *complaisant* was correct in Chopin's time (*Funk and Wagnall's Dictionary,* 1899).
2. This spelling of *mantel* was correct in Chopin's era (*Funk and Wagnall's Dictionary,* 1899).
3. *Brain fever:* A term for inflammation of the brain and fevers with brain complications. In nineteenth-century Louisiana, mosquito-borne diseases such as malaria, encephalitis, and yellow fever were endemic, with occasional epidemics killing more than 10,000 people in such cities as New Orleans and Shreveport. Any of these diseases, among others, might be referred to as brain fever or swamp fever.

Chapter X. Perplexing Things

1. "White as milk-man's cream": An unusual command on the part of the mother, since, at the time, an extremely pale complexion was desirable for women and girls, especially those of the middle and upper classes.

Chapter XI. A Social Evening

1. *Plymouth Rock:* An American breed of domestic fowl of moderate size which is usually well-fleshed.
2. *Pip:* A disease of poultry and other birds, characterized by the secretion of a thick mucous in the mouth and throat, often with a white scale on the tip of the tongue.
3. *Basse-cour:* Poultry.
4. *Loth* was interchangeable with *loathe* in Chopin's era (*Funk and Wagnall's Dictionary,* 1899).
5. *Six-handed euchre:* A card game, somewhat similar to bridge, popular in the nineteenth century. It was played with the 24–32 highest cards in the deck, depending on the number of players. Two-, three-, and four-handed versions of the game also were played.
6. *"Five on hearts":* A bid in euchre, in which the bidder is required to take five tricks, with hearts as the trump suit. This would be a very difficult bid to make, especially given the circumstances described above, and it is significant, since, earlier in the novel, Fanny has been established as a skilled card player.
7. *Waverley Novels* were a series of thirty-two novels and tales by Sir Walter Scott. Jean Racine was a seventeenth-century French playwright, best known for *Bajazet, Mithridate, Iphigénie en Aulide,* and *Phèdre.* He was friends with Molière, the father of modern French comedy, who is known for such dramatic pieces as *Tartuffe.* Edward George Earle Bulwer-Lytton was a nineteenth-century member of the British Parliament and an historical novelist. Shakespeare was found in the libraries of most Americans dating back to the colonial era. In fact, the three books owned most commonly during the nineteenth century were the Bible, *Pilgrim's Progress,* and Shakespeare's *Collected Works.* Rev. Alban Butler's multivolume work, *Butler's Lives of the Saints, Complete Edition,* ed. Herbert Thurston and Donald Attwater (New York: P. J. Kenedy and Sons, 1956), is still considered the authoritative source on Catholic saints, including their lives and deaths.
8. Saint Monica was the mother of Saint Augustine, here referred to by Chopin as Saint Austin, the English equivalent of his name. Monica is called the "ideal of wifely forbearance and holy widowhood." Saint Augustine of Hippo is the patron saint of brewers, in large part because of his "life of loose living" before he was converted. He is the author of *Confessions.* See Butler, *Butler's Lives of the Saints.*
9. *Con fuoco:* An Italian musical term meaning "with fire and passion."
10. *Vingt-et-un:* Blackjack (twenty-one).

CHAPTER XII. TIDINGS THAT STING

1. *Colfax* is located in Rapides Parish, near Alexandria, Louisiana. See Illustrations, map 2.
2. *Texian* is a nineteenth century variant of Texan, most commonly used in Texas and the surrounding states.
3. *Scapulars:* Of or pertaining to the *scapula* (shoulders). Also an outer garment meant to be worn over the shoulders.

CHAPTER XIII. MELICENT HEARS THE NEWS

1. Those of the Catholic faith believe that requiem masses should be performed following the death of a believer. Additional masses would be said for the deliverance of a church member's soul from an extended stay in Purgatory.
2. Melicent's English serving woman also would serve as a chaperone in the event that Melicent, a single woman of marriageable age, had male visitors. The woman's presence was a tacit indication that the behavior of Melicent and any possible guests was above reproach.
3. *Jardinière:* Window box.
4. *Visiting book:* A book containing the names of persons to be visited. One of the primary social obligations of a middle- or upper-class woman in the late nineteenth century consisted of paying and returning formal social visits, with an exchange of calling cards, to personal friends and the wives of her husband's business associates.
5. Georg Wilhelm Friedrich Hegel (1770–1831) was one of the most influential philosophers of the nineteenth century. His dialectical method of analysis greatly influenced the work of Karl Marx.
6. *Pinted:* In British regional dialect, pointed.
7. Guilds became very fashionable during the late nineteenth century. The term "guild" forms part of the names of various modern associations, with the notion of imitating the medieval guilds in object, spirit, or constitution.
8. *Passmantry:* Johannah's British dialect influences the pronunciation of *passementerie,* which are trimmings used to enhance garments. The trimmings might be heavy embroideries or edgings, rich braids, beads, silks, and so on.
9. Melicent assumes a less strict level of mourning than does Thérèse at the beginning of the novel, due to the less serious nature of the relationship between Melicent and Grégoire. Given that their relationship had ended, and had never progressed beyond casual friendship, Chopin's readers would have found it odd that Melicent engaged in any mourning rituals at all. See the selections pertaining to "Mourning" in the "Backgrounds and Contexts" section of this book.

CHAPTER XIV. A STEP TOO FAR

1. *Gibbet:* The projecting arm of a crane or gallows.
2. *"Muddy-Graw," or Mardi Gras,* is the celebration of Fat Tuesday, which lasts from Twelfth Night until Lent. During Lent, Catholics are instructed to deprive themselves of something in order to help prepare their minds and hearts for the coming of the Easter celebration. The Mardi Gras carnival season which precedes Lent is a season of feasting, revelry and celebration, prior to the restrictions of the Lenten season.

CHAPTER XV. A FATEFUL SOLUTION

1. A *tarpaulin* is often called a *tarp* in contemporary American English usage.

CHAPTER XVI. TO HIM WHO WAITS

1. *Toque:* A small, close-fitting, brimless hat. Also a pad used when dressing the hair in a pompadour style (old usage). See Picken, *Language of Fashion,* 156.
2. *Gros-Bec:* A grosbeak or finch; members of the most common family of birds indigenous to North America.
3. Hosmer refers to being able to "come to you free" when he meets Thérèse on the train returning to Place-du-Bois. Undoubtedly, he is referring obliquely to the obligatory mourning period following the death of his first wife, Fanny. See "Social Classes and Roles in Southern Society," in the "Backgrounds and Contexts" section of this book.

CHAPTER XVII. CONCLUSION

1. The proverbial "nine days' talk" refers to the amount of time that an item of gossip would remain in conversational currency.
2. *Sea Island Cotton:* Cotton of a particularly high grade, grown on the islands just off the coast of Georgia and South Carolina.

NOTES FOR BACKGROUNDS

THE TIMBER INDUSTRY AND CHOPIN'S *At Fault*

1. Per Seyersted, *The Complete Works of Kate Chopin* (Baton Rouge: Louisiana State Univ. Press, 1969), 742.
2. Claire A. Brown and Glen N. Montz, *Baldcypress: The Tree Unique, the Wood Eternal* (Baton Rouge: Claitor's Publishing Division, 1986), 30.
3. Brown and Montz, *Baldcypress,* 22.
4. J. H. Moore, *Andrew Brown and Cypress Lumbering in the Old Southwest* (Baton Rouge: Louisiana State Univ. Press, 1967), 87.
5. George Stokes, "The Day the Whistle Didn't Blow: Folklife Resources in the Louisiana Timber Industry," *Louisiana Folklife* 6, no. 2 (1981): 3.
6. Ibid., 1.
7. Brown and Montz, *Baldcypress,* 36.
8. Ibid., 37.

RECOLLECTIONS OF THE 1904 WORLD'S FAIR

[1.] Sham battle shows included "Cummin's Wild West, Indian Congress, and Rough Riders of the World" on the north side of the Pike, which claimed to re-create Wild West scenarios, and the "U.S. Naval Exhibition" at the west end of the Pike, which re-created naval battles using miniature reproductions of warships. The sounds of the "Boer War" re-creation of the battles of Colenso and Paardenberg are less likely to have been heard on the Pike, as that concession was located some distance south of the Pike beyond the Ferris Wheel and opposite the Palace of Horticulture. "Popular Prices," p. 19; "The Boer War Exhibition"; and MacMechen, "The Pike and Its Attractions," pp. 18, 20.

[2.] *Serpentine:* Long narrow strips of rolled colored paper thrown so as to unroll as streamers.

[3.] Water balloon.

[4.] A reference to "Hagenbeck's Trained and Wild Animal Show."

Catholic Morality

[1.] The more common kind of intoxication is that which results from taking an excess of alcoholic liquor. It is known commonly as intemperance or drunkenness.

[2.] Drugs are examples of intoxicating food.

[3.] Those who kill in self-defence or by executing criminals do not disregard God's right to be Master of human life, since He Himself, in His law, permits and approves of their action.

[4.] Scandal given in order to lead another to commit sin is known as *direct* scandal. The reason for which it is given is the gain, or pleasure, of the scandal-giver, as for example to irritate another for the sake of seeing him in a rage. If, however, it is given precisely in order that another may do himself spiritual harm, or that God may be offended, it is known as *diabolical* scandal, and is specially opposed to the love of God and one's neighbour.

Early New Orleans Society

[1.] The traditional approach to the Creole is most succinctly summed up by Roger Baudier in his "The Creoles of Old New Orleans" (typescript, Howard-Tilton Library, Tulane University, but is also to be found in practically every treatise on Louisiana. That this concept has become a matter of dogma with the present New Orleans Creoles is demonstrated by the study of Ben Avis Adams, "Indexes of Assimilation of the Creole People in New Orleans" (M.A. Tulane University, 1939).

[2.] *New Orleans L'Ami des Lois,* March 3, 1824; *New Orleans Louisiana Gazette,* June 28, 29, 1824.

[3.] [John S. Whitaker], *Sketches of Life and Character in Louisiana* (New Orleans, 1847), 83.

[4.] Everett S. Brown, "Letters from Louisiana, 1813–1814," in *Mississippi Valley Historical Review* (Cedar Rapids, 1914–) XI (1924–25), 571–79; Dunbar Rowland (ed.), *Official Letter Books of W. C. C. Claiborne, 1801–16* (6 vols., Jackson, Miss., 1917), III, 299; New Orleans *Argus,* May 15, 1827.

[5.] New Orleans *Argus,* Jan. 18, 1827.

[6.] G. W. Pierson, "Alexis de Tocqueville in New Orleans," *Franco-American Review* (New Haven, Conn., 1936–38) I (1936), 34.

[7.] Annie Stahl, "The Free Negro in Ante-Bellum Louisiana," in *Louisiana Historical Quarterly,* XXV (1942), 376.

[8.] New Orleans *Mercantile Advertiser,* Oct. 29, 1835.

Cane River's Creoles of Color

[1.] [Carl N.] Degler, *Neither Black or White* [New York: Macmillan, 1971], 107.

[2.] [James Hugo] Johnston, *Race Relations* [Amherst: Univ. of Massachusetts Press, 1970], 231.

[3.] [James M.] Wright, *The Free Negro in Maryland* [New York: Columbia Univ. Press, 1921], 109.

[4.] [H. E.] Sterkx, *The Free Negro in Ante-Bellum Louisiana* [Rutherford, N.J.: Fairleigh Dickinson Univ. Press, 1972], 34.

[5.] [John Hope] Franklin, *The Free Negro in North Carolina* [Chapel Hill: Univ. of North Carolina Press, 1943], 193.

[6.] Governor Bernardo de Galvez reported to Madrid in 1779 that these two companies "behaved on all occasions with as much valor and generosity as the white soldiers." Alice Dunbar-Nelson, "People of Color in Louisiana," part 2, [*Journal of Negro History* 12 (1929):] 374.

[7.] Ibid., 370, 374; [Laura] Foner, "Free People of Color," [*Journal of Social History* 3 (1970):] 416; Elizabeth Shown Mills, "Natchitoches Militia of 1782," *Louisiana Genealogical Register* 20 (Sept. 1973): 216, notes the presence on this roll of one "Zacherie," a free man of color, at the Natchitoches post.

[8.] Franklin, *Free Negro in North Carolina,* 193.

[9.] Charles Gayarré, *History of Louisiana* (4 vols.; New Orleans, 1903), 3:179.

[10.] Clarence E. Carter, ed., *The Territorial Papers of the United States* (Washington, 1934–), vol. 9; *The Territory of Orleans, 1803–1812* (Washington, 1940), 139, quoted in Foner, "Free People of Color," 421. Italics in Foner.

[11.] Foner, "Free People of Color," 421.

[12.] Sterkx, *Free Negro in Ante-Bellum Louisiana,* 161.

[13.] [Annie Lee West] Stahl, "The Free Negro in Ante-Bellum Louisiana," [*Louisiana Historical Quarterly* 25 (1942):] 316, 327; Gray, *Agriculture in Southern United States,* 1:524.

[14.] Johnston, *Race Relations,* 231. Italics added.

[15.] Quoted in Paul A. Kunkel, "Modifications in Louisiana Negro Legal Status," [*Journal of Negro History* 44 (1959):] 4.

[16.] *Adele v. Beauregard,* 1 Mart. La., 183 (1810).

[17.] Helen Tunncliff Catterall, *Judicial Cases Concerning American Slavery and the Negro* (5 vols.; Washington, 1932), 3:571.

[18.] Sterkx, *Free Negro in Ante-Bellum Louisiana,* 182–84; Third Census of the United States, 1810.

[19.] Wright, *Free Negro in Maryland,* 106–7.

[20.] Stahl, "The Free Negro in Ante-Bellum Louisiana," 318; Sterkx, *Free Negro in Ante-Bellum Louisiana,* 161.

[21.] [Theodore Brantner] Wilson, *The Black Codes of the South* [University: Univ. of Alabama Press, 1965], 27.

[22.] Kunkel, "Modifications in Louisiana Negro Legal Status," 4.

[23.] [Frederick Law] Olmsted, *Journey in the Seaboard Slave States* [New York: Dix and Edwards, 1856; reprint, New York: Negro Universities Press, 1968], 636.

[24.] Ibid.

[25.] Herbert Aptheker, ed., *A Documentary History of the Negro People in the United States* (New York: 1951), 26; [Charles S.] Sydnor, "The Free Negro in Mississippi," [*American Historical Review* 31 (1927):] 7–8.

[26.] Stahl, "The Free Negro in Ante-Bellum Louisiana," 315–19.

[27.] [Helen Tunncliff] Catterall, ed., *Judicial Cases* [Washington, D.C.: Carnegie Institute, 1932], 3:601.

SUGGESTIONS FOR FURTHER STUDY

PRIMARY SOURCES

FIRST EDITIONS OF WORKS BY KATE CHOPIN

At Fault. St. Louis, Missouri: Nixon-Jones, 1890.

The Awakening. Chicago: H. S. Stone, 1899.

Bayou Folk. Boston: Houghton Mifflin, 1894.

A Night in Acadie. Chicago: Way and Williams, 1897.

A Vocation and a Voice. Edited by Emily Toth. New York: Penguin, 1991. This work was prepared by Chopin but not published during her lifetime.

REPRINTS AND REISSUES OF WORKS BY KATE CHOPIN

Bonner, Thomas, Jr. *The Kate Chopin Companion.* Westport, Connecticut: Greenwood Press, 1988.

Chopin, Kate. *Bayou Folk and A Night in Acadie.* Edited by Bernard Koloski. New York: Penguin, 1999.

———. *A Vocation and a Voice.* Edited by Emily Toth. New York: Penguin, 1991.

Seyersted, Per. *The Complete Works of Kate Chopin.* 2 vols. Baton Rouge: Louisiana State University Press, 1969.

Seyersted, Per, and Emily Toth, eds. *A Kate Chopin Miscellany.* Natchitoches, Louisiana: Northwestern State University Press, 1979.

Toth, Emily, and Per Seyersted, eds. *Kate Chopin's Private Papers.* Bloomington: Indiana University Press, 1998.

Walker, Nancy, ed. *The Awakening,* by Kate Chopin. Boston: Bedford Books of St. Martin's Press, 1993.

Secondary Sources

Primary Bibliographies

Thomas, Heather Kirk. "Kate Chopin: A Primary Bibliography, Alphabetically Arranged." *American Literary Realism* 28, no. 2 (1996): 71–88.

Secondary Bibliographies

Green, Suzanne Disheroon, and David J. Caudle. *Kate Chopin: An Annotated Bibliography of Critical Works*. Westport, Connecticut: Greenwood Press, 1999.

Springer, Marlene. *Edith Wharton and Kate Chopin: A Reference Guide*. Boston: G. K. Hall, 1976.

Biographies

Seyersted, Per. *Kate Chopin: A Critical Biography*. Baton Rouge: Louisiana State University Press, 1969.

Toth, Emily. *Kate Chopin: A Life of the Author of the Awakening*. New York: William Morrow, 1990.

———. *Unveiling Kate Chopin*. Jackson: University Press of Mississippi, 1999.

Critical Books

Ballenger, Grady; Karen Cole; Katherine Kearns; and Tom Samet, eds. *Perspectives on Kate Chopin: Proceedings of the Kate Chopin International Conference, April 1989*. Natchitoches, Louisiana: Northwestern State University Press, 1990.

Beer, Janet. *Kate Chopin, Edith Wharton, and Charlotte Perkins Gilman: Studies in Short Fiction*. New York: St. Martin's Press, 1997.

Benfy, Christopher. *Degas in New Orleans: Encounters in the Creole World of Kate Chopin and George Washington Cable*. New York: Knopf, 1998.

Boren, Lynda S., and Sara deSaussure Davis. *Kate Chopin Reconsidered: Beyond the Bayou*. Baton Rouge: Louisiana State University Press, 1992.

Bryan, Violet Harrington. *The Myth of New Orleans in Literature: Dialogues of Race and Gender*. Knoxville: University of Tennessee Press, 1993.

Elfenbein, Anna Shannon. *Women on the Color Line: Evolving Stereotypes and the Writings of George Washington Cable, Grace King, Kate Chopin*. Charlottesville: University Press of Virginia, 1989.

Ewell, Barbara. *Kate Chopin*. New York: Ungar Publishing Company, 1986.

Koloski, Bernard. *Kate Chopin: A Study of the Short Fiction*. New York: Twayne/Simon and Schuster, 1996.

Petry, Alice Hall. *Critical Essays on Kate Chopin*. New York: G. K. Hall, 1996.

Taylor, Helen. *Gender, Race and Region in the Writings of Grace King, Ruth McEnery Stuart, and Kate Chopin.* Baton Rouge: Louisiana State University Press, 1989.

Critical Articles

Arner, Robert D. "Landscape Symbolism in Kate Chopin's *At Fault." Louisiana Studies* 9 (1970): 142–53.

Bonner, Thomas, Jr. "Christianity and Catholicism in the Fiction of Kate Chopin." *Southern Quarterly* 20, no. 2 (1982): 118–25.

———. "Kate Chopin: Tradition and the Moment." *Southern Literature in Transition: Heritage and Promise,* edited by Philip Castille and William Osborne, 141–49. Memphis, Tennessee: Memphis State University Press, 1983.

———. "Kate Chopin's *At Fault* and *The Awakening:* A Study in Structure." *Markham Review* 7 (1977): 10–14.

Fluck, Winfried. "Kate Chopin's *At Fault:* The Usefulness of Louisiana French for the Imagination." *Transatlantic Encounters: Studies in European-American Relations, Presented to Winfried Herget,* edited by Udo J. Hebel and Karl Ortsiefen, 218–31. Trier, Germany: W. V. T. Wissenshaftlicher Verlag Trier, 1995.

Gaudet, Marcia. "Kate Chopin and the Lore of Cane River's Creoles of Color." *Xavier Review* 6, no. 1 (1986): 45–52.

Gunning, Sandra. "Kate Chopin's Local Color Fiction and the Politics of White Supremacy." *Arizona Quarterly* 52, no. 3 (1995): 61–86.

Hotchkiss, Jane. "Confusing the Issue: Who's *At Fault?" Louisiana Literature* 2, no. 1 (1994): 31–43.

Leary, Lewis. "Kate Chopin's Other Novel." *Southern Literary Journal* 1, no. 1 (1968): 60–74.

Menke, Pamela Glenn. "Fissure as Art in Kate Chopin's *At Fault." Louisiana Literature* 2, no. 1 (1994): 44–58.

Ringe, Donald A. "Cane River World: Kate Chopin's *At Fault* and Related Stories." *Studies in American Fiction* 3 (1975): 157–66.

Shurbutt, Sylvia Bailey. "The Cane River Characters and Revisionist Mythmaking in the Work of Kate Chopin." *Southern Literary Journal* 25, no. 2 (1993): 14–23.

Warnken, William. "Fire, Light, and Darkness in Kate Chopin's *At Fault." Kate Chopin Newsletter* 1, no. 2 (1975): 17–27.

INDEX

At Fault was designed and typeset on a Macintosh computer system using PageMaker software. The text and chapter openings are set in Granjon. This book was designed by Cheryl Carrington, typeset by Kimberly Scarbrough, and manufactured by Thomson-Shore, Inc. The paper used in this book is designed for an effective life of at least three hundred years.